DIRECTION

OF THE

WIND

ALSO BY MANSI SHAH

The Taste of Ginger

THE

DIRECTION

OF THE

WIND

A Novel

MANSI SHAH

LAKE UNION
PUBLISHING

Published by Lake Union Publishing, Seattle

www.apub.com

Amazon, the Amazon logo, and Lake Union Publishing are trademarks of Amazon.com, Inc., or its affiliates.

ISBN-13: 9781542035422
ISBN-10: 1542035422

Cover design and illustration by Micaela Alcaino

Printed in the United States of America

For Tejas

1

SOPHIE

2019

Sophie Shah presses her slim body against the cold wall that separates her bedroom from her papa's. *What used to be Papa's*, she reminds herself, but can't dwell on that thought for too long. If she does, tears will flow, and it is senseless to let that happen again. A strand of her long, thick black hair loosens from her braid and falls across her forehead, irritating her eye. She does not dare tuck it behind her ear, fearful that if she moves even a centimeter, her fois will hear the thin gold bangles on her arms jingle and stop their conversation. She blinks hard, forcing her eyes to obey and not tear up again, and she concentrates on the exchange in the next room.

Sharmila Foi and Vaishali Foi, Papa's older sisters, are packing his clothing and personal effects. As a dutiful adult daughter, Sophie should have handled that task. But she couldn't. The clothes still smell of him—of the almond oil he used each morning on his unruly black hair and the talcum powder that kept his skin dry during the blistering summer heat in Ahmedabad. She cannot bear to see the dress shirts neatly pressed, folded, and stacked according to their muted tones inside the wardrobe, knowing Papa would never wear them again. Knowing that when he placed them inside, he did not know it would be the last time he would do that. His death was sudden. Heart attack. He'd been at his office, and an employee had found him on the cold white marble floor. Sophie often wonders what his last moments were like. Could he feel the life drifting out of him? Was he in pain? Has he moved to his next life already? Will his soul find Sophie again as she continues through this one? Will she feel his presence against her skin like a gentle breeze on a warm night?

Vaishali Foi has a ring of keys on a clasp tucked into the top of her sari slip, just below the exposed, doughy belly rolls that separate the top of the slip and her blouse. The keys clink against each other as she moves through the room. Sophie has grown up in this house and knows every corner of it, including the perfect place to cup her ear against the wall to listen to what is going on in the bedroom next door. She'd learned that spot as a little girl, when she used to hear her parents speaking in hushed tones.

"This will be better for her," Vaishali Foi says to her sister in Gujarati, their native language.

Sharmila Foi clucks her tongue. "Hah, it is the only way."

"Who knows how it will end up if we wait much longer, yaar. An unmarried girl her age living by herself would be unthinkable."

Sophie cringes. Papa passed away nine days ago, and these two women are the only family she has left. She has no siblings, and her mummy died when she was six years old. It has been her and Papa alone in this house for the twenty-two years since. She would give anything to stay in her home, but it is not proper for a twenty-eight-year-old woman to be living alone. Her fois made that very clear. And even if they hadn't, Sophie knows living in the house is no longer possible. Customs are not up for debate, and she has always abided by them. Well, almost always.

By this point, she should have been married and living with her husband's family. Her friends had all married years ago, like they were supposed to. Sophie has always been an avid rules follower, and not being married yet is the only custom she has broken, but she could not leave Papa. And now, after such a quick and unexpected end, it is she who is suddenly left behind. So, when her fois approached her not even three days after Papa's death to tell her that they had found a suitor available for her marriage, she agreed. What other option did she have? She had managed to avoid her arranged marriage for longer than most. People would raise their eyebrows after she passed the age of twenty-five and had yet to marry, but they assumed she was the devoted daughter looking after her widowed papa. And they hadn't been wrong. After her mummy died, she knew she had to take care of him. But now there were no more excuses.

"She's a good girl," Sharmila Foi, the younger and softer of the two, says. "She knows she cannot live in this house by herself. I just wish we had more time to give her."

"Time is not up to us," Vaishali Foi says. "The auspicious dates are running out, and then we would have to wait for the next propitious period. We are lucky the Patels are willing to take her at this point. Who knows if they will find someone more suitable if we wait? Young men these days are so fickle. It's not like it was when we were young. Now, they want too many choices and don't know how to work for the marriage, hah?"

"The Patels are a good family," Sharmila Foi says. "Local. Good biodata. Kiran has good height-body. Rajiv would have approved of this match."

Vaishali Foi clucks her tongue. "Whether he approves or not, it must be done. Sophie is smart with her numbers, but she knows nothing of the ways of the world. Rajiv made sure of that. She needs someone to take care of her properly."

"It is true," Sharmila Foi says. "We will not be here forever . . . someone must protect her when all the blood relatives are gone."

"That is the husband's duty," Vaishali Foi says.

Sophie hears their bangles clinking as her fois move about the room.

"It's good that it only took us two days to teach her to make a proper Gujarati meal," Vaishali Foi continues. "It would be such an embarrassment if after all of this, she cannot perform the basic duties of a wife. Rajiv let this go on too long, not teaching her the proper roles she must serve."

Sophie flinches, feeling the sting of their words. Her fois have served as her surrogate mummies since hers passed away, but she knows they have never understood why Papa didn't arrange her marriage earlier, when Sophie would have had her pick of the suitors. Their children had followed conventions when it came to beginning the marriage phase, and for the past three years they had begged Rajiv to make this a priority for Sophie so she didn't end up with a half-wit, or, worse still, alone. Rajiv made the occasional inquiry, but ultimately no one seemed worthy enough for his only daughter, and he could not bear to part with her. After he passed, her fois made it their top priority to find someone to take care of her when all of them were gone.

But their task was not easy because Sophie is damaged goods in the Indian marriage market. A now orphaned spinster whose papa allowed her to focus on her education, obtain an accounting degree, and pursue a career rather than forcing her to learn the ways of the kitchen and management of servants. Her fois were relieved to have found a man from a good family willing to marry her despite her untraditional lifestyle. Sophie knows marriage is for the best, but as she thinks about her future surrounded by strangers and the fact that she will never see her papa again, the cloak of loneliness wraps more tightly around her.

"Maybe if Nita had been around, Sophie would have been raised to do the right things at the right times," Sharmila Foi says.

Vaishali Foi scoffs, the keys at her waist jingling as she walks. "Like that woman could have taught anyone right. Look what she did with her life."

Sophie pushes her ear closer to the wall. Nita was her mummy, but Sophie recalls so little about her now. Just a few distant memories: the heady smell of paint while she worked on canvases near the dining room window, the round red chandlo between her brows signifying she was a married woman, the way she would stare at the sky when she sat with Sophie on the family's hichko in the front yard, that she brushed her hair with 101 strokes every morning and every night and did the same to Sophie, counting each one aloud. The main thing Sophie recalls about her mummy is that although she had never set foot in the country, she loved France.

That was why Sophie ended up with her French name. Nita had shunned the cultural norms that mandated that Rajiv's mummy select Sophie's name based on the location of the stars, and so Sophie has spent her entire life explaining to everyone in India why she doesn't have a normal name like Swapna, Reena, Ketan, or Atul, like her cousins do. As a child, she often wished that Papa had been less progressive and lenient with Nita and had forced the traditional naming conventions upon her so that Sophie could blend in. She had hated saying her name aloud in school or at work and having people stare at her. She took after Papa and did not crave the attention of others, and living in Ahmedabad with a name like *Sophie* meant she went noticed more often than she cared to be.

After Nita died, Papa and their family barely spoke of her. With the passage of time, Sophie's memories of her mummy started to fade, and with no one willing to speak about her, there was no way to revive them. Yet even though she remembers very little, Sophie still feels the urge to defend her mummy from her fois' words. After all, who else is left to do it?

Sophie begins to move from the wall when she hears Sharmila Foi say, "I wonder how Sophie would have turned out if she hadn't left."

Vaishali Foi murmurs something Sophie cannot hear, and then, in a louder tone, says, "She would have filled Sophie's head with all those crazy dreams of hers. She would have turned her into the same rebellious spirit who doesn't know her place. The best thing for this family was when she ran away. With her gone, Rajiv at least could teach Sophie duty without disruption."

Ran away?! Sophie's mind reels. Her mummy died.

As Sophie mulls over her fois' words, she scans her memories of the events surrounding Nita's death twenty-two years earlier. She recalls that she had been too young to attend the funeral. But she remembers her fois coming home from it and putting a garland of vibrant orange marigolds around the framed photo of Nita that had been added to the puja room. Sophie presses her ear even closer to the wall, sure she has misheard her fois because she would have known if the story of her mummy was something different. In Ahmedabad, the streets have eyes and the wind has ears, so secrets like this would have been impossible to keep from her for all these years.

Sophie wants to burst into the room and ask them what they are talking about, but she knows better. She would only be chastised for eavesdropping. *A good Indian girl should never speak out of turn* is what they would say while looking at her disappointedly. And she has been that—a good Indian girl—for as long as she can remember.

If only Papa were still here, she thinks to herself as tears continue to prick her eyes, *then I could ask him what they were talking about.*

The burden of truly being alone in the world sits heavy on her heart. Because it had been just Papa and her in this big house for most of her life, they had developed a tight bond—closer than the average parent-child relationship she saw with her friends and cousins. He would never lie to her, and she never lied to him. It is what made her such an obedient daughter. She never wanted to disappoint him, so she'd never snuck out of the house with friends or tried alcohol that someone in university had gotten from a foreigner with a liquor license. Instead, she always behaved as was expected. And she will honor him by continuing to do that even though she desperately wants to tell her fois not to speak poorly about her parents when her memories are all she has left of them.

~

Sophie had convinced her fois to let her stay alone in the bungalow for one final night before moving into Vaishali Foi's home until her wedding the week after, and then into her husband's family home, where she will spend the rest of her life among the strangers who will become her new family. She has never been alone in the bungalow she grew up in. There were always servants or Papa or another relative, but now the servants have been dismissed, and her fois are in their own homes tending to their own children and grandchildren after having spent the majority of the last week and a half dealing with Rajiv's passing.

The night is eerie as Sophie moves through the bungalow. The windows are open, and Sophie inhales the smells that waft in, letting them linger around her. Jasmine that blooms just outside the living room and releases the sweetest scent at night, the smell of fire and charcoal from the street vendor who roasts cashews with black pepper at his tiny cart, and lemon from the water the servants use to mop the floors. She will never smell this combination again. She will never smell home again.

Sophie hears a pack of dogs nearby, rickshas and scooters tooting their horns as they swerve through the streets, and firecrackers off in the distance. There must be a wedding somewhere, she thinks, knowing that October is the start of the wedding season in Ahmedabad. Her heart feels so broken and empty that she cannot contemplate celebrating anything. She cannot fathom that in a week she will be part of a wedding herself and embark on the most unknown chapter of her life. Who will greet her on the mandap? One of her fuas?

She glides across the cool marble floor and brushes her fingers along the ornately carved wooden dining room chairs. Last month, she and Papa were sitting in those chairs, going over the wedding schedule for this year. With so many weddings, each spanning a week or more, they strategized about which events to attend for which couple. They considered which families would have the best food and planned to go during mealtimes for those. They talked through which ones were all the way across town, requiring them to navigate hours of Ahmedabadi traffic, and came up with polite excuses. Of the nineteen weddings on the calendar between late October and the middle of December, before the auspicious period ended, none of those weddings were meant to be Sophie's. Until now. Papa's passing had made her Wedding Number Twenty for this season among their family and social circle.

She slowly climbs the marble staircase and pauses outside of Papa's bedroom. Her fois had left the door open, his bed littered with piles of clothing, evidence of their efforts to pack his belongings. Having spent today removing all the valuables and transporting them to the safes in their homes, tomorrow they will ask the servants to finish what remains.

She moves into the closet room and tugs on a door, wanting to smell Papa's shirts one last time. Memorize the scent. So she never forgets, the way she forgot the smell of her mummy. She knew it as a child, but it faded so many years ago despite how much she tried to conjure it, and she doesn't want that to happen again. She has a set of house keys fastened to the waistband of her panjabi, and she finds the right one and begins to unlock the wardrobe doors, opening them all. She touches Papa's button-down shirts and slacks, some still folded and wrapped in thick brown paper bundled together with twine from the cleaners. The paper crinkles as she unties the twine and exposes the shirts. She buries her face in the starched cotton and inhales deeply, knowing that unmistakable smell of Papa that lingers even after the clothes are washed. His

THE DIRECTION OF THE WIND

shoes are lined up along the bottom. Everything in its place. Just as he had taught her. She smiles as she pulls open the drawers. His watches and rings are now gone, tucked away in his sisters' safes; only the red velvet lining remains, and she imagines the items that used to be there.

In the very back of one drawer, she sees a box covered with dust. Her fois must have forgotten to look that far back. Wanting to make sure all Papa's treasured possessions are preserved, she removes it. It is the size of a shoebox but is ornately decorated, like her fancy jewelry boxes that are wrapped in cloth and adorned with colorful stones.

She lifts the lid, expecting to find watches or cuff links, but is surprised to see a stack of thin blue onionskin airmail letters. Papa used to send this type of letter to their distant relatives in America or Australia, and they would send the same back. *Par avion*, the envelopes say. *By plane*, she thinks, remembering the only bit of French Papa had let her learn.

The Gujarati lettering on them is a feminine scrawl. She knows these are private but is unable to resist the temptation to share in whatever memories her stoic papa had cherished enough to save all these years. She doesn't see a return address or sender name on the outside of the first one and opens it. It is addressed to Rajiv. Without reading the body, she quickly moves to the signature and sees her mummy's name scribbled at the bottom. An icy chill sweeps through her body. She turns back to the postmark on the letter and sees March 23, 2000. She freezes.

Sophie's eighth birthday. A year and a half after her mummy had died.

Then she sees the postmark from Paris, France.

She collapses to the floor, the letter falling from her fingers as if she has been burned by it. She had not misheard her fois. Her dead mummy is alive.

2

NITA

Nita Shah stared at her packed suitcase, the tough navy-blue fabric frayed at the edges. Visible signs of a life outside of Ahmedabad. She had longed for such a life, but the wear on the bag was not from hers. It was one of the many things she had inherited with her marriage to Rajiv. His finance work allowed him to travel to Europe. At thirty years old, Nita had never left India but had dreamed of going to Europe, a place she had experienced only through the pages of books. She'd begged Rajiv to take her with him on his trips after they married. Being able to accompany him on his business travel was one of the primary reasons she had agreed to marry him after her parents had suggested the match. But she'd become pregnant soon after their honeymoon, and once they'd had Sophie, Rajiv worried that she needed to be older to be left without both parents. Nita knew his overprotective nature would never allow him to feel comfortable until Sophie was herself married and out of their home. She knew she would never get to France unless she devised her own plan. Today, she would finally execute it.

The four thin gold bangles with tiny embedded diamonds that she always wore on her left hand jingled as she hoisted the suitcase from the bed she had shared with Rajiv for the past seven years. They had been a wedding gift from her mummy. It had been a tradition in her family to provide the new bride with a set of daily-use bangles that were delicate enough to be feminine but sturdy enough not to be damaged by her new wifely duties, like entertaining, child-rearing, and the occasional cooking when the maharaj was off for the day. Nita wore them every day of her marriage as a reminder of who she was meant to be. A wife. A mummy. Dutiful.

Her bag contained little more than her paintbrushes, some family photographs, and clothing but was heavier than she had expected. She supposed compressing the elements of her life into one small container would have weight to it. She wasn't accustomed to lifting luggage or doing any form of manual labor. That was something the servants handled, but today she could not call upon them. The price of exposure was too high.

After Rajiv had left for work and her six-year-old daughter, Sophie, had gone to school, she had sent the servants to do time-consuming errands like getting papad from the old ba across town who moved like her feet were stuck to the floor with tamarind candy, ensuring Nita would have the sprawling bungalow to herself. She tugged the suitcase across the cold white marble floor to the edge of the stairs. Leaving the bag poised at the top, she took a deep breath and crossed the hallway to Sophie's room. Like the other rooms in their home, it had stark white walls with no decorative items revealing anything about the occupant. In India, a bedroom was meant to be functional, not inspirational. That was part of the problem. Nita wanted to be inspired. She always had. Ever since she was Sophie's age, her parents had said she lived with her head in the clouds. She'd never understood why that was wrong. She'd seen countless movies from the West in which the characters did just that, and they seemed creative, happy, and joyful. She so desperately wanted to feel those things inside of her. It had been so many years since she had.

"This is not practical," her mummy would say when she would find young Nita in her room, painting a picture of the French countryside from a book she had spread before her instead of completing her chemistry homework. The greatest punishment her parents could inflict on her was taking away her paints. This had happened more often than she could remember, almost becoming a ritual of sorts, but the desire to re-create the fields of lavender or food markets along the Seine that she saw in colorful foreign books compelled her more than the deterrence of punishment could. Now, she thought of her parents in the way a child must think of them after they have passed. Nita knew they would be so disappointed when they learned what she had done. She would be bringing shame upon them, and there was no greater atrocity she could inflict. Her decision forced her to abandon everyone. And the fact that she was willing to do that in the first place was her proof that what she was about to do had never been a decision for her to make. It had always been decided for her.

She sat on Sophie's bed in the corner of the room and pulled the folded rajai at the end to her lap. She held the densely woven, heavy blanket to her face to smell the clean little-girl scent that followed Sophie wherever she went, baby powder and sandalwood soap. The smell was familiar to her, and she would be able to identify it, but she didn't inhale it the way that Rajiv did. She could see the love, adoration, and gratitude all over his face each night when he came home and wrapped Sophie in his arms, breathing in the scent of her hair. Nita kept hoping she would grow into that feeling. She told herself that it would come to her, the way it came to all mummies. But it hadn't. It wasn't Sophie's fault. She was innocent in all of this. But Nita had never felt like a mummy. Not the way she knew she was supposed to. Sophie was getting older now, and Nita was less able to keep up the charade than she had been when Sophie was younger. Rajiv wanted another child, and Nita came up with excuse after excuse because she still didn't feel the maternal bond she had expected with the child she already had. But how could she say those words to Rajiv? Sophie was his light. And with each passing year, Nita felt more and more darkness. Nita didn't know what was wrong with her—only that something was. If she stayed, she was afraid her darkness would encroach on Sophie, and that was the last thing she wanted for her child.

She clenched the rajai, the maroon fibers smooth against her fingers. She pictured her daughter wrapped in this blanket with her small head poking out, a smile on her face as Nita read her the story of Ramayan before bed. The image should have conjured tears for Nita. Part of her maybe even hoped it would jolt her into going back and returning to her life as if nothing unusual had happened today. As if she wasn't about to abandon Sophie and Rajiv. As if she hadn't been thinking about it for the past eighteen months. Longer, if she were being honest with herself. As if she hadn't started planning for it last year when she went across town to a place Rajiv would never visit and paid an agent in cash to begin the lengthy process of obtaining her French visa, with an added premium for not alerting her husband.

She released the rajai from her grip, smoothing it and questioning whether she could go back to being the mummy she had always been. But that was the problem. The mummy she had always been was an unhappy one. Picturing Sophie didn't make her change her mind, confirming that Nita was making the right decision for all of them. Motherhood meant giving all of herself to Sophie, and Nita didn't have anything left to give. Not beyond the jewels she had left for Sophie in the family safe at the bank. As her final maternal act, she had commissioned a local jeweler to create a set of four daily-wear diamond-and-gold bangles for Sophie, and she had left a note for Rajiv to pass those on to Sophie on her wedding day, just like Nita had received the family gift from her mummy when she married Rajiv.

Nita sighed, thinking about how Sophie's life was changing today. She saw what a great papa Rajiv was and knew that Sophie would be okay without her. The two idolized each other, and Nita had been on the outskirts anyway. She knew Rajiv would need to tell their daughter something about Nita leaving and had no doubt that he would deliver the news in the best way for Sophie, but she wondered what explanation he would offer. Tonight, when Sophie came home and slept in this bed, what would she think? Would she understand? Would she ever forgive Nita for leaving?

One of life's greatest cruelties was that those who were innocent suffered more than those who inflicted the harm. The flawed, the broken, the damaged—they moved on most quickly. Nita wondered if she were all three. In her mind, she was already picturing her life in Paris. She hated knowing that Rajiv and Sophie, the two most innocent souls she knew, would bear the brunt of her betrayal. They'd agonize over whether they had done something to cause the pain they felt at her leaving. They hadn't. But she knew no words she could ever say would absolve them of the hurt, doubt, and guilt they would feel. But she hoped that once those feelings faded, they'd find joy in the small family that remained.

Afraid that if she lingered longer, the servants would return and catch her, she placed the rajai back at the end of the bed, tucking its edges so it was a perfectly folded rectangle. She then returned to her bedroom—now Rajiv's bedroom—and placed a sealed envelope on his nightstand.

August 13, 1998

Dear Rajiv,
I have started this letter to you countless times but have never found the words. I'm not sure I have them now, but it is time. I am sorry I was not brave enough to say these things to you in person, but I've never had your strength. I took a vow to be your wife and Sophie's mummy, but I have not been honest with myself or with you.

You are a good man. But this life is not enough. It was never one that I wanted. It was the one our parents chose for us. I've done my best to grow into the wife and mummy that you and Sophie deserve, but it hasn't come naturally to me. I kept hoping it would, but the days pass, and the more I try to force myself into my maternal and spousal duties and repress the life I dreamed of as a girl, the more the weight of that burden crushes me. We were born into a culture that doesn't permit independence for any of us. Our roles were decided at birth. Maybe even before that. We could never have changed that. I did my best to play my part, but my heart craves more. Our life in Ahmedabad is suffocating me, and if I continue to ignore it, it will destroy me, or I will destroy our family. Sophie deserves better than that. As do you.

I need to become whole. To feel in control of my life for the first time. My body yearns to set foot in the country I have been thinking about since I was a little girl. To be in a city where dreams like mine come true. Where I can become like the artists whose paintings I have seen only in books. Where maybe one day my skills will develop so that you or Sophie will open a book in India and find my work. Please know I have not made this decision lightly. You must let me go. As for Sophie, you may tell her what you wish. Your judgment has always been sound. Do know that I loved her and you in the best way I knew how. I'm sorry it wasn't enough for all of us to be happy.

Nita

Taking one final look at the letter, knowing these words could not be unsaid, she switched off the light and left their bedroom. She struggled to get her suitcase downstairs, pulling the bag toward her small frame and leaning backward to counterbalance the weight. She was now embarking on a life of depending only on herself, so she had better get used to it. She closed the heavy front door to the bungalow behind her and, without ever looking back, made her way to the street to hail a ricksha.

~

Paris was emptier than she had imagined it would be. A few people passed Nita on the street and cast sideways glances. The warm, balmy August air made the delicate fabric of her parrot-green sari stick to her skin. People around her wore the Western clothing she had seen on satellite television in India—slacks, jeans, short dresses revealing their slim, pale legs. The women bared their shoulders, letting the sun color their fair skin. Her parents would have been appalled at the lack of modesty, but Nita relished the thought of joining them, letting the constraints of her sari fall away from her meter by meter.

The surly, large-eared agent at the airport desk had given her the name of a budget hostel in the Latin Quarter. She glanced at the navy street signs with green borders and white letters and tried to match the names with the piece of paper she had received from the tourist information kiosk at the airport. The lettering was so different from the Gujarati and Hindi signs throughout Ahmedabad. She used the small map he had provided her to search for Rue Saint-Séverin and finally saw it on a stone building at a large intersection.

She flung the pallu of her sari back over her shoulder and wheeled her rickety suitcase through the street until she was halfway down the block and saw a nondescript black door with the words **L'Hôtel Canard Volant** with a single star below them. The windows next to the door were covered with a crackling black film. The exterior was a far cry from the whitewashed walls of the expansive bungalow in Ahmedabad that had been home until she'd boarded the flight yesterday and an even further cry from the five-star hill stations in the Indian countryside where she and Rajiv would vacation each year with Sophie.

This door was much easier to push open than the heavy, solid block door to her home in India. She stepped inside and was immediately slapped with the smell of cigarette smoke and crinkled her nose, not accustomed to the potent scent of tobacco. Rajiv's only vice had been the occasional paan, and that left no odor behind. This room smelled like layers of stale scents had woven their way through the cumbersome purple-velvet-upholstered furniture and thick matching draperies framing the dingy, dark windows. The source of the immediate odor was a narrow-shouldered, mousy woman in her thirties who sat behind the reception desk, a slim cigarette dangling haphazardly from her burgundy lips while she flipped pages in a colorful fashion magazine.

"*Bonjour.*" Nita uttered the first French word to escape her lips in the faintest of whispers.

The woman glanced at a clock to her right. The hands were pointed to six twenty in the evening. Without looking at Nita, and returning to her magazine, she said, "*Bonsoir,*" emphasizing the last syllable.

Nita dropped her head, recognizing her mistake and wishing she had made more effort to learn French before she embarked on this journey. When she'd asked Rajiv to get her some French language-lesson books and CDs, he had not hesitated because she'd had such a long-established obsession with France that this request was in keeping with that. He'd had no idea she was planning for her life after him. Nita had learned in the mere hours since her arrival that trying to learn French from CDs was a far cry from having to speak it in daily life.

"Sorry," she said in English.

The woman placed her magazine aside and looked Nita up and down. She had a name tag pinned to her blouse that read "Cecile."

"Americaine?" the woman asked with a bored tone.

Nita shook her head.

"Londres?"

Again, she shook her head.

The woman sighed, tired of the game she had started, after only two guesses.

"English?" Nita asked as she approached the counter.

"If I must," the woman said with a thick French accent. She eyed Nita's sari, clearly unfamiliar with seeing people dressed in traditional Indian clothing. "Do you need help?"

"I need a bed."

"How many nights?"

The question surprised Nita even though it shouldn't have. She could not stay at the hostel forever, but she hadn't really considered her plans beyond getting to Paris.

"Can I pay week to week?"

The woman shrugged. "Seven hundred and fifty francs a week." She eyed Nita carefully before narrowing her eyes and saying, "Cash."

The woman's eyes widened as Nita pulled a stack of bills from her sari blouse. When she handed over some of the money she had just exchanged at the airport, the woman crinkled her face and held the bills with an outstretched arm as if disposing of a lizard. She gave Nita a key attached to a piece of wood much too thick and bulky to be placed in a pocket or purse.

"Key, you leave here when you go out," she said.

Nita took the large key from Cecile's outstretched hand and tucked it between her chin and chest as she grappled with lugging her suitcase up the narrow, winding stairway. Cecile returned to her magazine and made no attempt to help. Nita knew she was in for a massive lifestyle adjustment, but she would get used to it. She had to. Her new life had to be worth more than the one she had given up.

Nita unlocked the door to a large room with four sets of bunk beds. Most of them were unmade, with clothing strewn over them. She had not envisioned climbing a ladder in her sari and was grateful when she saw one lower bed in the corner with what appeared to be a clean set of sheets folded and resting on it. She sat on the edge of it and touched the linen. Scratchy, with pills on it. Another thing she would need to get used to.

What have I done?

She held her breath as she thought about the life she had walked away from. The people she had left behind. She calculated the time in Ahmedabad. Rajiv would have found her letter many hours ago. He had probably driven straight to the airport to stop her, but she would already have been in the air, moving away from her old life. Now she sat, weary and dirty from her travels. There would be no servants to draw her bath or go to the market, where they wouldn't even need to pay for her favorite sandalwood soap and could put it on the charge account that she and Rajiv had at all the local shops. No, now she had money tucked into her sari blouse, knowing it was all she had in the world and that it would not last forever. She had moved from her papa's home to her husband's, and financial matters were left to the men, so she had never had any glimpse into them. For the first time in her life, she thought about money. How vital it was, and how much she would need to survive. She had no idea how much was enough, but she knew that for the first time in her life, she needed to get a job.

She yawned, the fatigue catching up to her. Before allowing herself to succumb to sleep, she pulled out some more francs from the wad tucked in her sari blouse and went to buy the toiletries she needed to wash herself before bed.

At the store, she was overwhelmed by the number of different soap offerings in the small sundry shop down the street from the hostel.

There were dozens of them, their aromas competing, like a garden assaulting her senses. It seemed overly extravagant compared to the few choices she would have had back in Ahmedabad: sandalwood, rose petal, vanilla. She mentally converted the French francs to rupees and could not believe how much it cost to buy a single bar of soap! She wished she had brought these things with her when she'd left so she wasn't doling out her limited money now, but it had not occurred to her because she had never traveled to a place where those items would not have been provided. Her money, which had felt like a fortune when she boarded the plane, would not go far. She'd never learned accounting and budgeting and felt helpless realizing how necessary those skills would be. She thought about how easy it would be to go back. Rajiv was a gentle and kind man. He would welcome her. She could say she'd temporarily lost her mind and agree to give him the second child he wanted, and she knew all would be forgiven.

3

SOPHIE

2019

Sophie breathes in and out sharply as she sits on the floor of Papa's wardrobe. Her fingers tremble as she picks up the blue letter again, and her delicate gold bangles clink against each other. The sound echoes through the desolate room. She tries to read the single page, but she can't concentrate long enough to bring the words into focus, and they swim before her eyes. In the box are several more, each with the same familiar scrawl—each with a postmark from Paris. All of them after September 1998, when she'd been told her mummy had died. They go on for a few years after that tragic day that changed Sophie's life forever. The day that separated everything into a before and after.

"How can this be?" Sophie asks herself aloud.

Her words fall heavy in the quiet bungalow. There is no one to hear her. No one to answer her questions. There must be an explanation. There has to be. She rechecks the dates, making sure her eyes are not playing tricks on her, but the last letter she sees has a date of 2001, and there's no mistaking that Nita hadn't died in 1998.

~

Sophie thinks back to that time over twenty years ago. She still remembers it like it was yesterday but now examines it more carefully. Nita had been away for over two weeks, taking care of Ba in a village a couple hours from Ahmedabad. When Ba had first gotten sick, Papa had left as well to go help Mummy and Ba, and Sophie had been left with Sharmila Foi's family for a week.

When Papa returned alone to take her back home, he said Nita would be back as soon as she could. That week, after Sophie finished her schoolwork, she sat in the seat by the window where Nita did her painting and worked on drawings of the green mango tree and jasmine flowers that she wanted to send to Ba and Mummy. Then one day Sophie came home from school and found Papa sitting at their dining table with his head in his hands. Sophie felt the heaviness in the air around her and knew she had to be on her best behavior. Papa reached for her, and she silently moved toward him so he could put a shaky arm around her shoulders.

"Beta," Papa began, "there has been an accident. Mummy—" His voice caught on the word. He cleared his throat and took a deep breath. "Mummy is not coming back home."

His eyes misted, and Sophie did not know what to do. She had seen her mummy cry on occasion, when Nita was alone and didn't realize anyone could see her. Sophie would approach her and ask what was wrong, but Nita's expression would change quickly, and she would dismiss the tears and focus on the chores that needed to be done around the house. But Sophie had never seen Papa cry.

He took a deep breath, and his eyes rested on the photo of Bhagwan hanging in the dining room with the garland of fresh marigolds and rose petals taped to it. The servants changed the garland weekly so the blooms were always fresh.

"Beta, Mummy has died. We will not get to see her again. Not in this life. But hopefully in the next one."

Sophie considered his words. "How will we find her in the next life?" she asked.

Papa looked surprised by her question. "I don't know, beta."

"How will she know it's us?"

His face was strained. "She will know. Especially you. She cannot forget her daughter. She loves you very much."

Papa's eyes flooded, and a single stream escaped from each, slowly trailing down his cheeks. He looked to the seat by the window where Nita's easel still rested. Her paints that were usually strewn around it had been gone since Nita went to Ba's, and Sophie's colored pencils were there now. Papa clutched Sophie to him so hard that she could barely breathe, but she didn't protest. Later that day, she packed up her colored pencils and never brought them out again.

In the weeks afterward, Sophie remained quiet as her fois organized the pujas for Nita's passing. They both seemed mad, but they took a framed photo of Nita and added it to the mandir inside their home with a small garland of flowers. Sophie sat quietly behind them as they chanted the prayers and dotted Nita's photo with vermilion and a few grains of basmati rice and laid the flowers around it. Papa was not present for those ceremonies.

Each morning since, Sophie has gone to the mandir and said her daily pujas and touched the bottom of her mummy's framed photo to show her respect. Papa had never commented on her ritual, nor did he join her for it. Sophie had always believed it was all too painful for him. And she never wanted to burden him with that pain, so she bore hers alone, just as he did his.

~

Sophie now reels as she considers how many of these memories had been a lie. She has so much sorrow over Papa's passing, but rage fills her as she thinks about how much she did to protect Papa from his sadness.

That they could not grieve Nita's death together because Papa knew there had not been one. Why would he tell her that when it wasn't true? She could not fathom what would justify such a lie and knows she will never have the answer from him. She is bereft thinking about how his love and lies existed so seamlessly. Sharmila and Vaishali Foi obviously knew as well, based on the conversation she overheard. She clenches her teeth, wondering if everyone in her life knew and only she had been taken for a fool. She must learn why she was kept in the dark, but how can she trust those in her life who have maintained the lies for so long?

4

NITA

1998

The room was filled with sunlight when Nita woke up the next day. She rubbed the sleep from her eyes, feeling as though she had just awoken from the dead. She took in her surroundings and remembered she was not at home in Ahmedabad. She glanced at her watch face on the inside of her wrist. It was the middle of the afternoon. She had been asleep for fifteen hours. Never had she slept this many hours straight, not even during her pregnancy or after giving birth. But she had never traveled before. She now understood better the jet lag Rajiv had always suffered upon his return from his business trips abroad and that it wasn't simply a matter of discipline to get over the exhaustion.

She felt she could lie in that bed, rickety and uncomfortable as it was, for another day, but she needed to use the toilet, so she sat herself upright, slipped on her champals, and padded down to the communal restroom. As she drew near, she heard a female voice humming. Inside at the sink was the source of the melody: a young, upbeat Asian woman with thick, silky black hair and large, wide-set brown eyes. She leaned close to the mirror and applied bright-pink lipstick.

"Bonjour." She nodded in Nita's direction. "You have risen, have you?" she said, making eye contact with Nita through the mirror. She spoke with the British accent that Nita was used to hearing on the television programs she had watched in Ahmedabad, but Nita had only ever seen white people speaking it there, so it seemed misplaced coming from this woman.

"It was my first day here," Nita said shyly as she made her way to the farthest stall in the corner.

She wasn't accustomed to sharing this type of space with another person and sought the most privacy possible. When she exited the stall, the girl had moved from her lips to painting her eyelids a bold shade of blue—the type that an upper-caste woman in India would never have worn.

"You want some?" the girl said, holding out the compact.

"Oh, no," Nita stammered, surprised that the girl would offer to share such a personal item with a stranger she had just met. Did she not worry about passing germs?

Nita turned on the sink, and warm water spilled over her hands. She had learned yesterday that hot water flowed from the plumbing in a seemingly endless, almost wasteful, stream. There was none of the planning involved that was needed in India. There, she or the servants had to turn on the Gizzard to heat the water twenty minutes before she intended to use it, and then, because there was a limited amount, use it to fill up buckets to mix with cold water to get the right temperature. And that was for the privileged upper caste, who had an option of having any hot water flowing through the pipes at all. Here, it seemed everyone had access to it, whether wealthy or poor.

"Where are you from?" Nita asked.

"London. And you?" She leaned toward the mirror and puckered her lips, admiring her handiwork.

"Ahmedabad."

She scrunched her nose. "Where's that?"

"India."

She nodded. "My flatmate in Islington was from there. India, anyway. Not sure where exactly. Good spicy food, that stuff. Like the Thai food my mum makes. You won't find that here! It's all cream and butter." She smoothed her hair into a ponytail. "So, what's your name?"

"Nita."

"Cool. They call me Dao. Sangdao when I'm misbehaving," she said with a glimmer in her eyes. "So, what have you got on today?"

"I need to look for a job. Do you work?" Nita said.

"I've been bartending a bit in the Marais. Gets me by. Can you mix drinks? Shall I put in a good word for you?"

Nita was again taken aback by her friendly nature. The two had just met. Didn't she want to know about Nita's family history and upbringing before recommending her for a job? That was the way it would have worked in India. A person's reputation was everything, and recommending someone for a job was an extension of that. It was no matter, though. She had never even had a sip of alcohol. It was banned in Gujarat, and Rajiv was a rules follower who never let it cross their threshold even though some of their friends had access to it via foreign relatives who used their liquor licenses to stock up for their families. She knew she would not be skilled at anything involving alcohol.

Nita shook her head. "I think I'm going to look for work as a shop teller or something like that," she said. It was the first time in her life she had even considered getting any job, let alone such a menial one, but she had not been trained in the ways that would matter for employment. She could prepare a perfect Gujarati meal, as cooking was one of the few things that had come naturally to her as a wife and mummy, but there would be no need for that here. This was a city of croissants and crêpes, not rotlis and shaak.

Dao shrugged. "Whatever suits. Just make sure you have your papers in order."

"My papers?" Nita asked.

"You know, work permits and such. Some people will ask you to show it before they even hand you the application, as if they don't want to waste a piece of paper." Dao rolled her eyes. "Those cash jobs are harder to come by these days, if you know what I mean?" She winked at Nita through the mirror. "I somehow managed to find one even with my papers, but it wasn't easy!"

Nita felt her pulse quicken. Why hadn't she thought about that before she left? *Because you have no experience with the world*, she chastised herself. She'd never even thought about the fact that if someone had a job available and she had matching skills, there would be further barriers to entry. Work permits and such were not even a consideration in the life she'd led until that point. At least, it seemed, there was a way around that, and she now knew she needed a job that paid cash—just like the ones they had given to their servants in India. She got herself here and she would find a way to stay. Worst case, maybe she'd have to learn to bartend with Dao!

"I didn't think about how much goes into moving countries," Nita said.

"Everything looks romantic in the moonlight, but the sun always rises the next day." Dao laughed to herself. "So, what brings you to this fair city?"

"I'm an artist." Nita beamed at hearing the word leave her lips. Artist. She had been a daughter, a wife, a mummy. But never an *artist*.

"You've come to the right place, then, that's for sure. You can't throw a stone without hitting an artist."

As she spent more time in Paris, Nita would learn just how right Dao had been. Nearly everyone she met was pursuing some creative passion and thought of Paris as the gateway to success. Nita joined the flock but knew her dreams would be short lived if she didn't find work soon. Dao hadn't lied: many shop owners narrowed their eyes at her when she inquired about jobs and demanded to see a work permit. Her rupees were dwindling more quickly than she had imagined, and, for the first time in her life, she was dependent on herself rather than her papa or husband and had nowhere to turn to get more money.

~

Paris was not like she had dreamed. It was more. So much more. It was the opposite of Ahmedabad in all the ways that mattered. The streets were filled with fair-skinned people who were not used to seeing others who looked like Nita and had no preconceived notions about her or how her life should be. In fact, passersby glanced down at the sidewalks, hardly noticing her or anyone else except to avoid direct collisions. In Ahmedabad, people had stared, openly and pointedly, no matter where she went. Beggars and wealthy alike would look her straight in the eyes in a way that no one seemed keen on doing in Paris. That came with the stature of coming from a prominent family, and, while she should have been grateful, all she'd ever wanted was the anonymity she felt along the cobbled Parisian streets. She did not feel judged or scrutinized. She felt invisible and realized how freeing that was.

Nita did not know a soul in this country. And she did not care. Family and friends had surrounded her for her entire life, but they had heightened her loneliness. In this sea of strangers, she finally felt at peace. She had seen so many pictures of Paris in books that she felt she had been living there for years even though she had arrived just three days ago.

Paris was a city filled with intrigue and inspiration. The Eiffel Tower took her breath away by the sheer scale of it. It was the first place she stopped. The metal structure glistened in the sun, making its presence known no matter how far a person traveled from it. She strolled along Boulevard Saint-Germain and stopped in cafés like Les Deux Magots and Café de Flore, thinking about the great artists and writers, such as Pablo Picasso and Ernest Hemingway, who had frequented them. She could not afford to spend the little money she had in those spots, but she sat on the patio of Les Deux Magots, pretending to peruse the menu before discreetly leaving without ordering anything. During those moments, she thought that perhaps one of those ingenious artists had sat in that exact place, had taken in that same view, and she took that motivation and returned to her shared room in the hostel and pulled out her paints for the first time since she had arrived in Paris. She closed her eyes and focused on the images that appeared, begging to be put to paper so the rest of the world could experience them as well. Paris was more than a city of lights. For Nita, it was a city of hope.

Her favorite part of the city thus far was the stalls along the River Seine owned by the *bouquinistes*. She had seen so many as she walked back from the Eiffel Tower, taking in their distinctive green, like that of foliage in a lush forest, and the clean lines they made on the walls of the river's edge. The stalls were filled with local paintings and old used books. The musty smell she breathed in reminded her of Sophie's schoolbooks, but she quickly pushed that thought aside. She had given up that life and needed to forget it. The occasional stall had baubles for tourists, but it was the artwork that stood out, different pieces evoking different moods and feelings. She wanted to look at them all, touch each canvas, feel the texture of the paint against her fingers. The work by each artist was so distinctive, each one telling a different story captured from a unique perspective.

She passed a stall that had some paintings of a woman who looked to be in her twenties but had thin lines near her eyes, hinting that she could be older. She was fair skinned, with watery blue eyes that conveyed a hidden depth like glacial ice, and her lips formed a thin line as if they were forced closed but intimating that she had something to share buried deep inside of her. She seemed to repress so much underneath those soft pale features. Nita connected with the subject, a reminder of her life before this. The woman's eyes showed her story was deep and troubled and not yet over. Nita delicately flipped through the canvases, admiring the meticulous brushstrokes and marveling at how smoothly the colors had been blended, as if the artist had used watercolors rather than the opaque oil-based paint. She gingerly moved the paintings aside, hoping to piece them together like a puzzle to uncover their chronology and discover the woman's story.

"*Vous aimez ça?*" a deep male voice said from behind her.

He was so close that the tiny hairs on her neck stood up. She spun around and stared into a pair of crisp blue eyes, the left with a small jagged scar just above it. The man's hair was cut very short against his head, like he had shaved it and it was just starting to grow back, the dark hair poking through his milky scalp.

"*Vous aimez ça?*" he asked again, sweeping his hand past hers to see which canvas she had been studying.

She shook her head helplessly. "No French," she said softly.

"Do you like it?" he asked in accented but clear English. Like so much of the city, he, too, smelled of cigarettes and coffee.

Nita searched for the right words. "She makes you want to learn her story."

The man's lips curled into a half smile. "That she does," he said wryly.

"You painted these?"

He nodded, pulling a cigarette from the pocket of his worn jeans and tucking it behind his ear while he searched his back pocket for a lighter.

"They are beautiful. Especially the way the light strikes her face . . . the choice of shadows gives her so much depth."

"You like art?"

She nodded. "Very much."

"Take it." He gestured toward the canvas while he lit his cigarette with a practiced flick of his lighter. He inhaled deeply, holding the smoke in for several seconds before releasing it in a steady stream.

Nita resisted the urge to cough. "*Merci*, but I cannot take it."

"*Oui*, you can. Her face haunts me. Better you have it than me."

"No, I mean, I have nowhere to put it. I only just arrived here."

His gaze moved carefully from her head to her toes. Even though her canary-yellow panjabi covered every centimeter from her ankles to her wrists to her neck, she felt very exposed. Her cheeks were flushed by the time his eyes met hers.

"You're from India." He said it as a statement rather than a question. "I can keep the painting for you here, and when you get settled, you can claim it then."

She was surprised by the generosity. "That is very kind."

"*Bien sûr.* It means you will have to come again." His blue eyes glinted in a mischievous way that caught Nita off guard.

～

Rupees did not go very far when converted to francs, so Nita knew she had to be thrifty and think of ways in which she could earn enough to support her new lifestyle, modest as it was, free of servants and fine tailored clothing and fancy hotel meals. She did not speak enough French and had no papers, which were the largest impediments to getting work when she saw the NOUS EMBAUCHONS signs in shops, advertising that help was needed.

As she neared the end of her first week in Paris and her stack of rupees continued to dwindle, her nerves got the better of her, and she called her parents to ask them for help. When she left Ahmedabad, she had left a letter behind for them as well, knowing she could never have said her goodbyes in person. She knew their reaction must have been severe, but she had naively hoped they would understand. After all, they were the people who had tried to force her into a particular mold for her entire life and knew that she had never fit into it. And they were the ones who should want her happiness above all else.

Her papa answered the phone, his tone sterner than she had ever heard it. "What have you done?" he seethed into the crackling line of the collect call she'd had to make. "You have disgraced this family. Beg your husband's forgiveness, and stop this nonsense immediately."

"You have a daughter!" her mummy pleaded.

Nita knew that. She never forgot. But how could she explain to her own mummy that she didn't have the instincts and unconditional love that went with being a mother? That if those were learned skills, her mummy had not taught them to her. Or if they were innate, she'd been born broken. Nita was convinced her presence in Sophie's life would have ultimately harmed her daughter. Sophie had constantly sought Nita's approval and attention, and she had none to give her. How would that have impacted Sophie long term, to feel her mummy's disdain? To Nita, leaving Sophie felt like the most selfish and yet most maternal act she could have done.

"Nita, go back to your husband this instant!" her papa said.

"I can't," Nita said softly. "Even if I could, who knows if he would accept it."

"Of course he will!" her mummy pleaded. "He is there now! Looking for you! You must simply go to him."

"Yes, yes," her papa chimed in. "Just go to the hotel, and this all will be done."

Nita's blood ran cold. Rajiv was in Paris! He was looking for her. She scanned the room, as if he had been hiding there all along and would jump out at any moment to reclaim her.

5

SOPHIE

Sophie has never flown on an airplane. She's never even left India. In truth, she has rarely left Ahmedabad, other than a few trips by train to Delhi in the north and Goa in the south, and car trips to the hill stations for vacations. She knows her life experience is limited, but she does not care. Earlier that year, when Papa had insisted on getting her travel documents to join him on his business trips to London, Paris, and New York, she had allowed him to do it because she did not want to disappoint him, but the truth was that she had no desire to visit those places. She was not sure she would have ultimately joined him in the end because the thought of venturing outside of India had filled her with trepidation.

She had tried searching for Nita on the internet, hoping to avoid taking this drastic step of flying to Paris, but there was no trace of her. She is a ghost who haunts only Sophie. Sophie wonders if Nita changed her name in order to prevent being found. She had gone to such great lengths to leave that Sophie knows that anything is possible. Sophie's world remains in limbo and her questions unanswered until she can find Nita, and so she has had to push past her fears of traveling outside of India by herself.

As she walks through the bustling terminal in Charles de Gaulle, everything around her feels foreign and frenetic. She wishes she had gone with Papa on one of his trips so that she could have learned from him how to navigate another country. He had taught her so much. Because of him she knows how to balance any company's accounts with a speed and accuracy that is surprising, especially for a woman, as she is often told by her male clients. She knows how to hide the valuables so they are never temptations to their hardworking servants. "Loyalty should not be tested," Papa would say to her. She knows how to manage her often difficult fois, who are now the only family she has left, so this skill is more important than ever. He had taught her so much, but he'd never taught her how to be an outsider.

That is exactly what she is now, she thinks as she scans the large airport signs, trying to figure out where to go. No one looks like her. No one dresses like her. No one speaks her languages, so she can't ask anyone for help. She moves through the crowded terminal, following people from her flight who walk with purpose, as if they know the way. She finds the customs line and nervously checks around her to make sure the people around her are also carrying foreign passports and she has found the right one. Every uncertainty piles upon the last, and she feels herself fuming at Papa for being stuck in this strange new place because of his lies. She is here because he deprived her of her mummy. Is there any greater atrocity a parent could commit?

She is lost in her thoughts when the person behind her nudges her, pointing to an open station, and she gives him an apologetic smile before moving toward the kiosk.

"*Bonjour, bienvenue,*" the customs agent says to her in a monotone as she hands him her passport. He has light skin, dark hair, and a dry, bored expression.

With feigned confidence, Sophie hands him her passport, which still looks shiny and new, the spine tight as the agent opens it. He glances at her briefly, and her pulse quickens as she tries to think of how to explain the purpose of her visit. Business? Pleasure? What category does "searching for the mummy you thought was dead" fit into?

The agent presses the crisp pages open, glances quickly at the one with her visa, and takes his large metal stamp and slaps it down on her passport with a definitive motion. *"Au revoir, Mademoiselle. Bonne journée."*

She collects her documents and shuffles past him, surprised and relieved at how easy it was to get through customs. Papa had so often complained of hassles while traveling on an Indian passport. "Westerners are always suspicious of us," he would say. It was one of the reasons she had never joined him on his business trips despite his urging. She had no desire to willingly invite that into her life when she lived so comfortably where she was.

She finds the baggage claim area and scans the belts for her suitcase. She'd quickly packed some photos of Papa, photos of Nita before she died, and her own personal effects.

Left, Sophie reminds herself. Photos from before Nita left them. She feels equal parts anger and anticipation at the thought of Nita having done that. How could she? Had Papa done something to drive her away? Could Sophie have done anything to make her stay?

Sophie shakes her head to break her spiraling thoughts and focus on finding her luggage. She knew it would be cold in Paris in late October, so she brought her heaviest jacket and thickest shawl, but looking at the warm wool coats on people around her, she knows she is not prepared for the weather outside of the airport doors. Her valuables are always with her, namely several lakhs of rupees she took from Papa's safe-deposit box—the money that became hers after his death. Her fois now control those funds after Papa's passing, but Sophie knew the bank teller well enough to be granted access. She keeps the money in a zipped sleeve strapped around her hips underneath her panjabi and tries to carry herself in a way such that it will not be noticed beneath the thin fabric. In Ahmedabad, all her shopping was done on the home accounts she and Papa had at every shop they frequented, so she typically carried very little cash, and no one in India used credit cards. Carrying this much money makes her very nervous, but she knew she'd need more money for this journey than she has ever kept before.

As she approaches the conveyor belt, she cannot believe how smoothly it flows around and how patient and orderly the passengers are, standing respectably apart from one another, each one fixated on their mobile phone, nonchalantly waiting for their bags to arrive. It has none of the chaos of the Ahmedabad airport, with people pushing ahead of each other and directing servants to retrieve their belongings. As a child, she'd gone to the airport to meet Papa after his business trips because she was so excited to see him after his time away and begged her fois to take her so she wouldn't miss another second with him. As she got older, it had become their tradition right up until he passed away, and she had loved seeing his eyes light up when he would see her waiting for him after a long, weary flight.

She stands to the side, scanning the metal belt for her brown suit-case. It is easy to spot because she tied yellow synthetic rope around it to secure the contents, just like she'd seen Papa do before each of his trips. It surprises her that none of the other passengers took those same precautions to protect against theft.

The sea of faces around her is different from anything she has ever known. She has never been in a place with so few Indian people. In fact, she can probably count on her fingers and toes the number of non-Indian people she has seen in her entire life. Now, she sees many white faces, some so pale that thin blue veins can be seen through the skin. Then she sees a couple of Black men with trendy scarves tied around their necks and woolen jackets on their shoulders. Other than on American television shows and films she watched via their satellite, she has never seen a Black person before. These men look nothing like what she has seen portrayed on the screen and are instead dressed like the sophisticated businessmen in tailored suits she saw every day in India.

It is nerve racking for her as she tries to make sense of the signs and find where to exit. She is too self-conscious to ask any of these foreign-looking strangers for help and doubts they would understand her anyway. She worries about her half-baked idea to come to Paris and wonders if she should turn around and take a plane back home. It would look like she had been gone only a couple days. Her arranged marriage to Kiran could proceed as planned, and she would be back in a world she understood with people who understood her. As uncomfortable as she is, it's the thought of her marriage that gives her strength to continue with her mission. If she finds Nita, Sophie could have a different path. Perhaps one that does not include marriage to a stranger. Learning Nita shunned her marriage forces Sophie to think about options that were previously not even in her realm of understanding. But even if marriage is her path, she needs to know what happened to Nita, because how could she ever become a parent without knowing that? Lineage is essential to consider when planning a family. What if whatever caused Nita to leave also lives inside of her? She is apprehensive about what she will find, but this is one instance in which cautious, pragmatic Sophie, who balances the pros and cons of all situations as she would a profit and loss statement, thinks uncovering the unknown weighs as the better option.

"Are you waiting for someone?" a voice says from behind her in accented English.

She turns to see an Indian couple who appear to be in their early sixties, and she breaks into a smile.

"Are you Gujarati?" the man asks.

She nods, feeling instantly relieved.

"First time in Paris?"

Again, she nods.

He smiles, a bright open smile. His eyes are kind, with laugh lines around the edges. His hair is an equal blend of salt and pepper. He wears simple khaki slacks and a white button-down shirt tucked tightly into the waist. Just like her papa did. At his side is a similarly aged woman in a blue panjabi.

"Are you meeting your family here?" the woman asks.

Sophie hesitates, not sure how to respond. She'd gotten away with not having to share "I'm looking for my mummy, who I thought was dead" with the customs agent and knows it is too much to share with strangers, especially ones who are Gujarati. She fears that within moments of them speaking, they will uncover the family friends or distant relatives they have in common, and after that, the whole of Ahmedabad will know her family's gossip.

Instead, she says, "Yes, I'm meeting relatives in a few days' time."

"That's good." The woman nods her head from side to side in approval. "You are by yourself until then?"

Sophie pauses, again not sure how much to reveal to them. But she is no longer in Ahmedabad, where she knows people all over the city whom she could turn to. Here, she has no one. And this couple is the first who have even bothered to speak to her in this strange new world.

"What's your name, beta?" the woman says in Gujarati.

Papa had called her *beta* more often than he ever said her given name, and Sophie feels a tug at her heart upon hearing the word.

"Sophie."

The woman raises her eyebrows. "That's not a very Indian name."

"My mummy was"—she catches herself—"is very fond of French culture."

The woman nods. "This is Saumil." She gestures toward her husband. "And my name is Anjali."

"It's nice to meet you, Uncle and Auntie," she says, using the Indian conventions for those who are not blood relations. "I did not expect to find people from Gujarat when I arrived here."

Saumil Uncle laughs. "Sophie, you will see we Indians are everywhere. You only have to look."

"Where will you stay until your relatives arrive?" Anjali Auntie says.

"At a youth hostel." Sophie had done some quick internet research before she left and printed a list of places she could try when she arrived in the city.

Anjali Auntie shakes her head and turns to her husband. "We cannot leave her alone like this. She doesn't even speak French."

Anjali Auntie looks to Sophie, and Sophie nods her head slightly to confirm she is correct that Sophie does not speak French. Sophie looks from one to the other, eyes darting as if watching a shuttlecock pass back and forth over a badminton net.

Saumil Uncle says, "We have a hotel in the city. And an extra bed if you need one for a few days. Our son was going to arrive with us, but he had to work at the last minute, so we will wait for him before we all go home to Toulouse. He's a doctor in America, you know?" He says the last part with a twinkle in his eye. Many people she knew in Ahmedabad would get that same pride when talking about their children who had succeeded in America or England or any other part of the Western hemisphere. Having a relative who had succeeded in the West considerably elevated a family's stature.

Sophie considers Saumil Uncle's offer and starts weighing pros and cons. She is terrified about how she is going to navigate this new city, and it seems this new uncle and auntie could help her with that. She wonders if she should be cautious about their generosity, but then she thinks about all the times strangers from overseas had appeared on their doorstep in Ahmedabad and she and Papa had welcomed them in for a meal. They would be friends of friends of friends of someone, but they had the address of Sophie's family bungalow and would drop in unannounced for tea or meals and catch up as if they were old friends. She recalls some of Papa's stories about doing that when he would travel abroad and need a proper Indian meal. He would search for the common Gujarati names from their caste—Shah, Patel, Desai, Mehta—and phone the family to introduce himself. Sophie has never traveled before but has heard enough about Indians helping Indians. As she leans in favor of joining them, her ingrained sense of not wanting to take on obligation resurfaces, and she hears Papa's voice saying that debts were always collected at inopportune times, so it was best to avoid them.

"That's very kind of you, but I don't want to be a burden," she says, deciding it would be impolite to impose.

"If it were our son alone in a foreign city, we would want someone to do the same for him." Anjali Auntie puts her arm around Sophie's shoulder. "Now, we should go."

Sophie can see that, like her fois passing around a second helping of dal, Anjali Auntie will not take no for an answer.

"You have your luggage already?" Sophie asks, looking around them.

Anjali Auntie motions toward the medium-sized suitcase behind her husband. Saumil Uncle takes their bag and Sophie's and begins wheeling both in the direction of the exit.

~

Paris public transport is unlike anything Sophie has ever seen. Saumil Uncle and Anjali Auntie show her how to buy a ticket, and then they board the train from the airport into the city. Sophie cannot even imagine a public transport system in Ahmedabad. The poverty, homelessness, and meandering animals would make it impossible to maintain any such public service.

They arrive in a neighborhood called the Marais, and Sophie cannot believe what she sees. The streets are paved. All of them. There are no smaller dirt roads like the ones the rickshas travel along in Ahmedabad, clouds of dust being kicked up by their wheels. The buildings grow one right out of the other for an entire block, and people live in flats rather than bungalows. The buildings have elaborate doors in a variety of colors, and windows are dotted with tiny wrought iron balconies that would be impossible to put even a single chair on but house tiny potted plants, flowers, and herbs. Everything is so clean! There is no litter along the edges of the roads. Instead, there are green waste bags dotting the sidewalks, and, by their fullness, people seem to use them! Nothing is strewn on the ground around them. The only animals she sees are small dogs on leashes, padding patiently alongside their owners, who are dressed in warm coats, scarves, and hats.

The cold air whips through the thin fabric of Sophie's panjabi. She pulls her shawl tighter around her shoulders.

"You must have a proper jacket," Anjali Auntie says to her.

She nods. She has never had a need for warmer clothing before, given that Ahmedabad's winter has the same temperatures as Paris summers.

"Our hotel is just this way," Saumil Uncle says, steering her down a busy street and eventually stopping in front of a thick, ornate black door.

Sophie marvels at how different everything around her is. The door to the hotel has intricate moldings on it. She is used to doors like the one on her home, wide and sturdy with several sliding locks for security but no other frills. Functional, not decorative.

She waits in the well-appointed lobby with Anjali Auntie while Saumil Uncle speaks with the receptionist in rapid French. She cannot understand a word he is saying, but the receptionist nods several times and then hands him a plastic key card.

The three of them shuffle into a small lift that takes them to the third floor. The hotel room is clean but sparse. Not like the extravagant resorts at the hill stations she and Papa used to visit in the summers.

This room has two beds pushed together in the center and a cot along-side the far wall. All are fitted with simple white sheets and velour blankets resting at the edges.

Sophie takes her luggage and places it under the cot, doing her best to take up as little space in the room as possible so she does not take advantage of Uncle and Auntie's generosity.

Anjali Auntie opens the closet and points to the safe inside. "Do you have anything you need to lock up?"

Sophie thinks about the money belt fitted tightly around her mid-section but shakes her head. She vows to wear her thicker Western clothing, like her jeans and sweaters, going forward, as they will hide the belt better than her thin panjabi fabric.

"Your passport? Anything like that?" Saumil Uncle asks as he removes his shoes and sits on the bed, slowly rubbing the bottoms of his socked feet. "You must be careful with valuables."

A lifetime in India worrying about whether everyone from the servants to strangers on the street would steal from her gives her confidence that she knows how to be discreet with anything she doesn't want taken by the service staff at the hotel.

She sits on the cot and considers how she will begin her search. Her mobile phone has not worked since she left India. It now seems obvious to her that it wouldn't, but she has no idea how to fix the problem and had not considered what it would be like to roam the city without the aid of internet in her pocket. She saw a hotel computer in the lobby, and knows that is her best option for now. She can't wait to use it and map out directions for the place she hopes to find Nita.

6

NITA

1998

Nita pressed the phone to her ear and considered her parents' words. She heard them breathing rapidly on their side of the call. *Rajiv is in Paris right now and searching for me.* She could put a stop to this. Erase the past week. Return to Ahmedabad as if nothing had happened. Rajiv had such a soft temperament that she believed they were right and he would forgive her. She believed she could convince him of her remorse and fly back with him as if they'd gone on a trip and ignore what she had actually done. The problem was that while she needed money, she couldn't fathom her old life. Returning home would be returning to a life without options and with no ability to change her circumstances. She'd rather have the chance to be inspired and dream and hope that she might experience joy and peace, even if it meant living hand to mouth every day.

"I'm sorry I brought shame upon the family," Nita said humbly.

She was sorry for that. Reputation was everything, and she had tarnished her family's with her actions. Had there been another way, she would have done it, but in their culture, these things were intertwined and impossible to separate.

"We raised you better than this!" her papa yelled into the phone.

Softly, Nita said, "You tried to . . . you really did. I'm sorry," and then hung up.

She tinkered with her gold bangles, which she still wore every day. They were one of the last good memories she would have of her family because she suspected that was the last time she would ever speak to her parents. She was now truly on her own, to rise or fall on her own merit.

~

September 3, 1998

Dear Rajiv,
The truth is I thought it would be easy to walk away. Every day I think about Sophie and wonder what she thinks about her mummy being gone. What that must be like for a young child. But she is your daughter. Always has been. She is strong. Not weak like me.

My parents told me that you came here to find me. They also told me to come back and behave like a proper girl. I can't live that lie, and I think you know that. Rajiv, you cannot come here again. It is smaller than Ahmedabad, but it is still a big city. You will not find me. You are wasting time that you should be spending with Sophie. She needs you, especially now. You have always been her whole world. That's why I knew it was okay

*for me to go, but you . . . if she ever lost you . . . I
cannot even think about it. You are free now. You
are both free.*
    Nita

Her heart sank when she dropped off the thin blue airmail envelope at the post office that evening. She wondered how long it would take to reach Ahmedabad. She pictured Rajiv reading it at the dining table in their home. He was a stoic man, but she sensed that he would have emotion coursing through him. But she felt she had done the right thing. For all of them.

~

By her third week, her funds were running low. She had managed to pick up some shifts at her hostel when someone was on holiday or sick. The owners of Le Canard Volant—the nickname by which the hostel was commonly referred to—had been immigrants themselves and looked the other way in situations like hers in which the person had no work permit. Hostel travelers tended to speak English as their common tongue, and that was something she knew quite well. But the work was not steady and was not sufficient to keep her going. Art supplies, and everything else, were more expensive here than in India, or at least seemed that way after she converted the prices back to rupees.

After yet another shop owner told her she needed fluent French to apply, she was not sure what to do next. For the first time in her life, she worried about whether she would have a roof over her head and food in her belly. Cecile had made several comments about her late payments and seemed like she would be thrilled to throw Nita out if she were late again. In her dream country, she had more in common with the servants who had waited on her than the wealthy class into which she was born. She empathized with the many lower-caste people who had floated in and out of her life and wondered how difficult it must have been to live with this type of uncertainty every day. She'd been spoiled and sheltered and was starting to realize just how much.

Dejected, she picked up a takeaway *sandwich du fromage* and began her usual walk along the *bouquinistes* stalls of the Seine. The breeze near the river picked up, and she tightened her shawl around her shoulders. With all her concerns about money, she hadn't yet had time to truly focus on her painting and wondered when she would have produced enough to rent such a stall and fill it with her work. The irony was that she would have spent more time on her craft had she stayed in India because there she had nothing else to worry about, given that the servants managed day-to-day life.

She bit into the baguette as she walked along the south side of the Seine, letting the crumbs from the crusty bread scatter along her path, the occasional pigeon swooping down behind her to pick them up. She had gone past the handsome stall owner's space several times over the past couple weeks, but to her disappointment it had been closed, a large padlock signifying that the owner would not be returning shortly.

As she neared it that day, she saw it was open. Before she could get close enough to see if the man was there, she heard someone behind her.

"You've come back to claim your prize."

She didn't need to turn around to recognize the voice.

7

SOPHIE

2019

Sitting on the terrace of a small café just a few blocks from their hotel, Sophie scrunches her nose at the unfamiliar items on the menu, unable to tell which are without meat or fish or eggs. She studies the items, trying to find something safe, as she doesn't want to further burden her newfound companions by being a picky eater.

"Do you eat nonveg?" Saumil Uncle asks her.

She shakes her head.

"Okay, we will tell them to make three veg plates." He beckons a waiter to their table.

Sophie sinks into her wicker chair, grateful. She is famished after her long journey and ready to eat anything that was not once alive and able to move on its own.

Their plates arrive, and Sophie is surprised by how much she enjoys the vegetables, coated in butter instead of ghee and seasoned with salt, pepper, and herbs rather than turmeric, cumin, and red chili powder like her fois taught her to make in preparation for her wedding to Kiran.

As she savors the vegetables, she wonders what explanation was given to him. That she ran away? That she will return? Will her fois now speak about her the way she had overheard them speak about Nita? Kiran seemed nice enough during the single afternoon when they met. He had an average height and body, with the classic broad shoulders and skinny legs so common on Gujarati men. His hair was cut shorter, in a more Western way, but that made sense given the time he and his family had spent living in England. He wore glasses that at first appeared too large for his face, but as Sophie looked closer, she realized it was the style and was likely another trend he had picked up from his time in the West. His Gujarati was accented, if she listened closely, probably another remnant from his life outside of India. But despite his time away, he seemed to understand the customs and conventions of the local culture, which was a relief to her. But even if he hadn't, Sophie didn't feel like she'd had much choice in the matter when she agreed to marry him. It was time to move forward into that phase of her life, and Kiran was the one her fois had chosen for her, so that basically settled the matter.

She had been seated between Vaishali Foi and Sharmila Foi on one sofa, and he between his parents on the other. They had never shared a private word during the two hours that their relatives sipped chai and crunched on nasta while discussing their respective family trees. Kiran's gaze was fixed on the marble floor. He occasionally stole glances at her and smiled shyly. His hands were clasped together, and his right knee bounced slightly, revealing his nerves. Sophie remained stoic, demure. She had lost her papa five days earlier, and nothing seemed important. Not this man. Not her marriage. And not her future. She'd wondered if Kiran had known just how recently she'd lost Papa before coming that day and suspected he had. Everyone knew everything in Ahmedabad. That's why it is such a shock to her that the entire city had managed to keep this conspiracy about Nita from her for over twenty years. It must have been the gossip of the town when it happened, and somehow Sophie had been none the wiser.

"Have you eaten enough?" Anjali Auntie asks as she gestures toward Sophie's now empty plate.

She nods, surprised by how quickly she devoured her food, and sits patiently as her companions finish their meals. Like the diners around them, Uncle and Auntie don't seem rushed as they break off morsels of baguette to soak up the buttery sauce left on their plates the same way she would have torn a piece of rotli to get the last bits of her dal and rice from her thali. The temperature begins to descend for the night, and they are grateful that the restaurant has switched on the outdoor heaters. When the check arrives, Sophie tries to contribute, but Saumil Uncle waves her off. She hesitantly accepts and vows to do something kind for them before they part ways. Finding them was a true stroke of luck for her. Bhagwan found a way to smile upon her when she hadn't felt favored in a while.

"Which of your relatives are you meeting?" Anjali Auntie asks as they sip on their tea after their meal.

Sophie swallows the liquid, letting the warmth radiate inside of her. She can't bring herself to utter the word *Papa* without tears, so she knows she cannot say that. Instead, she says, "I'm meeting my mummy here." It isn't a lie. It is why she has come, and she hopes it will be true.

"You are brave to come by yourself," Saumil Uncle says. "You have no brother or sister to join you?"

Sophie shakes her head. "We have a small family." True as well.

Anjali Auntie glances at her left hand. Sophie is wearing the engagement ring that Kiran's family had given her a couple days earlier, a yellow gold band with twenty-five small diamonds embedded into a square on the top. "Your husband could not join?"

Sophie pulls her hand back modestly. "No. He had to work." Kiran probably does have to work, so this could be the truth as well.

Each technical "truth" is getting easier than the one before it. Even though she feels Uncle and Auntie are harmless, Papa raised her to be cautious with personal information, and it is a difficult habit to break. Personal matters and truths are hardly spoken of in India out of a sense of privacy and unwillingness to show any weakness to others outside of the home. Sophie prefers things that way because it also means that people don't ask her private things, like where her mummy is, and she never has to explain about her mummy's passing. Sophie now wonders how many people had avoided asking about Nita because they already knew the truth that Sophie is just learning.

~

That night, after Uncle and Auntie fall asleep, Sophie creeps out of the hotel room with her stack of letters and heads to the computer terminal in the reception area. The night clerk is a middle-aged man who gives her a disinterested nod before turning back to his book, the pages yellowed from time and the cover worn from use. She had put the letters in chronological order, hoping she could use the details as clues to help find Nita.

On the outside of one, Sophie sees a return address referencing Le Canard Volant. It's been twenty-two years since the date of the letter, and the writing is a feminine scrawl but doesn't appear to be Nita's, so Sophie can only hope that whatever that place was will still be around. She types in the name, and, instantly, there are numerous links to pictures and videos of ducks in flight, and eventually, toward the bottom of the page, there is a link to a one-star hostel. Her heart races as she clicks on it. She forces herself to calm down. It's not as if the link is going to transport her to her mummy, she reasons.

She jots down the address and sees on a map that it is in the fifth arrondissement. She has no idea where that is. She zooms out on the map and sees she is on the other side of the river from it. She's starting to plot a route for her to get there when she feels a hand on her shoulder.

8

NITA

1998

Nita spun around, quickly swallowing the bite of bread she had been chewing and hoping she didn't have crumbs littering her clothes but did not look because she was too self-conscious to show how self-conscious she was.

"*Bonjour,*" she said.

The blue-eyed man sipped coffee from a paper cup while staring intently at her.

"You remember me," Nita said, looking away shyly.

"*Bien sûr.*" He moved past her to his stall and put his coffee on the stone ledge behind it. He leaned against his chair in a way that was both carefree and enchanting. "What is your name?" he asked.

"Nita."

He nodded, as if filing it away so he could retrieve it later.

"And yours?" she asked.

"Mathieu. What do you do here?" he asked, looking directly at her with those penetrating eyes.

She boiled under his stare. In India men looked from afar, and when they made eye contact, it was different, more an observation and possible judgment. Mathieu stared at her as if he was intrigued. She glanced at the canvases around them. She could not tell this man with so much talent that she was a painter. It would have been like comparing herself to Chagall.

"I'm looking for a job," she responded instead.

"People always talk about work, work, work." He moved closer to her, and she froze, not sure whether to step out of the way. Then he knelt and readjusted some of the canvases near her feet, the heat from his arm radiating through her clothing just a few centimeters away. "Life is about passion." He met her gaze again from his stooped position.

"Passion comes at a price." The words slipped out before she could stop them.

He looked at her, amused, and stood up. *"En effet, Mademoiselle. Vous avez raison."*

She moved away from him, fingering the canvases as she took a few steps back. "I hope one day to live a life where I have a stall along the river as well. But I am not as far along in my work as you."

He smiled the half smile she had seen when she first met him. "You are an artist, then. I see."

She shook her head. "I am a woman who needs to work so she can learn more about her craft to one day become an artist."

"But you don't aspire to be a successful one?" he asked.

She was taken aback by his comment and felt her face falter.

"I only mean that you aspire to be a *bouquiniste*," he said. "People aspire toward fancy galleries and museums"—he gestured around him—"not to wooden, green boxes along a river. You must dream more grand, *Mademoiselle*."

She chewed her bottom lip. "It is hard to think of something such as that. It's a life I could not even begin to plan for."

"Planning can be quite tedious." He waved his hand dismissively. "Sometimes it is better to just do what you feel."

Nita thought about how she had acted on emotion to get to Paris in the first place. Given where things were now, she had serious doubts about whether she had made the right decision. But anytime she thought of calling Rajiv, of going home, the shame put her back on her path. He would have received her letter by now telling him not to come back to Paris and look for her. *There is no going back after what I have done*, she kept telling herself, because she needed to believe that in order to move forward in this new life.

"If only life could be that simple," she said.

"You don't think it can be?"

She shook her head. "There is so much pressure. So many people to consider. Being selfish is a luxury many do not have."

"Then we should consider ourselves lucky," he said.

She had already been selfish, but she wasn't sure if she would consider herself lucky. Selfishness was contrary to the core values of the collectivist society in which she had been raised but was further evidence that she hadn't belonged there in the first place and needed to escape those cultural handcuffs. Her current life wasn't luxurious like her old one, but this was the first time she had picked her desires over convention, and it had freed her mind and spirit.

"Have you ever lived outside of Paris?" she asked.

He shook his head. She envied him. How must it feel to know nothing other than the life one currently had and be so happy with it? From birth, her life in Ahmedabad had been prescribed in every meaningful way. She couldn't even blame her parents for it because the roles society expected her to play went far deeper than any single family. There was no place for someone like her—a dreamer who wanted a life beyond being a wife and mummy. Even her friends had not been able to understand her preoccupation with painting and curiosity about what existed in the world outside of India. Everyone—including her—had assumed her passion was a phase and the feeling would eventually leave her, but it never had. And more and more she had felt like she had to hide that part of herself as people's patience with her unconventional ideas began to dwindle.

"Do you miss your old life?" he asked.

It was her turn to shake her head. "I was ready for a change."

"Have you found it?"

She looked around them at the Parisians and tourists strolling along the River Seine, knowing none knew her or her family. None had expectations set out for her. None cared if she fit society's mold or created her own. None cared if she embarked on her dreams or stayed exactly where she was. They cared only about themselves, and it was this anonymity that gave her peace.

"I could not fathom being anywhere else right now."

~

A few weeks later, on a day that was especially warm compared to the weeks earlier, she treated herself to a rare tea in a café along the sidewalk on the north side of the river near Pont Neuf. Cecile had been on holiday for two weeks, and Nita had picked up all her shifts and had her board paid for the next month. It had eased her money woes for the short term as she only had to worry about food and sundries and didn't feel the constant stress that she might become homeless. She felt someone's stare on her as she sipped hot mint tea and sketched on the pad propped between her legs and the table. Looking up, she saw Mathieu standing on the sidewalk, no more than two meters away from her.

"I still have your painting, *Mademoiselle*," he said.

Nita slipped her hand over her sketch pad, turning it away so he could not see. She could not help feeling self-conscious around him.

"*Merci*," she said, knowing her French had improved ever so slightly since she'd last seen him. "I still have nowhere to hang it. You are not at your stall?" She silently chastised herself for stating the obvious.

"I needed a stroll. And the fates have made me run into you, so it was well worth it."

She felt her cheeks flush in a way they never had when Rajiv had looked at her.

He did not move his eyes from her. It was as if he didn't even need to blink. "Would you like to join me?"

"Now?"

"Pourquoi pas?" Why not? His lips curled into that half smile that had haunted Nita's thoughts since she had first seen it.

She felt her body standing before her mind had even made a conscious decision to go with him. She was wearing a light pair of jeans and a navy blouse she had purchased at a secondhand shop, and, in her new Western attire, she felt more and more local every day. After slipping her sketch pad into her oversize bag, she placed several francs in the small metal cup resting on her bistro table with the check peeking out of it. She draped her shawl over her shoulders and flung one side toward her back to keep it in place.

"Where will we go?" she asked.

"Anywhere we want," he said with a shimmer in his pale-blue eyes.

~

The Luxembourg Gardens were rather desolate on that late September day. A few tourists roamed about with cameras dangling from their necks, taking the obligatory photos near the center fountain with the Palais du Luxembourg in the background. The usual vendors with their ice cream and snack carts were not present. Some individuals were scattered about, reading or writing in journals. A few teenage couples sat on green benches, their lips suctioned together in an impenetrable seal. Nita still had not gotten used to the ever-present displays of affection she saw throughout the city. Such behavior was staunchly discouraged in India, and even if it had not been, she'd never desired Rajiv in that way.

They had stopped along the way, and Mathieu had purchased some pastries and a bottle of wine. Nita hadn't had the heart to tell him she didn't drink alcohol. Their shoes crunched against the gravel as they made their way to a particularly empty area at the side of the fountain. Mathieu pulled two grayish-green metal chairs closer together and placed the paper bag with the food and wine on a stone bench behind them. He sat and squinted as he looked up at her still standing.

She slowly lowered herself to the chair next to him, grateful that he hadn't chosen one of the benches where there would have been no barriers between them. She had passed through the gardens before but had not stopped to sit and take them in. The neatly manicured flowers that outlined the plush green grass created a bold color palette of purples, oranges, yellows, and pinks. Butterflies and bees flitted between them. The bees in particular had been difficult for Nita to get used to when arriving in Paris because they were everywhere. Nita inhaled and concentrated on the sweet aroma of the flowers. She stared at the carpet of bright-green grass within the flower border, and she longed to lie suspended on the thick blades. It was something she had never seen in Ahmedabad. The climate there was too hot and the city too congested for this type of nature to thrive. But she saw that people respected the INTERDIT signs and not a single person was breaking the rules, and thus she would abide by them as well.

"Do you come here often?" Nita felt silly the second the question left her lips.

He smiled at her, reaching for the bag. "I find inspiration here when it is not overrun with tourists."

He pulled out a pocketknife and revealed the corkscrew folded into its casing. There was a pop as he released the cork from the glass bottle with a practiced pull. They didn't have any cups, so Mathieu touched his lips to the rim first, letting the red liquid flow onto his tongue. Nodding in approval, he passed the bottle to Nita.

She hesitated, not wanting to tell him she had never tried wine. She didn't want him to see her as some innocent schoolgirl.

What's the worst that can happen? she asked herself as she took the wine from him.

The thick glass rim felt cold against her lips. She parted them slightly to take the tiniest sip. She felt sweetness on her tongue, followed by a burning sensation as she swallowed. She coughed and handed it back.

"You don't like it?" he asked, his eyes showing concern.

"I don't drink much wine," she said, knowing the best lies were grounded in truth.

He handed her the bag of pastries, and her face lit up. The sweets in France were a different story. She loved how the chocolate here tasted so deep and rich and luscious, a perfect complement to the buttery flakiness of the pastries. It was very different from the brightly colored mithai in India made with food coloring, milk powder, cornstarch, and oil. She pulled out a *pain au chocolat*, the flaky layers already falling from her fingers to the ground. The light, airy exterior surrounding the dense, rich chocolate center was much more pleasing to her palate than the wine.

"You do smile." His blue eyes shimmered as the late-afternoon sunlight bounced off his face.

She paused, midchew.

"You always look so serious," he continued. "It's intriguing. What makes you so serious?"

Thoughts began whipping around in her mind: *That I'm away from home. That I left my family. That I don't have any money or a real place to live.*

She shrugged noncommittally and swallowed her bite. "You ask a lot of questions."

"Is that not how one has a conversation?" He squinted as the sunlight fell across his face.

"I suppose so . . . it's just different where I used to live. People only spoke on the surface."

"That doesn't seem to be a very exciting way to live. It's always what's below the surface that's interesting."

He eyed her body, and she felt like he could see through her clothes to her skin. It made her tingle with electricity.

9

SOPHIE

2019

Sophie squeals, and her hand flies to her chest to feel her heart beating. She whips around, then realizes it was only Saumil Uncle who had touched her shoulder. The receptionist looks up from his book for a moment but then goes back to it after glancing at them.

"I didn't mean to startle you," Saumil Uncle says.

"No, it's okay," she says, catching her breath. "I was hoping not to wake anyone. I'm sorry if I troubled you as I left the room."

He peers behind her, trying to see what is on the screen, the way she's seen countless uncles do back in India. She knows uncles have no respect for the privacy of others if personal information is presented to them, so she positions herself in a way that blocks the monitor from his view.

"I could not sleep with the jet lag, so I thought I would research some of the places I want to see tomorrow," she says.

Uncle raises an eyebrow but lets her comment pass. "There is much to discover in Paris."

"Yes, I know," she says, her hand still covering her chest as she tries to calm her pulse. The quickness is from more than the fright she got.

She has an existing address that matches with the old letter! She feels the adrenaline surge through her because she hopes that by revealing the past, this city will unlock her future.

~

The next morning Uncle and Auntie say they are feeling groggy and promise to show Sophie around the city later that afternoon.

"Old age," Auntie jokes, her legs cracking as she stretches them in front of her. "Take advantage of your youth!"

Sophie does not mind because she is eager to find Le Canard Volant and see if there is anything left of Nita there, and that is something she must do in private. She is pleased that the hostel is only a thirty-minute walk from where they are staying.

There is a chill in the air as she crosses the bridge over the Seine. Fortunately, it is at her back and not blowing into her face, but she knows Anjali Auntie is right that she needs to get a warm coat. The thin jacket she brought with her is no match for the late-fall weather in Paris. Sophie follows the map that the receptionist had given her and notices she must cross two bridges because she is passing over an island that sits in the middle of the river. She looks around her and sees more bridges, each ornately constructed yet each one unique. The bluish-green water ripples beneath them, responding to the breeze. She hears bells to her right and sees the back of a large structure with two majestic towers looming in the distance. The part nearest her is blocked off by a temporary wall, but above its height she sees a blackened and burned building with scaffolding surrounding it for refurbishment. According to her map, it is a church: Notre-Dame. It looks so different from the Hindu temples she is used to visiting. After fully crossing the river, she finds the street she is searching for. She turns right and quickly walks until she sees the vertically scribed black sign bolted onto a narrow building face with white script letters saying **L'HÔTEL CANARD VOLANT** with a single white star beneath them, and assumes this is the right place.

She pauses for a moment, staring up at it, knowing Nita must have stood in the exact same spot. The sign looks new, or at least not more than twenty years old, so Sophie suspects parts of the view have changed, but she wants to believe she now shares a moment in common with Nita. As a child that was what she had always wished for, that she was doing the exact same thing her mummy had once done. In the months after she was told Nita had died, when Papa was at work, she would sneak into his room and sit at the vanity where Nita brushed her hair each morning and night. Sophie would take her brush, look into the mirror, and count to 101 in her head, as she'd seen her mummy do so many times. Now, she realizes that Nita could have been sitting on that stool for Sophie's entire life and just chose to be away from her. She feels anger rising in her. She has never been an angry person, but she feels it growing in her the more she sits with the lies she has been told. But for now, she pushes it down with the rest of her unprocessed emotions and focuses on the hope that she may find answers.

The windows of the hostel are covered in a black film, some of it cracked and peeling at the edges. Sophie pushes the heavy door, and, as it swings shut behind her, the low lamplight in the reception area eclipses the natural light that had snuck in while the door was open. Sophie's eyes adjust to the dimness. This is a room in which time stands still because one would never know if it were day or night outside its four walls.

Inside, there is a reception desk. A petite woman with chin-length dark hair speckled with gray who looks to be in her fifties sits behind it, holding her mobile phone so close to her face that she's almost cross-eyed. She taps the screen with her manicured pink fingernails. Sophie can't help but feel disappointed even though she should not have expected Nita to be sitting in this hostel, waiting for her long-lost daughter to appear. Still, some part of her thought maybe it was possible that she would see Nita when she pushed open that door, and that hope is dashed as she sees the white woman at the counter.

The woman puts down her phone as Sophie approaches. *"Vous avez une réservation?"*

Sophie looks at her blankly, finally registering what the woman must be asking based on the context. "Do you speak English?" she says.

The woman sighs and nods even though her expression suggests she is annoyed by the question.

Sophie pulls out a picture of Nita that was taken the year before she left. She is dressed in an ornate blue sari studded with white beads for a Diwali party. A radiant smile adorns her face, and it is still hard for Sophie to imagine how a woman who smiles like that could be willing to leave her life, her husband, her daughter.

"I realize this is very strange, but do you happen to know this woman? She would look older now, but she stayed here twenty-two years ago." She holds out the photo.

The woman raises her eyebrows in a way that could mean she is intrigued or annoyed but humors Sophie and takes the old photo. Her eyes narrow as she inspects it carefully, bringing it close to her face like she had done previously with her phone, then moving it away and peering over her red-framed glasses at it before bringing it closer to her face again.

"Why do you ask?" She looks at Sophie but does not move to hand the photo back to her.

Sophie has not thought through how odd the truth would sound to strangers and realizes she must alter it to avoid seeming crazy. She says, "She's my relative. I haven't seen her since she moved from India, and I'm trying to find her." It is somewhat close to the truth.

The woman points her finger to the photo. "This woman is your relative?"

Sophie nods.

"What is her name?"

"Nita." Sophie's voice has a hint of excitement.

The woman hands back the photo. Sophie sees that she's wearing a name tag that reads "Cecile."

10

NITA

"Well, you look like the cat that swallowed the canary," Dao said to Nita when she walked into their shared room at the hostel and sank onto the bed after her day with Mathieu in the Luxembourg Gardens. Dao's hair was wet, and she was using a towel to wring out the excess water.

Nita looked confused.

Dao waved a hand, dismissing the comment. "Just meant that you have a look on your face like you had some really good sex or something."

"No, definitely not," Nita said, bringing her hand to her chest.

"Well, then you're thinking about it," Dao said with a good-natured laugh.

Nita blushed even though she hadn't been. Nita had noticed in the last few weeks that Dao was able to relate most things to sex. She was far more open about it than Nita, and far more open than Nita expected any Asian person to be, but despite their very different outlooks on life, the two had developed a fast friendship. Nita enjoyed hearing Dao's stories about the people who came into the bar where she worked and the random escapades she went on with some of those men. "Life is for living!" Dao would say. As much as Dao seemed content with her carefree lifestyle, Nita could not picture the same for herself, nor did she want it. Her dreams were focused on her craft. If she could successfully connect with people through art, she believed she could finally connect with the world in the way that had left her wanting for so long.

Nita told her about Mathieu and tried to make things sound as platonic as possible, but Dao refused to humor her.

"Well done, you, mingling with the locals. It's about time you had a fling," she said.

Nita knew there was no point in telling her there was no fling to be had.

"Just be careful," Dao warned. "The accent will charm the pants off you if you let it. I should know!" She laughed to herself as she picked up her blow-dryer. "And you need to watch out for the ones that only like you because of some fetish . . . I know too much about that too! So many of these white guys are in it for the conquest!" She shook her head as she strode down the hall toward the bathroom.

~

Over the next few weeks, Nita began spending more and more time with Mathieu. He taught her about wine, and although she still didn't have much of a taste for it, it was a part of life in Paris, and she had to embrace that. She had also begun to watch him paint. He had called her his muse, saying he was producing more than he had in years and liked having her near him. Watching his moods change as he stroked the canvas and seeing his ultimate creation made her realize how much she still had to learn. She had become less timid about showing him her work, and he guided her through different techniques, always encouraging her to *peindre du cœur*—paint from the heart.

One afternoon in mid-October, she sat in his small apartment while he worked and stared at her own blank canvas.

"Qu'est-ce qui ne va pas?" he asked. What's wrong?

"Rien," she said softly, her French having improved considerably the more time she spent in Paris and the more time she spent with him.

He stood and came near her, then placed his hand on her back. "You cannot say 'nothing' when it is clear there is something."

She turned to face his searching blue eyes. "I'm worried that I haven't found a job yet. I'm not able to pick up many shifts at the hostel now that the summer holidays are over and no one is taking vacation. I fear I will run out of money soon."

"Oui, l'argent. It is always a problem."

She hesitated, not sure whether to share the rest with him, but ultimately deciding that she needed to share it with someone. "It's not just the money," she said, taking a deep breath. "My visa will be running out, and I thought I'd find work that would allow me to stay here, but it seems no employers want to take on that burden of helping me get a work permit. I'm afraid of what will happen to me after that time."

Mathieu's glacial blue eyes shimmered as he stroked her back. "I did not know you were carrying such burdens. I'm sorry this is happening, but we will find a way."

She forced a smile. "Life always works out as it should, *non?*"

"J'espère que oui." He pulled her to her feet and led her to the tiny kitchenette. "Let's have some tea."

He seemed lost in thought while waiting for the electric kettle to boil. Once it did, he poured hot water into two mugs and added loose-leaf tea to individual infusers before dropping them into the mugs to steep.

"I might be able to help you," he said, staring into the steaming mugs.

Her eyes grew wide in protest. "I could not. You have helped me so much already." She gestured toward her artwork. "I could not take money from you."

He laughed. "And I have none to give you. I meant that *mon ami* teaches art classes. They are often looking for models to pose for the students. It's all paid in cash, and he wouldn't question your visa status. You are quite striking, and I suppose he would like that for his class."

Nita was now even more embarrassed than when she thought he was offering her the money himself. "Me? I could not model. I wouldn't know how."

It was not a profession for upper-caste girls in India. It would have been the same as prostitution, as far as her family was concerned.

"You must only stay still. You seem as though you would have quite the discipline to do that," he teased.

"I don't know." She tried to quiet the thoughts of disgrace running through her mind. There was no one left in her life to witness any such scandal anyway, she told herself. It would be a terrible example to set for Sophie, but Sophie would never know. Neither would her parents or Rajiv. She looked at Mathieu and tried not to think about her husband, because her time with Mathieu would be the greatest shame of all.

She needed the money; that much was clear. Without looking him in the eyes, she asked, "How much would it pay?"

11

SOPHIE

2019

The woman behind the reception desk narrows her eyes at Sophie, as if trying to size her up before responding. "It is odd, no? If you are related, why have you not kept up with her contact details?"

Sophie can tell the woman knows something, and her pulse quickens. She has lived her life without telling lies as Papa had instilled in her the karmic canon that if she lies, a bigger lie will be told to her. But the rules she has lived by until now have failed her. While she struggles internally with wanting to be honest despite knowing that the world has deceived her, she knows she cannot leave this place without learning what this woman knows.

"I have never come to France before, and it is going to be a surprise to her to see me after so many years." She inhales sharply, knowing her words will be most convincing if she sticks to something in the realm of the truth. "Please, it is very important that I see her. My papa—her brother—passed away, and I have come to tell her the news in person."

The dew that forms in Sophie's eyes is no lie. It forms every time she must utter aloud that Papa is dead. That phrase has not gotten easier to say, and Sophie wonders if there will be a time when it will be. She hopes not. She fears if it is ever easy, it will be because she has forgotten Papa and the love he lavished upon her, and she never wants to forget. Even if she is angry at him now, she cannot forget the lifetime of love and protection he bestowed upon her. Especially as she learns the truth about Nita. Papa was the one who stayed. And for that, she will always be grateful. Because she is learning that there was another path. The one Nita chose. The one that abandons Sophie.

Cecile softens, a knowing look sweeping over her face. Loss is a universal equalizer. The raw and personal nature of it resonates with everyone.

She stands and hands the photo back to Sophie. "Why didn't you say she was your aunt? I knew her. The resemblance between you now and the way she looked then is striking. Strong family genes, indeed."

Sophie's heart beats faster upon learning that this woman knows Nita! The rational, analytic side of her knew this was a long shot, statistically improbable that she would find Nita in this massive city, and yet this woman knows her! Sophie reasons that no matter the odds against her, she just needs one break. She takes a step closer to Cecile.

"Do you know where she is?" The hope in her voice is unmistakable. Lightning has already struck once, and the odds of it striking twice are improbable. Improbable, but not impossible.

Cecile shakes her head, ruefully. "It's been many years, and many husbands, since I last saw her. She stumbled in here, much like yourself, when I was a young girl working this desk. Now, here I am, an old lady still working this same job." She shakes her head as if playing a slideshow of the moments in her life over the past twenty years.

"She stayed here? For how long? Why did she leave?" The questions swirl in her head, but she tries to keep the dialogue manageable, tries to keep Cecile engaged and talking.

Cecile gestures around the reception area. "Look at this place. It's not the most chic hotel in the city. People only stay here when they are passing through. But Nita . . . she stayed longer than most."

Sophie wants to know every detail this woman can remember, but before she can decide on the next question to ask, Cecile starts moving toward a room behind the front desk.

"Would you like a coffee?" she asks over her shoulder. "This trip down memory lane requires a coffee for me."

Sophie doesn't drink coffee but says yes. Anything to connect with this woman.

Cecile returns with two tiny mugs of espresso and moves to the purple velvet couch in the reception area, motioning for Sophie to follow her. The couch is old and dingy and has seen better days. A close examination reveals cigarette burn marks and dark stains from who knows what, but Sophie doesn't care. She sits next to Cecile and takes a sip of the strong coffee, forcing herself not to wince at the acrid taste and hot temperature.

"What is your name?" Cecile asks.

Sophie places her tiny mug back on the saucer and responds.

Cecile polishes off her espresso like a pro before saying, "Your aunt was such an enigma. She walked through those doors in a sari and was such a sight in this city! She didn't even have a pair of jeans to her name. After she started working here, we had to go shopping to get her some more suitable clothing."

Sophie remembers the parrot-green sari Nita had been wearing the last day she saw her and wonders if it was the same one, but she does not ask. She has far more pressing issues than wardrobe.

"She worked here?" Sophie asks.

Cecile nods. "She came here to pursue her art. Painting, if I recall correctly. We get so many artists through this place that it's hard to keep track. She had to start taking shifts at the desk here to keep up with her lodging. Poor thing didn't speak much French when she arrived, and jobs were hard to come by. Lucky for her, the owners had a soft spot for foreigners trying to find their footing in Paris." Cecile stares off into the distance like she's trying to remember more. "Actually, Nita was great for my dating life because I got to take on less work here and chase after more boys."

Sophie nods as if she understands even though she's never been on a date in her life, let alone had a boyfriend. She can't really count her fiancé, Kiran, whom she has met once and is likely no longer her fiancé if her fois have told his family that she's disappeared.

"Come to think of it," Cecile continues, "maybe it would have been better if I had worked more during those years! Might have saved me from landing with husband number one."

"How long was she here?" Sophie asks, trying to refocus the conversation.

Cecile cocks her head, thinking back. "Let me think . . . maybe six months? A year at most. It's hard to remember so far back."

"Why did she leave?"

A smile creeps across Cecile's face. *L'amour, bien sûr!*

Sophie stares at her.

"She fell in love," Cecile says in a wistful voice.

Sophie bolts backward as if she's been slapped. "She what?!"

Cecile laughs. "Don't be surprised, young girl. This is the city of *l'amour*. Love will happen to you when you aren't looking as well."

Sophie cannot tell this woman her shock is because Nita was married and had no business dating someone new, let alone falling in love with some stranger who was not her husband. She feels anger swelling up inside her as she considers the disloyalty to Papa. He was such a kind, generous man. He never even considered taking on another wife, even though he had a daughter to raise by himself and could have used a woman's help. His sisters had begged him to move on, but he would not entertain the thought. Sophie now realizes it was likely because he knew Nita was alive and he was not truly widowed. Papa had remained faithful to his wife for the rest of his life. If only he had known that Nita did not share that same loyalty toward him.

"It's been such a long time, so it's surprising to hear what her life outside of India was," Sophie says, trying not to grit her teeth. "Please continue."

"I don't know what else there is to say. She left to be with her new beau. She took on shifts here and there for a while but then stopped working here entirely. I don't think I saw her again after that." She holds up a finger and pauses. "No, I think I saw her a few times around Paris. Paris is such a small city. There was a bistro around the corner that she used to go to with her artist friends, and I saw her there a couple times, her beau's arm around her and a cigarette dangling from her lips like there was no place in the world she would rather be."

Sophie's eyes widen at the thought of her prim, polished, never-a-sari-pleat-out-of-place mummy with a cigarette. She does not know any women in India who smoke. Then she thinks about how happy Nita had been—away from Sophie and Rajiv—and her eyes fill with tears, the big fat kind that there is no way of demurely retracting. Before she can say anything, they spill onto her cheeks, and she swipes them away. She repeats Cecile's last phrase in her mind again and again: *Like there was no place in the world she would rather be.*

"Oh, *chérie*. What is the matter? Is it something I said?" She puts a hand on Sophie's shoulder to offer support.

Shaking her head, Sophie says, "No, you have given me so much with your words. I'm afraid the passing of my papa is still recent, and many things remind me of him."

"I lost my *maman* a few years back. I understand the wave of memories that come with such a tragic event." She walks to the reception area and returns with a tissue for Sophie.

Sophie dabs her eyes, collects herself, and manages a smile. "Do you know where she is now? Or where she went after?"

Cecile shakes her head. "I'm sorry, child. I know she moved in with her boyfriend, but I don't recall where. Maybe in the Marais? I know she was still able to walk here, so it could not have been far. It's been much too long since I last saw her to know where or what she is up to these days."

"Do you know his name? The boyfriend?"

Cecile shakes her head again. "I wish I did so I could tell you."

Even though she has learned more about Nita during the last twenty minutes than she has known in her entire life, Sophie's shoulders slump as she realizes she has hit a dead end. "Thank you for your help. It is most kind of you to share so much."

Cecile nods, standing to head back to the reception desk. "When you find her, tell her that Cecile says hello and she can still look me up here. I'd love to hear what happened to her. Hopefully she fulfilled those art dreams and had better luck with the men in this city than I've managed to have."

12

NITA

1998

A week later, Nita showed up at the Luxembourg Gardens in her most elaborate sari, just as Mathieu had instructed her to do. Her coat covered the intricate stitchwork and heavy jewels sewn into the border of the cream-and-burgundy silk fabric. Her wedding sari. She had considered leaving it behind, given its bulk, but then decided to bring it as a reminder of the life she had left. Rather than it being nostalgic, she saw it as a source of strength if her resolve to pursue her passions ever weakened. She had sacrificed too much to be in Paris, and the six meters of fabric represented the life to which she had once agreed but never wanted. One meter for each year she'd spent as a mummy.

Mathieu had instructed her to go toward the back of the gardens, away from the fountain where they had sat the first time they had come there together. She walked down the gravelly path littered with fallen leaves. Statues adorned the sides, and the occasional tourist stopped to pose near one. The grassy areas somehow remained a vibrant green even as the cooler autumn weather settled in, although the bright flowers along the edge were starting to wilt and lose their petals. The air felt chilly against her cheeks, and she was glad to be wrapped in the second-hand coat she had purchased a few weeks earlier. The weather here was much colder than Ahmedabad, and she would need to adjust to it. She had never seen snow and had been told that it did not often get cold enough for that in Paris, but hoped that people were wrong and she might be able to see it. Feel it on her skin, let a flake fall onto her lips.

Toward the back gate of the park, she saw Mathieu leaning against one of the statues, a cigarette dangling from his lips as though it might fall out at any second, but by now she knew it never would. He had a scarf wrapped around his neck and looked rather dashing as she approached him and another man. Behind them, she saw a group of artists with portable easels set up around them.

"*Bonjour*," Mathieu said, flicking the cigarette onto the gravel path and stamping it out with his shoe before kissing both of her cheeks.

The man next to him introduced himself as Simon. He was several inches taller than Mathieu, with broader shoulders and a more muscular build. He leaned in to give her *bisous* as well.

Nita was still getting accustomed to this French tradition of kissing people no matter the relation. It was quite different from the Indian way she had been taught to greet people, especially elders, by bringing her hands together in namaskar and then bending to touch their feet to show her respect. Kissing was reserved for her husband, and even then, it was used sparingly.

"*Oui, Mathieu.*" Simon turned to his friend. "*T'as raison. Elle est très jolie.*"

Nita felt her cheeks warm, knowing they were saying she was pretty. Here, those types of compliments fell fast from men's tongues like raindrops on the pavement, but she appreciated them all the same.

"You have a traditional dress on?" Simon asked her, his English sounding just like all the Hollywood movies she had seen.

She nodded, holding open her coat so he could see her sari. "You are American."

"Perfect," he said. "Yes, my accent is a dead giveaway, I'm sure." His smile was warm and inviting. "Originally from sunny California."

She nodded, knowing only what she had seen in the movies or on television, but what she had seen seemed like a dream. She understood why she would want to leave a place like India to come to Paris, but it must be a more difficult decision for someone like Simon, who already lived in such a remarkable place.

He gestured behind him at the eight students, who looked in their direction. "My students have been learning to paint the full form and master the art of shading. I've been teaching them how to capture the figure in different types of dress, and this will be a challenge they haven't faced yet."

"*Merci* for the opportunity," she said demurely. "What shall I do?"

"If you can just remove your coat—" He saw the way she was standing, with her arms folded around herself to lock in the warmth. "I'm sorry, *Mademoiselle*, as it is quite chilly today. Will you be okay?"

She knew she would be freezing within seconds but had been raised to accommodate and not complain when around strangers. "It will be okay." She smiled at him.

Relieved, he gave Mathieu a nudge to move him away from the statue. "The light here is good. Perhaps you can lean against this and tilt your face so that it catches the sun."

Nita removed her coat and handed it to Mathieu. She stood as Simon directed her.

"If you need to adjust periodically, it's okay. Just go ahead and do as you need to be comfortable," Simon said before turning to his students.

"*Alors, on a une personne originaire d'Inde où les femmes portent des vêtements de ce style. Vous avez une heure pour la peindre.*" His French was slow and measured, like the phrases she was learning, making it much easier for her to understand. We have a person from India, where women wear clothing such as this. You have an hour to paint her.

Nita remained as still as she could in the cold. Following instructions in class was something for which she had always strived for fear of having the teacher rap her knuckles with a ruler when she acted out. While others in class had never had the ruler touch their skin, she had seemed to encounter it on a weekly basis. She would often be caught doodling on her science homework or sketching on the back of her book cover, activities that were punishable offenses in her school. Here, though, she did her best to be the perfect student. She remained still, listening to Simon as he went from student to student, offering tips and suggestions. She strained to hear his words and absorb them like a dry rag soaks up spilled milk.

At the end of the class, he allowed her to see the work created by the students. Their interpretations were so different from one another. Some tried to copy her image exactly, while others tried to gather the essence of her shape in abstract art. And it was clear they had varying levels of talent among them. Abstract art was something she had never practiced and was not well versed in. She found joy in capturing a perfect, lifelike moment, so she lingered on the canvases of the artists whose styles most resembled hers. Simon explained some of the shading techniques that the students were working on incorporating to give depth to the folds of her sari. He described strokes to her in a careful and methodical manner, using an imaginary brush against the canvas to demonstrate.

Once all the students had cleared out of the space, with flushed cheeks he handed her a small white envelope with the hundred francs she had been promised. "I'm sorry, but the school doesn't offer more to the models."

"There is no need to apologize."

Mathieu joined them. "Shall we go get some wine?"

Simon looked at her and shrugged agreeably. "If you two don't mind me tagging along, I could use a drink."

Mathieu slung an arm around his shoulder. "*Pas du tout.* You are always welcome." He then winked at Nita. "Perhaps we should go somewhere nice now that you've got some cash."

She assumed he was joking but firmed up her grip on the envelope. She was so desperately in need of this money to pay her board at the hostel, so even a joke was not funny to her right now. She was not accustomed to paying when she was out with a man because until France, it had always been her husband, or papa, or a relative, and her money would never have been accepted, so there was no need to even offer. But men in Paris were not the same as those in India. She managed a half smile as she walked with them out of the park, tightly holding on to the cash.

~

At the café, she nursed a glass of wine, trying to fit in without Mathieu and Simon realizing they were the only ones refilling from the liter carafe in front of them. She had gone back to the hostel to quickly change out of her sari and into the jeans and sweater Cecile had helped her purchase a couple weeks ago. They were among the first items of Western clothing she had ever bought herself, and, while it was taking her some time to get used to seeing her image in a mirror dressed in formfitting tops and pants that traced the lines of her legs, she felt like she was blending in more. Fewer people glanced at her a second time on the street, and she continued to strive toward being invisible.

They sat at a small bistro table on the terrace, coats tightly wrapped around them as the sun began to set and the temperature began to drop.

"How is the wine in India?" Simon asked, exhaling from a puff on his cigarette.

Nita laughed. "Nonexistent."

He raised an eyebrow.

Nita continued, "The state I am from doesn't have alcohol. Those who get it acquire it illegally, and my"—she inhaled sharply, realizing she was about to say *husband*—"family would never have engaged in such illegal activity."

Simon nodded. "That's a real shame. Not sure I would have gotten through my twenties without it."

Mathieu said to her, "It's no wonder you wanted to leave." He refilled his own glass.

"Most importantly for me, art was considered a hobby there," Nita said, wanting to change the subject.

The cigarette smoke from both Simon and Mathieu had created a haze around them. Nita felt the stench absorbing into her skin, her hair, the fibers of her coat and sweater.

"No cigarettes either, I suppose," Mathieu said.

She didn't want to say that she often saw men smoking in India, but they were from the lower castes. Certainly, Rajiv and her family members would have never engaged in a vice worse than the occasional paan after dinner, letting the tobacco and spice-wrapped betel leaves linger in their mouths until their tongues were deep red.

"They probably didn't need them there," Simon said, smiling at Nita. "I never smoked in California. It's just so damn cold here that you need something to keep you warm."

"It does get much colder here," she agreed.

Simon winked at her. "You might find yourself turning to the tobacco stick soon. This isn't even the worst of the weather!"

Something about Simon made her feel at ease, and she reached for his cigarette. "No harm in trying," she said.

Mathieu looked between them curiously as she adjusted her grip on the cigarette. It warmed her fingers as she brought it to her lips and parted them slowly. It didn't seem that bad as her lips moistened the paper.

"You need to inhale," Simon said.

She slowly took a breath and felt the smoke in her mouth. The coughing was almost instantaneous, and she quickly removed the cigarette from her lips. The boys chuckled in a way that suggested her reaction reminded them of their first times smoking.

"You get the hang of it," Simon said, taking back the cigarette, his lips now covering the place where hers had just been.

"You just need practice, *ma chérie*," Mathieu said, passing his cigarette to her, the look in his eyes territorial, as if he wanted to make sure that if she were sharing a cigarette with anyone, it would be him. The waiter left the check on the table, and Mathieu retrieved some notes and coins to cover it. She was relieved that despite his comment earlier, he had picked up the bill.

She took his cigarette and tried again but had the same result. "Perhaps I will practice another time," she said.

And practice she did over the next month. Simon had been right. As the temperature dropped, she got past the coughing and found the warmth in her mouth a relief from the cold air against her face. Mathieu was generous with his cigarettes and seemed to have an endless supply. She hadn't bought a single one yet. When she wasn't with Mathieu, she was with Simon, serving as a model for his students, and then he supplied her with them to help fight off the cold. It was a habit she was beginning to crave and one easily satisfied by both men she was spending time with.

13

SOPHIE

2019

On her walk back to the hotel in the Marais, Sophie feels adrenaline surging through her. She met someone who knew Nita! What were the chances of it being that easy? She cannot help but wonder if Nita is somewhere around her. Maybe just a few streets or even mere buildings away from the hotel. Maybe Sophie would even pass by her on the street. What would she look like now? Would Sophie recognize her after all this time? Would she recognize Sophie? She realizes it is crazy and Nita could be anywhere, but it was also crazy to find the same receptionist at Le Canard Volant who was there when Nita had first checked in. The odds of that had to be one in a million, if not more. Bhagwan was smiling upon her today, so she had to keep hope.

She also could not believe that her mummy had a boyfriend here. And so soon after leaving India. Was it so easy for Nita to forget about her life in Ahmedabad and move on? The thought incites Sophie even though she remains desperate to find the woman who had abandoned her and Papa for this racy new life in Paris. Sophie had had so little to warrant anger or resentment as a child because Papa ensured that she had everything she wanted, but now she feels bitterness on so many levels. She tries to imagine a world in which Nita would have a cigarette dangling from her lips and her arm around a man other than Rajiv! The thought of it is almost cartoonish, but Sophie must recalibrate the person she remembers as her mummy and replace those images with the person she became.

She isn't sure what to do next to find Nita. She contemplates asking Saumil Uncle and Anjali Auntie for help. They have been so kind to her, and she doesn't want to impose further on them. But their help could go a long way. They know Paris much better than she does and speak the language, so they could be a valuable resource if she were willing to open up to them. By the time she gets back to the hotel, she has convinced herself that this is the right decision. The stakes are too high to rely solely on herself.

~

Sophie opens the door to their shared hotel room very quietly so she won't disturb Uncle and Auntie in case they are taking a nap. When she enters the room, she sees no one is there. The beds are still unmade. She scans the room, suddenly realizing there isn't a trace of them left. And her suitcase still sits in the corner where she had left it, but its contents have been tousled.

She races to the luggage and falls to her knees, digging through her clothing to the places where she had tucked away the bulk of the money she had brought with her, separating the stacks as an added safety measure, just like Papa had taught her. She knows the thick wads of rupees that convert to nearly €3,000 will not be there, but she removes everything from the suitcase and shakes it out, holding out the last bit of hope she has because what else can she do? She realizes that her mobile is missing, too, but that seems less troubling given that it hadn't worked here anyway. She knows she has been swindled by them, like in the plot of a Bollywood movie.

I'll have to call my fois to help me, she thinks to herself, dreading the phone call. They have control over the accounts Papa left to her when he passed. All her money is in those accounts, including the money Papa's friend paid her for her job. It was always understood that when she married, the accounts would transfer over to her husband like a modern-day dowry.

She cradles her head in her hands. She has been cautious her entire life, just as Papa taught her to be, and the one time she lets down her guard, she is punished for it. New anger builds on top of what was already simmering inside of her. But then she experiences something that dwarfs the anger. Despair.

It pushes against every muscle and fiber of her being, making her feel like she's sinking into the floor. Sophie has never been without hope before. She has never been without someone to help her through life's difficulties. She'd always had Papa. She realizes that she's been sheltered from most of life's adversities through the tireless efforts of him and their community in Ahmedabad. Without him serving as her shield, she feels alone, and her body begins to quiver. The new levels of loneliness she has felt since Papa's passing make her realize she has never truly understood the feeling before, even if she thought she had. Papa had always told her how independent she was. She was the only one among her friends who didn't get married by age twenty-five and start a family. She developed a career. Something unheard of for a woman in her community, and Papa had supported her in doing that, so it made it okay.

"Having a job that Papa helped me get didn't make me independent," she says to herself, kneeling before her suitcase with the contents now strewn around her.

It hadn't made her independent. She suddenly sees clearly that she's lived a very privileged and sheltered life. Her experiences have been controlled. She's never had to deal with situations like the one she is currently in, and she's unsure if she has the coping skills to get herself out of this mess. She reels at knowing that moments earlier her first instinct was to call her fois rather than to find a solution on her own. No, she is not independent. Far from it. Papa had tried to instill in her that she should be resilient, always telling her "Pavan ni disha na badali shako, pan amara sadh ni disha badali shako." *The direction of the wind cannot be changed, but we can change the direction of our sails.* He stressed to her how important it was to be nimble in the face of adversity, but then in reality, he removed most of her obstacles before she'd even known they were there. He'd been the one adjusting her sails before she even knew she needed to. But now he is gone, and she has to learn the lesson he'd meant to teach her as a child.

Had Nita had these same feelings when she had come over? She'd had a similarly sheltered and privileged upper-caste life in Ahmedabad. Sophie could not imagine that Nita had any better life skills than Sophie did. If anything, Nita would have been worse off, never having worked a day in her life. At least Sophie had some experience outside of the home. It is this final thought that pushes Sophie forward, making her stand and pack her remaining belongings. She has the money she carried with her to the hostel this morning. She will not run to her fois. Nita had found a way to survive here, and so will she.

14

NITA

1998

After one of Simon's class sessions, Nita was waiting for him to complete his rounds of critiquing the students' work. They were inside a classroom in the sixth arrondissement this time, sheltered from the cold. Mathieu had stopped coming to each of the classes for which she modeled, beginning to delve more into his own work, claiming that she was inspiring him to test his artistic boundaries. She and Mathieu would walk around the city for hours at a time, him striding next to her and always walking on the side of the street closer to the traffic. She found his chivalry endearing and enjoyed their long strolls and the new impressions of Paris she was forming as she saw the city through his eyes—those of someone who knew every nook and cranny of it the way she knew Ahmedabad. His love for his city and enthusiasm for painting had begun to inspire her as well. Between Mathieu and the tips she overheard in Simon's art classes, her work was getting better, and she was grateful for the free tutelage.

After Simon finished speaking with the students, he came back to her, bringing her coat.

"We should grab a drink," he said, holding the coat open so she could slide into it.

Nita had not spent any time alone with Simon outside of his classes. In the past, Mathieu had been with her, and the three of them would go to a café together. There couldn't be much harm in her going without Mathieu.

"*Mais, oui*," she said, practicing her French.

"*Allons-y*," he said, leading her by the elbow out of the classroom.

They sat in an intimate corner booth in a small café that overlooked one of the gates of the Luxembourg Gardens. Given the temperature, they had opted to be inside, near the window. Simon rubbed his palms together, trying to warm them.

"This weather still takes some getting used to," he said.

She nodded. "I never had a coat like this until I moved here."

They ordered a carafe of red wine, something Simon said he liked, and then ordered a plate of charcuterie, cheese, and bread to go with it. Changing her lifelong vegetarian diet had been an adjustment, just like developing a taste for wine had been, but Nita was determined to blend into the new world around her, and consuming the same things during meals was an essential component.

"How long have you and Mathieu been dating?" Simon asked as he filled both of their glasses, careful not to let any drops slide down the exterior.

"Oh, we, no," Nita stammered. She took a breath and collected herself. "We are not dating. We just met when I moved here and became friends."

Simon nodded, seemingly filing away her answer. "Have you ever been to the States?"

Her face lit up. "No, but I would love to go. I see so much of it on the television, and it all seems so glamorous."

He laughed. "I'm not sure if I'd call it glamorous, but it has its perks. We are spoiled by things like water pressure."

"I'm spoiled by what we have here," Nita said.

The constant flow of hot water in the showers still amazed her. It was hard to imagine that America had certain conveniences that were even greater than those she had seen in Paris.

"If you aren't dating Mathieu, then you should find a nice man to really spoil you."

Nita wasn't sure how to take Simon's comment and cast her gaze downward, avoiding his eyes.

"It's the Parisian way, after all," Simon said.

"I suppose it is the Indian way as well."

"Did you come here because you hadn't found that guy in India yet?"

Nita thought of her husband, who had tried to give her everything society had told him he should: a home, servants, jewels, clothing, children. He just didn't understand that what she wanted was different from what society wanted for her.

She shook her head. "I came because I knew if I didn't come now, I would go my entire life without ever setting foot in this country. Days would pass, the same as the ones before, and I couldn't let that happen."

That much was true. The love she felt for Sophie had grown at the same rate as the resentment she felt for the life into which she had been born. That resentment had begun to spill onto her precious daughter, who had done nothing to deserve it. Nita could not see a future in which she could be the mummy that Sophie deserved. She loved her daughter as much as she hated being a wife and mummy and had no idea how to reconcile those two things. She wasn't sure they could be balanced. That she could be fixed. In the months leading up to her decision to leave, she had realized she was becoming more and more short with Sophie. Scolding her when she was caught playing with Nita's bangles. Brushing her hair harder than she needed to each night. Growing more irritated as her daughter asked questions about the French landscapes she was painting. Parenthood came naturally to many, but not to Nita. And she had felt like she was getting worse rather than better.

"There's no time like the present, then." Simon raised his glass in a toast.

She clinked hers against his and sipped from it, wondering what the present looked like for Sophie and hoping that Rajiv was finding ways to bring Sophie joy through this difficult time. Above all else, she wanted Sophie to be happy.

~

Nita sat on the leather sofa in Mathieu's apartment, her sketch pad on her lap, untouched for the last several minutes. The pads of her fingers were blackened from the charcoal sticks she'd been using.

"*Qu'est-ce qui ne va pas?*" Mathieu asked her what was wrong.

She startled at hearing his voice break the silence.

"You look very far away," he said, kneeling before her on the couch so that his gaze was level with hers.

She could smell the cigarette smoke emanating from his clothes and skin, the thin green sweater seeming to have trapped it all within its fibers. She placed the sketch pad down.

"Sorry," she said, "my mind is somewhere else today." She took a deep breath. "It's just been very hard to find a steady job since I arrived, and I'm afraid of what will happen if I can't make more money soon."

He nodded. "Money is the greatest curse of an artist. We need it to live, but it takes away from our life."

She wasn't in the mood for one of his poetic musings. She was hitting a critical stage with her finances and was learning how necessary money was to survive. She had never thought about it like this because it had always been there. It was only when she had lost it that she realized how much power it held. And she had assumed that by now she'd have gotten a job that would have allowed her to extend her visa. How naive she had been. She'd never been in the position of worrying about whether she could be kicked out of a place that felt like her home, and that weight was exhausting to carry. There were so many things she'd never had to think about because they had been a given for her. And she realized she truly didn't know what happened to people when they ran out of money and security. She pictured the countless beggars she had seen on the streets in Ahmedabad and shuddered at the thought of that being her life here. Homeless people were periodically seen in Paris, but not in remotely the same numbers as in India. She wondered if there really were that few of them or if they were off somewhere, hidden. Either way, she hoped not to find out, but she also could not see a way out of her predicament. She could not become fluent in a new language overnight, and the circular logic of needing a job to get a visa and a visa to get a job was hard to overcome. She had felt trapped in her life in India, but now she was learning a new form of being trapped and wondered if people were always trapped by something, no matter what they did or where they were.

"I'm sure it will be fine," she said, forcing her voice to sound light and airy. She had been raised not to leave her problems with other people.

Mathieu's eyes bore into hers, showing he did not believe her facade. "How can I help?"

She shrugged, turning away from him. "I don't suppose there's much you can do unless you know someone willing to hire an Indian woman who doesn't speak French and pay her in cash." She tried to laugh it off, knowing that if such a person existed, she would have found them by now.

She could see his mind swirling, his desire to help written across his face. He had been so attuned to her needs as their friendship developed, and his empathy was the quality Nita most respected about him.

"There must be something you can do for work," he said, mostly to himself. Turning to her, he added, "We will find a way. Many people come to Paris just like you, and they find a way. We will too."

She felt her cheeks flush. "You've been such a good friend already. You don't need to take on this burden."

He gave her his half smile. "What kind of friend would I be if I didn't? Besides, I cannot have an unhappy muse! It's bad for business!"

She looked at him, grateful for her fortune that in a city with this many people, she had stumbled upon this one. She had never had a stranger become a friend and was often surprised by how much he or Dao or Cecile were willing to let her into their lives, having known her for such a short time. Her friends in India had been curated for her. As a child, she had been introduced to the daughters of her parents' friends, and then as an adult, it had been the wives of Rajiv's friends. She'd never been in the position of doing something for herself and meeting someone whose path she was not predetermined to cross. Her bonds with her new friends in Paris felt so much stronger than the ties she'd had to people she'd known for her entire life. She had chosen her people in France, and choice made all the difference.

～

A few days later, Nita was at the reception desk of the hostel, covering an evening shift. Cecile had a date that night with a guy she'd claimed was "the one" and had taken the afternoon to get herself ready for it. The concept of spending hours getting ready to meet someone was completely foreign to Nita. Then again, the concept of dating was foreign to her too. Nita was flipping through a fashion magazine Cecile had left behind, trying to read the French and work on her language skills, when Dao came down the stairs.

"I'd like to complain about my room partner," she said dramatically.

Nita gave her an exaggerated eye roll. Dao loved to voice her "complaints" whenever Nita was covering a shift. Seemed the joke was funny to her every time, although Nita had to admit she enjoyed the banter as well. Le Canard Volant was not exactly a hotbed of activity, so the job was rather dull, but Nita was grateful for any amount of money she could earn. She was at the point where she was practically surviving only on the wine and cigarettes that she shared with Mathieu and was growing rather thin.

"You off to work?" Nita asked her.

She nodded. "In a bit. Haven't seen much of you around lately, though. Seems you have to be doing a shift for me to find you!" Her eyes twinkled as she spoke.

"I've been working on my art projects."

Dao laughed. "Oh, is that what you're calling it?"

Nita blushed, knowing what she meant but wanting to set the record straight—for herself as much as Dao.

"Yes," she said definitively. "I know you love a good intrigue, but that's really all I'm doing. It's the reason I came here, and if I'm not focused on my art, then I may as well go back to India."

Dao leaned over to see the magazine Nita had in front of her. "Whatever suits your narrative," she said.

Nita knew there was no use convincing her. Dao saw the world as a never-ending romantic comedy. She'd confessed how stifling it had been for her when she lived with her parents in London and her immigrant parents had expected her to be laser focused on her schooling so she could get a good job and had frowned upon any sort of dating. Dao said she had fallen in love a thousand times with the characters on her television screen because they were all she had. But now that she was out from under her family's watchful stares, in a city that was entirely her own, she was going to turn each of those romances she'd watched into a real story in her life. While Nita could relate to the freedom of being in a city without fear of her family seeing and judging her actions, she could not imagine having such a rosy outlook about love and romance. Still, she was grateful to have someone in her life who saw so much good in the world around her. Nita had been having some very low moments as she contemplated what her future looked like, and Dao's energy often helped her pick herself up and try again the next day.

"And what about you?" Nita asked. "Is there not a young Frenchman at the bar who has caught your eye?"

Dao laughed again. "Please. There are several! It would be easier to count the ones I don't fancy."

Nita didn't think she could ever be that carefree with her heart, especially at this late stage in life. Dao's perspective seemed like one that had to be ingrained in a person from childhood. And it was so interesting to Nita that, given that Dao's parents sounded similar to hers when it came to tradition and a woman's place, Dao still managed to have that natural way about her when she dealt with dating. Nita couldn't imagine herself being anything other than awkward.

"I do think you should bring these friends of yours to the bar one day. I'd love to meet them. You never know, if you don't want them, then maybe I will have a go!"

Nita knew she was joking, but the thought of Dao and Mathieu or Simon together did not sit well with her. In just a few moments, she planned their entire life together. They and Dao had all been raised in the West, so they had similar backgrounds, even if Dao was Thai and they were white and there might be a racial caste disparity. They all understood the same jokes and cultural references to television shows and songs, and Dao knew all the foods they ate and wine they drank. And above all else, Nita had spent enough time in Paris to notice the numbers of white men holding hands with striking, slender Asian women with features and hair like Dao's and knew that Dao's type of Asian was a prize greater than Nita's. The thought of one of them with Dao unnerved her so much that she vowed not to introduce them. She couldn't give up her friendship with any of them, and the best way to keep things the same was to ensure they never met.

15

SOPHIE

2019

Sophie does not cry as she lugs her suitcase through the streets of Paris, unsure of where to go. She does some quick calculations and knows her remaining rupees are worth only about €200. She has put her cash and engagement ring into her money belt, vowing not to wear the ring again in this city and attract would-be thieves. She refuses to cry. Her tears lately have been reserved for Papa's passing. She will not let those two horrible people elicit the same reaction as her beloved Papa. "Bhagwan will take care of those who are bad," he would always say, and she remembers those words now as she stands at a busy intersection, waiting for the light to change so she can cross.

She has always believed these words. Lived her entire life according to them. Convinced herself that she always had to take the high road and never degrade herself to the lower levels of others. But now she wonders if that is true. If there is any justice in the world. If there were, surely Papa would not have been taken from her. Her mummy would not have left her. It's hard to believe the universe has a plan when everything around her feels random.

She cannot believe that people from her home country would scam her the way that Saumil and Anjali had. She could never even think of doing such a thing to another person. They must have made her their mark straight from the airport, and she cannot believe she had been so gullible. Her desperation had clouded her judgment, but she cannot be the doe-eyed victim again. Before, she hadn't been aware, but now she is, and she must start to take responsibility for herself. And she learned enough today about Nita that she needs to stay and discover the rest. They have already spent too much time apart and have a lifetime of stories to learn about each other. Nita owes her answers, and Sophie is determined to get them. Determined in a way she never was before. She convinces herself this is a simple equation, just like any other, and it is up to her to find the solution.

Sophie knows nothing of this city, and the only place she can think to go is the same place Nita had sought refuge when she first came to Paris. She knows the path this time and can get there quickly, which is good, given that her luggage is beginning to strain her arms after she'd hauled it behind her for thirty minutes.

Cecile is seated exactly as she had been earlier that day, her phone very close to her face. She smiles when Sophie enters.

"Did you find her already?" she asks. "How is our dear artist?"

Sophie shakes her head. "I'm afraid I was sidetracked. I came across some very bad people, and they took my money from me."

Cecile rushes to Sophie and puts her hands on Sophie's slumped shoulders to look at her carefully. "Are you hurt? Shall I call the police?"

Sophie shakes her head again. "It was my fault. I should not have trusted them. And I don't know what I could tell the police that would be helpful. I probably don't even know their real names." Sophie takes a deep breath, and her eyes meet Cecile's. She breaks from her Indian upbringing to never share problems outside of the home, and says, "Do you have a small room I can rent until I can figure out my finances? I have a little money left, but not much."

Cecile tightens her grip on Sophie's shoulders. "If only your aunt could see you now. This was how she came to me that first day she arrived in Paris. Come," she says. "We aren't full, and I can put you in one of the beds for a few nights without drawing attention."

Sophie reaches for her money, but Cecile wags a finger at her. "Put that away. I won't take your money like this." She moves back to the reception desk in search of a room key. "And people say we French don't help others," she scoffs, mostly to herself. She then hands Sophie a key before helping her maneuver her luggage up the winding staircase.

16

NITA

Nita arrived at the address in the Marais that Mathieu had written for her on a slip of paper. He had found her a modeling job that paid considerably more than her sessions with Simon, and she had been elated. She so desperately needed this money to get through the next month. Mathieu had not told her what to wear, so she decided on her best panjabi, thinking it was always safe to look polished. Underneath the wool coat, the pale-pink silk fabric felt soft against her skin, while the intricate embroidery and jewels around the neckline chafed her chest slightly, a feeling to which experience told her she would grow accustomed as the night wore on.

There were fourteen students seated on stools with easels before them. At the center of the circle of students was a wooden platform on which their subject would pose. Mathieu and another man stood chatting at the front of the classroom.

"*T'as raison*," the man said to Mathieu. You are right. He held a lit cigarette behind him as he nodded.

"Oui, toujours." Always. Mathieu had a glimmer in his eye as he spoke. *"Elle s'appelle Nita."*

She nodded politely as she approached them and heard her name.

"Bonsoir," the man said, leaning in to give her two quick *bisous. "Je m'appelle Julien."*

A nearby furnace kicked on, releasing a gust of hot air into the room. Nita removed her coat and draped it over her arm.

"I was not sure what to wear," she said, gesturing toward her panjabi.

He released a stream of smoke from his lips and fanned it away from them. "It is no matter. You can change there," Julien said to her while pointing to a little curtained-off area in the corner. Then to Mathieu, he said, *"T'as lui dit, n'est-ce pas?"* You told her, right?

"Pas de problème." Not a problem.

Nita looked surprised. "This is all I've brought," she said, glancing at Mathieu.

He took her arm and led her toward the curtained-off area. "You must pose nude," he said.

She stopped dead in her tracks, staring at him as though he had gone mad. "What are you talking about?"

"The students are learning to paint nude figures. That is why the pay is so good."

"I—I can't do that." Nita felt exposed even thinking about standing in this room full of people in nothing more than her bare skin. A thousand francs wasn't worth that!

He tightened his grip on her arm and leaned in toward her. "You said you needed money."

"Yes, but I didn't mean . . ." She searched the room for her quickest exit point. She would find the money another way.

"What is the issue?" he asked. "This is art. The human form is beautiful, and these students are trying to study it."

She felt like a wild animal trapped in a cage. Every student was now focused on their conversation and staring in their direction.

"Mathieu, I can't." Her voice was barely audible and began to tremble.

"Il y a un problème, mon ami?" Julien asked from across the room. Is there a problem, my friend?

Mathieu shook his head. *"Non, non. On a besoin juste d'un moment. J'ai oublié quelque chose."* We just need a moment. I forgot something.

He steered Nita toward the door she had entered moments ago. The icy air felt good against her face. Nita inhaled sharply, finally able to breathe again.

"What was that about?" His blue eyes narrowed as he glared at her.

She had never seen his kind face look so harsh. She took a step back. "You cannot expect me to pose nude in front of those people." Her voice was soft, timid.

"Julien has an entire class that needs a female model. You said you needed money. I pulled some strings to get him to approve you. It's too late to cancel."

"You should have told me," she shot back.

"Told you what?" He threw his hands in the air. "You say you are an artist. The human body is basic stuff for a serious artist." He lingered on the word *serious*, watching her reaction.

It was as if he knew how much that jab would disarm her. He had no clue how much she had given up to become an artist. Her expression turned hard, matching his. "You don't know me. I need to go home."

His face softened, and he changed his approach, coming toward her with his arms open in apology. *"Viens ici, ma belle."* Come here, beautiful.

He folded her into his arms, and she felt the warmth of his body radiate onto hers through the thin silk fabric she wore. "Your skin is so cold." He rubbed her back with long strokes, trying to make her feel more comfortable. He pulled his head back so he could look down at her face.

"You are beautiful. You should not hide that from the world," he said, staring at her with tender longing as he dropped his mouth to meet hers.

She stood frozen as his warm lips covered hers. The only other man she had ever kissed had been her husband. And that had been so different. His mouth didn't have the same fervor as Mathieu's did. His lips didn't have the same softness or thickness. She found herself responding to Mathieu by parting her lips and deepening their kiss. She brought her hands to his face, pulling it closer to her as if she were afraid he might pull away and leave her breathless and wanting more. She had never experienced anything like this and now understood what the scenes in the Western movies she had seen were trying to capture. There was an urgency in her that shocked her.

When he did finally release her lips from his own, she was indeed breathless and trembling and wanting more. His lids slowly opened, revealing those mysterious blue eyes, now with the gentleness in them she was accustomed to seeing.

"You taste as beautiful as you look," he said as he kissed her forehead and pulled her closer toward him in a tender embrace.

She could not find the words to express to him what she was feeling, so she mumbled a soft *merci* into his chest. He cupped her chin in his hand and lightly tilted her face to meet his kind eyes.

"*Ma belle*, we must go back inside."

The magic of the moment was broken, and she again filled with the terror she had felt when emerging from the classroom a few minutes earlier. She shook her head, feeling lost and confused. "I can't . . . ," she said, not wanting to disappoint him but not knowing what else to say.

He kissed her again, this time more softly, with a tenderness that made her believe he would protect her. "Let me help you. It will be over soon, *ma belle*, and then you will not have to mar your beautiful face with worry about money like you have these past weeks."

Before she could answer, he pulled a small cigarette from his pocket and lit it. This one looked different from his others, shorter and fatter and rolled by hand. He sat on the stone ledge outside of the art school and pulled her onto his lap. The warmth of his thighs radiated through his jeans and felt good against her cold legs.

"Take this." He nuzzled her neck as she took it from his fingers.

She held it awkwardly, not quite sure what to do with it. She could tell this was something different from the usual cigarette. She wanted so desperately to get through this night without scaring him off that she brought the white paper to her lips. She looked at him questioningly.

"It's hashish. Stronger than the other cigarettes. Breathe in and hold the air for a few seconds. This will help you relax."

He was infinitely more relaxed than she was, so maybe this was the answer. She coughed through it but tried to do as he said. The smoke was more pungent but sweeter than the stale cigarette smoke she had gotten used to.

After a few minutes, Julien poked his head out to check on them. *"Vous êtes prêts?"* Are you ready?

Mathieu looked at Nita before nodding. *"Un instant."*

A calm began to set over Nita, as if she wasn't in her body anymore. Her head felt light. She rested it against Mathieu, and he seemed happy to let her do so. He gingerly helped her rise to her feet and put his arm around her waist so she could lean against him.

"Once we finish here, it will be only us again."

The words he whispered in her ear left a warm, tingling sensation that stayed with her as they made their way back inside and to the corner with the curtain. This time, she didn't even notice the students in the room because the only presence she felt was Mathieu. He came behind the curtain with her and, with a delicate hand, undressed her, studying her body with his eyes as if they were the only two people in the room. A black robe hung on a nail, and he helped her slip into it. Her gold bangles clinked together, and she was about to remove them and slip them into her purse when Mathieu put a hand on her forearm.

"Leave them," he said, a twinkle in his eye.

Nita looked at them on her wrist, glinting as she moved. No, she decided. She could not have this last memory of her parents on her arm as she did something she knew would strip her family of their dignity. It was as if by her wearing them now, her parents would somehow sense who she had become. She slipped them off and put them in his palm, closing his fingers around them.

"You must take care of these."

He nodded. Then, giving her one last kiss, reminding her of what would come, he led her to the wooden platform at the center of the room. Julien had placed a chair there and asked her to sit with her legs crossed at the knees. Her dark hair fell over her shoulders in unruly waves, and Julien moved half of it behind her ears, revealing more of her face and creating a clean line of sight to her left breast.

"Try not to move so it does not disturb the shadows while the students are working," he said.

From the corner of her eye, she saw Mathieu leaning against the wall, admiring her, as if he knew that her body was already his for the taking. A shudder passed through her.

17

SOPHIE

2019

After leaving her suitcase in the room upstairs, Sophie wanders along the streets, not sure of what to do next. As she is walking along Rue Saint-Michel, she smells familiar scents from home—sautéed garlic and ginger with coriander, turmeric, and chili—wafting out of a restaurant and looks over to see an Indian bistro with the name Taj Palace written in red script on the door. A menu hangs in the window, but Sophie doesn't need to read it to know what dishes will be offered inside. The aromas make her feel as if home is not quite as far away.

"Come in. We have very tasty food," a man says with a thick Indian accent.

Sophie hesitates, doing the math and knowing she can't afford to spend her money on food like this. "I think I should not," she says shyly to the man, who appears to be in his late fifties. He has a head of thick black hair that is starting to show more gray, just like her papa did.

"Come now. The food is quite good." He cocks his head from side to side in that familiar Indian way.

"No, I did not mean to offend. I'm sure it is quite good. I have very little money right now." She looks at the ground as she makes her final statement, feeling ashamed to be speaking about money with this stranger, but she has never been robbed before, so money is on her mind more than usual.

The man stares at her in that direct, pointed way with which most Westerners are generally too polite to look at strangers, and after a few moments motions her in. "Please come. The meal is on me. You can try some of my new recipes to tell me if you think they are authentic enough. We have to make some changes for this Western palate, but I don't want to stray too far!"

Sophie wrestles with the idea of taking charity and what Papa would think if he were alive, but she is on her own now, and it is an offer she cannot refuse.

~

Taj Palace is cozy, with seating for about forty people, but there are only four patrons in the restaurant, two tables of two, all of them white and speaking rapid French to each other as they eat their meals using silverware. The walls are adorned with authentic beaded Indian artwork on black cloth. The pictures are of elephants and camels, and in the center of the main wall is a large beaded image of the Taj Mahal. Incense burns near the front door, filling her nostrils with the familiar scent of sandalwood as she follows the man into the restaurant. He gestures toward a small table in the corner, near the kitchen and away from the other diners.

"Are you Gujarati?" he asks.

She nods, already knowing from his accent and familiar features that he is Gujarati as well. She feels the weight of her body as she drops onto the cushioned chair he has pulled out for her. It has been a very long day, and she has had a lot of those lately, each one piling on top of the other.

"Will you like Indian spicy or Western spicy?" he asks.

She looks at him, confused.

He laughs and says, "I will make it like home. Saag paneer and channa masala is good for you?"

Sophie salivates at the thought of those familiar flavors, and she eagerly nods.

"My name is Naresh," he says, bringing his palms together and bowing at the waist in respect even though she is the younger of the two and it is she who should be bowing to him.

"Sophie," she responds.

His eyes flicker with the same quizzical look that crosses all Indians' faces when she tells them her name. He masks it quickly and makes his way toward the kitchen, where she sees another Indian man, younger than Naresh and probably closer to her age, in a white chef's coat, peering out from the pass at her, his eyes narrowed. Naresh and the chef exchange a few words, and the chef glances at Sophie and then nods, picking up a steel pan to heat it on the stove before disappearing into the back. There are some faint noises from the kitchen, and Sophie closes her eyes and lets the aromas transport her back to a simpler time.

She recalls her parents preparing for a Diwali dinner the year before Nita left. The bungalow had been filled with the smells of freshly made paneer and ginger and garlic sautéed in ghee. The blender was whizzing up the greens for the saag. In the background was the sizzling sound of the puri hitting the hot oil and puffing up to create a soft and chewy bread to accompany the vegetable dishes. The whistle on the pressure cooker sounded, signifying the rice was ready. Nita was rushing through the house, instructing the servants, the pleats of her blue sari rustling as she glided over the tiles, making sure everything was as it should be. Just before everyone arrived, Sophie found her sitting on her bed alone with her shoulders slumped. She straightened upon hearing someone enter but then relaxed her body again when she realized it was only Sophie. She held out her arms to welcome Sophie into them and pulled the little girl close to her bosom. "I hope you are better at this," she whispered into Sophie's thick dark hair. At the time, Sophie had assumed she meant planning a Diwali dinner, but after everything she has learned, she now suspects Nita meant more.

Naresh brings out a tray with copper bowls of steaming channa masala and saag paneer, both adorned with vibrant green cilantro leaves, as well as some garlic naan and fluffy white rice dotted with cumin seeds and verdant green peas. He also brings out a small dish of hot mango pickle and a plate of fresh cucumber, onions, lemon wedges, and tomatoes. He arranges them on the table in front of her with a precise and practiced hand.

"This is too much for me," she says, eyes wide.

It is a feast, and Sophie cannot possibly finish the food and tenses at the thought of wasting it. "There are starving people right outside our door, and we cannot waste," Papa would say. And it was true, any scraps of food left behind would be put on the street for the beggars. She doubts such a thing would happen here and assumes the food will be tossed into the garbage bin if she doesn't finish it.

Naresh waves her off. "Just eat what you can." He takes two large spoons and clamps them in one hand to use them to scoop rice onto the middle of her plate. Then he serves her the remaining items, arranging them around the rice, creating neat piles with bold colors from the different dishes.

The spices waft to her nostrils, and her mouth waters. She rips off a small piece of hot naan and wraps it around some of the deep-green saag. She closes her eyes while she chews slowly and savors the bite. The green chili lights up her tongue, followed by the brightness of the lemon and the sweet roasted garlic from the naan. She's not sure if it's the best Punjabi food she's ever had, but as she sits in that chair, she thinks it could be. Sophie has had a lot of meals in restaurants, between growing up without a mummy and doing her accounting work in this industry, so she thinks of herself as a credible food critic. She looks at the French patrons in the restaurant and wonders if they can fully appreciate how well flavored and balanced the food is here. If they went somewhere else, would they realize that it lacked the freshness and attention to detail of Taj Palace?

She finishes her meal in peace, trying to eat as much as she can, both so she doesn't waste and because she knows she will not get another meal like this for a while. She thinks about what she should do next now that she has little money. She has taken charity twice in one day: first with the hostel and now with this meal. She feels her cheeks flush at what Papa would say about this. She is failing him so soon after his passing, having run out on her job that he'd secured for her without a word, left the fiancé her fois found for her, and lost the money she'd brought with her. But then she reminds herself that he had failed her for much longer by keeping secret the true story of Nita. She unclenches her fists and pushes down the anger that continues to reside inside of her.

She fills herself to the brim with the tasty food before her and then rises to find Naresh to thank him for the meal. He nods in acknowledgment and holds the door open for her. Sophie is back out on the streets of Paris, away from the comfort and familiarity of Taj Palace, and so far away from her life in Ahmedabad. People rush by her on the streets, some jostling her as if she isn't even there, and she feels so alone and so invisible. Perhaps she is not her mummy's daughter. Perhaps Nita had the strength to flee her homeland in search of adventure, but Sophie has never craved such things.

With a full stomach and clearer head, Sophie starts evaluating the pros and cons of her current situation. She is alone in a foreign country with very little money on a far-fetched theory that Nita is somewhere in this city. She has no way of tracking her and doesn't speak the local language. The wise thing would be to go home. Not to give up the search for Nita but to do it once she is more prepared. She can hire people in

India to investigate and search instead. It has been so many years, and it could be that Nita met some untimely demise, just like Papa had, so perhaps the effort isn't even justified. If she goes home, she can lean on her fois for support. They may have more information they can share now that the truth has come to light. Sophie doesn't know what other secrets they've kept from her all these years.

As she slowly makes her way back to the hostel, she knows she has to go home. Back to Sharmila Foi and Vaishali Foi. Back to the life she is meant to live with Kiran. She convinces herself that it's what Papa would have wanted. And it is the least she can give him after the life he had given her.

18

NITA

There had been no courtship. No biodata matching. No approval from the parents. No consulting the alignment of the stars. No blessing from a priest. There was nothing sweet about the intimacy. Yet when Mathieu kissed her that night after her nude modeling session, she felt a fire ignite inside of her that she had never felt before. Something raw and animal-like, matching the way he had savagely ripped off her panjabi as soon as they had walked into his apartment. The delicate silk fabric lay in a pale-pink heap near the front door. He had not even taken her into the bedroom and had instead pushed her against the sofa in the living room and immediately mounted her like a tiger in heat.

She had not been expecting everything to happen so quickly. She had pictured more sweet kisses filled with passion but still restrained, like they had shared before the art class. But before her head and heart could decide whether this was something she wanted, she felt him inside of her. Their bodies had decided for them, and maybe that was how sex was meant to be. It certainly had never been that way with Rajiv, but then, of course, with him the intimacy had not been for pleasure but for a purpose—to make Sophie.

Sophie. The face of her six-year-old daughter rose to the top of her thoughts. She desperately tried to push it aside, shame washing over her as Mathieu thrust so quickly that she could not keep up, and then he stopped, and she felt a warmth inside of her. She didn't know if the shame was from leaving Sophie behind or moving forward with Mathieu.

He kissed her forehead as he pulled away. He then flopped onto the sofa next to her and lit a cigarette before pulling her toward him, his arm across her shoulders and his hand dropping down to cup her breast. It smelled like the same hashish they had shared earlier. He took a couple puffs and then offered it to her. At this point, there was no need for her to even hesitate.

She inhaled and held on to the smoke the way he had taught her earlier that night. He released a small cloud from his lips and then leaned against her, placing his other hand territorially on the inside of her thigh. It was a form of intimacy that she couldn't decide whether she enjoyed, but she didn't shift her body away from him. She had crossed so many lines today that there was never going to be a way back to her old self. And maybe that was what she wanted. Maybe it was what she needed. To move so far from who she was that her old life would be closed off to her forever.

~

Despite their rocky start on that first day, Cecile and Nita had fallen into a somewhat reserved friendship. She would be the first to tell Nita about open shifts that came up at the reception area. Nita had been spending more and more time at Mathieu's apartment, so she often went days without visiting her room at the hostel.

When she arrived for a night shift after spending an entire week at Mathieu's apartment, Cecile was waiting impatiently with her purse in hand.

"You're late," she said.

"I'm sorry." Nita rushed to get behind the desk.

"Just as well," Cecile said evenly. "Best to make the man wait for me." She had a date with someone she had met earlier that week. "Do I look okay?" She puckered her red lips into a faux-seductive look.

"*Très chic!*" Nita said, her French becoming more natural as she moved into her fourth month in France.

Cecile started to walk toward the door and then stopped and slapped her forehead. She turned around and gestured toward a drawer in the back of the reception desk. "*Ooh, là là!* I almost forgot. There is a letter for you. I put it in the locked drawer." She then turned and pushed the door open, letting a gust of cool air enter the reception area and tickle Nita's skin.

Nita unlocked the drawer and found a blue airmail envelope. The return address was her former home in Ahmedabad. The handwriting was Rajiv's.

December 9, 1998

Dear Nita,

I pray this letter reaches you. I have spent the last four months trying to find you. I'm not sure what has happened to you, but all can be forgiven. Sophie misses you. She has taken ill and contracted tuberculosis. I try to soothe her, but I fear that she needs you more than me. You are her mummy. If you tell me where you are, I will send money for you to come home. You need not come for me, but please come for her.

Rajiv

Nita read the words a dozen more times. She would have kept reading if the bell hadn't interrupted her when the front door opened and a guest walked in, laden with a large backpack and that weary look that came from lengthy international travel. The woman was an American who had come to Paris from Phoenix. Nita was not sure where that was but hurried to check the woman into her room and give her a key.

She read the letter again. The words burned right through her as if the paper was white hot. Sophie was sick. She had to go back. How could she let her baby suffer? Oddly, in her time away, she had developed more maternal instincts for Sophie than she had ever felt before. The absence of her daughter now created a hole in her heart that she feared could never be filled, but when she had been in India, Nita had felt Sophie was a chain forcing her to stay in a prison she could no longer bear. The truth was that were it not for Sophie, Nita would have left Rajiv and their life much sooner. The marriage had never felt right to her because it had never been her choice. She suspected Rajiv knew that as well, given how he had always handled her delicately, like approaching a goat on the street that he did not want to spook. But now, the thought of Sophie suffering nearly brought Nita to her knees, and she would have happily sat by Sophie's bedside and stroked her hair.

The American girl from Phoenix came back to the reception area and asked where the closest sundry shop was, and Nita quickly directed her.

As the girl exited and the door closed behind her, Nita knew she had to pull herself together. *What if it's not even true?* she asked herself. Maybe this was Rajiv's way of cajoling her into coming back home and Sophie was actually fine. She could see his eldest sister encouraging him to come up with such a ruse. Vaishali had always been cunning and domineering like that, and she had never cared for Nita. Nita's mind and stomach were churning, and it was easier to settle on thinking this was a hoax designed to bring her home. The most troubling part was that Rajiv had managed to send a letter to her at the hostel. He knew where she was. She must have been careless with the last letter she'd sent to him, and it must have had something on it that had pointed him to the hostel. She'd asked Cecile to drop it in the mail and had been careful to not leave any return address. Had Cecile seen the missing information on the front and filled it in before sending it? Nita could envision Cecile trying to be helpful in that way and realized she should have handled the task herself. Rajiv could show up any day and drag her back. Did she really have any power to stop him from doing that? She was his wife still. And if that happened, she would never see Mathieu again. She'd likely never paint again. Surely Rajiv would not allow her to fill her mind with dreams and ideas again. She pictured the prison she'd return to if she ever went back, and banished the thought. She could not do it. And she had to make sure he couldn't find her here. As staunchly as she tried to convince herself that the contents of the letter were a lie, she couldn't push away the feeling that maybe they weren't. She brought her palms together, bent her head, and began praying to the gods to protect Sophie above all else.

19

SOPHIE

2019

When Sophie returns to Le Canard Volant, she asks Cecile if she can use the phone for a collect call. She can hear Sharmila Foi's voice in the background even while the operator is asking if she will accept the charges.

"Sophie?" she asks.

Sophie cannot answer. She thought this was the right decision, but now she is not so sure. Can she really go home without learning the truth about Nita?

"Sophie? Beta, where have you gone? Come home. We are worried sick," her foi says.

Still Sophie is unable to speak. She knows Papa would want her to go back to her old life, and she had convinced herself it was the right decision, given the low probability of finding what she had come to France for, but she is not ready yet. And her old life is no more. She is as alone there as she is in this new country, so why not finish what she came to Paris to do so she can close this chapter without any doubts?

"I'm sorry, Foi," Sophie says. She inhales deeply, not realizing she had been holding her breath. "I'm okay. I will be coming back soon."

"Beta, come home, and we can help you. Whatever is happening, we can resolve it."

She cannot leave them wondering where she is and if she is safe. It is not how Papa raised her.

Sophie closes her eyes, thinking back to her sheltered life in India. "I'm in Paris."

There is silence on the other end. Sophie can feel that her foi has heard this answer before, more than twenty years earlier.

"Why have you gone there?" Sharmila Foi eventually croaks out.

"Foi, I found the letters."

"What letters?" Her voice is measured.

"That Mummy sent to Papa," Sophie answers.

Silence. And then a heavy sigh.

"Rajiv did everything he could to protect you from that shame," Sharmila Foi says. Her tone is heavy, but Sophie can also hear a trace of relief in it. The past is no longer hidden.

"I need to find her. Especially now."

"And have you?" she asks.

"Not yet."

"Sophie, I know you are going through a hard time, but Nita left decades ago and has not looked back. She did not want to maintain contact with our family. She even did not want to have contact with hers. Can you imagine? Casting aside her mummy and papa, who were disgraced and heartbroken by her actions. They said the last time they ever spoke to her was after Rajiv told her you had tuberculosis in the months after she left. She called them in the middle of the night asking if you were healthy, but did she come back? No, she got her answers and never spoke to them again."

Sophie remembers being sick at that time. She recalls the worry on Papa's face as he pressed a warm, damp cloth against her chest and face to try to soothe her. Even at that age, she could tell he wasn't sure what to do and wished Nita were there to help. Sophie knows the point of Sharmila Foi's example is to make her hate Nita and come home, but Sophie hears something different. Sophie hears that her mummy called to find out if Sophie was okay.

"Rajiv tried so hard to bring her back," Sharmila Foi continues, "but she did not want to be a part of our lives. I don't know what type of reception you'll receive if you do find her."

Sophie has thought through this already and knows her foi is looking out for her, but she cannot continue her life without knowing these answers. Her entire life was built on these lies, and now she doesn't know who she is meant to be. It explains why Sophie had to do the prayers for Nita's annual passing ceremonies with her fois instead of Papa. It had all been such an elaborate farce. The prayers had been done to protect Sophie from the truth, but it seemed Papa was never able to participate in the tangible parts of the charade.

"I know, but I need to see her."

"How will you find her? Shall Vaishali and I come to you? That way, we know you are safe."

Sophie hadn't expected her to offer to help. She'd certainly not expected her to offer to come to France! Like Sophie, her fois and their children had never left India. It was only Rajiv who'd had business outside of the country and had traveled beyond its borders. While she is grateful for the bond of her family, often dysfunctional as it is, she knows she must do this alone.

"I will be okay, Foi. All my life you have looked after me when Papa wasn't there. I need to start looking after myself."

"What about Kiran? What will we tell his family?" she asks.

Even though Sophie knows her foi is trying to secure a stable future for Sophie, she cannot fathom marrying this man who is a stranger to her. It is the furthest thing from her mind. She wrings her hands as she thinks about how to deliver this news.

114

"I don't know what is best. I know you worked hard on this, but I cannot be married next week. Maybe not even next year. I'm sorry to disappoint you, but it would not be fair to Kiran and his family. I don't know what I could offer as a wife right now."

"We don't need to make any hasty decisions," Sharmila Foi says. "I will tell them you had to go on a trip. When will you be back?"

"I'm not sure. But I hope not too long." She thinks about her lack of funds and knows she will run out of money if she doesn't find Nita soon, but she cannot ask her foi for help after the stress she has already caused. She'd have to explain how she'd been robbed by that nasty pair upon her arrival, and that would cause so much worry to her fois. She will find a way to make do for the few days or week it might take her to track down Nita.

"How can we contact you? Your mobile doesn't work. It goes straight to the voice mail."

There is no point in saying that her mobile has also been taken. All these details would cause stress, and her decision is made.

"I'm staying at a hotel." She gives them the information for Le Canard Volant to use in case of an emergency, although given that Papa is already dead, Sophie cannot imagine what such an emergency might be.

Sophie hangs up the phone, feeling better that her relatives know where she is and that she is safe. She hadn't meant to worry them, but she'd felt so abandoned and alone when she'd learned the entire family had conspired to keep the truth from her. She could not think past getting herself on a flight to Paris and the dream that she would reunite with Nita and all her problems would disappear. She'd been looking for someone to take the place of Papa when it came to sheltering and protecting her, and who better to take on that role than her mummy?

20

NITA

1998

"You seem distracted," Mathieu said breathily the next day as he raised his head from between her thighs and slid up her body, grazing her bare stomach and then her breasts, until he had propped his head just over her face. His eyes searched hers. "You are bored already?"

Nita averted her gaze.

"Non, mon cher. Juste fatiguée." Just tired, she said, even though she knew that wasn't it at all.

She couldn't tell him that she couldn't focus on the pleasure because all she could think about was her sick daughter. *Somehow that innocent girl is paying for my mistakes*, Nita thought, worrying that her bad karma had been transferred to Sophie somehow. It wasn't fair. Especially as Nita lay in this bed with a man who wasn't her husband. She could no longer even keep track of the number of her sins.

"C'est tout?" That's all? he asked with a devilish grin. "I will make you not tired again."

He slipped his finger inside of her—hard—sending a jolt through her that he probably intended as pleasure but that resonated through her body as pain. She stared into his eyes, trying to be present. She hid her grimace as he pushed deeper. She tried to let herself relax so that the pain would turn into the pleasure she was used to feeling with him. She had faked joy in this intimate position many times, but only with Rajiv, who had never been this forceful. He had always been courteous toward her, even during their acts of intimacy, and never pushed her or tested any limits. But with him there had never been the same passion she felt with Mathieu, and perhaps with passion there was pain.

She tried to make her body rock in time with Mathieu's as he climbed on top of her, his breathing and rhythm quickening until he was spent. He stroked her hair and smiled at her wistfully, placing a soft kiss on her forehead. She smiled back even though she had never felt so ashamed. Between her marriage and whatever this new relationship with Mathieu was, she'd become accustomed to hiding herself.

When he rolled over and began to prepare a joint for them to share, she was relieved. She just wanted to forget. Forget Rajiv. Forget India. Forget Sophie . . .

~

Although Nita tried to forget, the more she painted, the more Sophie wove her way into Nita's art. She began painting her daughter's face whenever she picked up a brush. When Mathieu commented that the faces in her work resembled each other, she waved him off, pretending she hadn't noticed. She painted a girl with laughter in her eyes and without a care in the world. A girl who didn't suffer from tuberculosis. It was the only way she wanted to see her daughter.

The drugs made it easier for her to escape her thoughts. It had started off with the cigarettes and then hashish, but then Mathieu brought home some pills that Simon had given him. The first one had made her head spin in the best way, fitting since Mathieu said it was called ecstasy. She would forget everything for hours, and when she woke up, she would crave that feeling again. What had started off as an occasional indulgence had turned into something she and Mathieu engaged in several nights a week. Mathieu would often paint in the middle of the night, when the pills' magic was at its peak. Even Nita could see that his work had improved. The pills allowed him to focus and unlocked the depths of his creativity. She hoped they would do the same for her, so she would try and paint alongside him. It was only when she woke up groggy after the pills had worn off that she realized that even though she had felt like she was able to forget, her painting from the night before was inevitably of a child with Sophie's face.

21

SOPHIE

2019

After hanging up with her foi, Sophie returns to Taj Palace. It is now empty, and Naresh raises his eyebrows, looking surprised to see her return.

"Did you forget something?" he asks, moving toward the front door from the kitchen pass.

She nods. "I cannot take your charity without paying."

He raises his hands in protest. "There is no need for any money."

Sophie surprises herself with the courage in her voice. "I'd like to work for the food."

He cocks his head, looking unsure of what she means.

Sophie takes a deep breath and stifles her need to be polite and tries to channel the Western women she has seen on countless television series—the ones who are not afraid to speak their mind and go after what they want. The ones who are probably more like Nita than she has ever been.

She looks directly at him. "I am in a difficult position, and I need a job." She hesitates, teetering between maintaining her privacy and knowing she needs his help. Finally, she accepts that the balance swings against her privacy. "I was robbed when I arrived here, and I need to earn some money. Do you have any work I can do? I can do anything. I'm not choosy."

Naresh looks at her, his warm eyes wanting to help her.

"Can you cook?" he asks.

Sophie hesitates. Less than two weeks ago, she would have been forced to say no. But her fois had just given her a crash course in Gujarati cooking for her upcoming marriage, and, while she can hardly consider herself an expert, she must do whatever it takes to get this job.

She nods but can tell Naresh is rightfully skeptical. Then she gestures toward the kitchen. "May I?"

He lets her pass through. The young cook who had prepared her food looks up when she and Naresh enter. He looks to Naresh for an answer as to why a customer is in the kitchen area. Sophie smiles at him, knowing she has only one chance to impress both men. She washes her hands with surgical precision in the sink toward the back. Then she heads toward a big mound of whole wheat dough for rotlis. She pulls off a small piece and begins rolling the cold, smooth wheat-flour-and-water mixture into a ball using the palms of her hands, just like her fois showed her. She then flattens the ball against the counter and dips the disk into the thali of rice flour nearby. Then she grabs a velon and begins rolling it like an expert, applying a little extra pressure to the right side so the circle automatically turns itself such that she can keep rolling it out into a perfect circle without ever having to stop to turn it. That was Sharmila Foi's trick. She then places the thin dough onto the warm skillet next to her and watches it start to form small bubbles. She flips it over, allowing the other side to cook. Finally, she holds her breath and prays as she places it directly on the heat. Like magic, it puffs into a perfect circle, just like her fois had taught her! She wants to clap her hands in elation and relief, but she knows she must seem like she is an expert at this and not revel in her beginner's luck.

She pulls the rotli off the flame and lets it deflate before adding a touch of ghee and presenting it to Naresh and his cook. The cook, still unsure of what is going on in his kitchen, looks at Naresh while he accepts the plate with the rotli from Sophie.

Naresh holds it up to eye level and smiles. "Manoj, could you use help in the kitchen? She needs to find work."

His tone suggests that the answer needs to be yes, and Manoj shrugs. "More help is always good," he says noncommittally, his eyes moving from Sophie to Naresh and back again.

"It is settled, then," Naresh says. "Sophie, you can help Manoj in the kitchen."

She beams, realizing this is the second job she's had in her life and the first one she's earned completely on her own, with no family help. It lifts her spirits to know that she has some survival skills outside of India, even if they are few and far between!

Naresh Uncle continues, "You must be willing to do cleaning and other things in addition to the cooking. I've taught my son here everything I know, so it will take time for you to learn the recipes as I like them." Naresh put his arm around Manoj's shoulders.

She nods eagerly. She feels good, knowing Taj Palace is a family-run business.

"We'll need to pay you in cash . . . I suspect you don't have any work permits."

Sophie smiles appreciatively. "Thank you, Naresh Uncle," she says, using the traditional conventions to show her respect for him.

While she is skeptical of Indians in Paris, given her experience with Anjali and Saumil, she knows she will get nowhere if she has no trust in her heart at all. She is a foreigner in this world, and if she has learned anything today, it is that the kindness of strangers in this city—regardless of the color of their skin—is the only thing that will help her survive and ultimately find Nita.

22

NITA

Dao had made Nita promise to come by the bar with Mathieu. She had insisted on meeting the mystery man who was stealing her new friend. Le Verre Plein was small, with a dark interior. There were couches along a stone wall and bistro tables spread throughout the center. Many red and green ornaments decorated the place in celebration of the upcoming Christmas holiday. The bar had white lights strewn along the front to add to the festive feel. Dao was standing behind it, pouring red wine into two glasses and chatting with the couple sitting on the barstools in front of her. Nita steered Mathieu toward two empty seats a few down from the couple.

"Why is it so hard to get a drink around here?" Nita said loudly.

Dao made her way toward them. "Probably because you are trying to order in English when you should be speaking French," she said, bringing her bright-red lips into a smile.

She leaned forward over the bar so Mathieu could give her *bisous*. "So, you're the one occupying our Nita's time. Very nice to meet you." She was far more outspoken than both Nita and Mathieu, whose temperaments were more reserved. He did not respond to her comment and instead pulled out Nita's barstool so she could sit.

"Quite the gentleman," Dao said with a nod. "What can I get you both?" She dried her hands on a towel. "Well, I suppose I know Nita will be having a water on the rocks, but what about you, *Monsieur*?"

Mathieu looked at Nita with questioning eyes. She jumped in and said, "Actually, I'll have a glass of white wine. Whatever you have open."

Dao's eyebrows raised. When she'd first arrived, Nita had told Dao that she hadn't grown up drinking and it was a rare occurrence for her. Dao had told her not to worry about it, saying it was so common for the women in her family not to drink either. Since then, Nita had not told her friend about the frequent drinking and certainly not about the drugs when she was with Mathieu. She knew that participating in those things with Mathieu was one thing, but voicing her behavior to a friend was entirely another. She preferred to keep her shame private.

"As you like," Dao said evenly, grabbing a bottle from the chiller.

Mathieu took a glass of the same, and the three of them chatted when Dao wasn't busy pouring drinks for other patrons in the bar.

"You should come and stay with me," Mathieu whispered into Nita's ear while Dao was tending to another customer.

"What do you mean?" Nita said. His breath against her ear and neck always sent a shiver down her spine.

"Just as I say. Why should you pay so much rent for a boarding room you hardly use?" He nuzzled his lips just beneath her ear, sending a tingling sensation from her neck to her toes. "We can find better uses for the money we save." He patted his coat pocket, the one where he kept his stash of hashish.

"You want me to live with you?" Nita said.

She knew she shouldn't be surprised. This kind of thing was common in France, even if it was forbidden in India. Her first day living with Rajiv had been after their wedding night.

"Bien sûr." He nuzzled softly against her neck, clearly trying to get her aroused. "I can think of nothing better than having my beautiful lotus flower all to myself."

She pushed him away when Dao returned, and whispered that she would think about it. It would solve some of her bigger problems, like paying for the hostel and the fear that Rajiv would show up there one day.

~

"He's very . . . *French*," Dao said to Nita as they both stood in the communal bathroom at the hostel the next day, Dao applying a deep-lavender eye shadow.

Nita was brushing out her long wavy hair, counting to 101 in her head, just like she'd always done since she was a little girl. It was a ritual she had never given up. Her mummy had done that with her own hair, making sure she ended on an odd number for good luck. Nita, in turn, used to do the same with Sophie's hair, also always ending at 101. She wondered if Rajiv had carried on the tradition after she left. She doubted it because she was not sure he had even known about it. Sophie's morning and bedtime routines fell under Nita's womanly responsibilities. She pushed the thoughts away and tried to bring her attention back to Dao.

"Does he always date foreigners?" Dao asked, now painting her lips a deep-mauve color.

Nita balked at her use of the word. "Probably not," she said. "He's never left France." In her head, she counted *seventy-one, seventy-two, seventy-three . . .*

Dao shrugged. "Plenty of people from all over come to Paris, so that doesn't really answer the question." She puckered her lips and admired her handiwork in the mirror. "He seemed a bit possessive. Not that typical laissez-faire attitude most of the men project."

Nita considered her words, not accustomed to having friends who were so outspoken with their views. *Eighty-eight, eighty-nine, ninety.* Her friends in India were always polite when speaking to her even though she knew they spoke their true feelings behind her back, just as she would have done to them. Her friendships in India had remained more on the surface, and it had taken some adjustments for her to get used to Dao's style, even though she had decided ultimately that she preferred it.

"I've only dated one French man, so it is hard for me to say the difference," she said as she completed her last stroke of her brush at 101.

Laughing, Dao said, "Well, that's fair enough." She faced Nita directly rather than catching her eye in the mirror. "I'm just saying girls who look like us need to be careful here. I just wonder if he needs someone exotic in his life. I meet those guys all the time in this city. You know the type—the pasty ones who think dating someone ethnic says something special about them, even though all they are doing is indulging their colonialist fetishes. I saw it all the time in the UK too. The English may have the top colonialist-fetish slot, but the French are not far behind!" She turned back toward the mirror. "Men can be dogs, and you just never know what they're really after. I should know. I've exclusively dated creeps in my life, so I'm quite the expert."

Nita pondered her words but knew she had no experience from which to form any opinions on the subject. Mathieu was the only person she'd ever dated—if what they were doing could even be called that. She wasn't sure it could, based on what she had seen on American television programs. All she knew was that she had very few people to rely upon in her new life, and she wasn't in any position to be choosy.

~

Nita continued to earn the bulk of her money from posing for Simon's and Julien's art classes. It had taken her several weeks to pose nude again for Julien's students, but the money from a nude session was ten times as much as she got from posing for Simon's students in her traditional Indian attire. The wad of rupees she had traveled to France with was long gone, and she had to live on only the money she earned. Realizing how difficult it was to save, she began thinking more seriously about Mathieu's offer to live together. She had overstayed her visa, and Mathieu had helped get her fake French papers so she could stay in the country and have something to show potential employers, but she was still far from fluent in the language. She accepted that financial woes would be a part of her new life, so his offer was the most practical solution. She just had to get over the shock of being an unmarried woman living with a man. Her cheeks burned whenever she thought about it.

Actually, she corrected herself, she had to get over the shock of being a *married* woman who was living with an unmarried man.

~

After posing at one of Simon's art classes that January, she helped him put away his paints, and they walked to a nearby bistro to have a coffee. Simon pulled out one of the round-backed, tan wicker chairs for her.

They sipped on two steaming cups of coffee in quiet company. Her friendship with Simon had grown to become very comfortable and easy, the two of them often sitting in silence, watching people pass by on the sidewalks, occasionally speculating about what a person's story might be. Nita loved that game. Loved guessing what led them to be walking along that street in that exact moment and where they would be going after they were out of Nita's sight. She knew people hid their most intimate secrets, herself included. She often wondered what Simon or Mathieu or Dao thought when they looked at her. What they thought her story was. She was sure they could not have suspected the truth, and that was why she assumed every stranger who passed her with hands tucked into a thick woolen winter coat and a smile on their face had a story far more sordid and complex than the easy stroll down the Parisian streets would suggest.

"It seems we see less of you these days," Nita said, staring at the people on the sidewalk.

"Oh?" Simon said.

"Mathieu tells me you have a new lady occupying your time."

Simon laughed. "Does he?"

"He believes it to be true."

"Seems like he's gotten rather chatty, having you with him constantly now," Simon said.

Nita had moved in with Mathieu on January 1, deciding she should start her new year embracing her new life. It hadn't been difficult to transfer her meager belongings, including the painting he had given her, to his place. He had made no attempt to display it and had instead rested it with the image facing the wall, as if haunted by its return.

"He said you seem smitten," Nita said.

Simon could not hide his smile. "I have met a new woman who doesn't run from my bastardized form of the French language."

It was Nita's turn to laugh. "Your French still surpasses my own."

"Men find a woman trying to speak their language charming. Women, on the other hand, find it tacky and trite when their language is being mangled!"

"You seem to have charmed her still."

"For now, yes."

"Tell me about her."

Simon's eyes lit up. "Call me superstitious, but I don't like to jinx myself by talking about it so early. Let's see if it lasts first."

Nita respected his privacy and went back to people watching. She was happy that he had met someone. He deserved to be with someone special, and she could tell by the way he approached the conversation that this woman already had a place in Simon's heart. It would only be a matter of time before Mathieu and Nita would meet her. Of that, Nita was sure.

Today was one of those rare moments in which she was living the life in Paris of which she had dreamed. She had spent the day working on a painting and then posing for Simon's classes, which had become like free art lessons, given how much she absorbed from him and the other students. Now, she was sitting in a café at which she had become a regular with a view of Notre-Dame, watching the myriad of people passing by on the street. She would go home to a man who devoured her mind and body with the same fervor. She hoped that in this moment, Rajiv and Sophie were as at peace in Ahmedabad as Nita was in Paris.

23

SOPHIE

2019

Naresh Uncle had been kind enough to give Sophie an advance on her wages, so she has been able to secure a room at Le Canard Volant beyond the couple nights that Cecile was able to help her with in the beginning. She is now sharing a room with five other girls and is surprised by how many people she's met at the hostel who have come to Paris to pursue creative endeavors, whether they be art, writing, or food. She has never had such dreams or ideals and cannot recall her friends in India having those types of impractical ambitions either. Her friends enjoy dancing or cooking or art as hobbies, but none would consider stepping outside the confines of their prescribed lives to leave Ahmedabad and pursue such an uncertain career, giving up the comfortable and privileged lives into which they were born. This desire for a life beyond the one you were given seems far more Western than Eastern in her mind, and she does not fully understand it. It seems much simpler to fall in line with what is planned for you, especially when you are given so much as part of it, but she now realizes it is easy to be content when you are born into the upper caste. Clearly Nita felt differently and must have had some part of that Western idealism inside of her to have chosen the path she did.

While Sophie sits in Le Comptoir, perusing the menu with so many foreign words, she wonders why she had the misfortune of ending up with a mummy who was such a rare exception to the Indian rules. She is in the café where Cecile mentioned Nita and her friends used to spend time all those years ago, and Sophie can tell that, like many of the places she has seen while walking around the city, it has not changed much in the twenty years since Nita would have come here. Indian cities are constantly striving to modernize and adapt to stay relevant, Ahmedabad included, but Parisians seem to favor tradition, and for that Sophie is grateful because it heightens her chances. The café has small chairs with rounded red padded backs against dark-brown wood frames. Between sets of chairs are small bistro tables. The patrons seem mostly French, which Sophie finds surprising, given the café's proximity to Notre-Dame.

Sophie scans the room for someone who looks old enough to have worked there when Nita would have first arrived but has not seen anyone of that age yet, so she chooses a small corner table with a clear view of the employees going back and forth to the kitchen. A lanky, dark-haired waiter who appears to be younger than Sophie arrives, and she manages to order a tea for herself, but she is unsure of the flavor she selected, given her inability to converse with the young man. He brings a small metal pot with steaming water and a tea bag wrapped in a paper pouch with a medley of flowers on it. Sophie is not used to the tea in France, which is more herbal and floral than the spicy, bold chai she grew up drinking. Papa had his chai twice a day, and she could set her watch by it: seven thirty in the morning after his yoga, prayers, and meditation, and then again at four o'clock in the afternoon. Sophie adopted his tea habit, but she is more flexible on this trip to France because she has less control over her schedule.

Finally, she sees an elderly man cross through the swinging door and take a seat on a barstool behind the back counter. He walks with the comfort of someone who has spent most of his life in this bistro and considers it a second home.

Sophie reaches into her purse and pulls out the photo she showed Cecile when she first arrived. She carries it with her everywhere.

"*Excusez-moi, Monsieur,*" she says as she approaches him.

He is wiping the plastic-encased menus with a damp white rag and looks up at her, waiting for her to continue.

"Do you speak English?" she asks, her eyes pleading that the answer be yes.

He nods, and Sophie lets out the breath she has been holding.

In a small voice, Sophie says, "I'm looking for someone who used to spend time here many years ago, and maybe she still does, but I am wondering if you happen to know her."

Sophie hands over the photograph, and the man wipes his hands on the white kitchen towel tucked into his black trousers before taking it from her.

He shakes his head. "She is quite beautiful, but it is hard for me to say." He gestures around the room. "So many people come every day."

"This is an old photo," Sophie offers. "She would be about twenty years older than in this." Her voice trails off at the end, like she is asking rather than telling.

The man shakes his head. "I could hardly recall someone I met yesterday and certainly could not guess what age would do to a person."

Sophie's shoulders slump. Even though she knows this search is a long shot, dead ends are disappointing all the same. Perhaps the universe is also reminding her that if Nita wanted to be found, then she would have made it easy. Sophie and Rajiv had lived in the same house with the same phone number since Nita left, as did all their other relatives in India. Finding them would have required no effort, and the fact that she had never reached out to Sophie is difficult to swallow. But Sophie pushes past those thoughts because things are different now that Papa is gone, and surely Nita would want to know that. Surely Nita would want to help her daughter, if only Sophie could find her.

24
NITA

Nita's art had so consistently gravitated toward Sophie that Mathieu pressed her on who the girl was one day.

"She haunts you, I can see." He lazed on the couch in the apartment they now shared. "Just like the woman in my paintings."

Nita sat on a stool in front of an easel in the area that used to serve as their dining nook. The small table had now been pushed against the wall to make room for the makeshift studio the two of them used when painting at home. Two easels stood back to back so that they could work together but not distract each other. She stared at the brown eyes pleading with her from the canvas, asking what she had done to make Nita run away.

The painting Mathieu had given her rested against the wall behind them, the picture still facing away. Nita knew it wasn't something he would ever want to display in his home, but she wasn't ready to part with it. It was the thing that had led her to Mathieu, and that seemed worth saving.

Nita gestured toward the canvas. "Will you tell me her story?"

Mathieu exhaled sharply. She was sure he was going to dismiss her question like he had the times she'd tried to broach it before. Nita had never pushed too hard because she felt the weight of her own secrets that she wasn't ready to share with him.

Today, however, Mathieu peeked out from behind the easel and nodded. He stood up, took her hand, and led her to the couch. She sat with erect posture, bracing herself for whatever he was going to say.

"She was my first love," he said with a sigh and wistful smile. "You never forget your first."

Nita realized she'd never had a first love, at least not in the way he meant it. She'd had a husband, but that was different. She wondered if the way she felt about Mathieu was love. She had nothing to compare it to but suspected that it wasn't. At least not yet. And she didn't know if it would be someday. She hadn't grown up dreaming of romantic love for another person. Her parents did not have it. She hadn't had it with Rajiv. Her friends hadn't had it with their husbands. It wasn't sought after in her community the way it was in France or in Hollywood movies. Nita had assumed she would go her entire life and not have that kind of love, but she didn't mind because she'd never longed for it. The love she had seen in India was the love for one's child.

That love seemed universal, no matter where a person was from. She'd seen it in Paris as much as she had in Ahmedabad. Her parents had shown her that kind of love, and she'd never questioned whether they would sacrifice every ounce of themselves for her. Nita had wanted to feel that love for Sophie. Rajiv had it. Year after year, she saw it expanding in him like an unhindered banyan tree, its branches and leaves reaching farther with each passing season, and she did not know how she could get to that same place.

She looked at Mathieu, waiting for him to continue.

"We met when I was twenty-six and she was a mere twenty-one. She was so innocent, and seeing life through her eyes gave me and my art a renewed sense of purpose. We fell in love instantly and planned the rest of our lives together. She made me feel true joy for the first time in my life. It's an interesting feeling, you know. Joy. It's completely surrendering yourself to a place from which you can only fall. There is no better place than joy, but it escapes us all at some point. And after joy comes pain. *Toujours.* I would have pledged my life to her. *Non,* I *did* pledge my life to her. But her family wanted more for her than a starving artist. She was to be with a lawyer or banker or investor. Her family did not want her to have the struggling life she would have had with me. And it turned out after several years, the romantic sheen had worn off for her, as well. You know," he said, running a hand over his head, "that is a genuine pain. Realizing you are not enough for someone after you have revealed your true self to that person. Such a thing will haunt every fiber of your being for the rest of your life."

Nita pondered his words. Every culture had its own caste system. There was always a hierarchy, and people were compared to one another to determine where one fell. This girl's parents had wanted the same thing for their daughter as Nita's parents had wanted for her. Rajiv had been their safe choice. Nita would never have even thought of ending up with someone like Mathieu if she were still in India. She didn't even know where a man who lived for his own whims and pursued passion for passion's sake would exist. Certainly, outside of her upper-caste community, in which people were born to fit into a limited number of molds.

But she understood not feeling like enough. Understood that part too well. With Rajiv and Sophie, she had known her heart was somewhere else when it needed to be with them. She always knew there was more of her to give that she was holding back. She knew she wanted more from her life than what they had to offer. And she knew she was more selfish than they realized. That she would do whatever it took to get that life she dreamed of. And, for that, she knew they deserved better. She wondered if it was this common feeling that had drawn her and

Mathieu together. Maybe they saw in each other the pain of knowing they had not been enough for the people who loved them.

"I know what you mean," Nita said. "But I think you can't carry that pain through the rest of your life. At some point, we must let it go and realize that even if we had not been enough in the past, there is still a chance to be enough in the future."

Mathieu nodded. "This is true. But letting go is easier said than done. And I suspect you know that all too well." He gestured toward her painting. "Who is she?"

Until then, Nita had always shrugged him off. She couldn't bring herself to be dismissive, but she also didn't want to tell him the truth. But given what he'd shared, she knew she had to say something.

"She's my niece." Her voice caught on the lie, but she regained her composure. "I miss her sometimes. Often, actually. Children have a strange way of getting under your skin like that."

He nodded.

"You don't speak about your family much. It's understandable. Families are complicated. You want your own?" He lit a cigarette, the end burning bright red until it settled into a steady stream of smoke.

"What?"

"Children." He inhaled slowly.

Even though she knew what he meant, it still shocked her to hear it. *Of course not! I have a child . . . that I left behind. It's clear I am a terrible mother and should never be one again.*

"I just need my paints," she said softly.

He leaned closer to her on the couch, placing his hand on her thigh. "Perhaps I shall convince you to have a little more than paints." His eyes glimmered as he pressed his hips against her leg so she could feel his hardness.

She pulled away. "I don't want children," she said with more force than she'd intended.

"Okay, okay," he said, pulling back with a smile, his cigarette dangling in that familiar precarious way. "I was just joking."

That's exactly the problem, she thought. *Children are not something to be joked about.* They were the most serious thing that could happen in one's life. Children highlighted every trait you lacked. And if you were not meant to be a parent, they stole your spirit in a way you could never get back.

~

That night, when she and Mathieu had sex, she felt him being harder and more aggressive. Almost like he had the same urgency as the first night, when it had felt primal rather than sensual. There was none of his usual foreplay.

Tonight, he kissed her so hard that his teeth bumped against hers, and, before she even realized it, he was inside of her. Within minutes, he had finished, and rolled onto his back, not caressing the inside of her leg like he usually did while catching his breath and not checking that she had been satisfied too.

He couldn't possibly be upset about her comments about children. He was a man in his late thirties who spent most of his time drunk or high to "focus" on his artistic passions. In Nita's mind it was understood that a man like that did not want the responsibility of a child. It would change his entire life in a way that he seemed ill equipped to handle.

He lit a joint and took a puff before passing it to her. She didn't comment on the roughness of the way he had taken her and accepted the cigarette, taking a few deep inhales before passing it back. She had the urge to rub the soreness between her legs but didn't want him to know he had hurt her. Instead, she curled into a ball, facing away from him, and told him she was tired tonight and couldn't go another round later.

25

SOPHIE

2019

That evening, Sophie is getting ready for her shift at Taj Palace when she hears Cecile's voice outside her door, telling her there is a phone call for her. Sophie already knows it is Vaishali Foi and braces herself for the verbal diarrhea she is about to hear.

"Have you lost your mind?" her foi says before Sophie can even manage a quick hello.

"Foi, please. I will only be gone a short time. A week or two at the most."

"Do you know what position this puts us in with Kiran's family? Hah? The wedding is just around the corner. What are we supposed to do about that?"

Sophie closes her eyes and nods even though her foi can't see her. "I'm sorry, Foi. It is hard to explain how it feels to learn your mummy might be alive after you grew up thinking she was dead." Her anger rises as she says the words, knowing Vaishali Foi was part of the conspiracy.

"We did that to protect you. Would you rather have been told that woman left you and Rajiv? That she left and never looked back. What can a woman like that offer you now?"

Her words sting because Sophie knows she is right. "I don't know. That's what I'm here to find out. Maybe you're right and the answer will be nothing, but I have to know."

"Beta, be reasonable. If word gets out about a failed engagement, we will not be able to help you find another. This family has had far too much scandal as it is, thanks to Nita." Her foi's disdain is plain on her tongue.

"It will be okay. If I don't marry, then I will manage."

"Don't joke about such things. Rajiv taught you nothing about survival. You must find a suitable husband."

Irritation and shame rise in Sophie's throat. Irritation that Vaishali Foi can't understand that this is bigger than finding a husband. Shame over knowing that her foi is right. Sophie hasn't learned to take care of herself in all the ways that are necessary to live a complete life. Her short time in Paris is showing her how few life skills she had when she was outside of her Ahmedabadi comfort zone.

"Foi, don't worry. Whether I marry or not, I will not be a nuisance to you."

"What has gotten into you, hah? You were never like this before. You were not raised to behave this way. We stepped in and cared for you like our own daughter after this mummy you so desperately need left. And this is how you repay us?"

Sophie sees Cecile return to the reception area and lowers her voice. "I'm sorry, and I hope you can see this is not about how much I love you and Sharmila Foi. I must go now. There are others waiting to use this telephone line," she lies. She never does that, but she does not even flinch at the karmic repercussions this time.

Sophie is emotionally drained as she hangs up the phone because she knows much of what her foi said is true. Sophie understands that regardless of what Nita's life in Paris is like now, the reality is that she left Sophie just as much as she left Rajiv. Sophie has spent her entire life believing that her mummy would have been with her if she could, but now she must face the fact that Nita *chose* not to be with her when she had tuberculosis as a child, or began her menstrual cycle and Rajiv didn't know how to handle it, or went to college, or had to agree to an arranged marriage because her beloved papa had died. Nita could have been there for those milestones but opted not to be a part of them. She had opted not to be a part of Sophie's life. But Sophie still needs to understand why. She needs to know what she did to drive her away. She needs to know if the love she'd felt from her before she left was real. In a matter of weeks, everything Sophie thought she knew about her life had been turned on its head, and she is now drowning and searching for a sliver of rope in the vast ocean to help her find her way back home.

Cecile files her nails and tries to look inconspicuous, as if she hadn't noticed Sophie's glum demeanor. After a few moments, she makes eye contact with Sophie.

"Are you okay?" she asks.

Sophie nods, because it is the habitual response to such a question and not because it reflects any truth.

"I should leave for work," she says.

Cecile's eyes light up. "Speaking of jobs, I remembered earlier today that your aunt had one after she worked here."

Sophie perks up. "What do you mean?"

"She had a job as a waitress. At this bistro in the second. I walked by and saw her there once. We made eye contact but didn't speak. She looked pretty beat down, if I remember correctly. Actually, looked a bit like you do right now." She says the last part with a laugh as if she still cannot believe the resemblance between the two women.

"Do you remember the name?"

Cecile's brow creases as she concentrates. "It's that place on Rue Bachaumont. It's a bit of a walk from Bourse station." She taps her knuckles on the reception desk while she continues to think of the name. "What's it called? What's it called? Paris can be such a small city sometimes, but then these things become so hard to remember." She snaps her fingers together. "Bistro Laurent! That's it! *Mince*, in my old age these things are getting tougher and tougher to recall." She smooths her hair back as if she had performed the physical exertion of running a race to arrive at that answer.

"Thanks for the tip!" Sophie beams at Cecile.

Her heart lifts. She has a lead! She desperately needed one, especially after the call with her foi. Her soul is reinvigorated upon hearing of a place she can check. She wants to go there immediately but looks at her watch and knows she will be insultingly late to Taj Palace if she does that, and she cannot disrespect Naresh Uncle in that way. She does a quick search at the communal computer and sees that the bistro should be open until eleven. If she hurries after her shift ends, then she should be able to make it just before close.

26

NITA

1999

As they got deeper into the winter months, Mathieu had not been selling as many pieces of his art as he normally did and became increasingly frustrated about money. Nita worried that he resented having asked her to live with him. She had moved from one life of obligation with Rajiv to another one with Mathieu. She tried to pitch in with money when she could, but she earned very little from her modeling sessions and still had not found a steady job. She knew that she was another person consuming food, and using utilities, and sharing cigarettes and drugs, and all those things added up.

He was painting less and spending more time getting high. He had started bringing home unidentifiable pills, saying the hashish and ecstasy weren't giving him enough focus and he needed something stronger. He would pop a little white pill and then crash out on the couch or bed, sometimes for days on end, moving only to use the toilet or pour another glass of wine. Occasionally, one of the pills gave him a voracious sexual appetite, and he would enter and release into Nita until she was raw and bruised. The romantic Parisian she thought she had moved in with was becoming a distant memory, and they'd only lived together for six weeks.

They no longer went on leisurely walks, holding hands and looking lovingly into each other's eyes. He no longer removed his sunglasses before staring at her because he did not want any barriers to their eye contact. They no longer asked each other questions about childhood and likes and dislikes, trying to learn every intimate memory of their partner. They were no longer partners at all. When they walked, Mathieu had taken to walking ahead of her, forcing her to rush to try to keep up with him as if she were a servant following her master. There were many times at which she wondered if he had genuinely forgotten she was there as she trailed behind him, but she never asked because she feared the answer was that he had.

She thought about leaving, but where would she go? And what would leaving accomplish in the end? She reminded herself that she had never dreamed of romantic love, so why did it matter that it seemed Mathieu was no longer interested in that? She simply needed a roof over her head and an ability to further her art. Still, it gnawed at her that he had given her a taste of something that made her rethink whether she should want romantic love only to take it away from her when she began to consider that perhaps she might want it. But then she reminded herself of the karma she had created when she abandoned her husband and daughter. Maybe now she was finally getting what she deserved.

"*Mon cher*, it's been a few days since you have opened your stall. Perhaps today is a good day to see if anyone is shopping for art," she said gently on a chilly morning in mid-February.

"People have no taste these days," he mumbled from beneath the covers.

"Then you must show them what is good taste." She lowered the covers enough to reveal his unshaven face, some white whiskers mixed in with the darker ones.

He squinted against the daylight in the room. His eyes drooped from the drugs he had taken the night before. His face was gaunt, like the beggars who had used to come along the outer wall of the bungalow she had shared with Rajiv.

"I can't be bothered today. I'm not feeling well." He whined like a sick child.

Given his mood swings lately, Nita was afraid to press him, but she had also counted the cash they kept in the kitchen drawer, and it was dwindling quickly.

"It might make you feel better to get out of the apartment for a little while," she said.

"I doubt it."

As gently as she could, she said, "*Mon cher*, we are running low on money, and we could really use some sales."

His face darkened. "Why is it my job to make the money?"

Remaining calm, she said, "I'm doing my best to earn what I can, but it is not enough."

His eyes fixated on her left arm, and he was silent for a few moments. "We could sell those fancy bracelets you wear. They're real gold and diamonds, right? Seems that would go a long way."

She took a step back and instinctively covered her bangles to protect them. Her mouth fell open, but no sound came out. She could never part with them. No matter how bad things were. They were her last piece of home. Her last piece of her family. Her last piece of who she had been before she came to Paris and met Mathieu and started a life that was so different from the one she had dreamed of for so long.

"See," he said, "you want to complain about money but aren't willing to do everything to get it for us. If you want the stall open so badly, why don't you go and do it? You have legs and know how to unlock it, just like I do."

She was no longer surprised by his harsh words, and instead of fighting back she decided to take him up on his suggestion. There was no reason she couldn't go try to sell some of his paintings.

She looked at the lump under the covers that she had become entirely dependent upon in this new life she had built—one far worse than what she'd had in India. She wondered if she was destined to always be at a man's mercy. She had never seen such darkness in Rajiv as she was now seeing in Mathieu. Maybe that was what bound them together. She could not look in the mirror anymore because the person she saw was too disappointing. She recognized her image but felt her insides had hardened in ways she couldn't even have dreamed were possible six months ago. The worst part was that given how quickly it all happened, she knew that this darkness had been living inside of her all along. It was that thought that kept her away from Sophie. She could not taint her daughter. So, at whatever cost, she had to make this life she'd built with Mathieu work somehow.

As she was buttoning her winter coat to head out, she saw some of the canvases she had done of Sophie and decided to take a few of them with her to get some feedback from passersby. She felt she was improving, but the true test would be if a stranger connected with her work. She craved the feedback because if she wasn't improving and wasn't becoming the artist she had dreamed of, then she had sacrificed so much for so little. She couldn't bear for that to be her life's story, so she needed to do everything she could to rewrite it.

~

The day was especially chilly, and Nita used a paper cup of hot coffee to warm her fingers through her gloves. The sky was overcast, with a light drizzle trickling down periodically. The sun was nowhere in sight, so Nita knew she'd have to stomach the cold for as long as she could before giving up and closing the stall again. She'd been there for three hours, and a few tourists had stopped in and idly perused a few of the canvases before scurrying off in search of a café or bistro to escape the weather.

She had kept her canvases of Sophie in a stack next to where she sat, eyeing them periodically, both hoping people would notice the work and not wanting to share Sophie with anyone else. She buried her face in a French children's book she had borrowed from the stall next door so she could practice her French while waiting for customers.

"Well, well," she heard a familiar voice say. "Mathieu, you get better looking every day."

She looked up and saw Simon nearing her, his arm comfortably around a pretty girl with dark hair, fair skin, and high cheekbones. She was very petite, and he stood easily a head taller than her.

Nita felt awkward exchanging *bisous* with him in front of his girlfriend but managed to shake it off and exchange them quickly with her as well.

"This is Élise," Simon said, cupping her hand in his. He couldn't keep himself from smiling even as he said her name. His dark-green eyes beamed as he looked down at Élise through his thick lashes.

"It is a pleasure to meet you," Nita said to her.

"*Toi aussi,*" she said, and then in her cute, accented English added, "Simon speaks of you and Mathieu often."

"Speaking of," Simon said, "why does he have you taking over business for him?"

Nita pictured her disheveled boyfriend, who couldn't be bothered to get out of bed and earn money that they desperately needed. "I thought it would be fun for me to try today," she said, keeping her voice breezy.

"You picked one of the coldest days in the year to try!" Élise said.

Simon added, "No kidding. You should've waited till spring!"

"It's not so bad," Nita said. "I just wish more customers were out and about."

Simon's eyes fell to the stack of paintings of Sophie near Nita's stool. "What have we got here?" He began flipping through the canvases, pulling them out and holding them up to get a better look at them.

Nita averted her gaze to the sidewalk. "Oh, nothing," she said softly. "Just some things I've been working on as practice."

Simon whistled. "Nita, these are great. Has Mathieu seen them?"

She nodded.

"Don't tell him I said this, but you need to be selling these instead of the same tired paintings he's had in this stall for years." Simon held up one of Sophie seated at a vanity with Nita behind her. The child used an oversize brush against her small head. Her expression was questioning, as if she weren't sure if she was doing it correctly but wanted Nita's approval from the reflection in the mirror.

"Who's the girl?" Élise asked.

"My niece." Nita found the lie easier to tell this second time.

"She's going to be a stunner one day!" Simon said.

He took the remaining two canvases and placed them side by side in a more prominent center place so that passersby would not miss them. Picking back up the one of Sophie with the brush, he turned toward Nita.

"I'd like to be your first customer and buy this one," he said.

Nita smiled at his kindness. "You don't have to do that."

"I'm not buying it because I have to." He reached for his billfold and removed a handful of francs. "Assuming I can afford it, of course! How much would it cost to have?"

Nita shifted her gaze to the painting, to Sophie's questioning eyes, which wondered what she had done wrong to make her mummy leave her. Had she not brushed her hair correctly, the way her mummy had showed her? And here Nita stood, again willing to give up her daughter and sell the painting to another person. She had not realized how difficult it would be to part with these canvases. Simon looked so genuine and earnest, and she knew she did not have a good excuse to refuse him. They did need money, even if it was charity from Simon.

"Forty francs?" she said, knowing Mathieu sold his for at least four times that but adjusting for her lack of experience.

Simon handed her two hundred francs and made her close her fist around the bills. "You should never undersell yourself."

His words warmed Nita's heart. It was *facile à dire, mais difficile à faire*—easy to say, but hard to do. She nearly hugged him for his kindness but refrained when she saw Élise squeeze his hand. It was easy to see why a woman would be lucky to have Simon as her boyfriend, bad French accent and all. There was no quality more desirable than compassion.

~

After those initial moments of feeling a sense of loss over the painting and reminding herself that it was going to a friend and if she ever truly wanted it back, it would be easy enough to get, she felt pride and excitement. She had sold her first painting! And for two hundred francs, no less! The most surprising thing she had learned about herself since arriving in Paris was that she could survive, no matter how dire the situation seemed. She didn't want to get ahead of herself, but if she could sell a few more at that price, she and Mathieu would be okay for a month, and maybe he would feel better and get back to his own work rather than sulking around the apartment all day.

With the drizzle turning into actual rain droplets and foot traffic stopping almost entirely, Nita decided to close the stall and share the good news with Mathieu. Even in his funk, she thought he would be able to appreciate this milestone in her artistic career.

As she walked along the river, passing other *bouquinistes* who were closing their shops as well, she couldn't help but smile at each of them. Having made her first sale, she felt like she now had a silent bond with the others who trudged out daily and earned their living selling art and wares along the Seine. She was now one of them, and it felt amazing.

As she neared their apartment in the Marais, she stopped in a local wine merchant and bought a bottle of Bordeaux so she and Mathieu could celebrate. She recognized a label that Mathieu had purchased before and handed the cashier fifty-four francs from the cash she had just received. This was the first bottle of wine she had ever purchased, and she realized that she was starting to become more French. Back in India, if things had been tight with finances, it would never even have occurred to her to spend some of her money on something frivolous, like a celebratory drink. Her family was far too practical for that. But here, she focused on living in the present and didn't worry about how the future would unfold.

She shook the rain off her coat before entering the apartment and hanging it on the hook behind their front door. She pulled the wine out of the now damp brown paper sack and could not wait to share her news with Mathieu. She heard some rustling in the bedroom, so at least she knew he was awake. That was a step in the right direction. Certainly, seeing the Bordeaux would help motivate him at least from the bed to the living area, where they could toast to her success. The French were far too civilized to drink wine in bed. She made her way to the bedroom with the bottle in hand, hoping this was going to be a turning point for them and both would focus on their art again and Mathieu would get back to being his old self.

She pushed open the bedroom door and saw Mathieu's face buried between the legs of a tattooed blonde girl who arched her head back while she moaned in pleasure.

27

SOPHIE

2019

She arrives at Taj Palace just after five in the evening and immediately heads to the kitchen, dons an apron, and ties back her hair so it is away from her face. Today, it is only Manoj with her.

She is anxious and agitated because she would rather be at Bistro Laurent but washes her hands and then approaches him. "What can I do to help?"

Manoj barely looks up from the haricots verts he is expertly chopping into bite-size pieces, his knife moving quickly back and forth in a rocking motion. He has a deftness in his work that Sophie admires. She is finding she enjoys cooking here under Manoj's tutelage much more than she had the cooking lessons that her fois had barked at her to prepare her for her marriage to Kiran. Those lessons had been forced, whereas these felt earned.

"You could get started on the cucumber and tomato."

Sophie glances at the counter behind Manoj and sees a pile of cucumbers and tomatoes that need to be washed, seeded, and chopped for the kachumber salad. She has been on salad duty since Naresh Uncle hired her. Manoj kept the real cooking within his control, still not fully accepting the arrangement of having Sophie join him in the kitchen. Occasionally when Naresh Uncle was around, Manoj had her make some rotlis or naan, but even those tasks were easy to master.

"Do you ever take a night off?" Sophie asks him while she prepares the salad.

Manoj laughs. "I need to be here."

"When do you find time to see your friends?"

"Here and there. I'm more of a loner, anyway. Growing up, we really focused on the family." He glances over his shoulder at her in a way that makes clear he thinks of her as an outsider.

Sophie can relate to prioritizing family over friends. Papa was her world, and everything else had come second.

"Was it strange growing up here?" she asks him.

He shrugs. "No, why would it be?"

Sophie puts her knife down and turns to face him. "It's a different country, different language. It must be strange, no?"

"Not to me. It's the country I was born in and the language I grew up with."

"But there are so few Indian people! It's not odd to you?"

He shrugs again. "What would be odd to me is being around only Indian people."

Sophie turns back to chopping the tomatoes. She wonders if Nita had felt the same way as Manoj and that's why she decided to leave. Ahmedabad has millions of people, all of them Indian. The diversity in Ahmedabad seems based on caste alone, and other than the handful of servants that cross her path, even caste differences are not a part of her daily life. Sophie has never thought twice about it, but perhaps there are people who crave more differences in the people around them.

"Have you ever been to India?" she asks.

Manoj shakes his head. "Papa went back about ten years ago, when his papa passed away. I had never met my grandparents, so it didn't make sense for me to go with him. Besides, someone needed to stay back and keep an eye on the restaurant." He gestures around him and then heads to the small pantry in the back to gather some spices for the shaaks, seemingly not interested in continuing the conversation.

Sophie cannot imagine a life in which she had never met her grandparents or relatives. Even if her fois drive her mad, they are family, and she can't fathom her childhood without them. Her entire existence had revolved around family until she came to France last week.

She finishes the salad and covers the large steel bowl with plastic wrap and places it off to the side.

"Can I help you with the shaaks?" She gestures to the medley of vegetables that are ready to be sautéed in large skillets with a combination of turmeric, red chili powder, ground cumin, cinnamon, fresh green chilis, and mustard seeds.

"I should be okay," he says as he drops some black mustard seeds into the hot oil and they start to sizzle and pop.

"Let her help you, yaar," Naresh Uncle says as he enters the kitchen with bags of groceries.

Sophie and Manoj startle and turn toward him. They had not heard him come into the restaurant. Manoj reluctantly shifts to the right to make room for Sophie to join him.

"That's okay, Uncle," Sophie says. "Your arms are full. I will help you put these away." She grabs a bag from him and nearly drops it, surprised by the weight.

Naresh Uncle smiles at her. "You are too eager," he says. "It's flour, so the bags are quite heavy!"

Together, they manage to get everything to the pantry, and by the time they return to the kitchen, it is heavy with the smell of sautéed spiced potatoes. Sophie never tires of these familiar foods and aromas. One of the best perks of the job is that she gets to eat comforting Indian food and drink chai when she's there. While traditional Gujarati food is not on the menu, Naresh and Manoj often make it for them to eat in the back as their dinner. Sophie's taste buds were awakened by the smell of khichdi when she arrived for her shift tonight. The simple meal of rice, lentils, and potatoes pressure-cooked with cinnamon, cloves, red chili, salt, lemon, ginger, and garlic made her feel most like she was back in Ahmedabad. It was the ultimate comfort food to her, the one her fois made her when she was sick, paired with tart homemade yogurt and mango pickle on the side so she could mix them in the proportions she desired. At Taj Palace, she does not have to worry about language barriers or fear that what she has ordered might have meat or alcohol or some other forbidden item. She has taken for granted how easy it was for her to do basic things like eat in restaurants in Ahmedabad. The entire city catered to her caste and diet, and she had taken that luxury as a given until Paris.

"He will come around," Naresh Uncle says to her.

"It's okay. I don't mind," Sophie says.

"No, he's thirty-two years old. He needs to learn to adapt. I won't always be here to smooth things over for him, and he must learn that."

Sophie smiles politely, wondering if Papa thought the same thing of her before he died. Did he question whether he had sheltered Sophie too much? Did he regret it if he had? Did he think her incapable of adapting to life if the path before her took any unexpected turns? Perhaps he would have been right to question those things, or perhaps he had underestimated her and would be surprised to see her coping now.

"Manoj," Naresh Uncle says in a stern voice. "Show Sophie how to make the cauliflower shaak."

Manoj pulls out the spice dabba and places it on the counter next to the stove and makes room for Sophie. She awkwardly joins him, feeling like she is caught in the middle of a long-standing papa-son battle, but her embedded obedience has her following orders.

"I need to tend to the books," Naresh Uncle says as he leaves the kitchen for the small office tucked away in the back. "Manoj, you'll be okay here, right?" His tone has a warning note in it.

"*Oui*, Papa. I will show Sophie the shaaks," he says.

After Naresh Uncle leaves the kitchen, Manoj teaches Sophie the spice ratios for the cauliflower shaak: equal parts turmeric and red chili powder and twice the amount of salt and the blend of ground cumin and coriander. She mentally notes them, as numbers and proportions have always come easily to her.

After they work in silence for a while, she asks him, "Have you heard of a place called Bistro Laurent?"

Manoj shrugs. "Why?"

"I need to go there after work," she says as she removes cauliflower florets from the head with a sharp paring knife, cutting from the base rather than the head, as Manoj had shown her the day before, so that the florets stay intact and the counter is not littered with cauliflower crumbs. She knows she'll always cut cauliflower this way now.

"Where is it?"

She gives him the street Cecile told her. He stops stirring the first batch of cauliflower in the large saucepan.

"You're going to go there after work?" he asks.

She nods.

"Why?"

Now she shrugs, not wanting to tell him the truth.

"You shouldn't go there that late. It's better to go during the day."

"It's not too far from here," Sophie muses. "It should be okay to make a quick stop on my way home."

"It's not very smart for you to be walking alone at night around there."

Sophie tries to brush off his warning. "I need to find someone. It should only take a minute."

"Someone who can't wait until tomorrow?"

Sophie realizes it is better to tell him what he wants to hear, so she says, "Maybe you're right. It can wait."

Manoj looks at her pointedly. "Your choice."

The two work in silence again, and she begins to roll out the dough for the naan. He takes it from her and slaps it against the side of the clay tandoor in the corner of the kitchen.

As she walks past the small office where Naresh Uncle is working, she sees him poring over ledgers with his head in his hands. His expression is pained.

"Is something wrong, Uncle?" she asks, wiping her hands on her apron as she stands in the doorway.

He forces a smile and looks up at her. "No, Sophie. Nothing to worry."

She sees a stack of bills next to him and knows the finances of a small restaurant like Taj Palace must be difficult. The place is rarely full of guests, and Indian food doesn't seem to be that popular with the locals, as they don't get many delivery orders either. She knows Naresh Uncle has had the restaurant for many years, so she assumed they had worked out a system, but she sees the worry on Naresh Uncle's face, and it is unmistakable. She has seen that look on countless clients of her accounting firm. She has helped restaurant owners in India rebudget their money to have the right ratio between food costs, labor, and marketing. Taj Palace has very little in the way of true labor costs, save Sophie, and she feels guilty knowing she is taking money from Naresh Uncle when it seems he has very little to give.

She considers the best way to offer some advice or help without insulting him but doesn't see a good opportunity now, so she moves back to her place in the kitchen and starts making mental notes of where the money in the restaurant is allocated. As she moves through the kitchen, she thinks about how much food in the pantry is wasted due to spoilage. She thinks about the cost of the menu items and how they compare to the portion sizes. Naresh Uncle's portions are quite generous, and the patrons of the restaurant leave a lot of food waste. She suspects that would be an easy fix to increase profitability. She thinks through the number of menu items and knows many are hardly ever ordered but require ingredients on hand in case they are.

While she and Manoj are working, she asks him, "Does your papa handle all of the finances for the restaurant?"

He looks at her skeptically. "Why are you asking?"

"I was just curious. My work in India was accounting, and I wonder if he might need some help. Restaurants were my area of expertise."

"I doubt it," Manoj says, and turns back to pureeing the toor lentils for the dal.

Sophie drops it, but his expression confirms that the restaurant is in trouble. She will think about how to raise her offer to Naresh Uncle in a respectful manner. For right now, she is focused on the clock and getting to ten thirty so she can leave and still get to Bistro Laurent before eleven.

28

NITA

Mathieu made eye contact with Nita while his face was buried between the woman's legs. His expression was steely, registering no emotion whatsoever in seeing her standing there.

Stunned, Nita dropped the bottle of Bordeaux. It made a thud as the thick glass hit the wooden floor. Only then did the tattooed woman open her eyes and realize that another person had entered the room. She didn't flinch, as if it were not her first time being caught in bed by another woman. She turned toward Mathieu to see how he was reacting, and he eventually rose to his knees, his flaccid penis now visible to both women. Nita knew that meant he had already satisfied himself in this woman and was giving her the "encore." Nita hadn't experienced the "encore" in a very long time because lately his sexual appetite had been focused wholly on himself. The woman propped herself up on her elbows, seemingly annoyed that they'd been interrupted before she'd finished.

Mathieu's lips glistened, and he didn't even attempt to wipe his mouth. "I thought you'd be home later." He reached for the cigarette and lighter that were on top of the nightstand near the bed.

Nita clutched the doorframe, feeling faint.

Mathieu lit the cigarette and let it dangle from his lips. He pulled the woman to a sitting position.

"Je pense que tu devrais partir." I think you should go.

The woman climbed out of the bed and pulled black leggings over her long skinny legs. She then threw an oversize sweater over her top. She hadn't bothered to put on her bra or panties and shoved them into her bag. She then reached into a small pocket in her purse and pulled out a clear bag containing white pills. She handed them to Mathieu and actually kissed him before scurrying past Nita and letting herself out of the apartment. Nita wondered if the woman could taste herself on his lips.

The entire exchange from the time Nita opened the bedroom door until the woman left had probably been no more than three minutes, but Nita felt as if hours had passed. Her legs felt stuck to the floor as if they had been cemented there.

Mathieu tucked the plastic bag with the pills into the drawer of the nightstand and inhaled deeply from his cigarette, his cheeks sunken as he held the smoke in for a few seconds before slowly releasing it. He used a tissue to wipe himself and then wadded it up and tossed it onto the nightstand before pulling up his underwear and then climbing into a pair of jeans that he'd picked up from the floor.

He walked toward Nita, but she still could not move her limbs or utter a word. As he neared her, she saw that his eyes were bloodshot, and she knew he was fading off his high from whatever pill he had taken earlier that day. Kneeling before her, he picked up the wine bottle and eyed the label.

"This is a nice one," he said while being careful not to drop the cigarette from his lips.

He moved past her into the kitchen, opened a drawer, and pulled out a corkscrew.

Nita finally found the strength to move and turned around to face him.

She could only eke out one word.

"Mathieu?"

The expression on her face conveyed everything else she couldn't say at that moment.

He made eye contact with her for the second time that night, this time without having his face pressed between another woman's legs. His eyes seemed to be asking what she was so upset about and suggesting she was overreacting.

Nita's hands clenched into fists. She put aside the Indian instinct she had been raised with to not speak out and found her words.

"What the fuck is wrong with you?!" She stomped toward him, fists balled so tightly that her fingernails almost pierced half moons into her skin.

He placed the corkscrew on the counter.

"*Qu'est-ce qui ne va pas chez toi?*" he asked her. What's wrong with you?

"Me? *Me?!*" Her body began to shake. "You just had your dick and tongue and whatever else inside of that—that—*thing*, and you are asking what's wrong with *me*!?"

"*Ma chérie*, it is not what you think," he said, adopting the sweet voice he had used with her when they first met. A voice she now identified as the act that it had been when she had first heard it.

Her eyes widened at the thought of him trying to explain away something she had literally witnessed minutes earlier. He came around the kitchen counter and moved toward her. She folded her arms across her chest, taking a step back.

"*Ma chérie*, she is the dealer I use," he said, as if this served as a fine explanation.

Nita shrugged him off as he tried to caress her arm.

"What difference does that make?"

Mathieu tilted his head down, gazing at her through his long thick lashes. His best attempt at an innocent puppy look. "We have worked out an arrangement. This way I don't need to pay her for our drugs, and everyone is happy."

Nita felt the walls closing in on her. She brushed past him toward the front door to create more distance.

"*Our* drugs? *Our* drugs? When did I ever say I wanted any drugs? And when did you ever say that you were trading sex for pills?"

Mathieu shrugged. "*Il n'y a pas assez d'argent. Je pensais que cela pourrait être un bon compromis.*" There is not enough money. I thought this would be a good compromise.

"Compromise? Compromise? You are having *sex* with someone else! How can you do that?" Tears began to prick her eyes, but she did not want to give him the satisfaction.

"It does not mean anything. It was easier than having to find the money."

"You thought those pills were so damned important that you should whore yourself out to have them?"

The sweet look on Mathieu's face while he was trying to curry her favor vanished. In its place was the dark, emotionless expression she had seen when she first opened the bedroom door that night.

He narrowed his eyes and focused his gaze on her. "I'm not the only whore in this room."

Nita's eyes widened at his insult.

Mathieu took a small step closer to her. "Funny that someone who takes her clothes off and lets people paint her for money has such high morals."

A tiny gasp escaped Nita's lips, as if she had been slapped. Her mind started racing, and she felt like she could not breathe. She wanted to hurl an insult at him that would hurt him as much as he had hurt her, but she was still reeling from what he had said to her. Mostly because part of her agreed with him. She hated who she had become. She did think she had demeaned herself, but she didn't know a way out. And she never forgot that he had led her down that path. If he hadn't, might she have returned home to Rajiv and Sophie? Might she have spared herself all the shame she now felt whenever she saw her reflection in a mirror? She grabbed her coat and purse, still damp from the rain, and opened the door.

The anger in her face had receded, replaced by hurt and sadness, the tears now dangerously close to sliding down her cheeks. "I don't know who you are," she said.

"Je m'en fous." I don't give a fuck.

To herself she thought, *I don't know who I am.*

She turned away so he wouldn't see her pain and closed the apartment door behind her.

29

SOPHIE

2019

Sophie leaves Taj Palace around ten thirty that night, and, despite Manoj's warning, goes straight to Bistro Laurent. By the time she arrives at the small street in the second arrondissement, close to eleven, she realizes she is among the few people still walking the streets that late on a weeknight. Perhaps she should have waited until the morning. The soles of her shoes against the sidewalk ring out into the empty night. She pulls her shawl tighter around her and keeps her head down as she walks. Several of the retailers on the street, like the *boulanger*, *pâtissier*, and *fromager*, are closed, given the hour. Many of the cafés as well. She hears a few voices coming from Bistro Laurent and is relieved to see it is still open.

She takes a deep breath before going inside. The few patrons turn to look at her as she enters. The restaurant is quite empty, but that is not unusual for this time on a weeknight. During the day, this area would likely be bustling with wayward tourists but has more of an eerie quality at night, when it is quiet and sullen. There is a tall, wiry man in his early twenties leaning against the door to the kitchen. He wears a white half apron, so she knows he is staff and probably the best person to ask.

"*Bonsoir*," Sophie says. "*Parlez-vous anglais?*"

The man nods. He has the lingering odor of cigarettes, and she suspects he'd rather be smoking one now than speaking with her.

"I am looking for someone who worked here before."

The man shrugs. "I'm new here. Only worked here six months, so I don't know many people."

"Is there someone else? Maybe an owner?"

He shakes his head. "Not tonight. The owner is Laurent"—he gestures toward the stack of menus with the name in large letters—"and he is only here during the day."

Sophie thanks him for his time and says she will return tomorrow.

As she exits onto the street, she is again enveloped by the night. There are few lampposts along these side streets, and, even though she does not have much money, she decides to find the metro station so that she isn't walking the entire thirty minutes back to the Latin Quarter at this hour. She starts heading east, thinking she will run into a stop without too much difficulty, given that is the direction of the Louvre and other tourist attractions. A man in a coat is walking along the opposite side of the road and looks up at her before putting his head back down and continuing on his way. Sophie is not used to being so isolated at night. There is nowhere she could have gone in Ahmedabad that would have had so few people out and about, even if it was because there were people living in shanties along the side of the road.

She hears tires crunching against pavement behind her and turns to see someone on a bicycle. She quickens her pace. After a few minutes, she wonders if she missed a street on which she was meant to turn and is trying to get her bearings. She should have seen a metro stop by now and hates the thought of being lost. While she stands on a corner, focused on the street signs, trying to remember which she should take, she hears bicycle tires approaching again. It appears to be the same figure from earlier, but he is not close enough for her to make out his face in the darkness. He is getting nearer to her, and no one else is around, so she makes a quick turn down a narrow street. She is not sure of the right way but starts walking quickly, her nerves setting in. She should have listened to Manoj.

The cobbles are uneven beneath her feet, but she goes as quickly as she can manage. A minute later, she hears the bike tires behind her again and knows it is the same man before she turns around to confirm. Her pulse quickens, and she breaks into a run even though she's not sure where to go, her shawl loosening around her shoulders and one end now flying behind her. She turns down the first street she sees, hoping to find someone—anyone—walking so she's not alone with the man on the bike.

She hears him quicken his pedaling and feels him catching up to her. Panic swells within her, and she turns down another street in search of anyone who can help, but there are no other souls around. She then realizes she's hit a dead end and knows the bicyclist is behind her. Her eyes dart from side to side, looking for an exit, but in the darkness, she can't make out another pathway. The man jumps off his bike and nonchalantly leans it against the wall before walking toward her.

"Are you okay?" he says.

The voice is familiar. She peers into the darkness, and, as the figure approaches, she recognizes Manoj.

She takes a deep breath. "What are you doing here?" Her voice is angry and agitated.

"I had a feeling you were going to come here even though you said you weren't."

Her breathing is still shallow, but she is relieved to see him. "But why were you chasing after me? You scared me half to death!"

He doesn't seem fazed. "I told you it was not safe to be here late. What if it hadn't been me on the bike, pedaling after you?"

"But it was!"

"My papa would be upset if something happens to you," Manoj says. "He seems to have taken quite a liking to you."

Sophie begrudgingly says, "You were probably right to have told me not to come tonight."

"Did you find the person you were looking for?" he asks as they start down the street, him walking his bike.

Sophie shakes her head. "No, I have to come back tomorrow."

He nods. "Let me walk you home. I'm not even sure you know where you are anymore."

He is right. She doesn't. And she is grateful she has company, even though he initially gave her such a fright.

After they walk a few minutes, she turns to him. "How did you know I would come here after I said I wouldn't?"

He laughs. It is the first time she has heard him laugh since she met him.

"Because you are stubborn."

She is about to protest. No one has ever called her stubborn. She has always been malleable and eager to please, but never stubborn. Her fois had called Nita stubborn when they thought Sophie was not listening. As they walk along the Seine, past all the locked stalls that are bustling and energetic during the day with tourists crowding around them, she realizes she might have some of Nita in her after all. The good and the bad.

"Even if I am, you don't have to make it your burden," she says, turning away.

Manoj continues looking at the path ahead of them. "So, what was so important that it had to be done tonight?"

She hesitates, unsure how much to reveal. She has been telling lies and half truths for so long, and she is tired of them. Manoj is the last person she thought she would confide in, but he has made her feel safe as she walks through the streets, and maybe that is enough.

"I'm looking for my mummy," she says.

He whips his head toward her. "Your mother is here? Then why aren't you staying with her? And why are you bothering to work at our restaurant?"

She takes a deep breath. "That's just it. I don't know where she is. She left India—left our family—when I was six years old. I thought she was dead all this time. It was only after my papa passed away a couple weeks ago that I learned the truth." She looks at him out of the corner of her eye. He does not flinch at her news, so she continues. "I thought I needed to find her now that I'm alone. But it's been hard, given how much time has passed, and I have very little to go on."

Manoj walks next to her, not sharing his thoughts. She lets the silence sit between them as they go another block.

"My mother died seven years ago," he says. "Really died. Cancer. We were with her until the end, so I don't have to worry about whether it happened or not. There is some peace in seeing someone who was suffering break free of that pain." He looks at her. "I'm sorry, Sophie. I cannot imagine what it must be like to think your mother had died and then to later learn she hadn't."

These are the first moments of kindness Sophie has felt from Manoj. He had let her glimpse past his hard exterior. She sees a young man, and she thinks maybe he is as lost as she is and just wants to feel cared for. She believes she sees the bravado he puts on for his papa so that his papa doesn't worry about him. She imagines that he goes into the restaurant each day and sees constant reminders of his mother and a different time in his life. Maybe it was she who helped him prepare the shaaks, and that is why he is so resentful of Sophie being in the kitchen with him. Sophie understands why he and his papa are so close and so invested in the restaurant that has been their family business for so many years.

"Everyone's path is different," Sophie says. "I can't change the fact that this is mine."

"Do you want me to help you find her?" he asks.

"Your family has already done so much for me," Sophie says, not wanting to add to his burden, especially now that she understands it better.

"I know this city better than anyone. I used to do deliveries for the restaurant on my bike, so I know every hidden street or alley. And you clearly need some guidance on which streets are okay and which are not!"

From her first few days of being in the kitchen with Manoj, she has not been able to fathom that a friendship would ever ensue. But now she can see the gentleness beneath his gruff demeanor. She knows how much he could help her and is desperate to find answers and move on to the next stage of her life—whatever that may be. But she knows she can help him, too, and has found the right opportunity.

"How about if we make a trade?" Sophie says.

Manoj cocks his head, intrigued by her suggestion. "What are you offering?"

"I saw your papa looking over the books and ledgers for the restaurant. I can see how much the place means to both of you. I know the finances are tight, but I have a real skill at balancing budgets and finding efficiencies. It is my job back in India, so if you can convince him, then maybe we can help each other."

Manoj looks at her pointedly. "You don't miss much, do you?"

"Neither do you," she says as they turn the corner to her hostel, a smile creeping onto her face.

30

NITA

1999

The rain had started coming down harder while she had been inside, and her umbrella did little to shield her from it. It was even colder now that the sun had almost fully set. She strolled aimlessly through the streets of the Marais, realizing she had nowhere to go and no one to turn to. Dao was visiting her family in England. Even if she had been in town, Nita could imagine the knowing look on her face after she explained what had happened. Dao had tried to warn her about Mathieu. She'd said that she didn't "get a good vibe from him" and that he "seemed more interested in himself than in her."

The only other people she knew in Paris were Julien and Simon. Julien was obviously out of the question, and Simon had always been kind to her, but he was Mathieu's friend. What could she even say to him?

Her fingers began to feel numb as the rain seeped through her wool knit gloves. She had 146 francs in her purse, so at least she could duck into a bistro and have a meal and tea while she thought things through. But then she feared spending that money, not sure if she would have a place to sleep or for how many days she'd need that money to last. She already regretted the fifty-four francs she had spent on the wine.

As she crossed over the Seine at Pont Neuf, she knew her feet had been taking her toward the only place she could think of going for the night: Le Canard Volant. The hostel looked so different to her now than it had when she had first arrived in Paris over six months ago. Or maybe it was that she had changed. Aged in the couple months since she had stopped taking on shifts there and had settled into her life with Mathieu and painting and posing nude. She hadn't been good at keeping in touch with Dao or Cecile and suspected that was because she was ashamed of them learning who she had become. They were the first two people she had met in France, and they had seen the version of her before Mathieu. She could hardly recall that person anymore.

She opened the door and was surprised to see Cecile with her bright-red lips visible from across the dark room.

"Well, look what the cat dragged in," she said, rising from the reception desk.

"Cecile!" Nita was elated to see a familiar face, even if it was one she felt guilty for neglecting.

The two women exchanged kisses on the cheek.

Cecile smiled at her and asked, "What brings you to our fair arrondissement? I thought you were off living with that mysterious artist in the Marais. A *rive droite* person now."

Nita's eyes welled up, and Cecile's expression turned somber. If there was a universal look that transcended all cultures and countries, it was the look of a woman with a broken heart.

"He's probably got shit for brains anyways," Cecile said as she led Nita to the old, battered couch in the lobby.

Nita smiled gratefully at the first person she had met in Paris. How far they had come. Or maybe it was more like how far Nita had sunk since that day. She was living a life she could never have predicted when she came to France to become the artist she had dreamed of. And yes, she had sold a painting that day, but at what price? Would she have been better off in Ahmedabad, painting at the window near their dining table? Rajiv, with his kind way, would indulge her curiosity and buy her picture books of France and Paris. It had all seemed so glamorous in the glossy pages, chic people with berets in cafés along the Seine, majestic views of the Eiffel Tower from all directions, lavender fields in Provence, pristine beaches in Saint-Tropez. Living the life was nothing like that. She had probably been too naive to realize that photographs were taken only of the good times. And she'd had far more bad times than good since she'd left. She considered this her karma. She had done such a selfish thing in leaving that it was bound to have negative repercussions. She had been crazy for not knowing that from the start and was now realizing she should never have left Ahmedabad in the first place.

"Are there any beds free for tonight?" Nita asked her.

Cecile nodded. "Let me check to see if I can finagle a private room for you so you needn't deal with the riffraff. There's a noisy group of British university girls who are impossible with their manners."

She went to the reception desk and flipped through some pages in the bookings ledger. She then returned with one of the oversize keys that Nita had not used in a while and a blue airmail envelope.

"It's good that you came by," Cecile said. "I've been holding this letter in case you ever did. Even told the staff to be on the lookout for an Indian woman who speaks terrible French," she said with a playful nudge.

Nita forced a smile and small chuckle. For the slightest moment she felt herself release from the pain and anger she'd been carrying with her. She took the letter, knowing what it was without having to see the handwriting. She wasn't ready to read it yet, though. It could say the thing she had feared most. That the tuberculosis had been real and Sophie had not survived it. She could not bear such news right then. There had been enough pain for one night.

31

SOPHIE

2019

The next afternoon, before her shift at Taj Palace, Sophie heads back to Bistro Laurent to try to find the owner. The neighborhood is lively and full of people, a stark contrast from the solitude the night before. Today, she does not feel unsafe at all, although she does keep an eye out for Manoj on his bike, expecting him to pop out from anywhere.

It is just after the lunch rush, and Bistro Laurent is still full of diners, but most appear to have finished their meals and are lingering over coffee and conversation before tackling the rest of their days.

A portly older bald man is behind the bar counter, drying some cutlery with a towel and placing it in a holder.

"*Bonjour, Mademoiselle,*" he says with a warmhearted smile.

"*Bonjour,*" Sophie says before confirming he speaks English and is Laurent.

The man has a much kinder demeanor than the gangly server she spoke with the night before. He wipes his hands on the towel before asking how he can help her.

Sophie retrieves the photograph of Nita from her bag and offers it to Laurent. "Do you remember if she worked here?"

Laurent's smile grows wider. "*Bien sûr.* I never forget a beautiful face. But I cannot recall her name. Her French was terrible, but a bit better as time went on. She was one of the first people I ever hired who was not French, but at that time, we had so many tourists who needed English servers, so it was okay."

Sophie's heart dances. "Nita Shah. She doesn't still work here, does she?"

Laurent laughs. "*Non, ma chérie*, not for many years."

It is the answer she had expected, but she still had not been able to stop herself from hoping for more. "Do you know how I could find her now?"

"*Désolé, Mademoiselle.* This job is not the type where people stay in touch after. She maybe worked here a few years before moving on."

"Do you know where she went after?"

"When she told me she was leaving, she said she was returning home. She'd had enough of France by then, I suppose."

Sophie processes his words. Nita had never come back to Ahmedabad. Or what if she had and had just opted to stay away from Rajiv and Sophie? Had Sophie come all this way when Nita was back in India?! It couldn't be. Ahmedabad was far too small for someone to hide in plain sight like that. The gossip would have trickled over to her family in no time. And Sophie's relatives on Nita's side would surely have known if that were the case, and they had never spoken of it either. Maybe "home" had come to mean something different for Nita, but Sophie couldn't imagine where else.

"Did she leave a forwarding address or anything? Maybe for her paychecks?"

Laurent laughs again. "I paid her cash on her last day, just like all the other times. We were not such a formal system back then. Not so many rules and regulations. *Pas trop d'avocats. Pas trop de règles.*" His expression suggests he preferred those times.

Sophie feels so dejected and realizes she must be wearing it on her face, because Laurent reaches out to rub her shoulder to comfort her.

"You know, my wife yells at me for hoarding all the paperwork for decades, but I think I might have her address where she lived at the time in the employee files. Wait here."

He disappears into the kitchen, and Sophie wrings her hands in anticipation of finding another lead and praying this one is not yet another dead end. Laurent is gone for over ten minutes before the black door with the round window swings back open and he emerges victorious, waving a piece of paper.

"Nita's employment application. It has an address. Looks to be in the Marais. Maybe the people there have a forwarding address for her."

He hesitates with the paper in his hand and looks at Sophie. "You resemble her. She is your family, no?"

Sophie manages a smile and nods. "Many people say that."

Laurent puts the piece of paper on the counter between them. "The laws say I should not be sharing this with you, but if I leave this old form here and you take it, I suppose there is not much I can do." He gives Sophie a gentle smile.

She searches his eyes before grabbing the paper and clutching it to her chest. It is the best news she could have possibly expected from this small round man with the shiny head. She could hug him but holds herself back.

"*Monsieur*, you have been such a big help. I cannot thank you enough!"

"*De rien.* I'm always happy to help a pretty lady in need." He winks at her in a good-natured, grandfatherly way, and she practically skips out of the restaurant.

32

NITA

1999

That night Nita lay in the bed in her private room at Le Canard Volant. The walls were thin, so she could hear the British girls stumble in drunkenly in the middle of the night and proceed to chatter on endlessly. Nita was relieved she had some distance between them. Rajiv's letter lay on her stomach, still unopened. She touched the gold bangles on her wrist, trying to remember what it had felt like to be safe and secure and know exactly what the next day held. She'd been bored in that life, but right now she would have given anything to go back to being bored.

The difference between leaving Rajiv and leaving Mathieu had been that the first time she'd had a plan. Tonight, however, she'd just stormed off, and she knew she needed to go back to that apartment at least one more time, and she was more than likely to run into Mathieu when she did. But she had to brave it. She had left behind the only things that mattered: her photographs and paintings of Sophie. She could not bear to leave those, could not comprehend walking away from her daughter a second time.

~

The next day, she contemplated her options and concluded that even though Simon had been Mathieu's friend first, he was the only person she could go to. With Dao out of town, he was her only real friend in the city. She walked to his apartment in the second arrondissement and hit the call button at the main door. After a harsh buzz, she heard his familiar American accent. He sounded surprised when she said who it was. She and Mathieu had stopped by Simon's building several times, on their way either to or from a drinking bender, but she had never been inside his home.

It was a small one-bedroom apartment, nothing fancy, but vastly cleaner than the one she and Mathieu had shared. Nita had constantly tried to keep their place tidy, but with Mathieu in his funk for these past months, it was hard to maintain any order amid the chaos of his binges.

Simon's home, on the other hand, had everything in a specific place. Except for a coat and sweater thrown over the back of the two dining chairs around his bistro table, there wasn't a thing out of place. He immediately reached for those two items.

"I'm sorry," he said, lifting them and moving them to the armoire near the front door. "I hadn't expected company . . ." His voice trailed off as if he was not sure why she was there.

"There is nothing to apologize for. You should see our place," she mumbled, perching on the edge of the couch.

Just mentioning their apartment brought back the scene from the day before, and her face fell.

"What's the matter?" Simon rushed to sit next to her, his brow furrowed.

She shook her head, unable to get out any words.

"Where's Mathieu? Is he okay?"

Nita clenched her fists at hearing his name. "He's an asshole, is what he is."

Simon's eyes widened at hearing her words and tone. She had never used such language around him. In fact, until yesterday, she hadn't really used such language at all. It was the one vice she hadn't yet picked up from Mathieu.

She stared at the wooden planks arranged in a chevron pattern on the floor and said, "I came home yesterday and found him—"

She couldn't finish the sentence, but she saw in Simon's eyes that she didn't need to. He put an arm around her shoulders and whispered "I'm so sorry" into her ear.

Warm tears slid down her cheeks, a single line tracing each one, when she saw he wasn't surprised. This reaction from a man who had known Mathieu for years said everything she wished she had known before she had ever met him. She wondered if she should have known from the start. But the reality was that she was a thirty-year-old woman who was dating for the first time in her life, if you could even call it dating, and she had no idea how the process worked. She had been sheltered and spoiled by the arranged marriage system as much as she had felt stifled by it. It eliminated the guilt that came from problems such as this because even if your husband was cheating, wives didn't blame themselves. The wife typically had little say in who her husband would be, so there was nothing she could have done to avoid an unhappy marriage. It's why Nita had never blamed herself for feeling suffocated in her life with Rajiv. There was nothing she could have done differently other than what she had eventually done: run away. But with Mathieu, the poor judgment had been her own.

"Has he apologized?" Simon asked, his voice low.

Nita met his eyes. "I didn't give him a chance. I left when I found them together. I didn't know what else to do. And I'm sorry I've come here. I—" Her voice cracked. "I didn't know where else to go," she finished softly.

"It's okay." Simon stared at the floor and shook his head. "He can make a real mess of things sometimes."

Nita realized the position she had put Simon in—having to turn on his friend—and felt it had been wrong of her to come. She started to stand. "I'm sorry. It's not fair of me to speak to you about this. You are his friend."

Simon grabbed her forearm, his hand strong and warm, and gently brought her back down to the sofa. "No, I'm sorry this happened. You needed someone. And I'm glad you felt comfortable coming to me."

She forced a smile, and her moist eyes looked up at him. For the first time, she noticed the painting of Sophie he had purchased resting against the wall behind him. She smiled that it was in such a prominent place and then thought again of the pictures and paintings she had left behind.

"The worst part is I must go back to that apartment," she said, still staring past him.

He looked over his shoulder to where her eyes had focused. "I need to hang it properly but thought that wall would be a good spot for it. That way I see it whenever I come through the front door."

"That's very kind of you," Nita said, her voice returning to normal. "It reminds me that I left some things that I need to get."

He turned back to her. "You mean you want to move out permanently?"

She was surprised he would think she would do anything else. "Of course. He's been with another woman. And in that bed!" She shuddered at the memory. "How could I not?"

"It makes sense," Simon said. "He's such a charmer, though. He's good at getting them back."

Nita fixated on him saying *them*. There had been others. She was not special or unique. She supposed it shouldn't have surprised her. She thought back to Dao's warnings after meeting him. Everyone around her had seemed to know the truth, but she'd wanted to believe in her Parisian fantasy. She'd wanted to believe that she had given up so much in India because she would get something better in France.

As if he could read her thoughts, Simon said, "I didn't mean anything by it. Only that in France, people seem less bothered by the occasional dalliance than perhaps you or I would be. It's a cultural thing, I guess."

Nita let his words marinate but still could not imagine how she could ever be in the same room with Mathieu again.

"I'm sorry." Nita rose to leave again. "Surely, you must have plans with Élise, and I'm taking up far too much of your time."

Simon pulled her back down. "Would you please stop making excuses to get out of here?" He smiled at her. "You are free to leave if you'd like, but I'm certainly not looking for a reason to get you out."

She nodded politely.

"In fact, why don't I make us some tea?"

"Thank you," she said, realizing how lucky she was to have made a friend in this city that was starting to feel as foreign to her as it had on her first day.

33

SOPHIE

2019

The sunlight feels warm on her face as she races back to the fifth arrondissement, worrying she will be late for her shift at Taj Palace but desperately wanting to run to the apartment in the Marais. Nita could still be living there! After all, Nita had lived in the same house in Ahmedabad for her entire life, until she got married, and Sophie has the sense that many Parisians do the same thing. What would she do if Nita answered the door?

Unfortunately, the address burning a hole in her jeans pocket will have to wait until tomorrow. That much she knows. Naresh Uncle has been so kind to her, and she cannot disappear when she has promised to help tonight, especially after the deal she made with Manoj. Sophie glances at her watch and sees she is eight minutes late and jogs the final block to the restaurant. She is breathless by the time she pushes the door open and races to the back.

"I'm so sorry, Uncle," she says while quickly washing her hands and then donning an apron and scanning the kitchen to discern where she can be helpful.

"Don't worry," Naresh Uncle says with a familiar bobble of his head. "Manoj was just saying he wanted to teach you the samosas today."

One glance at Manoj confirms that despite their conversation last night, he had not changed his attitude about teaching her the family recipes used in the restaurant. The filling and dough are already prepared and require only assembly. Manoj has kept the fragrant spice blends for the potato, onion, and pea filling a closely guarded secret since she began, calling them his magic masala. He had said it was his mother's recipe, and she had known not to delve deeper. Instead, she takes a nob of the lot and rolls it around between her palms, making a small ball. It has a hint of cumin as she rolls it out with the velan, crushing the occasional seed, just like Manoj shows her. She takes her flat circle of dough and cuts it down the middle and then forms a cone by pressing the sides of one half together. She fills the cone per Manoj's instructions and then pinches together the dough at the top to form the triangle that will go into the deep fryer when a customer orders it.

"That's not too bad, right?" Sophie shows Manoj her finished project.

He examines it and says, "It feels a little lumpy, but it will do."

Some behaviors are hard to change, and Manoj may never be overly friendly in the kitchen with her. She tries not to take it personally.

When they are alone in the kitchen, he asks her if she went back to Bistro Laurent.

Her eyes light up. "Yes! The owner had the address of my mummy's apartment when she worked there. I know it's a long shot, but it's worth a try!"

Manoj asks her for the address and processes the location after she hands him the piece of paper.

"Do you want me to go with you?"

"Is it unsafe?" she asks, thinking back to last night.

He shakes his head. "Not in terms of neighborhood, but you don't know who lives there now. And you don't speak French."

He is right. Going to a restaurant meant she was likely to find someone who spoke English and could help her. Going to a person's home is entirely another matter. She could probably use his help.

Sophie looks at him. "If you can take the time, I would be grateful for your help. Speaking of, have you talked to your papa about me assisting with the books?"

"Not yet, but I will tonight. Who knows? If we get lucky and find your mother, you might not need to work here much longer."

Her heart swells at the possibility of finding Nita. She has so many questions and cannot wait for the answers. Seeing Nita's face after all these years would make this crazy journey worthwhile.

"No matter what happens, I'd still like to help you both for your generosity," she says.

Manoj avoids her comment. "It will be too late to go tonight and show up unannounced like that, but we can go tomorrow before the lunch rush here."

34

NITA

1999

That night, Nita slept on Simon's couch, grateful to not have to spend more of her precious francs on another night in the hostel. Cecile had always been a stickler for rules, and she would never have felt comfortable risking her job to give Nita an off-the-books bed. Nita pulled the unopened blue airmail envelope from her purse. She quietly tore away the edges, revealing Rajiv's familiar scrawl.

January 23, 1999

Dear Nita,
Sophie's tuberculosis has broken, and she is starting to come out on the other side. But it is clear that she needs her mummy. She asks for you every day. I will come to Paris again and wait underneath the Eiffel Tower at five in the evening on our anniversary in the hopes that you will meet me and we can return home together. I

will not ask any questions of what has happened during this time, and all can be forgiven.
Rajiv

The first tears that sprang from her eyes were of joy. Sophie was okay! Relief washed over her. She felt calm and happy for the first time since she had caught Mathieu with that woman. She'd phoned her parents after receiving Rajiv's first letter and learned that Sophie was still alive and that her parents thought she would survive. But Rajiv's letter confirmed she was fully on the other side. Sophie was strong, and Nita was overjoyed. And then she pictured Rajiv standing beneath the Eiffel Tower, arms outstretched, telling her all was forgiven. It warmed something deep inside her to erase the pain she'd caused herself and so many others since August. But he didn't understand how much had happened in the time since she had left. She was no longer the woman Rajiv pictured in his mind when he thought of her, and she knew it would be evident when he laid his eyes on her. She was broken and damaged in ways someone with his pure heart could not comprehend.

She rolled over and curled into a ball, the old couch squeaking as she shifted her weight. She hoped it had not disturbed Simon while he slept in the other room. Tomorrow she would go back to the apartment and gather her things. Maybe it made sense for her to go to Rajiv. She was out of money, and when she left Mathieu, she would also be out of options. She couldn't sleep on Simon's couch forever. She'd already heard him speaking to Élise on the telephone in hushed tones, trying to explain that he could not see her that night. Nita could not continue to impose on him. Maybe after Dao returned, she could stay with her, but even that could last for only a short while. Nita's ability to find jobs had not improved much since she had arrived, and all the money she was currently making came from posing for Simon or Julien, so she could not count on that income when she was no longer a part of Mathieu's life.

She feared becoming homeless or worse. Maybe she'd already become worse. Rajiv was offering her a way out. A step back into the comfort she was born to have. It was February 17, and their anniversary was on April 8. In less than two months, she could go to him and erase everything she had done since August. Her thoughts bounced from one to another with the quickness of a shuttlecock until she let a restless sleep overtake her.

~

The next day, she awoke to Simon rummaging around in the kitchen. The smell of coffee tickled her nose, and she rose, wiping the sleep from her eyes. Sunlight was streaming in through the windows, a drastic change from the drab, dreary, overcast weather of the last couple days.

Simon set a steaming mug on the small table next to the couch. "Thought you could use some of this after a night on that rickety sofa."

Nita adjusted her shoulders a couple times, trying to work out the knots that had formed during the night.

Simon laughed. "You should have taken me up on my offer to sleep on the bed."

Nita smiled. "I could certainly not impose on you more than I already have."

"It's nothing. Really." He sat at the small bistro table near the couch. "I grabbed a couple croissants from the bakery downstairs, so hopefully you won't mind taking just one more thing. I certainly don't need to be eating both!" He patted his trim stomach, and Nita knew he would need to eat an entire truck of pastries before he would be in jeopardy of needing to lose weight.

Her stomach rumbled, and she gladly took one from the thin white paper sack, which was dotted with grease spots where the butter had soaked through. "I promise I will go after this."

"There's no rush."

"Thank you. But I must go get my things so I no longer have it hanging over my head."

"Do you want me to come with you?"

She wanted to scream yes, beg him to go and get them for her, but she had to do this herself. She couldn't put Simon between her and Mathieu any more than she already had.

"I have to do this myself," she said, determined.

"Do you want to come back here after?"

She had spent the better part of the night trying to figure out what would happen to her "after." The best she could come up with was that she'd take her share of the money she and Mathieu had stashed in the kitchen and then go back to Le Canard Volant. She would start over. She had done it once before and survived, and now she needed to do it again. Maybe this would be the turning point she needed. It would get her out of posing nude for Julien, something that still made her feel ashamed each time she did it. She was hopefully wiser, spoke more French, understood more customs, and would be able to make fewer mistakes this time around. And she knew that if things hadn't picked up by April, she could go to Rajiv and beg him to take her back to Ahmedabad with him.

"No, I think it's time I get back to what I came to Paris to do in the first place."

Simon looked at her painting behind him. "I understand why you feel that way. But you have a friend no matter what you do."

Nita embraced him tightly as she said goodbye. "Americans hug," he'd said to her as their friendship had developed, but the act had always seemed too intimate. She had struggled even getting used to giving and receiving *bisous*, but today she clung to him like the life raft he had truly been for her.

35

SOPHIE

2019

The next morning, the Saint-Paul metro station is teeming with people rushing to their jobs or errands, but Sophie has no trouble spotting Manoj leaning against the wall of a clothing boutique just north of the stairway leading underground to the station. There are several lanes of cars heading west as she waits for the light to change so she can cross the street to meet him.

They awkwardly say hello, and then he takes the scrap of paper on which she has written the address and starts walking away from the metro station. Sophie quickly follows. Within a few minutes they arrive in front of the address on Rue Elzévir. A turquoise set of double doors greets them with a panel to the left with buzzers for the apartments. Sophie looks back at the address on the paper and doesn't see an apartment number.

"I'm not sure which one," she says to Manoj.

The names on the call box are no help to her because the only one she would recognize would be Shah, and it is obviously not there.

He leans past her and buzzes the first name before Sophie can put out a hand to stop him. "We start with one until someone lets us in, no? This is how deliveries get made."

It is as good a plan as any other. It is not until the third apartment Manoj tries that someone responds. He asks to be let in, and the next sound is of an electric buzzer allowing them to push through the heavy doors and enter a dark hallway. There are ten mailboxes against the wall for the residents. It appears there are only two units per floor. They make their way up the first narrow flight of winding stairs, and Manoj continues walking to the next floor.

"Why not try these doors?" Sophie gestures toward the two apartments on the first floor.

"Those were the two that didn't answer just now. The buzzers go in order of the apartments." He continues up to the second floor.

She realizes how useful his help is and is grateful he's offered to lend it to her. She would never have been aware of these local norms.

At the second-floor landing, there is a young man peering through a slightly cracked open door. Manoj begins speaking to him in French, and Sophie is unable to follow the conversation. Manoj thanks him, and the man closes the door.

"He said he's only lived in the apartment for a few months and said we might want to check with the woman upstairs, who's lived here since the war."

Sophie knows this news is not promising but tries not to let her spirit fully deflate. Her feet are heavy as she climbs the next flight of stairs. "Bhagwan na nasib huse," Papa would have said to her. *It is God's will.*

Manoj knocks on one of the doors on the fourth floor. They hear some shuffling behind it and then silence. Manoj knocks again. More shuffling, closer this time.

"Madam," he calls politely. *"Pourrions-nous vous parler un instant?"* Could we speak with you for a moment?

"*Non, merci,*" comes back a scratchy voice.

"*S'il vous plaît. C'est important.*"

They hear a slow cranking of metal as the occupant turns the key in the door. Finally, it cracks open and an old, slight woman with white hair and a hunched back peers out at them.

"*Que voulez-vous?*" What do you want?

Manoj begins explaining to her in French and gestures over his shoulder to Sophie. She smiles softly at the woman, trying to seem innocent.

"Have you got a picture to show her?" Manoj whispers to Sophie.

The woman wags her finger. "*J'en ai pas besoin.*" I don't need it. To Sophie, she says in English, "The woman looks like you, isn't that right?"

Sophie nods.

"She was a troublemaker, that one!" The woman speaks quite forcefully for someone her size and age. She must be in her eighties. "Always carrying on at wee hours of the night, and so many strangers going in and out of the building. Good riddance to have them gone! It's much quieter ever since!"

The woman has no idea she's already answered the question that Sophie cares most about: Nita is no longer living in this building.

"Do you know where they went?" she asks.

"I do not care. Bad rubbish, I say!"

Sophie is shocked to hear someone speak of Nita this way. Sophie's memories are of the prim and proper woman who would be the consummate hostess to Papa's business clients, paint quietly near the window, and methodically brush her hair each night. What could Nita have possibly done to this old woman to warrant such ire?

"Madam, please. It's important," Manoj says. "If there is anything you can remember to help us find her, we would be very grateful."

"I am not getting involved in this," she says and closes the door hard. Then they hear the metallic sound of the gears turning in the lock. The conversation is over.

"I'm sorry that woman wasn't more help," Manoj says to a somber Sophie as they descend the stairs.

Sophie stops at the third-floor landing and stares at the door, trying to picture Nita living there with a man who is not Rajiv. It is incomprehensible, and yet she knows it is the truth. She pictures Nita climbing the same winding staircase, her hand holding the same banister the same way Sophie is now. Tries to imagine the man she is with, but he has no face in Sophie's mind. The building is a far cry from their home in Ahmedabad. What would make Nita choose this life over the lavish one she had back in India?

"Are you okay?" Manoj asks her.

She shakes her head to bring herself back to the present.

"Fine," she says. "Just disappointed."

"I know you really wanted to find her." He leads her down the remaining stairs and steers her away from the building and back toward the metro. "Maybe you still can. Have you got any other addresses for her?"

Sophie shakes her head. She is out of leads. Perhaps after a couple days the woman they just spoke to will be in a better mood and Sophie will be able to try and speak with her again. Or maybe she can ask Cecile to try and remember something else. She cannot have traveled all the way and come this far to turn back now.

36

NITA

1999

Her fingers trembled as she slid the key into the lock to Mathieu's apartment. She had never confronted someone in this manner and was ill prepared to do so. Part of her expected to find him straddling that horrible girl from two days earlier again. Another part of her expected him to be passed out from whatever drug du jour he'd ingested. What she hadn't expected to find was a freshly showered, clean-shaven, somber-looking man sitting at the bistro table in their recently cleaned apartment, the chemical smell of lemon solvent still in the air.

Mathieu looked like he had been expecting her and stood as she entered.

He smiled gratefully. "You came back."

Her expression hardened. "Only to pick up my things."

"*Ma chérie*, we must talk about this. It's been agony without you these last couple days. *Je suis désolé. Vraiment désolé.*" I'm sorry. Really sorry.

"*Vraiment désolé* is not enough, Mathieu," Nita said, pushing back her shoulders, determined to stay strong.

"*Je sais, ma chérie.* We can get past this. We must."

Nita clutched her purse to her side, not feeling comfortable enough to step farther into the apartment but also knowing she could not leave without her photographs and paintings.

Mathieu's eyes were melancholy, regretful. The light-blue pools held her gaze the way they had when the two had first met. Those eyes had haunted her since she'd arrived. He moved closer to her, gently, as if approaching a rabbit he did not want to scare. He never dropped his eyes from hers and eventually was standing in front of her. She could feel the tingle of his breath against her face, and it finally prompted her to move.

She pushed past him and marched toward the bedroom. "I need my photos. And my paintings and other things. Then I'm going."

He followed her, maintaining a comfortable distance so she could have some space. She went straight to the nightstand to retrieve her pictures. The chaos of the bedroom when she had last seen it had disappeared. The bed was freshly made, and she could smell that the linens had been washed. There wasn't even a cigarette or lighter in sight, let alone a bag of pills or hashish. She had no idea where he had stashed all the stuff, but it was clear he had tucked it away as a gesture to her.

As she inhaled the detergent smell, she couldn't recall the last time he had washed their sheets. That type of cleanliness had not been part of their regime. Now, she felt a shiver, wondering how many times she had lain in that bed on those sheets on top of the other woman's sweat, hairs, and fluids. Her stomach wrenched at the thought.

She opened the drawer and pulled out the handful of photos she kept there, the edges worn from the times she'd held them, staring at them and trying to put herself back in the exact moments they captured. Her suitcase was in the small wardrobe, and she pulled it out. After she placed it on the bed, ready to throw her meager earthly possessions into it, she felt the warmth of Mathieu's hand on her shoulder.

"You belong here, *ma chérie*," he whispered into her ear. "*Avec moi.*" With me.

His soft words tickled the small hairs on the back of her neck.

She spun around, her eyes narrowed. "You didn't feel that way when you were with that woman, did you?"

Mathieu looked sheepish. "*Non, ma chérie.* I made a mistake. A grave mistake. But that is all it was. I was in a dark place and did not feel like myself. Have you never felt that way, *ma belle*? Have you never made such a grave mistake?"

She looked at the pictures she had put into the mesh top compartment of the suitcase, and her shoulders drooped. She had made much bigger ones. She had left her child. She turned back to Mathieu. He looked so earnest and humbled. He slowly rubbed both of her shoulders.

"Nita, *je t'aime.*" I love you. "I cannot lose you."

They'd never said those words to each other. And Nita wasn't even sure either of them felt it, but in that moment, she could see that Mathieu, at the very least, thought he loved her.

"How can you say those words when you were just with another person?"

"Because with her, it never meant anything. It was a form of payment, that's it. And I've told her not to come by here again. You were right. The drugs were too much. And I won't use them again. We will go back to the life we had before that. We were happy then, *n'est-ce pas?*"

Nita felt stuck. She had been happy enough a few months ago but also had the awful image of Mathieu with that other girl. How could she stay with him and maintain her self-respect? If she even had any left inside of her. She felt confused and angry and defeated.

"*Ma chérie*, if you must go, then please let me at least see your smile one last time." His lips curled upward, encouraging her to do the same. "You are the most beautiful woman in the world when you smile."

He was laying it on thick, and she could not help but form a wry smile.

Mathieu managed a chuckle. "That's not the one, but if it is your best, then it will have to be enough. I meant what I said, Nita. *Je t'aime.* Will you remember that for me? Remember it always?"

Nita looked at the photos of Sophie in her suitcase. She had been determined to fill the bag with her belongings and go. She had already stayed longer than she had wanted, but her feet were stuck in place. There were no good answers, and she had no one to blame but herself for the lack of choices she now had.

As if he could read her thoughts, he said, "Where will you go, *ma chérie*? You should at least stay here for a few days, until you have a plan." He motioned toward the living room. "I can sleep in the salon if you need space. I just want to know you are safe."

Nita considered his offer and thought about the meager funds she had stashed in her pocket and knew there wasn't much left in the kitchen drawer, even if she took all of it. She was back to where she had been when she had first landed: desperate, alone, and in need of money.

She shook the thoughts from her head, knowing she had to get out of that apartment as quickly as she could. She snatched the photographs from the suitcase and clutched them to her chest.

"I have to go." She brushed past him. "I'll return for the rest of my things," she said, only half believing she ever would. She could sacrifice the paintings, her clothes, and anything else, but not her photographs of Sophie.

As the door to the apartment closed, drowning out Mathieu's pleas that she reconsider, she walked faster, nearly throwing herself down the stairs and outside of the building. The sun hit her face, and she gasped for air as if she had been drowning. She put her hand against the cold concrete wall to steady herself while she took in deep breaths. She hadn't even noticed the figure approaching her.

She rose with a start when she realized someone was next to her and then relaxed when she saw the familiar face.

"What are you doing here?" she asked.

"Making sure you're all right." Simon offered her his arm to steady herself so they could begin walking away from the building. "And making sure you are staying at my place again. This is no time to prove how much you can handle on your own."

Nita was lost for words. She simply nodded while they walked down the street toward his apartment.

They had gone a couple blocks in silence before Simon softly said, "You really surprise me."

"What do you mean?"

"I was pretty sure he'd convince you to stay. You wouldn't have been the first that he's managed to charm."

She looked up at him while they continued down the street. "Then why were you waiting?"

He smiled at her. "Because I had hoped you wouldn't."

~

Back in Simon's apartment later that night, he poured a couple glasses of red wine and handed her one. The two of them walked back to the couch and sat down.

"I'm guessing tonight you'll trust me and take the bed," he said with a grin.

Nita laughed. "I would still hate to impose on you more than I have. I can manage here."

"I'm afraid I'm going to have to insist. My mother would slap me silly if she knew I'd let a lady spend even a single night on this sofa, let alone two of them. Careless mistake for sure. She is a force to be reckoned with, so you're saving me the grief if you just say yes." He raised his glass, and Nita did the same.

"What are we toasting?" she asked.

"Your resilience," he said as he clinked her glass.

Embarrassed, she politely took a small sip. "We should be toasting your kindness."

He shrugged off her praise. "This wine needs some cheese." Simon went to the refrigerator and retrieved a wedge of comté and a small plate and knife. He cut a few slices and handed her the first one.

"Your mother did raise you well," Nita said. "Not like what we heard about in India."

"What do you mean?"

"My parents always warned me that people in the West always put themselves first. Not like the collectivist community mentality we were raised with."

She felt like an impostor, suggesting she was included in the collectivist mentality. Her selfishness had been unparalleled, so maybe that's why she had felt the strong need to leave India, and those values, behind her.

She let the saltiness of the cheese linger on her tongue. "Never mind that my parents had not left India to know for themselves. Such a detail did not stop them from being an expert on Americans!"

"Not having the facts doesn't stop any parent from acting like they know everything!" Simon laughed but then grew more contemplative. "I suppose there are different types of people everywhere: some good and some bad."

"It's true. You're the first American I've ever met, though, so you have set a high standard for the rest!"

Simon swallowed his cheese. "No pressure. And you? How is a girl like you raised in India?" He refilled their empty wineglasses.

"If you ask my parents, I'm afraid they'd say not very well."

He laughed. "Somehow I doubt that. I've never—make that almost never—seen you act out of sorts."

She sipped from her wineglass, enjoying the taste of the smooth liquid that had once burned her throat on the way down. "It's a different place with different expectations. You'd be surprised how obedient girls can be. Raised to dote on their husbands and rear perfect children, all without ever having a single sari pleat out of place."

"If that's the case, then I'm packing up and moving there tomorrow!"

Now it was Nita's turn to laugh. "I somehow think you wouldn't be so thrilled with an arranged marriage. And with you not having a place in the caste system, they wouldn't even know what to do with you! Sure, vendors want American money, but marrying their daughters . . . that's something else entirely!"

"Fair enough. Guess I better stick to where I am."

Simon opened a second bottle, and with the wine flowing, they talked for hours, sharing stories about growing up in their respective countries and trying to explain things to the other person, who had never set foot in it. He couldn't believe how straitlaced Indian children were meant to be, and she couldn't believe the brazen behavior American children engaged in. If she had done half the things Simon said he and his sisters had done while growing up, like skipping school to go to the beach and drink beers with their friends, her papa would have swiped her straight across her bottom with his belt. She may have had her knuckles rapped with a ruler in school, but even she knew the limits to avoid the belt. She couldn't believe that Simon's mother would let such behavior go with simply a warning and a promise to never do it again, though he assured Nita that they never kept those promises and were just more careful not to get caught.

Simon picked up the bottle of wine from the floor next to the couch and stared into it as though he were looking into a telescope. "Seems we've gone empty again. Time to replenish the supplies."

Nita shrugged, knowing she was already drunk. Her words had been slurring, but she was too far in to stop herself from drinking more. She was right in that danger zone, but it felt good to relax for a night. She heard the cork releasing from the bottle, and Simon handed her a freshly filled glass of wine.

"This is fun," she said.

He plopped onto the sofa next to her. "It is. Funny how more alcohol leads to more fun."

"No wonder my family in India was so boring." She laughed. They'd already discussed how her home state was dry and she'd never tried alcohol until that first time when she had tried it with Mathieu.

"Also explains why you are such a lightweight." Simon playfully punched her arm. "Although you are managing to hold your own today. Just like a regular French wino."

Nita took another long sip from her glass, the liquid tasting earthy and rich as it slid down her throat. "I'm a quick study."

Simon nodded and leaned back against the sofa cushions and stretched out his legs. As soon as he did that, she heard the thump of the wine bottle hitting the floor. They both swooped down to pick it up and hit their heads instead.

"Ow!"

They jerked their heads back, and then Simon finally righted the bottle, but not before most of its contents had spilled onto the floor. Nita brought her face back down to stare at the red mess. Neither of them moved to clean it up and instead just watched the liquid snake across the floor.

"Maybe the universe is suggesting we stop drinking," Nita said.

"Or it thinks that wine wasn't good enough for us and we should open a better bottle," Simon said in a low voice, continuing to stare at the floor.

Nita laughed, and he eventually joined her in her drunken laughing fit. The two began laughing so hard that they held on to each other to keep from falling backward. Nita had tears in her eyes, and Simon's were glistening as well. She wiped hers with the back of her hand and then stared at the moisture on her skin.

"It's kind of nice to know these are from laughing and not sad crying," she said to him. "These past couple days—"

Simon's warm wine-stained lips were on top of hers before she could finish her sentence. She felt her eyes widen and wasn't sure what to do. Just as quickly as he'd kissed her, he pulled away, keeping his face close to hers and staring, as if waiting for a sign. She could tell that he didn't know if she was going to slap him and jump off the couch.

37

SOPHIE

2019

The wheels are turning in Sophie's mind as she tries to think of other ways to find Nita, and she is completely startled when she walks into the reception area of Le Canard Volant that night after her shift at the restaurant and sees Kiran sitting on the grimy purple sofa. She freezes as soon as she lays eyes on him.

He stands to greet her. "Hello, Sophie." He shifts shyly. "Or perhaps I should be saying *bonjour*."

She glances from him to the reception desk, where Cecile has muttered an annoyed *bonsoir* to herself and is watching the two of them. Sophie then turns back to Kiran. "What are you doing here?" she stammers.

"I came to see you." His words are careful, and he watches her intently.

From the reception desk, Cecile says, "He said he was a friend of yours, and asked if he could wait for you." She loiters about, like a mother elephant observing her calf.

Sophie waves her off and manages a smile. "Yes, Cecile, it's fine. We know each other from India."

Cecile nods and disappears into the small office behind the reception desk.

When they are alone, Sophie whispers, "What are you doing here?"

Kiran matches her hushed tone. "I wanted to see you. I had to pry it out of her, but Sharmila Auntie told me where you are."

"Maybe we should go for a walk," she says, guiding him toward the door.

The cool air is refreshing against her skin. There are only a few people on the streets, striding with purpose, given the late hour. Sophie feels safe walking with Kiran, and something about his demeanor has always made her feel like it's in his nature to protect others. It reminds her of the way she felt around Papa.

"I'm sorry to have shown up like this," he says, hands stuffed into the pockets of his jeans, into which his checked button-down shirt is tucked.

Other than their brown skin, the pair of them look very Western as they stroll down the streets in the Latin Quarter. They could easily be tourists on a trip.

"Why did you?" Sophie asks. "I'm sorry for leaving so suddenly, but I had asked my fois to pass along the message to your family . . ."

He nods. "And they did. They said you were gone for a couple of weeks, and then we would set a new date when you returned." He stared at her with a wry smile. "But I guess I knew better and wanted to see you myself."

"Oh."

Sophie feels bad for adding this drama to Kiran's life. This is the first time the two have been alone together, but there is an ease between them. Maybe it is the familiarity of being with someone from a similar background who understands her life. The past week has been a series of new experiences, all of them far beyond her comfort zone.

"I'm sorry they were not honest with you," she says softly. She never wanted him to be collateral damage in the mess that had become her life. "I learned some things about my family that I needed to explore, and I didn't think it would be fair to involve you in that."

They find themselves along the bridge, the city lights twinkling on either side of them and the river shimmering below. It is peaceful and quiet compared to the bustle of the city during the day. They lean against the thick stone wall of the bridge and take in the view.

"It's okay. I actually lied to you too," Kiran says as he turns to face her.

"What do you mean?" she asks, feeling nervous.

"I knew you when we were kids growing up."

She scans her mind for any memory of him but comes up empty. She wonders if he is just another person like Anjali and Saumil who is out to swindle her in some way and now wishes she wasn't standing alone with him on this bridge.

"It's nothing bad." He holds up his hands. "At least I don't think it is. We used to play together when we were kids. My family lived in your neighborhood for a few months. You were five, and I was eight. We played cricket in your yard with some of the other local kids, and I remembered how fiery you were about wanting to play with the boys. The memories stuck with me."

Sophie recalls playing cricket as a child with the neighborhood boys, but she had stopped playing after she'd been told Nita had died. She had stopped doing a lot of things after that. Papa wanted to keep her under his watchful eye for as much of the day as possible, so Sophie spent more and more time at home with him or her fois. But she doesn't have any specific memories of the other boys. She remembers the ones she grew up with, but there were some, like Kiran, who came and went, and Sophie would never be able to identify them today.

"A few months after we moved, my mummy told me yours had died, and I remember how bad I felt hearing the news. I could not have imagined such a loss as a child."

"Yes, well, apparently we were all duped." Sophie is surprised by the anger in her tone and even more surprised that she would share something so personal with someone she hardly knows. But thinking about Kiran and his family sending condolences for the fake death of Nita inflames her. It makes the lies and selfishness of Nita, Papa, and the other relatives more pronounced.

"What do you mean?"

Sophie stares at the Seine shimmering beneath them, the reflection of lights from nearby buildings dancing along its surface. "My mummy didn't die. She apparently just didn't want to be my mummy anymore." She chokes on the last sentence, her eyes glistening.

Kiran ignores Indian conventions and puts his arm around her shoulders. "I'm so sorry. I did not know."

She swipes the salty streams from her face. "Neither did I. Until last week."

"That's why you've come here? She lives here?"

Sophie nods, the warmth of his arm across her back. "I don't know exactly where she lives or even if she is still alive, given how many years have passed, but when she left us, she came to Paris, and now I'm trying to find her."

"What will you say when you do?"

She hasn't gotten that far in her thinking. What will she say? *I grew up fine without you! Where were you when I needed you? You didn't even say goodbye or call on my birthdays. Would that have been so hard?* But the most important question she has is simply, *Why?*

"I suppose I won't know until I find her."

"You haven't seen her yet?"

Sophie shakes her head. "It's why I'm still here. I think I'm close to finding her, and I can't go back to India until I've done that. And even after that, who knows how I will feel about anything after meeting her." She touches his arm. "It wasn't fair of me to hold you hostage during that process. You should go and live your life. Find a woman who wants to be a wife and mummy now. You deserve to move on to that next chapter."

He stares at her hand on his arm, and she pulls it away, worried she crossed some line.

"You've removed your ring," he says solemnly.

She watches him stare at her naked left hand. She manages a small smile and pats her waist. "It is a long story, but I have it hidden beneath my shirt. I did not want to flash expensive jewelry and make myself a target."

He nods, looking relieved. He is silent for a few moments, staring out at the city. "I'm not sure that I want someone else. To be honest, when my parents first suggested you, I was excited because I remembered that spirited young kid who would not take no for an answer. I didn't want the typical docile woman that my parents would think is a suitable match. Then when we met, it seemed that fire was gone, and I thought maybe it was because you had just lost your papa." He turns to her and smiles. "But now I see you here, and I see that light again."

Sophie has never thought of herself as fiery. That was a trait people had attributed to Nita but never to her. Sophie had been demure, obedient, and risk averse, but maybe that was all to please Papa. He certainly had never encouraged any spirited behavior.

"I'm afraid you might not know me very well," she says.

"Maybe so, but I want to learn more. I think we could have a good marriage still, Sophie."

"Kiran, this is not something I can answer right now. My priorities have changed, and it would be misleading of me to suggest otherwise." Sophie knows marriage is the next step in her life after she finds Nita, but who knows when that will be. She sees a kindness in Kiran, but she cannot expect him to wait until she resolves her unknown.

"I understand. You can take your time doing what you need to do here, and we can see where things stand after that. My parents are eager to marry me off, so maybe they will have someone new waiting when I return home," he jokes.

"It would not be the strangest thing," Sophie says with a smile, knowing it would not be unusual at all.

Marriages in their community are arranged practically overnight. Her own parents had known each other only four days before marrying. In the end, maybe that had been the problem for Nita.

He walks her back to the hostel and then hails a taxi to his hotel near the airport. As Sophie stands on the street, waving him off, she wonders if she will ever see him again. This man who is meant to be her husband has left a strong impression on her, and, in this moment, it seems less crazy for her to become his wife. She can't believe that he did not turn away from her in anger upon learning the truth. Most men she had grown up with would have, and she can't say she would have blamed them. Perhaps it is because Kiran and his family have spent time outside of India that he has a different perspective on life and marriage. That he wants to be with someone who isn't docile and demure is unheard of. Sophie and her friends had spent their lives grooming themselves to be the perfect doting wives because that is what society expects of them, and she had never challenged it. She had never considered that there could be any other way. It was not until she left her comfortable world last week that she started questioning whether there could be a different life and different path. Nita certainly had. And she is a part of Sophie, so now Sophie questions everything she has ever desired for her future.

38

NITA

Nita stared at Simon, whose eyes were searching hers for answers. His expression implored her to speak, to know if he had offended her. Instead, she leaned forward until her lips were on his. After a second, she felt his shoulders relax, and he took her face in his hands.

She knew this was wrong, but in that moment, it didn't feel wrong, and the wine kept her mind free of the usual thoughts and consequences that would have filled it. Kissing Simon was different from kissing Mathieu. Simon was tender rather than forceful in the way he approached her. It was almost like those first kisses she and Mathieu had shared outside Julien's studio. The night everything changed for her. She was surprised by how comfortable she felt on the couch with Simon, their arms around each other. She and Mathieu had not been like that for so long now.

The spilled wine on the floorboards was long forgotten as their breathing grew heavier and their arms began to clutch more tightly around each other. Simon's shoulders and chest were broader and heavier than Mathieu's skinny frame. Nita felt as if she were holding on to a strong board, and she felt protected, having it so close to her. Without her even realizing, her fingers had moved under his sweater and were sliding up the sides of his torso. He pulled slightly from her again, searching her eyes.

Her vision wasn't entirely clear, given all the alcohol.

"Are you . . . ?" he began.

Her cold fingers were warming against his skin. She nodded and leaned in to kiss him, her hands now moving from his sides to his chest, and she felt him inhale sharply. With hesitant gestures, he moved his hands from around her back to her sides, staying on the outside of her sweater, and then eventually to her chest, cupping her breasts with both hands. It was her turn to take a quick breath. They stayed like that, kissing and exploring each other's upper bodies with their hands. Nita's pulse was racing at the anticipation of feeling his skin closer to hers, and she leaned back and pulled her sweater over her head so that now the only barrier between his hands and her was her simple black bra. She tossed the sweater behind her and pushed her body against him until she was lying on top of him.

They continued searching each other's mouths with their tongues while their hands roamed softly across each other's bodies. When her fingers rested against the fabric of his jeans, he broke from her and propped himself up on his elbows.

"What's wrong?" she asked.

He kissed her forehead. "Nothing. But I don't want to do this on this old couch like teenagers." He swooped her up in his arms, carried her to the bedroom, and then gently placed her on the covers of the bed.

As he stood over her, he asked again, "Are you sure?"

She nodded and pulled him toward her. Their remaining clothes flew off, and he took her in his arms and brought her under the covers before resuming his task of covering her entire body with kisses and gentle caresses. Nita had never before felt this kind of arousal, where her body was aching to be closer to his but also not wanting what he was currently doing to ever stop. She wanted to remain in those moments, where she felt both desired and safe. Everything about his movements felt like he was in control and wanted to give her whatever she needed.

She willed him to continue but he paused suddenly, frozen. Frustration crept across his face, and he buried his head in a pillow.

"What is it?" she asked.

"I don't have any condoms."

She didn't want him to stop. She and Mathieu did not use condoms. When she had once suggested it, based on Dao's advice, he'd said he didn't like the way they felt and had trouble maintaining his erection with them. She hadn't pressed because she was unfamiliar with them, too, having been only with Rajiv and Mathieu and not having used them with either.

"We can stop. I'm sorry I got carried away," he mumbled from the pillow.

Nita lifted his face so that she could see his eyes. She snuggled closer to his body, her cool skin craving the warmth he radiated.

"It's okay," she said softly, helping him roll back on top of her. "I want to."

She saw his lips move as if he were seeking more reassurance, and she put her finger against them to quiet him and then wrapped her legs around him. They maintained eye contact as their bodies connected, the grin on his face showing he enjoyed the urgency he was bringing out in her.

Mercifully, he started to move faster, and she knew he was as excited by her as she was by him. His brown hair stuck against his forehead, damp with sweat. She wiped it away from his green eyes while they continued moving together, the two of them completely entwined. Eventually, he pushed deeper, and she felt a warmth inside of her.

He then immediately pulled out of her and grabbed a tissue from the nightstand to wipe her clean. "I got carried away. I meant to pull out sooner."

She nuzzled her face into his neck, feeling just as spent. "It's okay."

And it was. Until the next morning, when she woke up and realized what she had done.

~

Her head pounded as she searched the floor for the jeans and sweater she had been wearing the night before. She had already pulled her underwear from between the sheets and slipped it on. She couldn't figure out if she was hungover or maybe even still drunk, but she was starting to come to her senses and realize the consequences of her actions.

She heard the bed creak as Simon rolled over and let out a groan.

"What are you doing down there?" he mumbled.

"Just grabbing my things." Nita tried to make her voice sound nonchalant as she knelt on the floor and pulled her thin sweater over her head.

Despite their actions last night, she was embarrassed to have him see her now without her clothes. She squirmed into her jeans while remaining seated on the floor and out of his view.

Simon poked his head over the bed until he made eye contact with her. "Are you going somewhere?" he asked.

"I should go back to my place," she said.

"Your place?" he asked. "I thought you were done with Mathieu."

She rose to her feet, bringing her hand to her forehead, trying to ease the throbbing she felt behind it. "I am. Er, I was. I just—I don't know what I'm doing."

Simon scampered up from the bed, the sheets bunched around his waist, and came closer to her. "What's wrong? Is it something I did?"

She shook her head.

"Nita, what is it? Please tell me."

His eyes bored deep into hers, and she had to look away. "We shouldn't have done that last night. You're with Élise. And this, what we did, makes me no better than Mathieu with that girl," she said softly toward the floor.

"You are nothing like him," Simon said, his jaw tight. "Please don't think that."

She shook her head again. "We let alcohol interfere with our friendship."

Simon sighed. "Maybe we needed it to prove we shouldn't just be friends. I will call Élise today. Tell her we shouldn't continue our relationship."

She met his eyes, knowing she was unable to give him what he wanted. She didn't deserve someone like him after the choices she'd been making. Decisions he knew nothing of and would never respect if he did.

"Simon, I'm sorry. I need to go back and either work things out with Mathieu or get my things and go. But I can't continue to rely on you to bail me out of this mess."

He wrapped the sheets more tightly around his waist so they wouldn't drop when he let go and put his hands on her shoulders. "We don't have to move into anything, but you don't need to run back to him just to get away from me."

Her heart sank at him even having that thought. "I'm not trying to get away from you. But I need to figure out where my life is supposed to go, and right now, I don't have any idea where that is."

She grabbed her purse, confirming the photographs of Sophie were still in the inside pocket. As she moved into the living room, she saw the dried wine still on the floor and felt bad leaving him with that mess, but she knew she had to get out before he convinced her otherwise.

She walked slowly down the Paris streets, taking in the tourists passing by her and the shop workers loitering on the streets for cigarette breaks. She had grown up feeling like she was never going to be the perfect, dutiful Indian daughter her parents had hoped for. She had known she was different from the other girls. But she had never realized that she was capable of such disgusting acts as what she had just done. It was more than even she had thought she had in her. She reminded herself of the Gujarati proverb "Even in Kashi, crows are black." She had heard the saying many times as a child but had never been to Kashi until a few months before her engagement. In that holy city, she had joined the throngs of Hindus who flocked there to bathe in the Ganga River, hoping to cleanse herself of the dark thoughts that had always surrounded her, so she could be pure for the man she would eventually marry. She'd observed the crows while she was waist deep in the river, holding her mummy's hand as they waded in. Some birds had circled over the river while others rested on wooden posts, cocking their heads at the humans as if the people were intruding on their home.

Here she had been in the city she'd dreamed of as sacred, and now she had fully felt the weight of those words as she realized that, like a crow, she would be black no matter what city or country she was in. She wondered if this darkness had always been inside of her and Paris had just unleashed that beast, or if Paris and her dreams for a different life had created the monster. She no longer saw any good inside of her. The emptiness in her now made her realize that the unhappiness she'd felt in India was only the tip of the iceberg. She wondered if she had been so evil in a past life that this one was her penance. Whatever the reason, a part of her felt she deserved what was happening to her. A part of her wondered if she would ever feel joy or light again. Had she even earned that right? A part of her knew that the best thing she had done for her daughter was take that darkness away from her.

~

"You're back." Mathieu sounded relieved and smiled as she closed the front door to their apartment behind her. "It's not just to get your suitcase, is it?" His eyes flickered with worry.

She tossed the keys onto the counter and sat across from him at the bistro table. "You said you wanted to talk yesterday, so talk."

He nodded, as though he understood he had one chance.

"I do not expect you to forgive me in a single day, and you were right that things had gotten very difficult for us. The drugs were too much. We came together because of a shared love for our craft, and I want to get back to that place." He gestured to his easel and rose to bring her the canvas from it. "I've started painting again."

Nita looked at the portrait he had started of her, sitting in the bistro, the day he had approached her and they had gone to the Luxembourg Gardens for the first time. She couldn't help but smile as she thought about that day.

"It's nice," she said, not knowing what else there was to say about a painting of herself.

"I have a beautiful subject," Mathieu said, smiling fondly at her. "I was worried about you last night. Where did you go?"

Nita said the only thing she could think of and the thing she should have done in the first place. "Le Canard Volant."

Mathieu nodded. "I don't want to worry for you like that again. Please come home, and we will find a way to work through this. I will sleep here until you are ready." He gestured toward the sofa.

Exhaustion took Nita's body and mind. She didn't have better options, especially now that she'd ruined her friendship with Simon.

"I will stay for a couple nights, and we can see what makes sense from there."

Mathieu could not contain his smile.

"But you are sleeping on the sofa," Nita added.

39

SOPHIE

2019

The next day Sophie brings Cecile a cup of tea while she sits at the reception desk.

"Could I speak to you for a minute?" Sophie asks.

Cecile sips the tea and nods. "Of course. What do you need? Is it about the young man who was here yesterday?" Her eyes light up at the possibility of romantic intrigue.

Sophie heads toward the purple couch where she sat with Cecile the day they met, and Cecile follows her. Sophie takes a deep breath.

"No, it's not about him. I was not honest with you before," she says softly.

Cecile straightens her shoulders and puts the tea on the stained coffee table. "About what?"

"About Nita." Sophie rubs her hands together in her lap. "She's not my aunt."

Cecile's eyes narrow. "But why did you—"

"She's my mother."

Her eyes now widen. "Why not say that?"

Sophie's face falls, the weight of her story coming down on her. "Because it is hard to admit. I was told she had died when I was young and only just found out that she wasn't dead . . . she just left us and came here."

Cecile puts a hand on Sophie's leg. "Oh, child."

Sophie meets her eyes. "You didn't know she had a daughter?" Her voice has hope that Nita had at least mentioned she existed.

"I'm sure whatever happened must have been hard on her too," Cecile says.

Tears slide down Sophie's cheeks. Cecile's answer confirms her fears. In Nita's new life in France, Sophie did not exist. They sit quietly, with Sophie's sniffling the only sound, but it is not an uncomfortable silence. It is a heavy but necessary one.

Finally, she says, "It is true that my papa died. Nita's husband. I don't have anyone left in this world, and I need to find her."

Cecile squeezes her hand.

"Is there anything else you can remember about her? Anything at all?" Sophie asks. "I've gone to the bistro where she used to work and found the apartment she moved into after staying here. All of them have been dead ends. People remember her but don't know where she is now. Most haven't seen her for many years, it seems."

Cecile shakes her head. "I wish I could be of more help. We really lost touch after she moved in with her boyfriend."

Sophie cringes and suspects she will always have that reaction when hearing Nita had a boyfriend.

Cecile takes her hand again. "I'm sorry, Sophie. No matter what you hear about her life in Paris, I'm sure it doesn't say anything about how much she loved you."

Sophie nods politely but is unsure.

"Actually, maybe there is one other thing you could do. There was another girl here that Nita had been friendly with. An Asian girl who bartended in the Marais. Her name was Dara or Sun or something like that. I heard she eventually took over ownership of that bar and is probably not too hard to find. Maybe she knows something more." Cecile's eyes shine as she recalls. "Sangdao! That's it. Her name was Sangdao. I think we all called her Dao, though."

Sophie perks up like a monkey around fruit. She is grateful to have another lead, no matter how tenuous it might be.

"What is the name of that place? *Je vais le chercher.*" I will find it, Cecile mutters to herself as she gets up and retrieves her phone. A few searches later, she says, "Le Verre Plein."

40

NITA

Before Nita knew it, a couple days had turned into two weeks. It had started off with Mathieu sleeping on the couch, as promised, but then about a week in, after they'd gone through a couple bottles of wine, he had managed to find his way back into the bedroom with her. And she had let him. She had once thought she could never get over the picture of Mathieu with that woman, but having slept with Simon somehow eased that burden. And she suspected her secret dalliance had meant much more to her than Mathieu's had meant to him. So, when she pictured him with that woman in their bed, she replaced the image with Simon and her in his bed. Somehow that tit-for-tat logic was starting to work on her, and the pain she'd initially felt began to drift away.

Mathieu had gone back to a routine of going to the stall and was selling more paintings. She hadn't seen him pop a pill the entire time. They smoked cigarettes, but nicotine seemed to be the only substance around their apartment these days. By their earning more money and spending less of it on drugs, the tin box in the kitchen where they kept their cash started to fill up again. Nita wanted to do everything possible to sustain this, but in the back of her mind, she often thought of Rajiv's letter.

As she and Mathieu settled into their new routine, Nita did her best to avoid Simon but eventually could not continue to offer excuses Mathieu would believe. They were meeting Simon and Élise for dinner because Mathieu had yet to meet her at all and had been trying to arrange this outing for several weeks.

"Well, if it isn't the happy couple," he said as they walked into the dark bistro on a quiet street between their apartments. He greeted Élise with *bisous*. "You are the one that has stolen our dear friend's heart."

Élise smiled. "Not stolen, but maybe just borrowed."

Nita tensely let Simon kiss her cheeks, trying not to think about the last time his lips had been on her.

"It's been a while since we've seen you two," Simon said, placing the napkin on his lap and making eye contact with Nita.

Mathieu motioned for the waiter. "Nita has been keeping me busy with work. Trying to make an honest man out of me." He nudged her playfully, his eyes shimmering in the candlelight on their table.

"Is that so?" Élise said. She looked at Nita. "You'll have to tell me your secret to tame men so I can use it on this one too!"

Nita couldn't hide her surprise. *But Simon is already wonderful*, she thought.

Élise laughed, seeing the look of discomfort on Nita's face. "I'm only teasing. I had to import a gentleman from overseas because you Frenchmen can be so fickle with relationships." She directed her last comment to Mathieu.

He brought his hand to his heart, feigning pain. "You quarrel with our impeccable manners and love for love? At least we know how to select a proper wine."

They all laughed at the banter, and Nita tried to join in but was having a hard time masking her discomfort. After they placed their orders, she excused herself to go to the washroom. On her way out of the stall, she saw Simon standing by the communal sink.

"What are you doing here?" she whispered.

"Checking on you," he said.

She peered behind him, her anxiety rising. "What if one of them comes and sees us?"

"Then they'll see two friends who ran into each other in the bathroom."

Her movements around him were short and staccato, like a hummingbird flitting from flower to flower. "Simon, please."

He held up his hands in defeat. "Just tell me he's treating you well. I only want to know you are okay."

"I am. But I can't do this right now," she said curtly before brushing past him and pasting a smile on her face while she joined Mathieu and Élise back at the table.

~

That night, when she and Mathieu were at their apartment, lying in bed, Nita was the one to suggest they smoke some hashish. Mathieu raised an eyebrow but didn't question it and pulled out a joint from the nightstand and lit it before handing it to her. She inhaled deeply, holding the smoke as if that would also hold her thoughts. She wanted to forget about Simon, and drugs and alcohol were the best ways she knew how.

Mathieu grabbed her wrist and brought her fingers that were holding the joint to his lips so that he could take a drag. He closed his eyes, a peaceful look creeping across his face. Getting high had been an indulgence since Nita had returned, and it was a delicate balance that he tried not to disturb.

"Sometimes it's nice to not think about anything else," Nita said, taking another hit.

Mathieu nodded. "It's liberating."

"Liberating." Nita repeated the word slowly. It had been a while since she had gotten high, and she had forgotten how good it could feel.

The smoke lingered between them and around the bed while they finished the joint.

"Feeling better, *ma belle*? You were very quiet at dinner," Mathieu said.

"Was I?" Nita said absently.

"*Oui*. You did not like Élise?" he asked.

She shook her head. "No, she's fine. Why do you say that?"

"Just saw you did not speak to her much."

"Probably because I don't know her well," Nita said. "You know I take some time to warm up to people."

Mathieu leaned in to snuggle her neck. "Yes, *ma chérie*. That is true."

His breath tingled against her skin, and she moved closer to him. "Maybe I wasn't feeling well."

"Are you feeling better now?" he murmured.

"I don't know."

He tilted her head toward him, their hazy eyes making contact. "It seems something is the matter. You can tell me."

"I just want a night where I don't have to think about anything." She turned her head away but kept her body close to him.

"You're sure you want that?"

She nodded, staring off into space.

"I can help you with that, if you really want it."

She looked at him curiously. "What do you mean?"

He got out of the bed and started rummaging around in the wardrobe before sliding back under the covers, his fist clenched tightly around something.

"What is that?" she asked.

"I saved them for a rainy day." He kissed her forehead before opening his palm to reveal a stash of white pills like the ones he had said he'd stopped taking.

Nita didn't even challenge him about why he had them in the first place. Instead, she took two and popped them into her mouth without a second thought. She might not get high often, but she knew that for the rest of the night, she wouldn't be worrying about Simon or Mathieu finding out or anything else.

Mathieu smiled as he also took two pills and then encircled her in his arms and began kissing her body, removing any layers of clothing that stood in his way while he worked his lips down. The sex was a blur that night, but Nita didn't care because all she remembered was that she was able to pass out into a comatose sleep. It was the least burdened she had felt in years.

～

Two weeks later, Nita stared at herself in the bathroom mirror. Her hair was oily and stringy around her face. She hadn't washed it in over a week. Her eyes had wide dark circles beneath them, and her face was gaunt. Getting high had become routine again, and it meant her appetite had lessened considerably. She didn't ask Mathieu how he had managed to get more pills after they ran out of the ten he had initially presented to her. The answer didn't matter. What mattered more to Nita was that she had the pills at all.

But then she had woken up today realizing it had been seven weeks. She had always been so regular, but it had been seven weeks. Seven. The woman staring back at her from the mirror had the answer, but she wasn't ready to admit it. Her hand grazed her stomach, sunken in from the lack of food. It was already too late, and there was nothing she could do. She didn't tear up or feel distraught. She hadn't felt anything in such a long time that she didn't expect to now. She was used to feeling empty. She knew her world was going to change dramatically for the second time in the past year, but she couldn't bring herself to care. What she didn't know was far more important. She didn't know who the father was.

41

SOPHIE

2019

Le Verre Plein is small and dark, like so many places in Paris. Manoj and Sophie stride to the bar and take a seat on the round vinyl stools and wait for the bartender to finish chatting with some other customers. After pouring two glasses of wine for a couple at the other end, the bartender makes her way toward them.

She looks to be around the same age as Sophie's fois. The woman has thick black hair pulled into a bun, with silver hair around her temples. As she moves closer to them, her gaze fixes on Sophie. She falters for a moment and then catches her balance. A look of recognition flickers across her face before she shakes it off. Sophie feels the energy around her change, and she senses she is meant to meet this woman.

"How can I help you?" Her accent is British.

"Are you Sangdao?" Sophie asks, already knowing the answer.

"Only when my parents were yelling at me for misbehaving. God rest their souls," the woman says. Her makeup is heavy, green eye shadow and thick eyeliner, a stark contrast to the demure coloring

Sophie has seen on the French women throughout the city. "You can call me Dao. What can I get for you?"

Sophie feels Manoj's stare, urging her to get to the point.

"I'm staying at Le Canard Volant," Sophie says. "Cecile suggested we come here."

Dao's face lights up. "Oh, Cecile! Love that bird. I'd say I can't believe she's still at that place, but then people would say the same thing about me." She gestures around her. "Everyone comes to Paris with dreams. Whether they come true or not, no one ever leaves. We all settle for the next-best thing if it means we get to stay."

Sophie inhales sharply. "Cecile said you might have known my mother."

Sophie watches for that flicker of recognition again, but Dao is stoic for a few moments, processing what Sophie has just said.

Then, she says, "I think I did. But I didn't know she had a daughter." She looks intently at Sophie. "You are the spitting image of her. When you first came in, I thought I was seeing a ghost." She shakes her head, her mind seemingly now in the past.

Sophie's pulse quickens. "Do you know where I can find her?" Her voice is laced with hope and desperation. This woman is the one who is going to lead her to Nita. She feels it in her bones.

Dao's eyes widen at the question. She stares at Sophie a few moments longer, as if caught in the headlights of oncoming traffic. The wine bar is bustling, and the background noise becomes deafening while Sophie waits for an answer. Finally, Dao motions to a server. A blonde, petite woman in her thirties approaches, and Dao asks her to cover the bar for a bit.

To Sophie she says, "Let's talk in the back."

42

NITA

The next day, Nita met Dao in a café along Rue de Rivoli for some tea. Dao had reached out several times this past month to catch up with Nita, but Nita had been avoiding her. Dao's disapproval of Mathieu was not well hidden, but these were desperate times, and Nita needed a woman's advice.

"How is your family doing?" Nita asked her while they both blew on the steaming mugs of black tea in front of them. They hadn't seen each other since Dao had returned from London over a month ago.

"Dysfunctional as always. Upset that I'm not doing more with my life. Not living up to the weight of their sacrifices, blah blah blah. But they're family, so you have to love them no matter what, right?"

"Right." Nita took a deep breath, trying to push the thoughts of her own family aside.

"I take it you're still shacking up with our favorite Frenchie?" Dao studied Nita's face through her heavily lined eyes.

Nita had not told her about Mathieu's cheating or her affair with Simon. By the time Dao had returned from London, things were back to the status quo, so there didn't seem much point in poisoning her mind about Mathieu any further. Or in having Dao think as little of Nita as Nita currently thought of herself.

"Yes, still in the same apartment." Nita put her mug on its saucer. She traced the outside of the saucer with her finger, trying to figure out what to tell her friend.

Dao, who could easily fill silence with chatter, was being unusually quiet.

Nita knew she needed to just say the words, so she leaned over and touched her friend's arm. "I'm pregnant."

Dao's eyes did not leave Nita's face as she put down her mug as well. "You're sure? You went to a doctor and everything?"

"I haven't been to a doctor, but I'm sure."

She was sure because she'd been pregnant before. She knew the subtle shifts in her body that only she would notice: the tenderness of her nipples, which became irritated from wearing her bra; the light-headedness she felt after climbing the stairs to their apartment; the loss of appetite followed by an intense craving for spicy or sweet. Pregnancy was an unmistakable feeling, and she just knew.

"You can't be sure until you see a doctor. For all we know, you could be suffering from stress or indigestion or whatever. We've got to take you to a doctor."

"Dao, a doctor will tell me what I already know. It won't fix this. I told you because I need a friend to help me through this."

Nita could see Dao processing and holding back words that were desperate to leap from her lips. In Dao's expression, Nita saw that she understood that this was bigger than their usual unfiltered conversations.

"You haven't told Mathieu, have you?"

Nita shook her head.

"But you will?"

Nita nodded. "I must." To herself she added, *Or maybe I should be telling Simon.*

Dao's next sentence came out very measured. "He, uh, seems like he will, er, be a good father, right?"

Nita laughed at the lack of confidence in her friend's statement. "I know he wants to be a father, so maybe that is enough."

"Do you want to be a mother?"

Nita thought about her life leading up to now and answered in the most honest way she could. "I didn't grow up dreaming of being a wife and mother."

Dao leaned toward her and said softly, "Well, then maybe you should consider other options. You don't have to be a mother."

Nita would be lying if she said she hadn't thought about it. In some ways, it would be best for everyone, probably even the baby. But another part of her knew she couldn't. When she was pregnant with Sophie, it had been through obligation. She had known she was meant to have Rajiv's children, but it wasn't her dream, and she hadn't relished the task. But when she held Sophie in her arms and smelled her skin for the first time and felt the soft wisps of hair, something had changed in her. As she watched her start to grow up, Nita had grown to love her in her own way. Her time away from Sophie had taught her how much she loved that child and how much sacrifice was required to be a parent. Even though Nita had been a far from ideal mother, she couldn't imagine a world without Sophie in it, which was why she couldn't give up this child.

"I don't have that choice," she said.

Dao squeezed her arm. "I understand. And I'm here for you. Whatever you need."

Nita fell into her friend's arms and let herself feel the warmth of the embrace. The words "I'm here for you" had a power in them that was greater than any other, even the phrase "I love you." "I'm here for you" showed solidarity and acceptance and conveyed in the best way possible that one was not alone. Nita had felt alone in some way for most of her life, and her heart swelled at Dao's support for whatever decision Nita made. She was going to be a mother again, and, in this moment, all she needed was for someone to hold her and comfort her as if she were a child.

~

A little over a week later, on April 8, Nita found herself again thinking about Rajiv's letter. It was their anniversary, and she knew he was in Paris somewhere and would be at the Eiffel Tower that evening at five, just as he had said he would. He was always punctual. Several days earlier, she and Dao had gone to a clinic to confirm her pregnancy. She had not told Mathieu, and she wondered if it was because she had not yet made up her mind about Rajiv.

She told herself there was no point in going there. What could possibly be gained? It was not as though she could return to her old life and pretend none of the past eight months in Paris had ever existed. Especially now.

Still, as the sun began to creep down from the sky, her feet led her toward the Eiffel Tower. There was a chill in the air, and she tucked her hands into the pockets of her coat as she walked along the Seine on the north side of the river. Her hair was safely tucked into her beret to keep it from swirling around her face. She could see the Eiffel Tower to her left, looming larger as she moved from the second arrondissement to the first. She crossed to the south side of the river using the bridge near the Musée d'Orsay. Her pace slowed as the iconic landmark grew larger. As she neared the metal structure, the crowds of tourists enveloped her. The most popular place in Paris was the easiest one to disappear in. She knew she could go there without being seen.

It was also the part of Paris that reminded her most of Ahmedabad. The throngs of people milling around and hawkers selling cheap novelty items, like Eiffel Tower magnets and coffee mugs, from wooden crates suspended around their necks reminded her of the chaos of India. The people yelling "Souvenirs" and haggling with tourists made her think of nights she had spent in the Law Garden in Ahmedabad, a bustling outdoor market with street vendors and small stalls set up along the perimeter. There, too, people were selling knickknacks and harassing passersby to unload some rupees on a shawl or brass trinket. Rajiv had never liked the Law Garden because he preferred to avoid noisy crowds, and she suspected he felt the same way about the scene at the base of the Eiffel Tower.

Nita walked slowly down Avenue Gustave Eiffel, careful to look inconspicuous. She stopped behind a guided tour group, the leader explaining the history of the landmark in German. She peered between people, trying to see if she could spot Rajiv. It was only four forty-five, but she knew he would be there already. Not seeing him, she ducked through the tour group and moved a bit closer, now standing behind a crêpe cart with a long line of people. She heard the sizzle of the batter hitting the hot plates before the vendor deftly spread it into a perfect circle using a T-shaped wooden spatula. She inhaled the smells of sweet chocolate-hazelnut spread and caramelized sugar and lemon. She peered around the cart and scanned the crowd ahead, seeing many families and couples posing for photographs they would cherish for years to come. She did not see Rajiv and feared something had happened to him. It was the only reason a man like him would miss such an appointment. Her thoughts cascaded toward him being in a car accident or something happening to his plane and Sophie being left without a parent. His two sisters would then be left with the job of raising Sophie, and they had never been overly kind to Nita. She worried they would not treat Nita's daughter as their own. She'd have to return if that were the case. Leaving Sophie with her loving papa had been difficult enough, but leaving her in the care of anyone else was unthinkable. Nita would have to do what she and Dao had discussed with her pregnancy. She could not have a second child and show up in India again.

As her thoughts tumbled around her, she saw him. Standing in a camel-colored trench coat that she had commissioned from their local tailor several years ago, shifting his weight from right to left while his eyes searched for her face. He was no more than ten meters away from her. Gray hairs dotted his temples, standing out against his jet-black hair. He looked skinnier and frailer than she remembered. Her husband. She saw the faintest glimmer of hope in his expression, which otherwise reeked of doubt. He held an envelope the size of a flat sheet of paper, and she wondered what it contained. She also saw the thick gold wedding band he still wore on his ring finger. She had left hers behind on their dresser the day she walked out of their house and out of his life.

A lump formed in her throat, and part of her wanted to go to him, but her legs felt as though they were cemented to the ground. She watched him scanning the crowd for what seemed like an eternity.

"Did you want to order something?" the crêpe vendor asked her with his nose in the air, clearly suggesting she should move away from him if the answer was no.

"*Désolée,*" she said without taking her eyes off Rajiv and backing away from the cart to another place where she could still see him without being seen. Night fell as the hours passed, and it would have been even more impossible for Rajiv to have found her then, but he remained in place. The lights on the Eiffel Tower sputtered on, and revelers began photographing the monument again in a flurry. Rajiv pulled his coat more tightly around himself as the temperature dropped.

Rajiv was a man who had done nothing but care for and try to protect her. He represented honor and dignity, both of which she felt she no longer had. She remembered how young and innocent he had seemed—they both had seemed—on their wedding day. She had been twenty-three, and he had been twenty-five. Two kids who hardly knew each other or the ways of the world, about to embark on a life together. The concept was crazy. She'd always wished her culture permitted dating and allowed people to form genuine connections before marriage.

Having had that experience with Mathieu, she knew one thing for sure—she would never marry him. She knew enough to know that he would never make a good husband. Perhaps if she had dated Rajiv and seen his kindness before she had become his wife, she would have felt more like it was her choice—like she was less trapped. Perhaps none of this would have happened, and they would have lived happily ever after, and the baby growing inside of her now would have been Rajiv's—the long-anticipated sibling to Sophie that he had dreamed of. She shook her head free of the thoughts because that was not how life had worked out and there was no sense in pretending as if it had.

It was not until eight thirty, after over three hours of Rajiv standing in place and Nita watching from a distance, that Nita saw him move and sit on the raised cement blocks encompassing a small garden area. His shoulders slumped, and he stared at the envelope. He occasionally looked up and scanned the crowd, but Nita maintained her cover and watched from a distance. At ten thirty, he stood and started walking in the direction of the crêpe cart and her. Nita's pulse quickened, and she turned her back to him and slunk behind a group of tourists. He crossed no more than two meters away from her, and she could smell the talcum powder and almond oil that he used every day. She inhaled deeply. Even after this much time had passed, she knew the scent of her husband. It had not changed, even though she had. She stood and watched him walk away for several moments before turning and heading in the other direction, wrapping her arms tightly around herself to brace against the cold wind blowing against her.

~

"Where have you been so late?" Mathieu asked her when she walked into their apartment that night.

Mathieu was lying on the couch, a book propped open and resting against his chest. Nita crossed the room to join him, picking up his feet and sliding under them before placing them on her lap. It was an intimate gesture. One she'd never done with Rajiv and hadn't seen any wives do with their husbands in India.

"We need to talk about something."

Mathieu sat upright, worry crossing his face. He seemed perpetually afraid she was going to leave again anytime her mood was different. "Is something wrong?"

She closed her eyes and took in a deep breath, then released it slowly. Without looking at him, she said, "I'm pregnant."

She felt his legs tense on her lap. After a moment, he yanked them off of her and knelt on the sofa next to her, grabbing her shoulders and turning her toward him.

"*Tu es sûre?*" Are you sure?

She nodded.

His face broke into a huge grin, and he kissed her passionately. "This is good news! *Mais non.* This is *great* news!"

She forced a smile, not sure she agreed but trying not to spoil his moment.

He leaped off the couch and clapped his hands, pacing frantically around the room as if not sure where to go or what to do.

"We must celebrate!" He grabbed a bottle of champagne from the fridge and held it up victoriously. He popped the cork and filled two flutes with the bubbly liquid. He handed her one and then paused. "We will get married?" He asked it matter-of-factly, as if he were asking her if she planned to paint tomorrow, not revealing if he were leaning one way or another.

Nita panicked at the thought. "No, we don't need to do that."

"Okay," he said, raising his glass to meet hers. "We don't get married." He smiled again, his blue eyes shimmering. "But we have a baby. Beautiful baby." His eyes widened. "Baby boy, like me!" His voice was childlike as he said it. Then he shook his head and took her hand. "No, beautiful girl like you, *ma belle.*"

In France, marriage wasn't a prerequisite to having children the same way it was in India. Several of Mathieu's friends had had children out of marriage and continued living together as they had before. She could hardly believe she and Mathieu were about to join that club.

Nita looked at her stomach, and Mathieu put his hand gently against it as if he were afraid too much pressure would break the baby.

"Yes," she said. "We will have a baby."

Gnawing at the back of her mind as she said "we" was whether the baby was even Mathieu's to begin with. But it no longer mattered. In this moment with Mathieu, she had decided the baby was his, and now it had to be. She knew she was tainted with a darkness that affected everyone she was close to, so she could not bring Simon further into that fold. He would be a great father and husband, and he should have that choice, with Élise or anyone else he deemed worthy. Nita could not burden his future with her mistakes. She and Mathieu were having a baby.

43

SOPHIE

2019

Sophie and Manoj follow Dao through a cramped passageway leading to a tiny office that has papers littered over every flat surface, some coated with what looks like years of dust.

"Sorry, it's not the tidiest office. Filing has never been my forte," Dao says.

She moves some papers off two bistro chairs across from the desk so Sophie and Manoj can sit. She then moves some items off the desk chair and sinks onto it like a rock. She holds Sophie with her gaze as if she is afraid to drop her.

"So, Nita had a daughter," she says, finally. "How old are you?"

"Twenty-eight."

"Twenty-eight," Dao repeats to herself, rocking slightly in her chair. Sophie can feel her counting backward in her mind.

"You grew up in India?" Dao asks.

Sophie nods. "All my life. This trip is my first time leaving home."

"Nita had a daughter," Dao says again to herself, closing her eyes and pressing the spot between her eyebrows.

Sophie sees Dao's expression change, as if she has put together the final pieces of a puzzle that she had been trying to solve for years.

"I'm so sorry you've come all this way," Dao says. "And I'm even sorrier to be the one giving you this news." She locks eyes with Sophie. "She did many paintings of a little girl—always the same face—and I'm sure they were of you."

Sophie feels Manoj near her, leaning forward and hanging on to each of Dao's words.

"Nita was a good friend to me. One of the most interesting women I've ever met in my life. She had spunk, that one. Grit and determination, when she first arrived in Paris." Her eyes are wistful. She leans closer to Sophie, her expression sympathetic. "I'm sorry to tell you this. You have no idea how much. But Nita died many years ago."

Sophie has been told Nita had died before, but this time is different. Even though she believed it to be true when she was a child, as an adult she now feels the weight of it. The words replay in her mind, all other sounds drifting away. Her mummy has died a second time to Sophie.

Sophie is surprised she's not crying upon hearing this news. She is more confused than anything else. While she had always known it was a possibility, she hadn't let herself believe that Nita could be dead because it seemed too cruel a fate. Finding the letters had felt like her destiny. She had thought the universe was sending her a sign that she could reconnect with Nita and they could forgive the past and move forward as a family. Now she feels angry. Not only had Nita abandoned her and Rajiv twenty-two years ago, but her lies had led to this recent bout of hope for Sophie, at a time when hope was hard to muster.

Even though nothing has changed, everything has. She had started to believe that these leads, these snippets into Nita's past, could not have been for naught. They were leading to a new path in Sophie's life. A rekindling of a long-lost bond between mummy and child that could survive the twenty-two-year hiatus. But those hopes and dreams have just been dashed. And in some ways, it is a relief. Sophie reverts to the person she was before this journey. The person who thought that Nita had missed her birthdays and Diwalis and dance recitals because she had died many years ago. Some part of that is true again. Only now, Sophie's thoughts shift to whether Nita would have missed those events in Sophie's life even if she had been alive. She'd certainly missed some by choice before she died, and why should Sophie think she wouldn't have gone Sophie's entire life without ever seeking her again?

"What happened to her?" Sophie says slowly. Her quest now is just one for answers.

Dao sighs, and her expression hardens. "She had taken up with a man here. Someone who did not bring out the best in her, or in anyone else for that matter." Her tone makes evident what she thinks of him. She looks at Sophie as if trying to decide how much to say to the child of her old friend.

Sophie's eyes plead with her to share everything. The two women say more to each other in this silence than they could have ever said with their words.

"Your mother was an amazing woman," Dao says, "but she had her weaknesses. This man was among them. When she arrived in Paris, she had the innocence of a saint! Had never smoked, drank, dated. It was amazing to see a woman in her thirties who had been so sheltered! She was easy prey for a debonair French artist searching for his muse. I think she was that to him, in the beginning—his muse. He doted on her like a puppy chasing after its master. But then he turned, as men often do." Dao's face clouds over. "He had many vices. It started off with drinking and smoking, but eventually he introduced her to harder drugs, and she was in too deep to think straight anymore."

Sophie gasps. How can this woman be speaking about Nita? Cigarettes and alcohol were hard enough to imagine, but drugs were something else altogether!

Dao reaches across the table for Sophie's hand. "I'm sorry to tell you this. She was a beautiful woman, and maybe it's better if we stop here."

Sophie shakes her head, urging her to continue, knowing she needs to summon the strength to hear these words.

"Are you sure?"

Sophie looks at Manoj and sees his unwavering support, and then she nods.

"Mathieu was so good at getting her to bend to his will. As I got to know her, I learned your mother had a lot of pain buried deep inside of her. She was very troubled. She tried to keep it to herself, but occasionally she would slip and reveal how much she was struggling to find her place on this earth. It chewed at her constantly. She'd often mutter to herself that crows are black everywhere, and whenever I asked her about it, she said it was an old Indian proverb, but I think it was something more to her. A burden she carried, and I think she used the drugs as an escape. It seemed like she was trying to run from so many things. Something would happen, and she would tell me she was cleaning up her life again and going to pick up her painting and get back to why she had come to Paris in the first place, but then Mathieu would come along, and they would slip back into their old ways. I guess that's the struggle of addiction, though. One step into the light, and then four steps back into the darkness. It was a very sad spiral to watch." Dao squeezes Sophie's hand. "Such an ugly disease. And one that affects the people left behind as much as, if not more than, the person with it. When you lose someone you love like that, it haunts you every day. Always wondering what you could have done better or differently to help." Dao leans closer and takes Sophie's hand in both of hers. "She did want to be better, though. She tried. I really believe that she did."

Sophie swallows the lump in her throat that has formed while Dao has shattered her images of Nita. Sophie rolls the name "Mathieu" around on her tongue and can almost taste its bitterness. With a name, she can now conjure up a whole persona and life story of this villain she's been concocting in her mind. Still, she gestures for Dao to continue. The truth, however hard, is the only way she can move forward.

Dao inhales sharply. "The saddest part was that she had finally decided to leave him and go back to India and get away from all that madness with him. It had seemed real that time. Not like the ones before, which were halfhearted in their delivery. It really seemed like she had turned a corner and was going to beat the addiction this time around. She knew it was the best thing for her and Vijay, and if they could just get on that plane—"

"Who's Vijay?" Sophie cannot stop herself from interrupting.

Dao's eyebrows raise. "Nita's son."

Sophie's eyes widen. Son? *Son?!* She has a brother?!

44

NITA

1999

To solidify her decision, she'd been rather deft at dodging Simon after sharing the news with Mathieu. If he suggested meeting Simon and Élise, she would say she wasn't feeling well and wanted to rest because of the baby. It was her free pass to avoid anything, and Mathieu always obliged and would let her stay home while he went out.

So, when she exited their apartment building one morning and found Simon leaning against the wall waiting for her, she was not surprised. He had a navy scarf tied around his neck, and his face was tinged red, as though he had been standing in the cold for some time. Even though it was late April, the frigid winter had not yet relented.

"You've been avoiding me," he said, his voice even but his eyes showing his concern.

"I have," she said, staring at the ground.

"Is it because it's mine?"

She whipped her head to meet his eyes. "It's not."

"How do you know?"

She hoped the baby was Simon's. She hoped it with every fiber of her being. He was a good man, far better than Mathieu, and she could admit that to herself now even if she couldn't have before. A child with Simon's heart had a much better chance in life than one with Mathieu's. Yet she had made her choice, and she was locked into it now.

"I just do."

He took a step closer to her. "But we didn't use—"

"Simon, it's not. And thank the gods. How could we ever explain that to Mathieu or Élise?"

He looked hurt. "So right after we were together, you jumped back into bed with him?"

She let out a slow breath. "Isn't that what you did with Élise?" she said, her tone not accusatory but matter of fact.

"I would break up with her and raise this baby with you if it's mine."

And she knew he would. That's why she hoped the life growing inside of her was half of this man standing before her. A man so good that he made up for her bad.

She smiled appreciatively. "Fortunately, none of us have to do that."

Softly, he said, "I would break up with her and take care of you and the child even if it's not mine."

Nita could not fathom how a person like Simon could exist. So kind and resolute in his goodness. She had to believe that it was something he had been born with. Something she had not. Something she hoped the baby would have inside of it.

She put her hand against his cheek, wishing she could agree to his generous offer and change her story. If only he had the power to do that. But she worried more that she'd change his. That she'd drag him down to where she was and he would lose himself trying to save her.

"Mathieu would never allow that," she said. "And it would not be a good life for you either. Simon, you should be free to pursue every dream you have in life. Go make beautiful art and beautiful babies with a woman who is less complicated."

His face fell, the resolve seeping out of his expression. He thrust his hands into his pockets, seemingly disappointed by their conversation but accepting her decision. He motioned for them to walk down the street in the direction she had been heading when she first exited. "Mathieu seems very excited," he said.

"He's been talking about a child for a while and was hoping I would come around. It seems the decision was made for us."

"You didn't want to be a mom?"

"I didn't know."

"And now?"

"As I said, the decision has been made."

"I think you would make a great mom."

He had no idea how wrong he was, but she said, "Thank you."

"Has Mathieu cleaned up his act?"

She shrugged. "He's being very attentive."

"I meant has he stopped with the drugs?"

Nita paused. It hadn't been like before, where he would get high and stay in bed for days on end, but after she learned about his secret stash of pills, he became more comfortable pulling them out, and she hadn't been able to resist the urge to join him. The feeling of floating away for even a short while was euphoric. She knew all too well the sleepless nights filled with noisy crying and dirty diapers that awaited them, only this time there would be no servants to help her with the child-rearing. She'd convinced herself that if she didn't indulge too often, it would be fine, tucking away the voices in her head that knew she was harming her baby and the ones even deeper within her that said it wouldn't be a bad thing to lose the baby and keep it from entering such an unstable life, but she couldn't share any of this with Simon.

Instead, she said, "People don't change overnight, but he's gotten better."

As they neared the corner where Simon would continue straight to go to his apartment and Nita needed to veer left to go to the market, Simon turned to her and said, "If you ever need anything, I want you to come to me. It doesn't matter what it is."

Her heart ached for this man who was willing to offer her so much more than she had ever deserved.

"We're going to be okay," Nita said, trying to convince herself as much as Simon.

~

Around the fifth month of her pregnancy, Nita was now showing in her normal clothes. Mathieu had tired of being the devoted boyfriend and future father and had moved from the ecstasy pills to powder cocaine that he would snort off a small mirror. Nita had tried it once and found herself energized and happy. The two of them had had so much fun that night, jumping on the bed like schoolchildren until they were out of breath. She was surprised they hadn't broken the springs. Or the baby. She was constantly conflicted, wanting to do better by the child than she had done by Sophie but also afraid that she was incapable of doing any better. She wondered if her inability to stop her reckless behavior was an attempt to dislodge and save the child from the life it would have with Nita and Mathieu.

Now that her body was feeling more run down and she had less energy, Mathieu was tiring of having to do everything around the apartment and worrying about having enough money to support them and eventually a baby. He was also getting increasingly irritated that she wasn't in the mood for sex, complaining that with all his added work he needed a "release" when he came home. Nita tried to oblige him every few weeks, letting him mount her and do what he needed, but he could tell her heart was not into it, and it became a mechanical act for them both. This was a far cry from the life she wanted, but it was the life she had, and she had no one to blame but herself, so she swallowed the pain and an occasional pill to calm her enough to get through the days.

As she delivered their baby boy in late November, part of her couldn't believe that she had carried him to term. She had taken so many risks with her health and his that it was a miracle to have delivered a healthy boy. When the nurse handed her the small baby wrapped in a cloth, crying and thrusting his arms and legs, she wept uncontrollably. He should not have been as perfect as he was, given all the anguish Nita had put him through during her pregnancy. She saw similar features in this new boy and Sophie. Would she be better this time? Would she be able to care for him without leaving him the way she had left Sophie? She gritted her teeth, asking herself what kind of person had another child when she'd already left the first one. She didn't deserve this second chance, and she knew it. She could not stop the tears.

Mathieu thought her tears were of joy. He could not fathom the depths of her despair at holding her second baby. He, too, wept the first time he held the boy in his arms, but his were the pride and love of a new father, and Nita hoped he would always be the father he was in that moment. Perhaps it would be a turning point for them both. In the first days that passed with her new baby, she tried to convince herself that she would step into the mother role to which she had not been able to commit with Sophie. But then she would feel guilty for thinking that. Why should this child get more of her than she had given her firstborn? But she pushed that thought away as well. The innocent boy with the light-brown eyes and dark hair deserved the best of her. He had not asked to be brought into this world, and she could not blame her circumstances on him. The best she could do was find a way forward and trust that Sophie and Rajiv had built a happy home for themselves. One that was more stable and loving without Nita in it.

~

Nita named her son Vijay, meaning victory, because she sensed this child would need to persevere through much, given the life she had built around them. In India she'd fought to give her daughter an unconventional French name, but now that she could name her child anything she wanted, she had opted for a name from her home country. Mathieu found it exotic and had always despised how generic his name was in France, so it was no trouble to convince him to go with an Indian name.

The baby's cries filled the room in the middle of the night and forced Nita and Mathieu awake. Mathieu groaned and rolled over, covering his ears. "Can you deal with him?"

Nita knew there was no point in arguing. The novelty of fatherhood had already worn off for Mathieu by the time Vijay had turned a year old. Nita rolled out of bed and made her way to the crib that occupied the space in the living room that had once served as their art studio. Dried paintbrushes had been thrown into a box in the corner, and neither of them had bothered cleaning them since Vijay had been born. The child had sucked the energy out of them, and there was none left to carry out their creative passions.

Nita picked up Vijay and held him close to her chest, swaying from side to side to coax him back to sleep.

"It's okay, beta," she said, using the same term of affection she had used with Sophie and her parents had used with her.

Vijay continued to wail, an impressive sound coming from his tiny mouth, his eyelids clenched tightly and showing no signs of relenting. She paced around the room, murmuring to him, but he was inconsolable. After a few minutes, she saw Mathieu standing in the doorway of their bedroom, his hair disheveled from his head being against the pillow.

"Can't you shut him up?" he asked groggily.

Nita glared at him. "If I could do that, don't you think I would have by now?"

"It seems like something is wrong with him. He cries way too much."

"He's a baby."

"Yes, but this doesn't seem normal even for a baby."

She sighed. "Of course it is."

"How would you know?" he spat out at her. "You've had the same amount of time with babies as I've had."

She turned her back to him, pretending she was adjusting her grip on Vijay. "I just do."

"There has to be a way to shut him up," Mathieu said again.

Nita kept pacing around the room, exaggeratedly bouncing her step to calm her son. "You were the one who wanted children in the first place."

Mathieu began to retreat to the bedroom. "Just give him a bottle or something so he can't fuss that much. I need some sleep."

Nita rolled her eyes, knowing Mathieu was going to self-medicate again by taking some morphine to help him sleep. It had become a ritual for him and, occasionally, for her.

Nita looked at the writhing, screaming child in her arms as she paced around their small apartment. She would have traded anything for Rajiv and the servants who had helped her care for Sophie. Doing everything on her own was so challenging, especially with Mathieu sinking back into one of his funks, during which he would stay in bed for days on end, or, if Vijay was too loud, leave in the middle of the night without a word as to where he went, only to return a few days later, unshaven and unkempt. Sometimes he said he went to Simon's, but Nita suspected that was a lie. They'd seen very little of Simon since the baby had come.

"Please go back to sleep," she begged the child. "I'm so tired, and I just need to sleep for a few hours. Then we can start this game again." She dropped onto the couch, cradling the boy in her arms as she rested her head against the back cushion. She closed her eyes, trying to tune out the noise for a few moments, but could not. She unbuttoned her top, hoping that feeding Vijay would calm him down or at least make it difficult for him to scream for a few minutes. She exposed her breast and brought him to it, allowing him to latch on and begin suckling.

Finally, peace at last, she thought while she fed him. She prayed that when he was finished, he would be satisfied enough to return to sleep so she could do the same. After a couple minutes, he began fussing again and turned his face away from her breast. As soon as he had cleared it, he let out another wail.

"I don't know what you want," Nita implored him, but he kept going, and she closed her eyes.

A few minutes later she heard Mathieu enter the room. He was wearing jeans and looked restless. She had stopped asking him where he could possibly be going in the middle of the night while she cared for their crying baby.

"When will you be back?" she asked.

He shrugged as he slung his satchel over his shoulder and shuffled out the front door.

"I hope he's not your father," she said to the boy whose caramel features did not reveal whether he looked more like Mathieu or Simon. "Please have Simon's goodness inside of you," she said as she cradled the screaming child.

Nita tried to rock Vijay, but she was exhausted. Maybe she should have listened to Dao and taken care of her pregnancy when she'd had the chance. Then she could have gone back to India with Rajiv and returned to her old, comfortable life. It was not as if she were pursuing her painting anymore. She couldn't remember the last time she had held a brush in her hand. Most of the art Mathieu sold at the stall now wasn't even theirs, and it was work produced by friends or Simon's or Julien's students, and Nita and Mathieu kept only a small portion of the sales as a commission. It was partly why they were so broke all the time.

~

When Mathieu returned home two days later, his eyes had bags underneath them and his face was dotted with whiskers poking through his skin. Nita was washing bottles while Vijay slept in his crib. She shushed Mathieu the second he opened the door, pointing to the sleeping child. He nodded and motioned for her to follow him to the bedroom. He produced a paper sack from his satchel and dumped the contents onto the bed. A spoon, a needle, a lighter, and some heroin.

"I thought you could use some sleep," he said.

She had tried heroin once before with him, and it had been the best sleep she had ever had. Half a day later she felt like she had risen from the dead, in the best way possible. Not even the baby's cries had gotten through her slumber.

Her exhausted body quivered at the thought of peaceful sleep. "Who's going to take care of Vijay when he wakes up?"

"How long has he been asleep?"

Nita closed her eyes to think. "Maybe twenty minutes."

"He will be asleep for a while, then. We should be fine."

Nita was not so sure, but she couldn't turn down the prospect of rest. "Just a little," she said, lying on the bed while Mathieu filled a syringe and held it up to his face and flicked it a couple times to make sure there were no air bubbles. She closed her eyes, having always been afraid of needles, and let Mathieu adjust her to expose the vein in her elbow crease. She felt a pinch as the needle pierced her but knew the pain would be worth it when she was resting. She felt pleasure take over her body, like being wrapped in a warm towel after stepping out of the shower, while the drugs worked through her body. Her mouth became dry, but her limbs felt too heavy to move, and she had no energy to get up and find water. The drowsiness set in, and her thoughts and worries about Vijay and everything else melted into the background as a small smile spread across her face. She was going to be free . . . even if only for a few hours.

~

By the time Vijay was two years old, Nita had given up on her art entirely. She didn't even think of it anymore. Her French was now good enough that she had managed to get a job waiting tables at a bistro in the second arrondissement. Most of the patrons were tourists anyway, and they needed English servers, so the owner did not care that her French was heavily accented. Her wages had become the only steady income used to support Mathieu, Vijay, and herself. Mathieu had found himself bouncing between highs and lows, depending on his drug du jour. Nita often worried about leaving Vijay home alone with Mathieu, but she had no choice, given she was the only one willing and able to hold down a job. She had begun to crave the drugs, too, so she didn't even ask Mathieu how he managed to procure them with so little money. She knew how resourceful he could be when he needed a fix.

She came home from work exhausted one night around midnight and found Mathieu and Simon sitting on the couch, smoking a joint and listening to some music on the radio. Vijay was crawling around the living room, pushing a red toy ball around the floor. He brought his little body to standing when he saw her and reached his arms toward her. She scooped him up and gave him a kiss before turning to the adults.

"What are you doing?" she asked. "I told you to put him to bed by nine."

Mathieu's eyes were bloodshot, the same as Simon's. Crumbs from the half-eaten baguette on the coffee table dusted his shirt.

"What time is it?" he asked.

"After midnight," she said, her lips pursed.

He turned to Simon. "You said you would remind me at nine!"

Simon stared at his watch, narrowing and widening his eyes as if trying to put it into focus. "She's right. We're late."

"How long have you been high?" she asked, cradling Vijay on her hip and taking him to the refrigerator in their small kitchenette. "Did you even feed him?"

She opened the door to the fridge and saw the full bottle of milk and had her answer. She would have been furious had she been less tired. The truth was that she had wanted to come home after her eight-hour shift and find a sleeping Vijay so that *she* could smoke a joint and relax before she had to wake up tomorrow and do it all over again. Vijay nuzzled her neck while she heated his bottle, and tears stung her eyes.

How did everything get so fucked up? she thought while looking at Simon and Mathieu.

Simon moved to stand from the couch. "Sorry, Nita. We should have taken better care of the little guy."

She glared at him. "Yes, you should have." Her look said that she expected better from him than she did from Mathieu.

"Won't happen again. But you should know it was my fault and not Mathieu's." Simon approached her and Vijay and ruffled the soft dark hairs on his head. "Sorry, buddy. Your dad and I got carried away because we'd had a rough day."

Nita's eyes asked him what he meant. If Mathieu was going to be in one of his moods again, she wanted to know why so she could avoid a fight. She was too tired to argue with him.

"Élise and I broke up. No big deal. Probably for the best."

"I'm sorry to hear that." She didn't want to pry into Simon's personal affairs, so she brought the warmed bottle to Vijay's mouth and readjusted him so he could drink.

"Turned out she didn't want to settle for an artist long term when her parents were able to set her up with a stable banker." He ran his hand through his hair, trying to seem nonchalant about it.

Nita wondered if Mathieu had shared his story of losing his first love. Seemed there was a theme between women and starving artists, and only Nita had been dumb enough to stay.

"She's wrong to think that," Nita whispered so that only the two of them could hear. "A good man isn't measured by his money."

Simon shrugged. "No need in her staying if she's not happy."

Nita looked past him to Mathieu, who had passed out on the couch. She wasn't happy, and she was staying. But that's because she had made a mess of her life and was saddled with a child now and had no other options. Élise had been careful not to put herself in that position, and, for that, Nita was envious.

~

Nita's thoughts were jumbled and cloudy, but she heard a familiar voice. She squinted her eyes to discern where it was coming from.

"Maman?"

The room felt like it was shifting beneath her, and she tried to steady herself even though she was already sitting on the floor. Sunlight crept through the narrow slit between the curtains above the bed. Her heartbeat quickened upon her not knowing who the stranger in the room was.

"Maman?"

The high-pitched voice was closer now. The sun was blinding her, and she could not see anything beyond that light. She stretched out her hands, trying to find the voice but feeling nothing other than the air around her.

"Maman." It was more urgent now. She felt a tug on her sleeve and brought her focus to the small hand pulling at her. Her eyes followed the skinny limb to a bony shoulder that eventually led to a gaunt face. She knew that face. She strained her mind to give it a name. Vijay. She

felt her pulse lower upon identifying the source. The tugging continued, and she forced her eyes to remain open.

"Maman, j'ai faim." I'm hungry.

Nita's head rolled from looking at her four-year-old son to the sunlight peeping through the curtains. She glanced around the room, trying to orient herself. She had no idea what time it was. She couldn't even remember the day.

"Maman, j'ai faim."

She brought her attention back to her son, blinking and squinting to bring his features into focus.

"J'ai faim," Vijay said again, his voice a cross between whimpering and resigned. *"Tu es encore malade?"* Are you sick again?

Encore. She mulled the word over in her mouth, tasting it like she could taste the metallic tinge of the heroin on her tongue.

Finally, she could muster words. *"Il y a du pain sur la table."* There is some bread on the table.

Vijay shook his head. *"Je l'ai mangé hier."* I ate it yesterday.

Yesterday? What day is it? she asked herself.

"Où est ton père?" Where is your father?

"Il est malade aussi. Dans le salon." He's sick too. In the living room.

Nita's maternal instincts to help her son were repressed by the drugs still coursing through her system. She saw the needle she had used was just under the bed beside her. An easy target for Vijay to grab, and she could have done little to stop him in her current state. She couldn't remember how it had gotten so bad. They only got high when Vijay was asleep so they could care for him when he woke up. That had been the rule. But she couldn't remember if they'd followed the rule this time.

"J'arrive." I'm coming, she said, telling herself she would close her eyes for just a moment and then go find Vijay some food. That was the last thing she remembered when she woke up again. This time the room was pitch black.

She found Vijay curled on the floor of the living room, sucking his thumb. She stumbled toward him and cradled him in her arms. Vijay did not react to her and continued sucking his thumb. Mathieu was passed out on the couch, oblivious to them. Tears slid down Nita's face and onto Vijay's soft brown hair.

"I'm so sorry," she repeated as she rocked back and forth with him and wept. His body felt frail and delicate, like the beggars who'd used to pass by her house in India. "I'm so sorry."

Vijay's stomach grumbled, and she scampered to the kitchen, throwing open the cabinets and fridge to find something to feed him. The fridge had some soft cheese that had grown mold; the milk smelled sour. The cabinets had some condiments but no real food. On the counter were stale bread crumbs from the baguette.

"Why are you making so much noise?" Mathieu grumbled from the couch.

"Because our son is starving!" she barked at him, continuing to frantically open drawers and cabinets as if some food might magically appear.

Mathieu squinted and looked around the room with one eye open until he landed on Vijay. "He's asleep. He's fine."

"He's not fine! None of us are fine! He hasn't eaten for god knows how long and doesn't even have the energy to sit himself up."

"Then why don't you get him something?" Mathieu asked, his voice groggy.

"*Putain!* What do you think I'm doing? We have no food!" She eyed the brown paper bag that had their stash of heroin in it and flung it to the ground. "All we have are these damn drugs!"

Fresh tears sprang, and she fell to the floor. "It has to stop!" She gasped for air, but it wouldn't come to her. She could not catch it in her mouth. Her breathing heavy and shallow, she said again, softly to herself, "It has to stop."

While she knelt in the kitchenette, her body convulsing from her erratic breathing, she felt a small hand reach out and touch her knee. She covered it with her own hand, her gold bangles catching the light, and managed to smile at her son. "Beta, it's going to stop. I promise." She pulled him toward her and kissed the top of his head. "We are going home," she said, with the fiercest of determination.

In that moment, she decided that no matter what happened to her, she had to give this innocent boy a better life. She could not do that with Mathieu. And she could not do that in France. She had to go back to Sophie and Rajiv and her parents and her life in India if she were ever going to feel whole again. She had to hope that they would take her back. That they could move past the hurt she had caused. At least in India, she had help, and Vijay could be taken care of even when she failed to do it herself. He would be warm and well fed and educated. He would have a chance at life. He deserved that. He did not deserve to suffer in the hell she had created for them.

Part of Nita had died the day she left Sophie, and the rest of her was dying now as she watched Vijay suffer because of her inability to control her own actions. She had been so broken and so lost in the depths of her mind for so much of her life. She couldn't recall being any other way, and yet she knew the people around her—people like her parents and Rajiv—didn't share those same struggles. She had convinced herself that she just had to find the right situation, and then she would feel the same contentedness that they felt. She had to change her circumstances and had gone to such great lengths to do it. But what she found on the other side of that was even more pain than she had known before.

It was only ten days until her anniversary with Rajiv, and she knew he would be standing at the Eiffel Tower, waiting for her, just like he had done every year since she left. Each year she had watched him from afar, but now she knew she must approach him and tell him she was ready to go back home. She had dreaded the thought of India for so long when she had first arrived, but now it felt like salvation. It felt like an escape, as much as Paris had when she had first left Ahmedabad. She had been young and immature and, above all else, selfish. She could not undo her past wrongs, but she could try to make amends in the future. If Sophie and Vijay had happy, healthy lives, then she would have done enough. She would have left the world with more good than the bad she had wreaked upon it.

Even if her family didn't accept her, they had to accept this child. Rajiv was the most compassionate man she had ever met. If he wouldn't take her son, then she would have to curry favor with her parents again. But she knew Rajiv would take them both. Vijay was Sophie's brother, and Rajiv would never deprive her of that. Nita had a lifetime of sins to atone for, and she knew she had to do whatever it took to do so. The people in her life whom she had abandoned deserved that from her. She deserved that for herself. She had to leave this world a better person than she had been for the past six years.

As she felt the cold floor against her legs, she was reminded of one of Rajiv's favorite proverbs: Pavan ni disha na badali shako, pan amara sadh ni disha badali shako. *The direction of the wind cannot be changed, but we can change the direction of our sails.* He had constantly said that to Sophie. Trying to teach her to accept what life threw at her and to adjust her responses. He had said it often, and Nita had wondered if he was saying it as much to Nita as to Sophie.

She looked at Vijay, shivering in her arms, and vowed to him that she would change their lives. She would get them to India and away from the drugs. She would get clean. She would become the mother he and Sophie deserved. She had allowed the wind to blow her about for far too long, and she was finally ready to adjust her sails. They just had to hold on for ten days.

45

SOPHIE

2019

Dao squeezes Sophie's hand tightly, as if she is drowning in the ocean and Dao is pulling her to safety. "I'm sorry you didn't know. It seems your mother was a woman of many secrets, and I'm so sorry to be the one to deliver them to you."

Sophie feels claustrophobic in this tiny office and shimmies away from Manoj's hand, which is lightly touching her back to offer her some comfort. There is too much to take in! She has a brother. She cannot even comprehend such a thing. Nita had left when she was so young that Sophie had never contemplated siblings the way her friends had. Hers was the only one-child household among their social circle, but she was the only one without a mummy, so it made sense to her. The math added up. Having a dead mummy and a new brother did not create a balanced equation. And Dao said Nita was going to go back to India. So maybe she would have been in Sophie's life. She jolts as she wonders whether she was wrong and Nita wasn't coming back for Sophie and instead was planning on coming back with this Vijay person and building a future with him. A do-over life because she'd been so unhappy with the one she'd built with Sophie and Rajiv. Sophie doesn't know Nita at all. She can hardly predict the whims of such an enigma.

"When did she die?" Sophie finally asks, trying to decipher the first time Nita was out of Sophie's life due to death rather than choice.

Dao leans back and closes her eyes, concentrating hard on the answer. "I think it was about seventeen or eighteen years ago. Vijay was four years old at the time, maybe five, if I'm remembering correctly."

"She was still so young." The words croak out of Sophie's mouth, and she feels her voice wavering, the emotion of what she is hearing setting in. "I would have been only ten or eleven years old then."

I was young enough to still need a mummy, Sophie thinks and wonders why hers hadn't returned to her. She braces herself for what comes next. She's relieved that her emotional state is so numb from everything else she's heard that the new blows cannot pummel her further. She looks to Manoj, and he remains stoic, a quiet, unjudging pillar of support.

"I think she had a hard time with all of it. Being here and away from home, that is. Mathieu started off as a savior to her but quickly became a warden of sorts. She felt trapped with him but also felt like she had nowhere to go and maybe like she deserved to be in that bad place. Karma and whatnot. Still, after she got pregnant, she tried to clean up her act, but it was a hard thing to do when Mathieu always had drugs around and was high, and the baby was colicky, and sometimes she was so tired from working and caring for him that she just needed to slip into oblivion for a short while before picking it up and doing it all over again." Dao's eyes dampen as she recounts these memories. "She decided she was going to leave him. Leave Mathieu, that is, and go back to India. Take Vijay with her. She said she could give him a better life there. Her family could help her care for him. It all made sense to me, considering she had come to Paris to follow her art dreams and all of that had fallen by the wayside. The little she had shared about her life in India seemed a lot more glamorous than the one she'd been living in Paris. But then a few days after she told me she was heading back, she had one last bender, and it was, unfortunately, one too many. Even when she was determined to move forward, the addiction she'd developed would not let her go. She overdosed, and Vijay sought out a neighbor to help him 'wake *Maman* up,' but she was already gone at that point." Dao wipes the tear sliding down her cheek. "I wish I could have done more. It seemed like Paris had been a prison sentence for her and she was finally getting her reprieve, only to have everything taken away from her."

Sophie wishes she could go back in time to the point at which all she knew was that Nita had died in a car accident on her way home from caring for Ba. That perfect image she had of Nita—the woman who died in furtherance of her attempts to help others—is now shattered and replaced by this. It was the cruelest twist of fate she could have imagined. Nita had given up her life with Sophie and Rajiv for this dismal existence that Dao just described. And it had taken her years to consider returning home. Years, and another baby.

"What happened to the boy?"

Dao grits her teeth. "He had an arse for a father, no doubt. That man could not care for a cactus in the desert, let alone a child. The best thing that could have ever happened to that little boy was Simon." Her expression lightens as she says his name. "He was an American chap that your mother had grown rather fond of. Anyway, he took over legal responsibility for the boy and raised him. Much better off, if you ask me."

Sophie wonders if this boy knows she exists or if he was left in the dark, just as she was.

"How can I find him?"

"Simon and Vijay lived in Paris a bit after Simon started raising him, but then Mathieu would stumble over drunk or high sometimes and wreak havoc on their lives. Simon thought it best to take Vijay back to America. His mother would be able to help raise the boy, and it all made sense. I'm not sure they've ever been back to Paris since.

Can't fault them. Not sure this fair city holds many good memories for either of them anymore. He used to send me the occasional photo of the two of them on the beach in California. It looked like a good life. Certainly, better than the one the kid would have had here with that no-good father of his."

As muddled and bewildered as Sophie is from everything she is learning about Nita, as resentful and angry as she is that she will never get to confront her for all her wrongs, Sophie feels one thought pierce through the haze like a beam of light shining directly on her.

"I have to find them."

Dao nods. "It's been several years since I last heard, but I have some letters at home. I also have some of your mother's things that I think you might like to have. I've never been able to part with them all these years, thinking one day Vijay would want them. But now I suspect I was meant to hold on to them until I met you."

46

That evening, Sophie stumbles into Taj Palace as if she's in a daze. Manoj tried to convince her that she is not in the mind frame to leave Paris, but now that she has her answers, Sophie wants to make good on the promise she made to Manoj to help Naresh Uncle with the finances before she leaves.

Sophie makes her way to the kitchen and finds Manoj scrubbing the grit off bushels of carrots. Naresh Uncle is in the small office, poring over the books again, his face strained. He still manages a smile when he sees Sophie. She goes to Manoj first.

"Does he know?" she asks him, hoping he kept her confidence as she had requested because she wanted to explain it all to Naresh Uncle herself.

He shook his head, and she felt relief. She shouldn't have worried, because even in this short time she has spent with Manoj, she has sensed that his word means everything to him.

"Have you spoken to your papa about letting me help?" she asks.

He nods, a half grin on his face. He gestures to the office. "Yes. That's why he's back there, looking over everything in the hopes of trying to find an answer before you find one for him. Trying to save himself the embarrassment."

"Good," Sophie says. "If it's okay with you, I will need to spend tonight helping him with that. Now that I will be leaving Paris very soon, I want to make sure this is done before I go."

"You are leaving?" Naresh Uncle asks, coming into the kitchen.

She nods.

"Uncle, I must tell you more about why I was in Paris and how much your generosity has meant to me." She eyes Manoj. "How much both of you have meant to me."

The three sit at one of the dining room tables near the kitchen while the restaurant is closed, and Sophie updates Naresh Uncle on the events that led her to Paris in the first place. He listens with a sympathetic expression and occasionally turns to Manoj, seemingly questioning why Manoj doesn't seem shocked by any of Sophie's story.

"Since I started working here, Manoj has been kind enough to help me try to locate her."

Naresh Uncle looks to Manoj with surprise but also pride.

Sophie takes a deep breath. "Yesterday, I met an old friend of my mummy's and learned the truth. Manoj was with me." She smiles at him gratefully. "Even though my mummy had been living in Paris for some years after my relatives told me she had passed away, she did in fact die here many years ago. None of my family in India would have known because she had lost contact with all of them during those first few months in France. I guess in some ways, it was better for me to have thought she was dead all along, since that is where the story ended up anyway."

Naresh Uncle puts his hand on her shoulder.

"Beta," he says, "that is a tremendous burden to carry on your own. Your parents would be very proud of the daughter they have raised. Any parent would."

She smiles at him and then looks to Manoj.

"I didn't find my mummy, but I did find something else," she says. "She had another child while she was here. A boy. Vijay. He moved to

America many years ago, but now that my search for my mummy has ended, my search for my brother has only begun. I could never have fathomed a sibling, but I must find him."

Naresh Uncle cannot hide his stunned expression.

"Now you will go to America and look for him?" Naresh Uncle finally asks.

"I have to. I've come this far. He is the only family I have left in this world, and I have to find him. Or at least try."

"How can we help?" Naresh Uncle asks.

She shakes her head. "You've helped me more than you will ever know. Especially Manoj. He gave me the answers that I have needed for so long." She smiles hesitantly at him again. "The only thing you can do for me now is let me help you with the books and find you some ways to save. Your kindness has allowed me to go on this journey, and I cannot believe my good fortune to have met you. I want to make sure the two of you and this wonderful place will be secure for many years to come."

Sophie thinks about Saumil and Anjali from when she first arrived and how much Naresh Uncle and Manoj helped her at a time when it was hard to trust strangers. That little bit of faith that she had, and their generosity, helped pull her through and ultimately allowed her to discover the answers she had needed to continue with her life.

Manoj gestures toward the office. "Why don't you two manage the books tonight, and I will handle the kitchen."

"You will be okay cooking on your own?" Naresh Uncle asks him.

Manoj scoffs and does not look at Sophie. "I've done it for years before now, and I will do it again after."

Sophie is surprised by his tone, given how much they have shared in the past day. She feels they are starting to form a bond, or at least she had thought so. But she follows Naresh Uncle to the office, determined to tackle that task first.

The desk has a laptop in the center of it and different piles of papers around it. Sophie sees a stack of bills and asks if she can start with those.

She sits, and Naresh Uncle pulls up a chair next to her. He translates the French on the different invoices, and she begins creating a spreadsheet.

"I've never used this program," Naresh Uncle confesses, running a hand over his head.

Sophie smiles at him. "It's okay, Uncle. I will teach you how to use it. I will set it up so each month you only have to enter the new amounts and it will tell you all of the data you need for that month automatically."

Naresh Uncle looks appreciative. "My wife—I don't know if Manoj told you—but she used to handle the finances for the restaurant. Manoj and I did the kitchen and front of the house. As you can see, I've never been much good at the numbers."

"Maybe we were meant to help each other, then," Sophie says. "I've always loved working with numbers. With maths there is a right and wrong answer. No gray area. I like the security and certainty that comes with that."

For the next several hours, Sophie works with Naresh Uncle on creating a program that will manage the expenses and revenues. She looks at all the expenses and finds a few areas in which they could cut down on costs, like switching to a lower-tier internet plan, given how little they use it at the restaurant, and buying certain food supplies in bulk online rather than from the more expensive local vendors. She shows him how to determine the food costs of each dish based on the ingredients and says she has been observing how much food waste is being created. She uses the program to show how much more profitable the restaurant would be if they reduced the portion size by 30 percent and kept the pricing the same. The new portion size would more accurately reflect what people eat, with the benefits of less waste and more profit. She shows him how to turn the raw data into charts and tables that can help them identify the dishes that are the most profitable for them so they can cut back on their menu items and eliminate the ones that have very few sales but require many ingredients on hand that will spoil if the dish isn't ordered by customers.

"I did not know how much having this information organized in such a manner could be so helpful!" Naresh Uncle's eyes light up as he watches Sophie change one number in the spreadsheet and sees it automatically flow through a series of formulas and cells to change the bottom-line profits or losses.

Sophie taps the laptop. "Yes, Uncle. This little device will be your guide. I'm confident that you can get to the profits you want now that you are armed with the accounting knowledge. The food you and Manoj prepare is delicious, and now you just need to make sure it is working for you as well. And if you have any questions, I will just be an email or phone call away!"

He smiles at her. "I think you were right before. I think we found each other at a time when Bhagwan deemed it so."

She nods. Her life had to work out exactly the way it had for her to be in the same place as Naresh Uncle and Manoj, and in her short time with them she feels she has made a difference to them, just as they have to her.

Naresh Uncle looks at Manoj working in the kitchen. "You may not realize," he says to Sophie, "but your time here has affected him. He does not have friends. Not since his mummy passed away. He's a good man. So determined to help me with the restaurant that he does nothing else. I feel guilty for the life that has been taken from him with these burdens."

Sophie had suspected that was the case from her conversations with him.

Naresh Uncle continues, "He's just a boy, though. He grew up early because he had no choice, and, as a papa, I wish I could have protected him from that."

Sophie touches his arm. "Don't be sorry, Uncle. He's grown into a fine adult. That is because of the example you set for him. Just like my papa tried to set a good example for me, but I now realize that he protected me too much." Her voice catches as she thinks of him.

"What do you mean? It is a parent's job to protect," Naresh Uncle says.

"In some cases, yes. But if you protect too much, the child never learns to grow up and develop any resiliency. I was dependent on Papa for everything until he died, and I did not realize how much so until I came here. I'd never taken care of myself—or anyone else, for that matter—and I think that is a lesson better learned much earlier in life." She looks at Manoj. "I think that is something you managed to teach Manoj long ago, and he is stronger for it. I admire his strength. It is something that I will aspire to after I leave here. I may have learned the lesson later in life, but at least I'm learning it now, and I can grow and take care of myself."

Her journey, self-discovery, and new insights about Nita and Vijay are just starting, and she is excited to see where they lead her, but they don't change the fact that her papa is gone and has left a hole in her heart. Even if she is angry at him for hiding these facts from her, he was still the person she ate dinner with each night and spoke to about her day. He was the person who protected her from life's evils, even if he took that role too far. He was the person whom she loved, and who made her feel loved, every day of her life. No amount of anger can replace that.

Naresh Uncle looks kindly at Sophie. "I have no doubt that you will accomplish everything you wish in life." He looks from her to Manoj. "It was nice to see him have a friend."

"It was good for me, too, especially in this strange new world."

"Perhaps you can still stay in touch and be friends after you return home." His expression is hopeful.

Sophie touches his arm. "I'd like nothing more. With both of you."

She goes into the kitchen. Manoj is chopping onions with fervor. Beads of sweat form on his brow, and his nose is running.

"I've created a profit and loss program for the restaurant," Sophie says, not wanting to startle him while he's wielding a sharp knife.

Manoj glances in her direction. "Thank you. Hopefully it's not too complicated for Papa to use."

"I tried to keep it simple, but I thought I would show it to you as well in case he has trouble. And you can reach out to me if there are any issues."

He nods. His demeanor is all business.

"Do you mind if we step away from the onions for a minute?" Sophie asks, tears pricking her eyes.

He wipes his hands on the white apron tied around his waist and moves to where she is standing.

"I really want to thank you for your help this past week. I know it wasn't an ideal situation to have me here, but I think perhaps life does work out for a reason. You helped me find answers that I have needed to know for my entire life, and I'm not sure there are any words that can repay that. You didn't have to help me, but the fact that you did made this painful journey easier."

"It was nothing," he says. "You didn't speak French, and you needed help."

"You have a lot on your plate, and that you took on my problems as well says a lot about your character."

He tries to shrug off her compliment.

"I hope we can stay friends," she says.

He raises an eyebrow, as if he realizes for the first time that they did become friends.

She laughs. "Don't let me pressure you into it!"

He now laughs too. "No, it's not that." He grows more solemn. "It's just been a while since I focused on something other than this place."

She nods. "I know. That's why I appreciate it so much. Maybe one day you will come to India and I can return the favor."

"Perhaps I will. I should probably go one time in my life."

"Whenever you do, you will have someone waiting. And in the meantime, I want to hear how the restaurant and the two of you are doing. I'm now invested in the success of all three!"

Manoj looks at his papa and then turns to Sophie. "We will be okay."

"Yes," she says, "I think we all will be."

"And you'll let us know you are safe in America?" he says, his hard demeanor giving way. "No dark alleys alone at night?"

She laughs. "I promise. And I speak the language, so I hope it will be easier there."

Her eyes convey the gratitude that her words cannot. This person who was a stranger to her a couple weeks ago has changed the course of the rest of her life. How can any words capture that?

As she leaves the restaurant that evening, she thinks about how much her world has expanded in such a short period of time, and in the most unpredictable ways. With the passing of Papa, she had felt lost and hopeless, then clung to the idea that Nita was alive like a life raft in the vast Indian Ocean. She realizes that when she came to Paris, she was seeking answers, but she was also seeking someone to replace Papa. She hadn't been equipped to go through life without that crutch of a parent paving her way, and now she is heading in that direction but is no longer as afraid. Less than two weeks have changed her past and her future. She is now a confirmed orphan, but the weight is not as heavy as she had expected, perhaps because her hope has shifted to this new brother who has been living a world apart from her. She knows she is meant to find him and knows this series of events is the way her life had to unfold for her to do so.

47

The next day Sophie meets Dao at her apartment in the Marais to collect Nita's belongings. Manoj had offered to join her, but she knew she needed to do this part on her own. He still insisted on giving her clear directions and making sure she repeated the steps to him three times. The apartment is on the top floor of a fifth-floor walk-up on Rue de Sevigné, and Sophie is out of breath by the time she reaches the top landing. The door is open a few inches, and from within it, Sophie hears Dao say, "Come in."

She gingerly pushes the door open wider and finds Dao rummaging through a small navy-blue suitcase that looks worn and old. There are some canvases leaning against the wall behind her.

Dao looks up to greet her. She stops rifling through the suitcase, and her hand flutters to her heart. "You really do look just like your mother did. Your hair is straighter than hers was. She had these waves in her hair that would form like magic even when she air-dried her hair, but your features are identical."

Sophie's cheeks warm. Speaking of Nita had always been taboo in her home, but she'd often heard relatives whisper the same sentiment when they thought she wasn't listening. "It must be hard for Rajiv to have the ghost of Nita in his house," they'd say. Sophie had wanted to look like Nita—it was a way to feel close to her—but also didn't want to cause Papa any more pain, so she'd always been conflicted when some-one made a comment about her resemblance. Hearing Dao, who knew a completely different side of Nita, say it in a positive way is refreshing.

"I wish I had known her better," Sophie says, approaching Dao and the suitcase on the small dining table between them. She sees that it is from the set Papa had used. "The woman I remember is so different from the one you knew."

Dao cocks her head sympathetically and motions for Sophie to sit before taking the seat next to her. She puts her hand on Sophie's forearm.

"None of us are just one thing," she says. "Your mother was as complex as I'm sure you are. I'm certain that was true of her time in India and her time in France."

Sophie isn't so sure. As she looks back on her own life, it feels very one note. But this journey she's been on since Papa passed has changed her. In ways she likely has not even processed yet, but she sees her flaws more clearly now and sees strengths she never knew she had.

"What do you remember most about her?" Sophie asks.

Dao's brow furrows as she ponders the question. "I think the thing that stood out most, especially toward the end, was that she was lost."

Sophie straightens. "What do you mean?" Sophie's memories of Nita are of a bold, self-assured woman.

Dao stares at the suitcase on the table in front of them. "She always seemed like she was in control. But as you got to know her, as you got past the exterior, she seemed scared and lost. From that first moment when I met her at the hostel, her jaw was set in determination that she had made the right decision to come to Paris. But when she thought no one was looking, you'd see her eyes flicker with the insecurity and doubt of a child. She was like that until the last conversation I had with her, when she told me she was going back to India. That day, I felt that her steely gaze and set jaw were more than an act and were genuine. I could see how badly she wanted to pull herself out of the spiral that time. Now, having met you, I wonder if she was lost because she had left you and felt restored after deciding to go back to you. She loved Vijay so deeply that I'm sure she felt the same way about you. It must have devastated her to leave you like she did."

Sophie lets Dao's words sink into her. It seems senseless that Nita stayed away if she felt so lost. Sophie, too, had felt lost after she left, and they could have found their way home through each other rather than spending the rest of their lives apart. Sophie will never know what motivated Nita to stay away for so long or what caused her to decide to come back. There is some comfort in knowing that she had planned to return, though. Sophie was wanted, and she just needed someone in Nita's Paris life to tell her that she hadn't been forgotten. There is no worse feeling than thinking your mummy has left you, and the feeling has gnawed at Sophie until this moment. She feels herself start to release tension that had woven its way into every fiber of her being since she had found those letters.

"I thought she had left because of me," Sophie says softly, not realizing until the words are out that she had felt that way. "That I must have done something to make her unhappy. To make her go away."

Dao shakes her head emphatically.

"How can you be so certain?" Sophie asks, her voice small and innocent, just like she is six years old again. "She didn't even mention me for all the years you knew her."

Dao stands and moves toward the wall on which the canvases rest with their backs to the room. She brings them over and turns them so Sophie can see. Sophie's eyes drift to the one of her as a little girl with Nita's bangles strewn around her and a look of disappointment on her face because she knew she would be scolded. She remembers that day so well and is surprised to see a painting of it. She had been five years old and had snuck into Nita's wardrobe room and pulled all the bangles from their neat rows and jumbled them in a pile on the floor, a colorful mess of glass circles in varying thicknesses. Nita's face had been soft initially, so Sophie didn't realize she had done anything wrong. And then Nita's face grew dark, and she jerked Sophie up from the floor, chastising her for having made such a mess. "Your papa likes order," she said. "You must never disturb that!" Sophie had sulked away with tears in her eyes for having disappointed her parents. She heard the gentle clink of the bangles as Nita sorted them and put them back neatly in rows organized by color.

The other was of her sitting on the hichko in the front yard of their bungalow with her small feet barely dangling off. She must be three or four years old in that painting. She has spent so many hours on that bench swing since that time. Sophie has fond memories of Nita sitting with her chai on the hichko, and ever since she left, Sophie has sat on that swing to feel closer to her, the same way she stared out the kitchen window where Nita had kept her easel in the bungalow.

"She had painted many more of you," Dao says gently. "I could not keep them all. Simon took some with him. Not sure what happened to the rest of them. But you were constantly on her mind. I think that's why Nita felt so unsettled here. She tried to follow her dreams while leaving her heart with you in India. A dream without heart is nothing at all. She did everything she could to get back to you. I really believe that. In the end, I think Mathieu saw that she could change and rise above the addiction, and he knew he couldn't, so he did everything he could to keep her at the bottom with him. He tried everything to shake her confidence, from gaslighting her, to yelling at her, to trying to keep her financially dependent on him. She had a lot of forces working against her, and even in perfect circumstances, addiction is hard to recover from."

Sophie feels Nita's pain as if she had experienced it herself. She cannot grasp Nita spending the last years of her life with someone who wanted nothing other than to keep her down. And even worse, her heart breaks that Nita wasn't strong enough to leave someone like him and rebuild herself. She knows Nita had fire in her, and for someone to enter her life and dampen that spirit is unfathomable.

Sophie gingerly touches the canvases. Nita had real talent. She had so expertly captured the emotion Sophie had felt on that day when she was caught playing with the bangles. Sophie may not be able to fully describe her feelings with words, but this painting speaks volumes. Sophie begins to understand why Nita's art was so important to her, but she still does not understand why she couldn't have pursued her dreams with Rajiv and Sophie. Sophie knows she needs to accept that there are questions, many of them, to which she will never have answers. The thing she understands better now is that Nita was deeply troubled and unhappy, suffering from addictions, and those things did not have to do with Sophie. Those addictions prevented Nita from making logical, reasonable choices for herself or anyone else in her life. The best Sophie can do now is make sense of the information she has and find a way to move forward.

Dao then reaches into the top compartment of the suitcase and pulls out a small red velour bag. Sophie instantly recognizes it as an Indian jewelry bag. She has many at home and in their safe-deposit boxes. Dao unzips it and pulls out some gold bangles and hands them to Sophie, who slips them onto her left arm. Four thin gold bands with tiny diamonds embedded in them. They jingle back and forth as Sophie traces her fingers over them. She closes her eyes and absorbs the familiar sound.

"She wore these every day," Sophie says, more to herself than Dao. She remembers them on Nita's arm. She remembers the sound of them growing more pronounced as Nita neared her and swooped her up in her arms to carry her to her room for bed.

"She did. It's a small miracle that Mathieu didn't pawn them during one of his benders, but I suppose the only reason he didn't is that he would have had to pry them off her. After her death, he banished everything that reminded him of her from the apartment, so I've held on to all this stuff since then. I thought I'd be giving it to Simon and Vijay when they were ready, but seems fate had another plan."

She next pulls out some worn photographs: pictures of Sophie that Nita had kept with her after she left India. It warms Sophie's heart to see that Nita had not abandoned all memories of her. The pictures are creased and tattered at the edges, and Sophie hopes that it is because Nita loved those photos and held them often. There are a few pictures of a baby she does not recognize, who must be her little brother. She still cannot believe that she has a sibling. A part of Nita lives on in another person the way a part of her lives on in Sophie.

As Dao continues with the contents, there are also a few pairs of jeans and sweaters, clothing Sophie had never seen Nita wear in India and now has a hard time imagining. At the bottom of the main compartment is Nita's wedding sari, zipped into a pouch like the saris Sophie has in her closet back in Ahmedabad. Beneath that is a parrot-green sari. Sophie recognizes it instantly as the one Nita was wearing on that last morning when Sophie saw her before school. It was that day, she realizes. Nita sent Sophie to school in the ricksha with the other kids, and she left India that very same day. She lifts the sari to her face and holds it against her skin. The fabric feels smooth and cool, just as it did when Sophie hugged Nita goodbye twenty-two years ago, not knowing it would be the last time in her life that she'd feel her mummy's arms around her. Sophie breathes it in. It smells musty from having been packed all these years, but underneath that is the smell of sandalwood and rose petals that had once been so familiar to her. She locks it in, the way she had done with her papa's shirts, so that this time, she never forgets.

Dao then hands her some blue airmail letters that are bound together with a thin white ribbon. Sophie recognizes Papa's scrawl.

"I never opened these," Dao says, handing them to her. "It seemed too private."

Sophie takes the letters and knows these will be the other half of the ones she found in Papa's closet. She will see what Papa wrote to his wife, who left them. Sophie puts them on her lap, knowing she needs a private space to read them, and Dao seems to understand without a word.

Finally, Dao hands Sophie a few white envelopes. "Here are the pictures Simon sent of him and Vijay from Los Angeles. His address is on them. It looks like the last I heard from him was six years ago. Vijay was just starting high school. Hard to believe he would be at university now, but I guess a lot of time has passed since we were all young kids just starting off in France."

Sophie takes the photos and studies the young, light-skinned boy with dark-brown hair and light-brown eyes who stares into the camera. He has a shy smile, like he's afraid to entirely commit and let someone see him fully. He is standing with a white man who is several inches taller than him, Simon, who has his arm around Vijay's shoulders. Simon has an easy smile, and his emerald-green eyes have deeply embedded laugh lines around them. Even from photos, Sophie can see that his demeanor contrasts with Vijay's more reserved stance. Simon looks jovial and happy, and Sophie is grateful that Vijay was part of a loving household, just as she had been.

"You haven't heard anything for six years?" Sophie asks, looking up from the photos.

Dao nods. "Seems so. The older you get, the more you can't understand where the time goes. Somehow you blink and years have gone missing." She looks over Sophie's shoulders at the photos in her hand. "I'd always left communication up to them. They were starting a new life, and I cared about Vijay, but I also understood the need to start over and leave everything behind. It's what I did when I came to Paris. It's what your mother did too. Sometimes a person needs to close a door to open a new one."

Sophie stares at the photo, seeing parts of Nita and herself in Vijay's face. The half smile and demure stance are like Sophie. His large eyes are Nita's shape, even if his eye color is lighter than hers. She marvels at already having things in common with this stranger whom she did not even know existed two days ago. And now, he is the closest relative she has left in this world.

48

Sophie calls Sharmila Foi that evening from Le Canard Volant. She answers after a few rings.

"What's happened?" her foi asks. "Have you found Nita?"

Sophie sighs. "Yes and no."

"Is that her?" Sophie hears in the background, and then a click and another voice.

"Sophie, what are you doing? You need to come home right now!" Vaishali Foi says. "We are worried sick!"

With them both on the line, Sophie can share the news once, and launches into the story of Nita's death many years ago, leaving out for the time being the part about Vijay and being intentionally vague about Nita's addictions. Sophie knows those details will be met with judgment rather than empathy. After Sophie finishes her tale, Vaishali Foi is without words for the first time in Sophie's life. Perhaps this journey was worth it just to experience that!

"She would have been much better to stay, clearly!" Vaishali Foi eventually says. "What a waste of Rajiv going back and forth all of those years."

"What do you mean?" Sophie asks.

"She knows everything else, so you may as well tell her," Sharmila Foi says to Vaishali Foi.

Sophie's pulse quickens. What more could she not know?!

Vaishali Foi clears her throat. "Rajiv went to Paris to try and find her after she left. He jumped on a plane the next day."

Sophie remembers him being away and spending a week with her fois before he returned.

"He could not find her," Sharmila Foi jumps in. "Was silly to even try with no address or anything. It's not like India, you know, you cannot just ask someone on the street and get a straight answer. He did not even speak the language, yaar. Then, when we found an address for some cheap hotel she was staying, he went there, but they said she had moved on. He used to send letters to her at that hotel because he could tell she was still getting them somehow."

"I said he should put an investigator outside that hotel!" Vaishali Foi quips.

"Oy, yaar!" Sharmila Foi says. "For what? To kidnap her and bring her here? She is an adult. She wants to go, then she goes."

"Maybe, but then we should know what is wrong with her to do this, yaar! But probably it wasn't worth it: us spending more money chasing her, hah? Rajiv was already spending so much on these plane tickets back and forth."

Sophie can hear in their voices that her fois have debated this topic many times in the past and have never agreed. She clears her throat audibly so they can be reminded of the purpose of this call.

"So, what I was saying," Sharmila Foi continues in a loud voice, signifying she is ready to move on. "He told her he would come every year on their anniversary, and she could come back home with him. And he did! For years he made this silly trip every year. Waiting for her under the Eiffel Tower. She never came. It took us eight or nine years to convince him to stop and focus on you. You were getting older, and he needed to be home to care for you, not flitting off to Europe, chasing something impossible."

Sophie remembers Papa having a "business trip" around that time every year and being gone for four days. She realizes it was the same four dates every year, and now she knows those last few years Nita wasn't even alive to have met him. But those first few years, she wonders if Nita thought about it. And that last year, maybe that's what she meant by going home when she had said that to Laurent at the bistro. Maybe that had been her plan when she told Dao she was returning to India. Maybe she was going to meet Rajiv that year and died before she could see it through. Sophie wonders what would have happened if she had survived and she had gone to Rajiv with Vijay in tow. Would they have all come back together? Would they have lived as one happy family in the house she grew up in? How would he have explained that in India? There are so many variables that it's hard to imagine such a life, but Sophie does not think it would have been a bad one. They would have made it work. They would have had no other choice.

"There's one other thing," Sophie says, drawing in a long breath. "She had another child. A son. With a man she met here."

If Vaishali Foi had been speechless before, she was likely in a coma now.

"She what?!" Vaishali Foi says.

"His name is Vijay," Sophie continues.

"How could she do that to Rajiv?" Sharmila Foi eventually blurts out, wounded on behalf of her brother. "Thank Bhagwan that he is not alive to hear what she's done to him!"

Sophie knows her fois are wondering the same thing she is: Why did Nita have another child if she couldn't handle caring for the first one? But Sophie does not want to pull at that thread. There is no answer that will satisfy any of them. They all just have to accept it and try not to apply logic to it.

"I want to find him. He's gone to America."

"Why? What will you say to him?" Vaishali Foi's voice is defensive.

"He's my brother. I have to meet him . . . which is why I called. I need your help to get to Los Angeles. I need you to use some of the money in my accounts to get me a ticket and wire some spending money."

Sophie feels guilty asking for help with something her fois surely do not approve of. She wishes she could do this journey on her own now that she knows how much the adults in her life have done everything for her in the past. But now is not the time to be prideful about her newfound independence. She will have a lifetime to grow into the woman she is meant to be, and she knows that now that such a path has been set before her, she will choose it. But life requires practicality as well, and she would need many shifts at Taj Palace to buy herself a plane ticket to America, and she needs her fois to help get her the money Papa left for her.

Before Vaishali Foi can challenge it, Sharmila Foi jumps in and says, "Of course. We will call our agent and get you a ticket."

"This seems crazy to go all the way there, no?" Vaishali Foi says. "And last minute, the ticket will be so expensive. Why not send an email or something and arrange a time to meet? Maybe after your wedding." Her tone is pointed, but also hopeful.

"Vaishali, please," Sharmila Foi says loudly. "Let her do as she wishes."

It is rare for Sophie to hear Sharmila Foi stand up to her big sister, and Sophie wishes she could see the look on Vaishali Foi's face. She is used to giving orders, not receiving them.

"Be practical, yaar," Vaishali Foi says to her sister. "She is Indian. She cannot just bhangra into America like that. She needs to go through the proper steps: come home, get a visa. Otherwise, they will think she is a terrorist!"

"Hah, this is true," Sharmila Foi says, clucking her tongue.

"I have a visa," Sophie says, and her fois go silent.

"How did you manage this?" Vaishali Foi says.

"I didn't," Sophie says. "Papa did. He wanted me to start joining him on his business trips, so he got my visas for France, America, and the UK. Bhagwan na nasib huse. I only hope that my trip to America doesn't force me to use the last visa and end up in England!" Her fois are silent, and Sophie gives them a few moments to absorb the information. "So, the only help I need from you is the plane ticket."

Sharmila Foi clears her throat. "This is important for her, and she must do it. It is her money to spend as she wishes. And we cannot ignore that somehow Rajiv, or Bhagwan, or whoever, knew she would need these visas, and Rajiv managed to get them before his death. This type of thing is no coincidence," she says to her older sister.

Vaishali Foi grunts in response, but that is all the affirmation that Sophie needs.

"Thank you," Sophie says, knowing she is one step closer to finding Vijay.

~

The mood at Le Canard Volant is somber when Sophie tells Cecile she will be checking out in the morning and heading to Los Angeles. Cecile is rapt with attention as Sophie tells her the full story of Nita and the brother she is now off to find in America.

Cecile looks exhausted after hearing the tale. "That poor thing," she says of Nita, shaking her head. "I'm sorry that she went through all of that. I'm not sure I would have made it any easier for her if I had known, even though I'd like to think I would have." She puts her hand on Sophie's forearm. "Things were so different back then. None of this talk of addiction or mental health. Not the way you young people talk about it now."

Sophie ponders her words. Even today, she doesn't hear many of her friends in India speaking of mental health issues. She doesn't know a single person who goes to see a therapist, or at least, no one who has admitted to it. When she thought her mummy had died as a young girl, there wasn't any consideration that she would need anything more than what her family could provide to cope with the trauma.

"I don't think it's that common to discuss it in India yet. And it would have been worse twenty years ago," Sophie says.

"Maybe the whole world needs to change." Cecile sighs. "The truth is that your mother was in so much pain and shouldering it all on her own. But we were all expected to sweep our problems under the rug at that time. Depression, anxiety, addiction, any mental health issues—those weren't something anyone advertised. Now, I do see it talked about more. I guess that's something, right? There seems to be more acceptance and less blaming of the person who is going through something."

Sophie nods. "I have so much to think about. Mostly, I'm just sad that she was so lost. There is so much more I need to learn about addiction, but I just wonder if I could have done something to make her happier than she was—something that would have avoided all this pain for her."

Cecile shakes her head. "Please don't put yourself through that. You were a child, and that was your only job back then."

Sophie hopes that she can file away Cecile's words and recall them when she revisits these thoughts, as she surely will. Even though she knows Cecile is right, it is hard for Sophie to accept that she had no control over the situation. And she cannot help but wonder if those issues have been passed down to her by Nita.

As if reading her thoughts, Cecile shakes her head. "You are your own person, just as your mother was her own person. I've only known you a short while, but I think you'll always stay in control of your destiny. And when things get tough, like they are for you now, you'll figure out how to claw your way back home."

Sophie exhales a breath she didn't realize she had been holding. "I can't believe I have made such supportive friends in this short time,"

Sophie says. "My mother was lucky to have known you, and I'm lucky to have met you now. You were a link in time that I could never have imagined. Without you, I'd still be searching for her. I'd still be searching for myself, really."

"Life hardly ever works out," Cecile says, "but on those rare occasions when it does lead you to the right place, it is a thing of beauty."

Sophie takes this advice to heart and knows she wants to see this journey as a positive, pivotal point in her life. While she would have loved nothing more than to reunite with Nita, she has found something she could never have expected. A brother. A family member whom she feels a responsibility to even though she's never met him. She finds herself needing and wanting to take care of someone else instead of constantly looking for someone to take care of her. She is ready to take care of herself and does not expect anyone else to do that for her. She is ready to turn self-reliance into independence because she now understands the difference between the two. She is ready to face what comes next, whatever that may be. And it starts with Vijay.

49

Sophie is grateful that Sharmila Foi has booked her on a direct flight to Los Angeles. She is mentally, emotionally, and physically drained as she boards the plane and embarks on the second international flight in her life, heading toward yet another country and continent to which she has never been and where she does not know a soul. The mobile number Dao had for Simon was out of service, as was the email address for him, so Sophie is armed only with an address in a place called Santa Monica. But Sophie is resolute. She's worked with less in the past week.

Her fois have booked her a hotel room and wired some money so she does not have to struggle as she did in Paris, and she is even more appreciative of her comforts now. She can think of no better way to spend some of the money Papa has left to her. Her fois made clear that after this journey she is to return home, where they can keep a watchful eye over her and make sure she is safe, and Sophie does not mind. She is ready to go home. Nita might have been searching for the place in which she felt at peace, but Sophie is lucky enough to know that place is Ahmedabad for her. And her travels outside of it have confirmed that.

When she reaches Los Angeles, Sophie is surprised by the pleasant temperatures in November. It is much warmer than the chilly streets of Paris, but that is only the start of the differences. Other than the fact that the city is filled with Westerners, she cannot find another similarity. There are hardly any people walking on the streets, and the city is so spread out that everyone is in cars. There is traffic and congestion like Ahmedabad, but it is more orderly than back home. There are no animals on the roads, and people obey the traffic signs and slowly move along wide multilane highways in neat rows, like ants marching toward a mango peel.

She has given the taxi driver Simon's address and considers what she should say when she arrives. She is dropped off in front of an average-size white house with light-gray shutters along the outside of the windows and curtains on the inside. A white picket fence surrounds the perimeter, and there is a well-manicured garden with flowers and fragrant herbs along the front of the house. There is short green grass expanding from the house to the fence, and Sophie has not seen lush greenery surrounding homes like this. Ahmedabad is so dry and arid and polluted. She tries to picture a little boy—her little brother—playing in the yard. It looks nothing like the life she has in Ahmedabad, but she hopes it has been a good life all the same. She is wielding both her suitcase and the one Dao had given her with Nita's belongings and realizes she probably should have gone to the hotel first and dropped them off. Surely, Simon will find it odd to see her laden with luggage as if she intends to stay indefinitely.

The air is cool and crisp, and she can smell the salty water of the nearby ocean. The only time she has ever seen the ocean was when Papa took her on a trip to Goa for her fourteenth birthday, and she already knows she differs from her brother in this way.

Sophie pushes open the small gate in the white picket fence, makes her way up the sidewalk, and tries to tuck her suitcases off to the side before she rings the doorbell. A chime sounds within, and she is surprised to hear a dog barking inside and paws padding closer to the door.

She hears a woman's voice from inside as a latch turns. "Nigel, stay back and let me see who's at the door."

Sophie cannot believe her luck that someone is home. When the door opens, she sees an elderly white woman with wispy gray hair tossed into a haphazard bun. She is wearing a blue plaid buttoned shirt that appears to have some soil marks on it, and light-blue jeans that are cuffed to her midcalves. The woman is holding back the sandy-colored dog by its collar and cracks the screen door open a bit.

"Can I help you?" she asks.

"I hope so. I'm looking for Simon Harris."

The woman's eyes narrow, and she looks Sophie up and down. "May I ask why?"

Sophie shifts her weight back and forth. "It's a bit of a long story, but he knew my mother many years ago, and I was hoping to be able to speak with him."

The dog tries to leap outside and get closer to Sophie while the woman restrains him. She focuses on Sophie and notices the suitcases to the side of her.

"Have you just arrived from somewhere?"

"Paris, but I'm from India. I don't mean to take up too much time. I came straight from the airport and will head to my hotel soon." Sophie wants to assure this woman that she has no intention of moving in.

"You must be tired then, dear." She opens the screen door wider while maintaining her grip on the dog. "Come on in for a second."

Sophie squeezes through the opening and tries not to startle at the rambunctious dog, which has even more energy now that a new person has entered the home. Even though animals are everywhere in India, pets are not common. There, the animals roaming the streets are nonplussed by the human inhabitants, so Sophie has not come across an animal who is actively trying to engage with her.

"I don't think I caught your name," the woman says.

"Sophie."

The woman extends her free hand. "I'm Maggie." She pulls the dog toward another room. "Let me just put Nigel in the family room, and you and I can have a chat in the kitchen."

Seated in a brightly lit, warm kitchen, Sophie takes in how different it feels from hers back home. The kitchen in her bungalow is a sterile room that is used by the servants to prepare meals and make chai. The only time Sophie has really spent in it, other than getting a snack, was when her fois were teaching her to cook as part of her new wifely duties. Here, this kitchen is a focal point and a room she can tell is filled with love. It is a room in which much time is spent, and the warmth makes it easy to understand why.

The woman washes her hands at the sink before joining Sophie at the table. "Sorry, I had been doing some gardening, so I'm a bit of a mess. Now, how was it that you said you know Simon?"

Sophie reaches into her purse to pull out the envelopes Simon had sent to Dao. "I didn't know him, but I was told that he knew my mother many years ago. Back when he lived in Paris."

Maggie's posture stiffens as she waits for Sophie to continue.

"I'm afraid I don't know too many of the details, and I was hoping Simon could help me fill them in. Does he still live here?"

The color drains from Maggie's face, and Sophie is wondering if it was wrong of her to come. Perhaps she should have investigated further. Maybe even hired someone to do so, like her fois had suggested.

"He used to," Maggie says. "He was my son."

Sophie has experienced enough death lately to catch her use of the word *was*.

"What happened to him?" she asks gently.

"Car accident. He was hit by a drunk driver almost two years ago. The hospital told us it was quick and he did not feel much pain. Thank God for that."

"I'm so sorry." Her tone is deflated. She does not know why she hadn't considered the possibility that Simon might be dead, just like Nita. She had prepared herself for finding a stranger who had never heard his name and having to investigate new ways to find him but wasn't prepared for being at his house and learning that he was not alive. "Do you know what happened to the boy who was with him when he returned from France? Vijay?"

Maggie's eyes widened. "Why?"

Sophie knows there is no turning away from the truth now. "He is my brother. We had the same mother, and I just learned about him and am hoping to find him. It's a very long story," she says apologetically, her hands resting on her lap.

Maggie's hand goes to her chest. "You're Vijay's sister? Nita was your mother?"

Maggie studies Sophie's face like she is searching for clues to an unanswered question, while Sophie is surprised to hear Nita's name roll off this woman's tongue so easily. The woman manages a small smile. "Life is just full of surprises, isn't it?"

Sophie looks at Maggie, confused. Maggie rises from the small dining table and heads to a built-in bookcase that is filled with cookbooks and photos, and brings one of the frames to Sophie. It is a high school graduation picture, and she sees a young man with the beginnings of a mustache smiling at the camera. He is standing with Maggie and a handsome man with emerald-green eyes. The boy is wearing a square, flat cap with a tassel, and the people around him are beaming.

"This is Vijay at his high school graduation. We were all so proud of him."

Sophie stares at the picture of an older boy than what she had seen before, searching Vijay's face for signs of Nita, and she sees the resemblance in his eyes remains. Even with the tan, his skin is lighter than Sophie's, but it is still possible to identify their common parentage. The boy in that picture looks like he is surrounded by a loving family, and there is no reason to shatter that idea. Sophie wonders if she made a mistake, intruding on the life that was built and reflected in that photo.

"Do you know where I can find him?"

Maggie reaches out a hand to Sophie and squeezes her forearm. "If I were a betting woman, I'd say he's probably upstairs, glued to those video games he's always playing."

Sophie's eyes widen. *He's here?! In this house that I've been sitting in?*

50

Maggie knocks on the closed door that leads to Vijay's room while Sophie holds her breath. She hears loud music from behind it.

"It's sometimes impossible to get him to pay attention," Maggie says ruefully as she raps harder on it. "Vijay! Open the door," she says sternly.

There is some stirring inside, and then the door cracks open and Vijay's head pokes out from behind it. He is wearing thickly padded headphones and has pulled one side back so he can hear her.

"What is it? I'm playing a game with my friends online," he says in the irritated tone that young adults have when dealing with parental figures.

"Take those off your ears," Maggie orders, and Vijay drops the headphones around his neck. Maggie steps to the side so that Sophie is in view. "We have a guest I'd like you to meet. Turn off your game and let us in. The world will not end if you return to it later."

Shoulders slumped, he opens the door wider and kicks some clothing on the floor to the side so Maggie and Sophie can enter. The room is cluttered with comics, clothes, and stacks of papers. The only hint of neatness is that the bed is made, and Sophie suspects that Maggie had more to do with that than Vijay. It is a far cry from the sparse bedroom that Sophie grew up in, where there was never a thing out of place.

Vijay's room would have been so different if Nita had made it back to India like she had intended. His entire life would have been different. She wonders if he even knows there was an alternate plan for him, or if he was too young to understand at the time.

Vijay stands near a beanbag chair that is against the wall near his desk, atop which is a large computer monitor and a controller. On the screen is a fighter jet game, and Sophie sees planes using lasers to attack a large robot. Maggie and Sophie enter and stand near him.

Maggie gestures to Sophie. "Vijay, this is Sophie. She's traveled all the way from India to meet you."

He raises an eyebrow. "Why?"

Sophie wrings her hands as she approaches him.

"I wanted to meet you because"—she struggles to find the right words—"well, because I just learned I am your sister. I mean, we have the same mother. Or did, I should say. She died many years ago."

Vijay's face hardens, and he stares at the carpet. "I know. I'm the one who found her on the bedroom floor."

His voice is laced with venom, and he doesn't seem surprised or curious about the fact that he has a sister and that she is standing in his bedroom only a few steps away from him. There is none of the excitement Sophie had felt when she learned of his existence, and instead there is only tension and irritation. He has the same look in his eyes that Nita used to get when she was angry. The same one she had when she caught Sophie with the bangles.

Maggie looks at him sternly. "Let's have better manners for our guest, who has traveled a long way to see you."

He plops onto the beanbag chair and crosses his arms.

Sophie says, "I'm sorry to have come unannounced. I just learned about you a couple days ago, and I only had this address to try and find you."

"How did you find me?" he asks.

"It wasn't easy." Sophie manages an uncomfortable laugh to ease the tension in the air. "My—our mother had a friend named Dao who had saved the envelopes and pictures of you that Simon had sent over to her. I tracked Dao down while I was trying to find our mummy."

Vijay nods. "Yeah, I remember Aunt Dao. She used to drop around our apartment in Paris before we moved here. She was a friend of Dad's."

Sophie is intrigued by his use of "dad" and wonders if he's referring to Simon or Mathieu.

"Did you ever know about me?" Sophie asks.

Vijay shrugs. "I guess so. You were in India, right?"

Sophie nods.

"Yeah, I guess I did know. *Maman* would occasionally mumble something about a sister in India. It just didn't seem like a big deal. I hadn't really thought about it again after she died."

Sophie flinches at his callous attitude. This is far from the reaction she'd been expecting. He knew about her, probably always had, and had done nothing to try to find her, so perhaps that explains his behavior. He's not as interested in having a sister as she is in having a brother. He has a new family in America and does not seem to yearn for anything more.

Sophie takes a different tack. "Do you remember much about her? I was young when she—when she left. My memories are fuzzy, and I am just now learning of her life in France."

Vijay's eyes go dark again. Sophie feels Maggie's arm on her shoulder, and, in a soft voice, Maggie says, "Vijay has a hard time speaking about his mother. It seems things were quite rough for him during his early years in Paris."

"I'm sorry. I don't mean to cause you any distress," Sophie says to him.

He pretends to shrug it off, feigning nonchalance.

"I'm not sure what you want me to say?" Vijay says to her. "The woman was an addict. She was high all the time. Talked about some

283

fancy life she had in India only to give it up and chase drugs down the streets of Paris. Seems like a bad trade, if you ask me."

Sophie feels a lump form in her throat. She agrees it was a bad trade, but as she looks at Vijay standing before her, she knows that without that trade there would be no Vijay and this moment she is having with him would not exist. It hurts to see how much animosity he has toward Nita because Sophie's memories of her are not filled with any of that turmoil.

"To me, she was nothing like that. To me, she was a beautiful woman who always smelled of rose and sandalwood, and hummed while she brushed her hair, and creased her brow when she was concentrating intently on a painting she was working on."

Vijay looks surprised, clearly not knowing this side of Nita.

"Maybe I will leave you two alone for a minute, and you can catch up?" Maggie says it more to Vijay to gauge if he feels comfortable with that.

He shrugs, which is probably as close to a yes as she's going to get, and she takes her cue to step outside of the room while saying, "I will be downstairs if you need anything."

Vijay traces a circle on the carpet with his foot, avoiding eye contact with Sophie.

"I'm sorry if this is hard for you," Sophie says. "I only just learned about you because, well, I was in Paris trying to find her, and—"

"You didn't know she was dead until now?" Vijay asks, staring at her.

Sophie sighs. "Yes and no, I suppose. Do you mind if I sit?" She gestures toward the bed.

Vijay shrugs, and Sophie sinks onto it, her body feeling weary.

Her voice quivers as she says, "My papa died a couple weeks ago. He was my whole world." Her tone is soft and low, as if she's mainly speaking to herself at this point. Then she meets Vijay's gaze. "He raised me alone from the time I was six years old. I came home from school one day, and he told me that Nita had gone to the village she was from to care for my ba. I didn't think anything of it. And then a couple weeks later, I came home and found Papa sitting alone at our dining room table, waiting for me. That's when he told me she had died in a car accident." She wills her tears not to spill, fearing that will make Vijay more skittish and uncomfortable than he already is. "So, for most of my life, yes, I thought Nita had died when I was a little girl. And I only just learned that when I thought she had died, she had in fact only moved to Paris and left Papa and me behind." She keeps her eyes on him and sees he is rapt with attention. "When I was cleaning out his closet after he . . . well, after . . . I found some letters Nita had written to him, and they were a few years after she had left. I had just lost my only family, and I thought Bhagwan was sending me a sign that she was still out there. That I wasn't really alone. So, I went to find her, using an address on the letters. It's silly, I know. But I had a feeling that this was the answer. But then I learned that she had really died, even if it had happened several years after I had thought. And I was back to being alone again. Until, that is"—she smiles shyly at him—"I learned about you."

"I'm sorry to hear about your dad," he mumbles. "My dad died too."

Sophie senses Vijay thinks of Simon as his father and does not want to bring up Mathieu. "Yes, your grandmother told me about Simon. I'm sorry to hear that. Do you know how he and our mother met?"

"I know Simon's not my real dad, if that's what you're asking. I was old enough to remember that jerk Mathieu by the time I moved in with Simon, but Simon's the only real parent I've ever had, so he's the only one who matters."

Sophie cannot even imagine what happened in his childhood to have caused this rancor in his voice in speaking about Nita and Mathieu. She has never felt anything but love for her parents, even after she learned Nita had left them; she was angry, but underlying that was still the love she'd felt as a child. But she can see that his childhood was very different from hers.

"You've had a better life here?" Sophie says. "With Simon?"

Vijay scoffs. "Easily. Dad was great. My grandmother is awesome. The weather is amazing. Dad taught me how to surf when we moved here."

"How old were you when you came to California?"

"Six," Vijay says. "I was four when I found *Maman* dead on the bedroom floor." He lifts his gaze to meet hers. "So, I guess I don't have to wonder if she's really dead, like you did. Mathieu was out. Probably getting more drugs. That apartment was a used-needle haven by that point. Dad said it was a miracle I didn't stab myself to death. Just got needle sticks when I was a kid, goofing around and not realizing that one of them had dumped one under the bed or in the closet or whatever."

The way he speaks so indifferently about his childhood makes Sophie cringe inwardly. How could the mummy she knew have ended up raising a child in that environment? Sophie's upbringing in India had been idyllic in comparison. The most she'd ever worried about had been a scraped knee from running too hard when playing cricket.

"I'm sorry she wasn't a better mother to you," Sophie says.

"It doesn't sound like she was a very good one to you either."

Sophie tries not to flinch. While she has always loved Nita, the fact that she was abandoned by her hasn't fully woven its way into her consciousness. "It's complicated because before all of this, I thought she was a great one. Do you have any positive memories of her?"

Vijay shrugs again. "I guess she had some stretches where she was lucid and had her shit together. Right before she died, she had a stretch that lasted a few days—maybe a week. She was clean and yelling at Mathieu all the time to get the drugs out of the house. It was so loud. One of the old neighbors kept coming down and telling them to be quiet, but she was kind of a nuisance anyway, so they never listened to her. There was food in the fridge every day because she wasn't off on those benders and losing track of time. She kept talking about going to India and what a great life we would have there. Saying it never snowed or got cold. That I'd have a big sister to take care of me. Guess that was you."

"What happened then? If she had a plan to come back?" Sophie is desperate to learn every detail of why Nita and Vijay never made it back to India.

"Who knows? She and Mathieu had some big fight, and he stormed out of the apartment. She was shaking and agitated and said I needed to take a nap while she relaxed. I woke up and was hungry and kept trying to wake her up. No one else was home. After I couldn't wake her for a while, I was so hungry that I went to the neighbor across the way and asked him if they had any bread or cheese I could eat, and then he followed me back and called the police. They came and stuck her on a stretcher and carried her out. Mathieu had come home around that time and was wailing about her being gone and telling me that it must have been something I did to cause her to take too much. Maybe I had been crying too loudly or whatever. That she knew the right dosage, and I must have distracted her." The disgust and pain on his face are evident as he speaks of Mathieu.

"I'm sure it was nothing to do with you," Sophie says quickly, already feeling a sense of responsibility toward him. "It sounds like she was in a bad place. Maybe even before she left India. But it wasn't anything to do with you."

"Yeah, maybe. She was an addict, so maybe it was silly for her to think she could ever have gotten clean. Dad kept trying to tell me all this good stuff about her, but all I could remember was her being an addict."

Vijay tries to make light of the heavy subject, but Sophie can see in his expression that he has thought often of this time in his life and has many demons surrounding it.

"How did you end up with Simon?"

A wry smile crosses his face. "Mathieu only lasted for a few months as a single parent. And even then, Dad took care of me most of that time. Sometimes Aunt Dao helped, too, but mostly just Simon. One day Simon packed up my things and said I was going to go live with him. I was so happy to get out of there, I never questioned it. I think Mathieu was high when we left, so maybe he didn't even remember it happened. I saw him every now and then after that. He came by the apartment a few times and yelled at Simon. Once, he tried to convince me to leave with him, but I knew better. And Simon wouldn't have let him take me, anyway."

Sophie wants to put her arms around Vijay and offer him the love and comfort he hadn't received from his parents. They are two orphans, bound by blood, and she feels an instinct to protect him. They both lost fathers they loved. They both grew up without their mother. Their circumstances were so different and yet so similar.

"Have you kept in touch with him? Mathieu?"

Vijay scoffs. "Never seen him since we moved here. Don't know where he is, and don't care. Simon's the only dad I need. And I've got Grams, so I really don't need anything else."

Sophie looks around the room. "This does seem like a great family and good place to grow up."

"It was better than where I was, that's for sure."

Sophie realizes that behind his blasé, carefree demeanor is a very emotionally mature man. One who struggled and saw more adversity in the first few years of his life than she has seen in all twenty-eight years of hers. It was naive of her to think she could protect him, because he has already learned to protect himself and has been doing it for far longer than Sophie has. He has been forced to develop a perspective that she is only now grappling with. There is quite a lot that she can learn from this young brother of hers.

"And Simon and our mummy? They were friends?" she asks.

"Yeah, I guess so. I remember Dad always being around before she died. He brought me toys from California a couple times. *Maman* always said he was a nice man and I should learn those qualities from him." He fidgets in his beanbag. "Truth is that after she died, I could tell he didn't like talking about it. We moved here so Grams could help out, I think. Dad might not have been ready to have a kid when he ended up with one."

Sophie smooths the comforter beneath her. "Did you ever wonder about your other family? The side from India?"

"Dad and Grams became my family. I didn't need anyone else, so why bother wondering about it?"

Sophie tries not to appear wounded. She cannot fault Vijay for not feeling the same way about her that she does about him. He still has family. He's not as desperate for a connection as she is.

"Now that you do know about me"—she tentatively meets his eyes—"I hope we can get to know each other more. There are relatives in India—"

He holds up a hand to stop her. "Look, I kind of said before that I've got all the family I need. Maybe you've got better memories of *Maman* than I do, but either way, I said goodbye to her and everything that came with her a long time ago, and I don't see any reason to go back."

Sophie inhales sharply as the only family she has left tells her he's not interested in having her in his life.

"Okay," she says softly before rising from the bed. "I'm sorry to have bothered you." With her hand on the doorknob, ready to pull it open so she can leave, she turns and says, "Did you keep anything of hers?"

He stands. "Just this old painting my dad had." He rummages around in the closet and produces a dusty canvas with an oil-painted image of Sophie as a child with Nita. The painting is of a woman and child looking in the mirror. In the mirror's reflection, the child is seated at a vanity table, running an oversize brush through her hair and looking up at her mummy, seeking approval, like she's trying to make sure she's doing it correctly. Sophie's heart warms at realizing that ritual she shared with Nita was something she never forgot either. Sophie still feels closest to Nita when brushing her hair at night. Looking at the painting,

Sophie feels like Nita felt the same way and that after she went to Paris, when she brushed her hair at night, she thought of Sophie.

"You can have it if you want," Vijay says. "My dad loved it, but it's just been sitting in this closet since he died."

Sophie shakes her head. "You keep it. I've got some of her other paintings being shipped to me from Paris."

Sophie doesn't need it. She is going to continue living that image every night and every morning, just as she has for the last twenty-two years.

"It's of you, isn't it?" he asks.

She nods.

~

Maggie is sitting at the kitchen table when Sophie emerges downstairs. The two women meet each other's gazes, and Sophie tries not to look away. She's afraid her emotions are written clearly on her face, and her Indian instincts are to hide those feelings from the rest of the world. Yet she does not want to do that now. She feels a kinship with, and gratitude for, Maggie, the woman who helped raise her brother and give him a happy home.

"It seems like he has had a really good life here with you," Sophie says, fighting back her tears. "I'm sure our mummy would have been grateful for all you've done for him."

Maggie crosses the kitchen and puts an arm on Sophie's shoulder. "We love him very much. But remember that he's a twenty-one-year-old boy, and sometimes they struggle with adult situations. This is a lot for everyone to take in."

Sophie manages a half smile, knowing it's not easy for her at twenty-eight years old either.

"Simon always said things in Paris were hard," Maggie says. "We missed him so much and were so thrilled when he came home with Vijay. But that was a hard adjustment for such a young child, especially one with such a tumultuous life leading up to that. Those things stay with you, no matter how far away you go."

Sophie nods, knowing how much the loss of Nita affected her. "Yes, it's hard to lose your mummy at such an early age, but I'm glad he had such a good father. It looks like we had that in common. I wish I could have met Simon and thanked him for all he's done."

Sophie feels an almost maternalistic pull toward Vijay. Family has been such a bedrock for her because Nita left when Sophie was so young, and Sophie then clung dearly to those who remained. Now she feels herself clinging to Vijay and wanting to take care of him as she would have if Nita had ever made it back to Ahmedabad. She knows that's what Nita wanted for Vijay, and, despite everything else, part of her heart is drawn to fulfilling Nita's last wishes for her son. For Sophie's brother. They are family, and Sophie will always see him that way.

Maggie looks wistful as she says, "Simon had a heart of gold. You would have liked him. And I'm sure he would have liked you too."

Sophie looks around the kitchen and into the living area. Both spaces are warm and well lived in. However his life started out, she knows he ended up in a happy home. Sophie wants nothing more than to build a relationship with Vijay and live out the childhood that Nita had wanted for them both before she died. She can imagine years of running around the bungalow with him and conspiring against their mother and Rajiv in the way that only siblings can. She had been envious of her friends and cousins, who all had siblings. As devastating as it is to know Vijay doesn't want her in his life, her older-sister instinct has already kicked in, and she wants to do what is best for him. At the moment, that is letting him process these life changes in the way that he needs—even if that is without her. Even if that means their paths never cross again.

"Would it be okay if I leave you my contact information in India, just in case Vijay changes his mind?"

Maggie's face looks like it registers all the emotions going through Sophie's head and heart. "Of course, dear."

51

Sophie is restless on the long flight from Los Angeles to Ahmedabad. Her emotional and physical journeys have started to catch up to her, and she thinks about how much she has changed in such a short amount of time. For a girl who had never left India before and never experienced much struggle, she now feels as though she has traversed the world and managed to come back in one piece. Before these past couple weeks, she never had to learn to pick herself up and move forward because she'd never fallen before. As painful as it is to fall, she has never experienced such growth and strength as she has in these last weeks, and she is proud of herself for pushing forward when it would have been so easy to allow others to fix her problems.

She is going back home but still is not sure what that home will be. Some things haven't changed since she left. Her parents are still gone, and she still must build a life without them. And she had no siblings before she left, and while this may not be technically true now, Vijay has made clear that he doesn't want or need a sister, so she's an only child, just as she was before. Everything has changed inside her, while everything has remained the same on the surface.

And then there is Kiran. Sophie still cannot believe he flew to France to speak with her. The way he thinks of her, with spark and determination, based on her playing as a small child still mystifies her because she's never seen herself this way. France was the first time she realized that she is her mummy's daughter and part of Nita would always live on in Sophie. But she is also her papa's daughter and thrives on rules and stability. It is okay for her to be both.

On the last leg of her flight, Sophie wraps the thin airplane blanket around her and leans her head against the window as she tries to drift to sleep and escape the swirling thoughts. She doesn't realize how deeply she has slept until the jarring motion of the plane touching down in India awakens her. She is home. And now she must figure out what that means.

~

Sharmila Foi embraces her when she emerges from the airport with her luggage in tow. Vaishali Foi has her arms crossed as if she is still annoyed, but when she hugs Sophie, Sophie can feel the tension release from her foi's arms upon knowing for herself that Sophie is okay.

"What were you thinking, running off like that?" Vaishali Foi mutters as she releases her grasp on Sophie. "What if something had happened to you, hah?"

"I'm okay, Foi. In fact, I'm better than okay. For the first time in my life, I know the truth about my family."

Their driver arrives and collects her two suitcases, and her fois usher her through the throngs of people to the car, each of them holding her hand as if she is six years old and crossing a busy street with them. She lets them. Sophie welcomes feeling taken care of, even if it is only for a few moments. No matter how trying they can be at times, her fois are her family, and she is more grateful for them now than she has ever been. She appreciates that even though her family's story isn't typical, she is more fortunate than so many, and hopes she never loses that outlook.

Once she gets settled at Vaishali Foi's bungalow, she cannot help but wish she was in her own room. She knows the house is vacant now, but she hasn't been in a place that felt like her home since she started this emotional journey. Her heart aches at knowing she might never have a place that feels like home again. She wonders if any place ever felt that way to Nita. Certainly, Ahmedabad did not. From what she's learned of her life in Paris, she can't imagine that felt right either. Sophie is grateful that Ahmedabad is her home. It's where her memories of Papa are. And it's where those few memories of her mummy live. She knows she will never leave it.

As she makes her way downstairs, she hears her fois rummaging around in the kitchen and giving directions to the cook, who will be preparing dinner.

There are steaming mugs of chai at the dining table, the thin layer of malai already forming across the top. Her fois join her as Sophie sinks into a chair and uses her spoon to skim the malai off the top and droop it over the edge of her mug. The familiar taste warms her from the inside out. She then dives into what she learned in Paris and her meeting with Vijay, leaving out the part about Nita being addicted to drugs, deciding some things are better left unsaid. Her fois need nothing additional to think poorly of Nita. They do not react strongly to Vijay not wanting to be a part of the family, and Sophie realizes it is because he's not technically part of *their* family. He has a different papa, and a non-Indian one at that. His existence casts more shame onto their family, which had already suffered a scandal when Nita left all those years ago. They are ready to put it in the past and leave it there.

"We think maybe it's best you stay here until we figure out the next step," Vaishali Foi says.

"Okay. And I think I should speak to Kiran."

Sharmila Foi perks up even though Sophie can see she is trying to remain neutral. Surely, they know he went to Paris to see her. There are no secrets in the Ahmedabad gossip circuit.

"Oh?" Sharmila Foi says, her voice anything but nonchalant.

"I'd like to speak with him alone, if I can."

Seeing him alone is a far from normal request, given the potential for gossip, but Sophie is a long way from normal these days.

Her fois exchange glances. "We can call his parents and ask," Sharmila Foi says hesitantly.

"Maybe I can just call his house and ask for him. I'm sure you know he came to France to see me, so if we're worried about what people will think, then we've got bigger problems."

They both widen their eyes at Sophie's directness. She has never spoken out of turn like this before. Sophie can't help but wonder if part of their reaction is to her behavior reminding them of Nita.

Sharmila Foi goes to her purse to retrieve the handwritten pocket address book she always carries with her. It is worn and creased from decades of being carted around in her purse. It is organized in a way that would make sense only to her because it is not alphabetical. She flips to a page and hands it to Sophie.

"When you are ready, here is the number."

~

Kiran and Sophie meet at her house, which she realizes is where they first met when they were kids. She arrives before him, wanting to spend some time alone in the bungalow. While the personal effects have all been removed, the custom furniture is still there, and she knows it will stay with the home and go to the new owner. Her fois are ready to sell it and move on. Sophie, however, is not ready to let it go.

She pictures Nita in this home. Not the woman she missed throughout her childhood but the one she has now come to know. The one who felt stifled and wanted to run from this life. She looks at the nook near the dining table where Nita used to set up her easel for painting. The window faces a narrow ridge of trees in their backyard, and beyond that are the upper levels of other bungalows in the neighborhood.

Sophie never knew what Nita was thinking about as she stared out of that window while Sophie played near her, but she now believes Nita was dreaming of France. And of a life in Paris that was very different from the one she ended up having. Sophie thinks Nita looked out that window and painted to escape the life in India in which she felt so trapped. Given how things turned out, Sophie wonders if she ever regretted her decisions. Perhaps the closest she will get to an answer is the fact that Nita seemed ready to come back to India. Maybe even to the family she left behind, if they would have her. And Rajiv's forgiveness was limitless, so Sophie knew the choice would always have been Nita's to simply return.

Sophie slides her fingers along the cool metal railing of the stairs as she heads up to her room. Her fois have left it alone, waiting for her to pack it. It's the only area with any personal items left behind. Sophie has lived every single day of her life in that room, and it was not until Papa's death that she really contemplated the fact that she would someday have to build a life outside of these four walls.

She ventures into her parents' bedroom and pictures Nita sitting at the vanity, brushing her hair. She envisions Papa in the closet, untying his tie and changing into his lengha while they discussed the plans for the next day. They did this every day even though the plans were always the same: Sophie would be at school, Rajiv would be at work, and Nita would be home or running errands until Sophie returned. It was a simple life. One that had made Sophie happy.

Her thoughts are interrupted when she hears tires pulling into the gravel driveway. She switches off the lights in the bedroom and goes downstairs to meet Kiran.

His keys dangle from his fingers, and he smiles as she opens the door. He looks rather Western in his red plaid shirt and medium-wash jeans, but with his shirt still tucked in and his jeans belted, he still could not pass for a native Westerner. Sophie has always felt that Kiran falls somewhere in between Indian and Western, never quite passing fully for either. He removes his shoes in the foyer and follows Sophie to the living room.

"I'm afraid my fois have cleaned out most of the home, so I can't offer you any chai or nasta," Sophie says as she gestures for him to sit on the L-shaped sectional.

He holds up his hands in polite protest. "Not to worry. I have just come from lunch and could not eat or drink another bite."

She sits on the other portion of the sofa so it's easier for them to face each other while speaking.

"Did you get the answers you were hoping for on your trip?" he asks.

Sophie mulls over his question. "I got the answers I needed to start the next chapter."

Kiran nods.

"If we married, you would still be marrying an orphan," she says.

He shrugs. "Nothing has changed since we first met to discuss marrying, but I am sorry for your loss. Again."

On the surface, yes, but for Sophie everything has changed.

"You surprised me very much by coming to Paris. It was kind. Thoughtful. The type of gesture from a man Papa would be proud to see me marry."

"So, you are still considering it, then? Us marrying?"

"You would still want to go forward, even after learning the scandal of what my mummy did?"

"That depends." He meets her gaze. "If we marry and you are not happy, will you speak to me about it first before running off to Europe?"

Sophie laughs. "It is a fair question. I can't promise that we will be happy all the time or even forever, but I know India is my home. Not because it's obligated to be but because I want it to be. There were so many strange things in France and America that I could never get used to!" She wrinkles her nose. "The people keep completely to themselves. No one says 'Hi, how are you?' when going down the streets. It's a very different life, and one that is not for me."

"I'm not sure if you answered my question," Kiran says.

Sophie smiles. "I would not leave without telling you. And I don't think I will ever want to leave Ahmedabad."

He nods, satisfied. "If you want to go to Europe or anywhere else, let's just have a chat about it, and we can plan a trip!"

"That is a deal. But there is more you should know." Sophie inhales sharply, knowing she cannot move forward without revealing this.

"My mummy, she . . ." Her voice trails off as she searches for the words. "She suffered from some addictions while she was in France." Kiran's expression does not change. "I don't know if that is something that lives inside of me too . . . something that I could pass on to our children." She blushes and drops her gaze to the floor. "That is, I'm assuming you want children," she says in a faint voice.

He nods slowly and considers her words. Addiction and mental health issues are not discussed openly in their community. Certainly, their upper-caste Ahmedabad circle would consider them taboo. If his parents knew the true story of her parents, especially of Nita, then they would surely call off the engagement. It is best not to marry into such problems when there are so many young women from other families that do not have such scandals—or at least none that are known to the public. Sophie now believes that, like her family, the others in their community must also harbor many secrets. When it comes to protecting a family's reputation, people will stop at nothing, and hers had been no exception. Her eyes are open now in a way they had never been before.

Kiran shifts his body, drawing Sophie's gaze back to meet his. "Do you feel like you have the same tendencies as your mummy did?"

Sophie recoils. "I could never do the things she did." And this is true, but addiction comes in many forms beyond drugs and alcohol and leaves similar wreckage in its wake. "I don't know everything about her mental state, and it is something I will seek to learn more about, but I suspect that her addiction was rooted in her unhappiness with the life she was given. It strikes me that she sought to change herself by changing her location or her circumstance. But I believe happiness comes from within."

Kiran hasn't flinched at anything she's said so far, so she feels emboldened to continue.

"I'm not unhappy with the life I have been given. I have learned so much more about how privileged I am compared to so many in this country—in this world! I grieve the loss of my parents, as any child would do, but Papa built me a happy life in a place where I have always felt safe. My mummy may have been born in the wrong time or body or place, because she seems to have always longed for something different. I hope that in her next life, she has found the peace she never had in this one."

Kiran says, "I hope that for her too. To have malcontent is a large burden for anyone. And I thank you for sharing such difficult things with me."

She holds her breath as she awaits his answer. She thinks Kiran would make a good husband and partner for her and is now afraid that her burden is too much for him to accept. But she steels herself, because even if it is, she will survive. She has gone through the great hardship of losing her papa and mummy, so she can endure the loss of Kiran if she must, but she does not regret telling him the truth of her family. She is more worried about the toll secrets and lies would take on them.

He clears his throat. "I am sorry for what your mummy went through. I wish her story had turned out better . . . for both of you. But the past is written. You have shared more with me about yours than any other woman I've met has or likely ever would in this situation of securing a marriage, when everyone is trying to present themselves and their families as perfect. But we all know that no person and no family is without flaws. I do think I'd still like to build my family with you. If we can speak as openly in our future as we are right now, then I think we can find a happiness that works for us."

He gives her a shy smile, and she feels like he really is giving her as much permission to decide as she is giving him. It feels so different from the way her friends spoke about their engagements or husbands, always making clear that they had less input in matters compared to the men. Kiran seems to be offering her something different from the life she had expected she'd have, and she believes in that life as much as she's starting to believe in him.

"I'd like to build this next phase of my life with you too," she says, returning his shy smile with her own. "So, we will put the engagement back on?" Sophie asks. "Our families will be so happy."

"I never thought the engagement was off," he says. "My family never told anyone anything different. Now it's just up to them to find the next auspicious date."

The conversation has been less businesslike than their first and made Sophie feel as if they, rather than their families, were making the choice.

"We're lucky, I think," she says. "We've gotten to know each other better than most of our friends and relatives were able to do before their own marriages."

"Yes, I suppose we have. Hopefully that means we will have a better marriage than some of them. That was one of the things I craved from my years in England: a marriage to a partner that was more than a parental decision to join two families. I knew I could never date and have a truly Western experience, but I wanted to know more about my wife than her biodata notes before agreeing to marry."

The look on his face conveys the sentiment she now feels: all families are dysfunctional in their own way but still find a way to love each other somehow. Marriage isn't meant to be perfect, like in the movies she saw as a child. It's complicated and messy and often a gamble. For Nita, it hadn't paid off in the end. Sophie hopes she will fare better. The one difference between her and Nita is that Nita still had her own family to fall back on if the marriage failed. Sophie is on her own, but then again, maybe not having a safety net is what will ensure that her marriage succeeds.

"I know we are not married yet, but I have one request of my new husband," Sophie says. "And it is an unconventional one."

Kiran raises an eyebrow.

"I'd like to live here. In this house." She looks around her, a memory evoked from each place her eyes land.

It is customary in their community for a newly married couple to move into the husband's parents' home so that they can care for his parents as they age. It is less common for a couple to move into a place of their own, and unheard of for a couple to move into the wife's childhood home. But Sophie cannot bear the thought of selling this bungalow, which harbors the last memories of her parents, and seeing strangers live among these walls. Or even worse: tear them down and build new ones. Sophie wants nothing more than to spend the rest of her life in this house and watch their future children play cricket in the yard and laugh while rocking back and forth on the hichko in the front.

"I am the eldest son, and my parents are very traditional," Kiran begins. He clasps and unclasps his hands as he ponders his words. "This is important to you?"

Sophie nods emphatically. "This house is all I have left of my family. Without it . . . well, I can't imagine my life without it . . ."

"Okay. Then we will find a way."

Sophie's heart leaps at knowing she will still have her home and her last piece of her parents. Kiran is making a big sacrifice, and she takes comfort in knowing that if they both compromise, their marriage might have a chance. She hopes they will have children who will run around this house, and maybe even a little girl whom Sophie will teach to brush her hair with 101 strokes every night. Now, with Kiran, maybe Sophie has a chance to live out the dream Papa had for this house when he first married. And the dream she feels is slowly starting to seep into herself as well. She can build a new family here while feeling the spirit of the first family she once had and lost.

52

Two weeks later, after what was a long engagement by Ahmedabad standards, Sophie is getting ready for her wedding. She put a smile on her face during the sangeet yesterday, twirling around with the other guests as they did garba and raas, and she knows to smile through the tears today. Her tears are not out of fear of what her life ahead will hold. That would be normal on a day when she is marrying a man whom she has known only a short while, but she appreciates the fact that she is situated differently than other brides before her, because she knows her groom better than most in her position.

Her tears today are in memory of her parents. Her fois have showered her with the same affection with which they'd showered their own daughters on their wedding days, but Sophie still feels the loss of her parents. Nita is not there to make suggestions about how to be a wife, but maybe that is better, given that Nita might not have been the best person to dole out such advice. Papa is not there to tell her how proud he is of his beautiful daughter. Sophie is marrying into another family, which will do their best to love her as their own, but it's always different when people don't share the same blood. Kiran's family will always choose Kiran, just as Rajiv's family chose him when Nita ran off. And she does not fault any of them. The bond between blood relatives should surpass the bond of marriage, and it is what she has always expected.

Sharmila Foi shuffles into the room, her bangles jingling as she approaches with a large red velour box. She kneels before Sophie, careful not to undo her pleats as she bends. Sophie is dressed in a red-and-white sari with a thick red border, and her arms and feet have intricate designs made with mendhi. She knows the patterns have meaning, but she never learned what they are. She touches the places where her name and Kiran's are woven into the intricate design, wondering how long it will take him to find them when they are alone together after the reception. Sharmila Foi unlatches the gold-colored hinges and reveals a very elaborate diamond set. It is heavy and intricate, the stones glinting in the sunlight streaming through the window. Sophie thought she had seen all the family jewelry when they did an inventory after Papa died, but she would have remembered seeing something so grand.

"Where did that come from?" she asks.

Sharmila Foi unscrews the backing of the ornate earrings and hands one to Sophie to wear. "This set has been sitting in my safe for a very long time. Until this day, actually. Nita had put it aside when she left, telling Rajiv that this was for your wedding day. He did not like keeping anything of hers in the house, so he gave it to me many years ago, and I've kept it safe since." She comes behind Sophie and helps clasp the necklace.

Sophie looks at herself in the mirror and brushes her hand against the diamonds and gold dangling from her neck and ears. Sharmila Foi then hands her matching bracelets. Four delicate bangles with diamonds embedded into them to create shine but still be smooth when Sophie runs her fingers over them. *My everyday bangles*, Sophie thinks as she carefully takes them into her hands.

"These are the wedding bangles Nita had made to give you on this day."

Sophie removes Nita's gold bangles that she has been wearing since Dao gave them to her, takes the new ones, and alternates them with the old before putting all eight bangles on her left wrist. She eyes herself in the mirror with her new jewels adorning her body. Nita believed she was never coming back when she left. Sophie had never thought differently, but having the weight of Nita's final gift to her makes her feel as though her mummy is here. That she always intended for a part of her to be with Sophie on this special day. And even though she knows so much more now, for today, she wants to remember Nita as she always had. The spirited woman who loved to paint and always had time for Sophie's questions. The woman who Sophie always believed would have given anything to share her daughter's milestones with her. Surviving tuberculosis. Her high school graduation. Passing her accounting exams. Learning how to make her first rotli. And, of course, her wedding day. The woman who, in her own way, loved Sophie as best she could.

Sharmila Foi's eyes water the way Sophie would have expected Nita's to do.

"He would be very proud of you," she says, holding tightly to Sophie's hand. "And so would she."

Sophie's never been an overly emotional person, but her eyes fill with tears as her foi says the words Sophie hopes her parents would have uttered if they had been here.

There is a rustling outside the room, and then Vaishali Foi sashays in, her sari pleats swishing as she moves. She holds a paper plate with a half-eaten samosa on it, and Sophie smiles. After Naresh Uncle and Manoj learned of her wedding, they insisted on shipping Manoj's secret samosa seasoning mix with explicit instructions on how to make them. Manoj didn't trust anyone else with the spice blend recipe and assumed they would botch it even if they had the right measurements. It is a small thing, but having their samosas at her wedding makes it feel like her new friends are with her.

"You look beautiful, beta," Vaishali Foi says, her voice warm with affection, as she places the plate to the side.

Sophie smiles shyly.

"There is someone here to see you," Vaishali Foi says.

"Who?" Sophie asks.

"It's best you just greet them."

There is something unusual in her voice, and both Sharmila Foi and Sophie give her questioning looks.

"We will be starting soon, no?" Sharmila Foi says. "Why doesn't she meet everyone who attends the wedding after. We don't want to be late and miss the auspicious hour."

Vaishali Foi shakes her head. "We won't, yaar. There is time still, hah." Her tone suggests there will be no stopping her. "I will bring them now. Sharmila, come with me."

Sharmila Foi follows her older sister's directive. Her fois could be so silly sometimes. Sophie thinks it must be some relative from Kiran's family whom they are afraid to offend. Her fois have been on edge, thinking that any small act of impropriety could cancel the wedding, so they have been especially accommodating to Kiran's family members.

Sophie touches her bangles again, feeling like she is not alone as she enters this next phase of her life. There is some murmuring outside the room, and then Vaishali Foi is back. Peeking out from behind her is Vijay, and behind him is Maggie, with Sharmila Foi bringing up the rear.

Sophie takes a step back, startled.

"But what—" she begins, unable to finish her thought.

"I believe you know these two," Vaishali Foi says. "They have traveled a long way to be here, and I thought it was important for them to see you before we begin."

"How did you—" Sophie's eyes widen.

Maggie steps forward so that she is now at Vijay's side, her hand on his shoulder. "Your aunt called us a couple weeks ago." She gestures toward Vaishali Foi. "And Vijay and I discussed it and thought it was important for him to be here. Isn't that right, Vijay?" She nudges him toward Sophie.

"Yeah," he mumbles. "I figured this whole marriage situation was going to be a one-time thing for you."

Sophie manages a smile. "I hope so."

"Yeah, and I've never been to India, and Grams and I had been talking about it, so it just seemed like maybe now was as good as any other time."

"We were thrilled to hear about your engagement," Maggie says, coming to give Sophie a warm American hug while her fois look on, surprised. "Congratulations, my dear. You look absolutely radiant!"

Sophie is stunned that Vijay and Maggie are in Ahmedabad and standing in her dressing room on the day of her wedding.

"I can't believe you've come all this way!" Sophie looks at Vijay, surprised she is seeing him again.

After their conversation in Los Angeles, Sophie had resigned herself to the fact that he didn't want her in his life and she needed to accept that and move forward with hers.

"We'll give you two a minute," Maggie says, taking charge and ushering Sophie's fois outside of the room so that Vijay and Sophie can have some privacy.

"You look really pretty," he says when they're alone.

"Thank you," she says, taking in his Western-style navy-blue suit and gray tie. "You look very handsome as well."

She suspects Maggie made him shop for something appropriate for a wedding. The suit doesn't quite fit him, in the way that is common for young men who haven't yet fully filled out their form, but Sophie can tell it is the most formal thing he has ever put on his body.

"It means a lot that you are here," she says.

He nods, staring at the floor. "I just wanted to say I'm sorry if I was rude when you came to LA. It's just, well, I mean—my memories of my mother—our mother, I guess—are different from yours, and I put all that stuff out of my head a long time ago. That time . . . the way she was . . . it's not something I want to remember. I don't have happy memories of her and Mathieu."

"You don't need to apologize. I understand. She was a complicated woman. I suppose everyone is, deep down, and I can't imagine what you went through. I'm sorry your memories of them aren't pleasant, but I hope you know none of what they did was your fault."

Vijay's face clouds over, and Sophie can see how traumatic these memories are for him.

"You don't have to tell me anything, but if you ever want to share something, even if it's something bad about her, I'm ready to listen," Sophie says.

He nods. "Maybe one day."

"And for what it's worth, I'm sure she loved you. She loved us both, even though she couldn't really show that to either of us. But after unraveling the things I have, I think that's why she wanted to bring you to India. She loved you too much to keep you in that life, and she was willing to sacrifice herself to change that for you. But the addiction that gripped her mind was stronger than the love she had for us. I have to accept that too. That she somehow thought leaving me was the best way she could love me." Sophie's eyes shimmer as the pain that has lingered around her begins to rise to the surface again. "But I know how hard it will be for both of us to make peace with what she did."

Vijay shifts uncomfortably, and it's clear he isn't sure what he should do if she starts to cry.

"Who knows what went through her mind," he says and then manages a half smile. "But today I hear you are getting married, and we should stay positive."

"Maybe so." She hesitates for a moment and then says, "There is a tradition where the men on the bride's side carry her in on a wooden dolly. I don't really have any direct relatives, so my fuas and cousins were going to handle it with some of their friends. Would you like to join them?"

Vijay pauses as he considers this. "I don't speak Gujarati or Hindi or anything, so I'm not sure if I'd need to know that. I don't want to mess anything up."

Sophie laughs. "You'd just have to walk with them. And everyone speaks English, so you'll be fine. If you feel up to it. If you'd rather stay with your grandmother, then no pressure."

Vijay shrugs. "I guess I could. But won't people wonder why some random stranger is in the wedding?"

Sophie puts her hand on his shoulder. "You aren't a stranger. You're my brother, and there's no one I'd rather have join me today."

He smiles a half smile again that reminds her so much of their mummy. "Okay."

Sophie's face lights up as she takes his hand and leads him out of the room toward her wedding ceremony. They step outside into the warm, humid Ahmedabad afternoon. She immediately feels beads of sweat forming underneath the heavy sari she wears and suspects Vijay must be feeling the same way as his dark suit absorbs the sun's rays. They walk across the gravel toward her fuas and cousins, who are waiting with the wedding dolly on which she will sit for her final moments as an unmarried woman. She pauses and turns to Vijay. She sees her mummy's familiar eyes. She squeezes his hand, and he does not pull it away. It's not the family she expected to have on her wedding day, but it is still family. She hopes he will continue to be part of the new family she is building. The new people she will call home. With family by her side, she will never be alone. She feels a light breeze at her back and welcomes the coolness against her skin. Her body tingles, and she senses Papa's presence in the wind and allows it to push her forward.

ACKNOWLEDGMENTS

Having gone through the book publication process once before, I have a much greater appreciation for the village it takes to turn a story into a book. My dream had always been to publish *a* book, but now having the opportunity to publish *multiple* books has been life changing. None of this would have been possible without the sage advice of my agent, Lauren Abramo, who plucked me from her slush pile and saw something special in my writing and storytelling that she wanted to bring to readers. Thank you for encouraging me to do the restructuring that I knew was the right format for this novel but had avoided doing because of how much work it would be! I am also fortunate to have the most supportive editor in Alicia Clancy, who lets me tackle controversial topics through my stories and helps me elevate them to new levels. These two talented women have allowed me to build a career I could only have dreamed of as a young girl.

I am so grateful to the team at Lake Union, who have taught me so much over the past year with the utmost patience and support. A huge thanks to Danielle Marshall, Gabe Dumpit, Rosanna Brockley, Nicole Burns-Ascue, Elyse Lyon, and Stephanie Chou. I've had the fortune of having both of my covers designed by the creative genius that is Micaela Alcaino. Her dedication to understanding my stories and then crafting the right visual has been nothing short of brilliant, especially for this author, whose only input is to say what I don't like on a cover!

My publishing journey (and my sanity) would not have been possible without my fellow APub Debut Sisters who have supported me, encouraged me, and taught me the ropes. These talented women traverse so many genres, and I've learned so much from each of them through their incredible storytelling and the friendships we have built. Eden Appiah-Kubi has been my rock as we navigate publishing stories that center around race, identity, belonging, representation, and equity. Jennifer Bardsley is so generous with her industry knowledge and so prolific in her writing. I could write an entire book filled only with the things I've learned from her, but I think she should write that book herself so every writer can benefit! Sara Goodman Confino writes some of the snarkiest, funniest rom-coms, all of which I hope are turned into films. Elissa Dickey is one of the kindest and bravest people I've ever met. Her writing about her autoimmune condition has helped so many people feel seen and understood, me included. Paulette Kennedy introduced me to the gothic fiction genre through her stories, allowing me to discover that there are still new genres for me to love and explore. She is also one of the most compassionate, empathetic, and strong women I have ever met. Watching her poise and strength in the face of adversity has been inspiring. Last but certainly not least, Kate Ward Myles is my fellow Hollywood-by-day, author-by-night friend. Knowing such a talented author who was going through the same balancing act was so helpful to keep me going when it felt like there weren't enough hours in the day.

There are also so many friends who have supported me along the way, and I am a better person and writer for having each of them in my life. Bestselling author Jennifer Pastiloff has continued to improve my life by developing my writing through her retreats and workshops and being an unwavering support system. She has selflessly championed me and my books, and I am honored and grateful to call her a friend. Nicole Chambers has been a wonderful sounding board and cheerleader, and I'm a better writer and person with her in my life. Aashna

Patel has forced me to do more with my self-promotion, and I'm lucky to have her as my one-woman production team! Srivitta Kengskool helped inspire and name Dao, and the book is better for it. Thanks to Paula Sloyer and Kim Mills for supporting this new career and for joining me in Paris during a pandemic to help me finish my research to flesh out the details of this book. And so many others have championed me and my writing and lifted me when I needed it, and I am immensely grateful: Penelope Preston, Cynthia Wood, Gabi Lozano, Jill Girling, Kirbee Miller, Elisha "Ishy" Seaton, Marion Karrer, Cheryl "Cece" Francis, Miriam "Mimi" Feldman, and Lina Iorgovan.

Some very busy authors have gone out of their way to help me, whether through providing blurbs or advice or helping to get my name and books out there, and I'd like to give a shout-out to Marjan Kamali, Barbara O'Neale, Saumya Dave, Suzanne Redfearn, Emily Giffin, Julie Buxbaum, Allison Winn Scotch, Lyn Liao Butler, Gian Sardar, Sonali Dev, and Yoojin Grace Wuertz. I cannot tell you how much I appreciate all you have done for me.

A warm and heartfelt thanks to my readers. I am beyond grateful to those who have read my books, reviewed them, posted on social media, emailed me with your touching stories, and requested your local libraries to order my books. The publishing business is difficult, and without your support I'd just be a woman with very long Word documents saved on her laptop. Thank you for giving my stories a place in this world and in your hearts.

And none of these books would have been possible without the love and support of my family. As I get older, I realize how fortunate I am to have grown up in a stable, emotionally secure, loving family and try not to take that for granted. My parents always encouraged my love of reading as a child, and it is clear those frequent trips to the libraries made an impact. While my dad is not much of a reader, he is an unrelenting supporter of anything I want to achieve in life, and I never doubt that he is proud of me, so thank you, Dad, for always being my champion. Mom, I'm grateful that our relationship is nothing like those of the daughters and mothers I write about, and I know that my creativity and perseverance come from you. Thank you for always encouraging me to be passionate and independent while balancing my life with being practical. For Tejas, you've taken care of me since birth, and you are the person in this world who knows most of my life story . . . I hope we never forget who we are and where we came from.

ABOUT THE AUTHOR

Photo by Ron Derhacopian

Mansi Shah lives in Los Angeles. She was born in Toronto, Canada; was raised in the midwestern region of the United States; and studied at universities in Australia, England, and America. When she's not writing, she's traveling and exploring different cultures near and far, experimenting on a new culinary creation, or working on her tennis game. She is also the author of *The Taste of Ginger*. For more information, visit her online at www.mansikshah.com.